TRUMP TOWER

Also By Jeffrey Robinson

FICTION
A True and Perfect Knight
The Monk's Disciples
The Margin of the Bulls
The Ginger Jar
Pietrov and Other Games

NONFICTION
The Takedown
There's A Sucker Born Every Minute
The Sink
Prescription Games
The Merger
The Manipulators
The Hotel
The Laundrymen
Bardot: Two Lives
The End of the American Century
The Risk Takers: Five Years On
Rainier and Grace
Yamani: The Inside Story
Minus Millionaires
The Risk Takers
Teamwork
Bette Davis

AS CO-AUTHOR
With Gerald Ronson
Leading from the Front

With Ronnie Wood
Ronnie: My Life as a Rolling Stone

With Joseph Petro
Standing Next to History:
An Agent's Life Inside the Secret Service

Official Website: http:/www.jeffreyrobinson.com
Follow Jeffrey Robinson on Twitter @writingfactory

TRUMP TOWER

A NOVEL

JEFFREY ROBINSON

Vanguard Press
A Member of the Perseus Books Group

For Barbara and Mel

Published by Vanguard Press,
A Member of the Perseus Books Group

Books published by Vanguard Press are available at special discounts for bulk purchases in the United States by corporations, institutions, and other organizations. For more information, please contact the Special Markets Department at the Perseus Books Group, 2300 Chestnut Street, Suite 200, Philadelphia, PA 19103, or call (800) 810-4145, extension 5000, or e-mail special.markets@perseusbooks.com.

Designed by Jeff Williams

Library of Congress Cataloging-in-Publication Data
Robinson, Jeffrey, 1945–
    Trump Tower : a novel / Jeffrey Robinson.
        p. cm.
ISBN 978-1-59315-735-7 (alk. paper) — ISBN 978-1-59315-736-4 (e-Book) 1. Trump Tower (New York, N.Y.)—Fiction. 2. Rich people—New York (State)—New York—Fiction. I. Title.

PS3620.R859T78 2012
813'.6—dc23

2012010191

10 9 8 7 6 5 4 3 2 1

List of Characters

Residents

Mr. and Mrs. Prakash Advani and daughter, Amvi (40th and 41st floors)

Rebecca Battelli (19th floor), owner of Scarpe Pietrasanta shoe company

Cyndi Benson (59th floor), model and former face of Chanel and Dior

Mme. Odette de La Chabrillan (58th floor), French cinema star from the 1940s

Tina Lee Cove and David Cove (45th and 46th floors), traders in distressed cargoes

Katarina Essenbach (41st and 42nd floors), longtime, wealthy resident

Zeke Gimbel (39th floor), Hollywood agent

Mikey Glass (31st floor), television sitcom star

Dr. Robert Gildenstein and Dr. Susan O'Malley (37th floor), married, orthopedic surgeons

Alicia Melendez (Haynes) and Carson Haynes (52nd floor), she's the anchor of *News Four New York*; he's a former tennis player, now cochairman of First Ace Capital

Ricky Lips and his son, Joey (32nd floor), rock star/bass player with the British group "Still Fools"

Roberto "Espiritú" Santos and his mother (61st floor), center fielder, New York Yankees

Trump Tower Staff

Pierre Belasco, vice president and general manager

Brenda, resident services

Harriet, commercial services

Little Sam, human resources

Big Sam, building engineer, maintenance

Bill Riordan, head of security

Anthony Gallicano, director of operations at Trump Organization

Antonia Lawrence, assistant to the director of operations

FRIDAY

1

Donald Trump only thinks he rules Trump Tower.
Pierre Belasco reminded himself of that every morning as he stepped into his antique-filled office.

But he doesn't.

He was always tempted to say that out loud.

Because I do.

But he couldn't say it, and he wouldn't say it—even though he knew it was true—not to anyone, not even as a joke. After all, he'd been raised in a business where the first rule in the list of The Ruler's Rules is . . .

"Sir."

. . . ultimate discretion.

"Sir?"

He'd just come in and hadn't even had his coffee yet. "Tanya?"

An attractive redhead in a black Trump Tower concierge uniform was standing in the doorway. "I'm afraid there is a very irate young gentleman . . . "

Belasco pushed the large, high-backed, ornate chair away from the eighteenth-century Louis XV table that he used as a desk, straightened his dark blue suit, and was about to follow her out to the small reception area when Tommy Seasons—currently the toast of Broadway in the smash revival of *Who's Afraid of Virginia Woolf*—barged in wearing faded jeans, a tight black T-shirt, and a very weary up-all-night expression.

"Get your thrills dude," he said, "then tell the slut she can't do that to Tommy."

"And what is it exactly," Belasco asked quietly, "that Madame has done to Mr. Seasons?"

"What is it exactly," he mimicked Belasco's slight accent. "You mean, what did Mr. Seasons do to Madame? Well, exactly, he said, *bon appétit*. You know what that means? Ask Madame. And fuck you, too, dude."

With that, the actor, widely acclaimed as the next Richard Burton, stormed out of the residents' foyer and disappeared down Fifty-Sixth Street.

Tanya seemed shocked. "Did you understand . . . "

Belasco told her, "Make certain that he does not go back upstairs."

She asked again, "But did you . . . "

"Yes," he said, waited for her to leave, then went to the French sideboard behind his desk—where he kept his three favorite Ming ginger jars—opened the drawer on the left, took out a small, brown leather pouch and put it in his pocket.

Turning to the large French cherry-wood Louis XV armoire along the far wall, he unlocked the doors with a small metal key. Built inside was a huge safe with a digital combination lock and a card reader. He took his card-key out of his pocket, inserted it in the slot, then punched in his eight-digit code.

The door clicked open, electronically registering that he now had access to the contents.

On the left there was a bank of computer hard drives, which served as the secondary backup for all the security cameras in the Tower, plus the office phone logs. On the right there was a grid with several hundred keys, each lying in their own little slot, each electronically tagged so that as soon as one was removed, a digital time and date stamp would show that the key had been taken out. Another digital time and date stamp also noted when the key was returned.

He took two keys from the slot labeled "Benson-59," put them in his pocket, shut the safe, relocked the armoire, and left his office.

One of the three elevators was waiting. He told Tomas, the uniformed operator, "Fifty-nine, please."

Tomas nodded, "Good morning, sir," but that was all either man said until they arrived on the floor.

Belasco stepped out, waited for the doors to close again, then went down the dark, carpeted hallway to his left. Now there were two large, darkly painted doors. Neither of them had a number. In fact, none of the apartments in the Tower was numbered.

He knocked on the door to his right.

No one answered.

He knocked again, waited a few seconds, then took the two keys out of his pocket and let himself in. "Miss Benson? It's Pierre Belasco."

There was no answer.

"Miss Benson?" Still nothing.

From the marble-floored vestibule he walked into the large living room that looked west over Fifth Avenue and south to the Empire State Building, where a fabulous palace-sized silk Kasan rug, circa 1900, covered the floor and where designer, modern furniture covered the rug. On the far wall there was an enormous painting that looked exactly like Manet's *Olympia*, except the nude woman lying on the couch was Cyndi Benson.

"Miss Benson?"

He peered into the dining room, which lined the Fifty-Sixth Street side of the building, where a beautiful Tabriz rug lay on the floor. There was a huge Italian refectory table, that he liked very much, and on the wall six large Warhol prints—two soup cans, one Elvis, one Jackie, one Marilyn, and one Mao—which he could have done without.

"Miss Benson?"

He moved back toward the vestibule, then along the marbled hallway.

"Miss Benson . . . it's Pierre Belasco."

That's when he thought he heard a whimper.

The door to the second bedroom was open—the room was so filled with clothes that you couldn't see any furniture—but the door at the end of the hallway, leading to the master bedroom, was shut. He went to the door and knocked on it twice. "Miss Benson?"

Now he heard her very clearly—whimpering.

Slowly opening the door—"Miss Benson?"—there she was, completely naked and gagged, her arms above her head, handcuffed to the top of the brass bedstead, with her legs tied to the bottom of the bedstead, stretched wide apart . . .

"Miss Benson . . . "

She began cursing, with the gag in her mouth, struggling helplessly to get free.

He picked up the black silk sheet that had spilled on the floor and covered her, but not before noticing she had a new, tiny tattoo near her bikini line on the left side—it looked to him like a ripe tomato on a vine—to go with the small double-C Chanel symbol that she had on the other side from her Paris days.

Removing the gag from her mouth, he said, "Miss Benson."

"That fucking bastard," she screamed. "Fucking bastard Tommy fucking Seasons . . . "

"Miss Benson . . . " He sat down on the side of the custom-made, extra-large king-sized bed, deliberately leaving her still handcuffed.

"I'll kill that fucking Tommy . . . "

Hanging on the wall behind the bed was a giant Lucien Freud nude portrait of Cyndi. Above the bed was a soft, gold-tinted, smoked-glass-mirrored ceiling.

" . . . fucking bastard Seasons . . . "

At seventeen, standing five-foot-eleven and weighing 116 pounds, she'd been the hottest fresh-faced American model on the Parisian catwalks. At nineteen she was the face of Chanel. By the time she was twenty-one she had her own clothing line and perfume, "À Poil," which means "naked." At twenty-three she left Chanel to become the five-million-dollar face of Dior. Two years later she was lured back to Chanel with a $10 million bonus.

When she was twenty-seven, Hugh Hefner offered her a meager $1 million to do a centerfold. She refused. Instead, she posed nude for free for PETA, the animal rights group, as part of its "I'd Rather Go Naked Than Wear Fur" campaign. But when His Excellency Sheikh Ali Mohammed Khalifa Bin Salman al Khalifa—a minor but extremely rich member of Kuwait's ruling family—offered to buy her a two-bedroom apartment in Trump Tower if he could visit six weekends a year, she bargained him down to four and accepted.

A month after that, Count Giacomo Albarco di Livenza, patriarch of a Venetian fortune and the future finance minister of Italy, paid for the same apartment in Trump Tower so that she would become his American mistress. She accepted him, too. But he never bothered showing up.

Later, His Excellency bought her a fabulous A-frame at Breckenridge, in Colorado. He went there once, decided he hated snow and never went back. But she always spent Christmas and New Year's there with friends.

When the Count realized he couldn't see her over the holidays, he bought her a beach house in Jamaica, where she stayed with friends every February. She never told His Excellency about the beach house, and the Count never visited there, either.

Now at thirty, she had one Trump Tower apartment in her name, the money for the same apartment in her Cayman Islands bank account, two other homes, and checks from each man averaging fifteen grand a month to cover apartment maintenance and charges.

She also still had her career, commanding $150,000 for a catwalk show, more if she did underwear, and up to a quarter of a million for a standard photo shoot.

Although she'd lately added blonde mesh highlights to her dark hair, her big, hazel eyes were the same as when they helped to make her famous, and her high cheekbones were the same, and her legs were the same but, as Belasco had already discovered—being two or three pounds heavier than she'd been as a teenager—she now had absolutely gorgeous breasts.

"I'll murder that fucking bastard son of a bitch prick . . . "

"Miss Benson."

" . . . cut off his balls and stuff them in his mouth . . . "

"Miss Benson."

It was several minutes before she finally calmed down.

"Miss Benson," he said to her once she stopped screaming and looked at him with those eyes. "This really must stop."

"I don't . . . it wasn't . . . he . . . oh Belasco . . . " She sighed and shook her head sadly. "Thank you, yet again."

He nodded, got up, went to the foot of the bed, and untied her legs.

"I hope you didn't mind the view." She pretended to blush.

"Miss Benson . . . " He gave her his best disapproving look, then pointed to the handcuffs. "Do you have the key this time?"

"No."

"We discussed this last time."

"This time he swallowed it."

"What?" Belasco wasn't easily shocked, but that stopped him. "Last time he simply . . . " Shaking his head, he mumbled "*bon appétit*, indeed," and said softly, "This must stop."

Her eyes opened wide like a child who's thought of a good idea. "We could ban him from the Tower, the way we banned Babaloo Facinelli."

"Who's Babaloo Facinelli?"

"The reggae singer."

"Miss Benson . . . " He took the small, brown leather pouch from his pocket, found an oddly shaped, very thin, cold steel instrument inside—like something a dentist might use—and went to the head of her bed. Taking the handcuffs, he fiddled with them, using the instrument to pick the lock. " . . . the Tower has never banned anybody named Babaloo."

"It wasn't him? You sure? Then it must have been George because he and I . . . "

"George who?"

"George Timothy Daniels."

"And who is George Timothy Daniels?"

"The astronaut," she said, as if it was obvious.

"No, not Mr. Daniels, either."

The handcuffs snapped open.

"Damn things . . . " she grabbed her wrists and rubbed them . . . "they hurt." She showed him the marks they left. "Someone stole my mink-lined handcuffs . . . the blue mink . . . I loved those . . . remember them? And Tommy . . . that fucking bastard, I will kill him . . . he said he got these from a cop . . . " She looked at Belasco. "Maybe it was Tony Curtis . . . poor Tony is dead . . . maybe he was the one who stole my blue mink . . . are you sure we didn't ban George?"

"I'm absolutely positive," he said, "that we have never banned any astronaut."

Pulling the sheet around herself, she sat up, crossed her legs Indian style, clasped her hands and said to him tenderly, "Poor Belasco, I am afraid that you have become my faithful knight in shining armor."

"You will need more than a knight in shining armor if His Excellency finds out about this."

"Hah." She agreed, "I'll need twenty-four-hour bodyguards."

He asked delicately, "And . . . *Il Conte*?"

"Pussycat," she assured him. "I never see him. Sometimes he phones late at night and we have . . . well, you know . . . and I keep telling him that if he put a camera on his computer then we could have Skype sex . . . but he can't figure out his computer." She shrugged, "Anyway, Italian men are cool about these things. He has his wife, and he has at least one mistress that I know of . . . she's in Venice . . . and come to think of it there might be another somewhere else. I suppose she's in Rome. After all, he's a very good-looking man." She thought for a moment, then decided, "But you're right, if His Excellency ever finds out . . . Arabs, you know, are born possessive. Especially Kuwaitis. It must have something to do with the water they drink. All that seawater after they take out the salt. He told me once that when he had this mistress in Brazil . . . she was a stewardess he picked up on a flight to somewhere, or from somewhere, I don't know . . . but he started showing up there regularly, which is how he found out that she was also sleeping with some soccer player. Let's face it, Belasco, every Brazilian girl I know is always sleeping with soccer players. Anyway, he found out and had the poor guy beat up by his bodyguards." She made a face. "Kuwaiti princes aren't as cool as Italian counts. In Kuwait they don't do *non c'è problema* . . . that's what the Duke says all the time, *non c'è problema* . . . no problem. In Kuwait they do, *Imma gonna breaka you legs*." She giggled, "Did that sound more Italian than Kuwaiti?"

Belasco smiled politely, then headed to the door. "These little peccadilloes with Mr. Seasons . . . they really must stop."

"Peccadilloes? Is that Swiss for fucking?" She looked at him and grinned shyly, like a child caught saying a dirty word. "Whoops." Then she nodded several times, "I suppose I do need to call Tommy and tell him it's over." She stopped, nodded again, and added in a deep voice, "*Imma gonna breaka you legs.*"

"You suppose wisely," he agreed.

"Thank you, Belasco." She gave him a little wave goodbye. "Can you believe he swallowed the key?"

He headed for the door.

"Oh, Belasco?" She called after him. "I thought it was George, but even if it wasn't him, or poor Tony . . . maybe we should put Tommy on the list?"

"If that's what you want."

"Because you're right . . . if His Excellency ever finds out . . . "

"I will notify security and Mr. Seasons won't be back to see you . . . unless you change your mind." He turned again to leave.

"Oh . . . Belasco?"

He stopped and looked at her again. "Miss Benson?"

She paused, then said quietly, "If I am ever found dead . . . you know, murdered in my bed . . . beaten up and bloodied or stabbed or shot or strangled or all of those things . . . if someone kills me, it won't be *Il Conte*."

BACK IN his own office, Belasco added Tommy Seasons to the long list of people who, for whatever reason, were banned from coming into the Tower.

Their names and faces were circulated to everyone on the security staff. Tommy would be easy for them to recognize because his face was on billboards and in all the subway stations. There was no worry about preventing him, or anyone on the list, from coming up in the elevator because no one could get into an elevator without first being cleared and, even then, invited guests were always escorted upstairs. The idea was to prevent these people from hanging out in the atrium or in the immediate vicinity of the building and, perhaps, causing an incident there.

"We do not need another Chapman," Trump himself once warned his chief of security, referring to the man who waited for John Lennon on the sidewalk outside his apartment at the Dakota and murdered him.

So from now on, if Tommy Seasons was spotted anywhere near Trump Tower, a "Chapman Alert" would be sent to everyone on staff.

Belasco replaced the keys to Cyndi's apartment in the armoire safe, locked it, then sat down and opened his laptop. Looking through his long list of bookmarked pages, he located the one he wanted—a company called B&L Loomis—and logged onto its site. He found what he was looking for—one set of blue mink-lined handcuffs—and ordered them.

When he clicked the button, "Take me to checkout," a small pop-up appeared. It read, "Perhaps you would also like . . . " and listed a few additional items.

He agreed, "Good idea," and checked the little box next to "An extra set of keys."

2

David Cove carefully lined up his putt. "Hundred bucks. Y'all okay with that?"

Gavin agreed, "Hundred bucks."

"Hundred bucks . . . " David gripped his Scott Cameron Tour Titleist triple black putter—"See, it's signed Scott, not Scotty," he pointed out to prove it was handmade—pulled the putter back ever so slowly, then moved the perfectly weighted club face right through the ball, sending it straight for the cup.

Suddenly, Barry put the G-4 into a sweeping left bank.

"What the fuck?" David bellowed.

The ball swerved sharply, hit the storage unit, then bounced into the little galley up front where Wendy, the stewardess, was already starting to clean up for landing.

"Sumbitch!" He shouted to the cockpit. "Y'all did that on purpose."

"Hundred bucks," Gavin put out his hand.

"Sorry," Barry called back from the cockpit.

"I get a mulligan," David insisted.

"Hundred bucks." Gavin held out his hand.

"On our way down," Barry said. "I need Gav up here 'cause there ain't no such thing as a mulligan landing."

"Sumbitch," David tossed the putter onto the cream leather couch, then bent down to pick up the little aluminum putting cup. "Sweetheart?" He asked Wendy, "Can y'all find that golf ball. Don't step on it, now, and tumble. It's down there at your feet, somewhere."

Gavin was still standing there, with his hand out.

David glared. "What?"

"Hundred bucks, boss. Beat you fair and square."

"You call that fair and square?" David reached into the front pocket of his golf slacks and pulled out a wad of bills. He peeled off $100. "How much of this does Barry get for sucker-punching me?"

Gavin handed the money to Wendy—"This is a tip from Mr. Cove"—then went into the cockpit and climbed into the right seat.

"Thank you," Wendy said, found the golf ball, brought it back to David, hesitated, then showed him the $100. "This isn't really mine."

"Y'all buy yourself something nice." He sat down, buckled up, checked his watch—it was after seven—grabbed his iPhone and went through some e-mails.

"Copper wire," he noticed. "We love copper wire." Then he spotted, "Fasteners. Good." He scrolled quickly through some others. "Airplane parts. Love airplane parts."

Reaching for the phone on the table in front of him, he got a connection and dialed his apartment.

Inside the large duplex that took up the entire eastern half of the forty-fifth and forty-sixth floors, a phone rang once, then stopped.

The apartment was dark.

No one was home.

TINA LEE COVE'S cell phone picked up the forwarded call, rang once, then a second time.

She opened her eyes.

It rang a third time, and now she hurriedly leaned across the bed and grabbed it. "Where are you?"

"Landing in twenty."

"How'd you do?"

"Good. Wait 'till you hear what I won off Trump."

"Okay, I'm getting into the shower . . . "

"See you when I see you. I love you."

"I love you too," she said, hung up and looked at the big, dark eyes on the weathered face of the skinny guy lying there next to her. "I have to go."

Ricky Lips reached for her. "One more . . . "

She moved away from him, swinging her legs off the bed, turning her back to him, stretching and yawning. "No way."

"Don't be so mean, luv. It's not only me who likes you . . . look at Little Ricky." He pointed to himself.

"Little Ricky needs to be . . . " She leaned over, put her middle finger on her thumb and flicked at it.

"Ouch," he said.

" . . . little again."

Now she noticed that on his night table there was a strange kind of clock. It was a square, black metal box with a red LED face and three columns—hours, minutes, seconds—that seemed to be counting down.

It read, "244 hours, 41 minutes, 50 seconds."

Then it read, "244 hours, 41 minutes, 49 seconds."

Then it read, "244 hours, 41 minutes, 48 seconds."

"What's that?"

"I got it from NASA," he said. "Awesome, isn't it?"

"But what is it?"

"It's a launch clock. See . . . two hundred forty-four hours, forty-one minutes, and forty-two seconds to launch . . . forty-one seconds . . . forty seconds . . . "

She pointed to him. "If you're planning to launch Little Ricky, you need to put wings on it."

"Not that." He pointed to his ankle bracelet. "That. Comes off in . . . two hundred forty-four hours, forty-one minutes, and thirty-five seconds . . . thirty-four seconds . . . thirty-three seconds . . . "

"How long has it been on?"

He said, "Six months, minus two hundred forty-four hours . . . "

"I get it," she said, standing up and going to the full-length mirror on the back of his bedroom door. She studied herself in the mirror, then turned to look at herself over her shoulder. "Bastard . . . look what that thing did to me."

He sat up on his elbows, stared at her, pointed to her, then pointed to himself. "Look what that thing is doing to my thing."

She inspected the small red welt on her upper back. "Why don't you take that thing off when you're home?"

He stretched his right leg into the air and stared at the electronic bracelet attached to his ankle. "I can get it off. Easy. But the bloody thing sends a signal when I take it off. They know. Something to do with body heat."

"Body heat?"

"Some sort of thermometer or something in there, and when it gets too cold, you know, too cold 'cause it's not attached, it sends a signal."

"What about when it is attached and gets too hot?"

"That too. It tells them my temperature."

She started shaking her head. "So they see your body temperature go up, and they know you're fucking."

He grinned. "Never thought of that."

She moved away from the mirror, picked up her clothes from the floor, and went into the bathroom to shower.

When she came out fully dressed, Ricky was still lying in bed, naked, looking at his ankle bracelet. "You got me thinking, luv, maybe they can hear, too."

She glared at him. "There's a microphone in there?"

"Dunno. Maybe one of them little video cameras."

"It's your ass if there is."

"When are you coming back, luv?"

"Next time I'm feeling charitable." And, with that, she left the apartment.

"Me visiting shag-the-nurse service," he said to himself, got out of bed, and walked naked—except for his electronic ankle bracelet—into the living room.

The place was a mess. The couch cushions were on the floor, and there were empty pizza boxes and beer bottles scattered around. Some guy was sleeping on his couch, but he couldn't see who it was.

Large paintings of himself and the band looked down from the walls.

"Got to get me a housekeeper replacement."

Whoever that was on the couch, stirred.

Ricky leaned down and tried to look at the man's face. But it was buried in a cushion. "Who the fuck are you?"

The man didn't answer.

Just then Ricky heard some noise down the hall. He followed it to the second bedroom, opened the door, and saw a naked guy on top of a naked girl. He didn't know either of them.

"Oy."

The guy looked over but didn't stop. "Hey Ricky, I'm Bugs. She's Shari."

"Don't mind me." Ricky stood there.

Shari looked up, half-waved, and brought her feet up. "Pleased to make your acquaintance."

He watched them for a moment, then stepped into the room and got into bed with them.

"When you're done with him, luv," Ricky said to Shari, "you get on top of me. Just be careful this bleeding ankle bracelet don't leave no marks."

IN HIS SENIOR YEAR at Texas Tech, David Cove moved from safety to defensive end and was a runner-up on the ESPN All-America team.

Nephew of the legendary oilman, R. D. Cove, he might have had a shot at the NFL but never wanted it enough. He was a better golfer than he was a football player, and anyway, "Uncle RD"—as everyone in the family called him, even his own brothers and sisters—promised that he was going to make David the best damn spot-oil trader in the country.

"Y'all gonna make my All-America team," he bragged, and for the next five years, Uncle RD trained him well enough to keep his promise.

By the time David was twenty-six, in 2004, he headed his own spot-oil trading team at Lehman's.

That's where he met Tina Lee.

A year older than him, she was born in San Francisco, grew up speaking Mandarin and Cantonese, and graduated summa cum laude from Stanford.

Courted by the US State Department and just about every business in the Silicon Valley—all of whom were looking for "power women" fluent in Chinese—she opted instead to learn the foreign exchange business. She spent three years in Hong Kong, another two in Shanghai, then one at Harvard getting her MBA. Lehman recruited her there and brought her to New York to trade currencies where, at the age of twenty-seven, she quickly became known as "Princess FOREX."

In 2007, when David and Tina saw that Lehman was in a tailspin and about to crash and burn, they opted for an early out. They got married the day before officially walking away with a package worth a couple of million dollars between them—it was tax-efficient to marry first—then set themselves up in Trump Tower.

For a while he played only in oil, and she played only in currencies, but then they discovered "garbage." And when it came to garbage trading, the Coves were everyone's first-choice All-America team.

BARRY PUT the old G-4 smoothly down on the runway.

Five minutes later he had the wheels chocked and the engines off at the hangar.

Wendy opened the door and lowered the steps, and before either Barry or Gavin could even stand up, David shouted, "See y'all . . . leave the clubs on the plane . . . thanks . . . " and was gone.

He climbed into his latest toy—a Ferrari 612 Scaglietti with a special 1950s dark red *vinacci* trim and *sabbia* beige interior—and made it to I-95 in no time. But he got stuck in morning traffic and had to sit on the 495 for over an hour waiting to get into the Lincoln Tunnel.

By the time he pulled up to the front door on Fifty-Sixth Street, it was after nine o'clock.

The tall Puerto Rican kid from the garage was waiting for him. David gave him his usual "Y'all be Goddamned careful with that car" warning as he handed him the keys, said hello to the doorman Roberto and to Tanya behind the concierge desk, and rode upstairs in the elevator with Jaquim.

"How's the baby doing?"

Jaquim pulled a photo out of his pocket and showed it to David. "Seven kilos already. That's the clothes you and Mrs. Cove bought for him. He like a lot."

"Seven kilos. Good." David had no idea if that was good or not, but he knew he had to say something nice.

Jaquim pointed to his chest and nodded, "He like his mama's titties a lot."

They arrived at forty-five. "Y'all have a good day," he said, getting out, then turned to tell Jaquim, "Great-looking baby." Jaquim smiled proudly as the elevator doors closed.

David mumbled, "I'd probably like his mama's titties, too," and, instead of using his key, he rang the bell.

Tina opened the door wearing shorts and a tank top. "How come you're still in your golf clothes?"

"Had a couple of drinks, then flew home." He stepped inside, kissed her, and shut the door. "Didn't have time to change."

Tina called to Luisa. "Please put Mr. Cove's filthy clothes in the wash this morning."

The maid came running out of the kitchen. "Yes, Madame," and stood there, as if she was waiting for David to get out of his clothes.

"I'll leave them on the hamper," he promised.

"Yes, sir," she nodded and went back into the kitchen.

"What's happening?" he asked Tina.

"Everything is dead."

"Copper wire? We like copper wire."

"Nothing."

"One of my e-mails said there was copper wire. And I saw something about fasteners."

"No fasteners, and the copper went away. Don't you believe me? I'm telling you, there's nothing."

"I also saw airplane parts."

"Way out of our league."

"Big money in that shit."

"Big downside because we could never cover it." She took a deep breath. "Maybe someday when we grow up and get really rich. You get any sleep?"

"Not a lot."

"Go take a nap . . . "

"Y'all coming with me?"

"One of us has to work for a living."

"I'll take a shower and . . . "

She turned toward the big corner study they used as their office.

"What's that?"

"What's what?"

"That bruise on your back?"

"Nothing," she said. "While you were away, I was screwing some convict and he got a little rough."

"Yeah," David laughed. "It's that sauna thing in the shower. Got me the other day, too. Why would they put it right where you can bang into it?"

"Bang, bang," she showed him the victory sign and went inside.

3

Although Belasco's office was just off the Resident's Lobby, his staff of six worked out of a small suite of offices on the southwest corner of the twenty-fourth floor.

"Brenda?" He pointed to the heavyset, middle-aged woman who was in charge of Residents' Services. "Please. Go."

"The Advanis return tomorrow after five months away," she began her weekly report.

Eight people were sitting around the table that took up most of the tiny conference room, where Brenda's four avocado plants took up most of the rest of the floor space, and glass walls looked out onto one of the few open balconies in the Tower.

There were Belasco, his staff, and Antonia Lawrence.

Brenda continued through a short list of matters that concerned the residents and ended with, "Shannon will be coming back after maternity leave.

Her temp replacement, Gilbert, will be leaving. He's a nice young man and asked to be considered if a post opens up. Will you sign off on a gift?"

"Of course," Belasco said. "Invite him to choose three shirts and ties from the boss' collection in the atrium. Is there a Mrs. Gilbert?"

Brenda said, "No."

"Then . . . his mother. Let him choose something for her." He turned to Brenda's sister-in-law, Harriet, who was in charge of Commercial Services. "Please. Go."

She read through her list, noting that Scarpe Pietrasanta, the designer Italian women's shoe company on the nineteenth floor, had missed their rent payment and that no one had responded to the follow-up.

"We told you that the guy died," Brenda reminded Belasco.

"Yes. Under the circumstances . . . "

"That's no excuse," Antonia cut in.

Belasco was surprised. "What?"

The twenty-nine-year-old assistant to the director of operations for the Trump Organization—who thought of herself as a Minnie Driver look-alike, except she was shorter and heavier than the dark-haired actress—had been attending these meetings for several months at her own request. "The lease belongs to a business. The business is still there. The rent is due on the first."

Harriet suggested, "Death isn't quite the same as the check's in the mail."

Antonia wasn't having it. "If you must, send flowers and a sympathy card. But this is about business. We don't do family problems."

"We don't do family problems?" Belasco repeated in amazement. "Actually . . . yes we do."

"Why?" Antonia shot back.

"Because compassion is always the right thing to do." He pointed to the human resources supervisor known to everyone as Little Sam. "Please. Go."

"It's bad business," she said. "Can you imagine the signal that sends . . . "

Belasco answered sharply, "I know exactly what signal it sends. And that is precisely the signal that I want to send." He turned back to Little Sam, "Please excuse the interruption. Go."

Little Sam hesitated until he was sure that Antonia wasn't going to interrupt again. "The Carlos Vela matter. I got with the lawyers again yesterday. They reiterated that theft is a de facto firing offense."

"Except," Belasco said, "we don't know if there was a theft. Or, if there was, we don't know that Mr. Vela had anything to do with it."

"He was the only one with opportunity," Bill Riordan pointed out. The ex-NYPD detective headed up the Tower's security team. "If it quacks like a duck . . . "

"There are two maids in the apartment," Belasco reminded Riordan. "And she has a chef."

"They've been cleared."

"By who?"

"First by me. Then by the police. It's Vela."

Belasco argued, "But Mr. Vela says he's innocent."

"Guilty people don't just say they're innocent, they swear to God they are."

"The police said they're not going to charge him."

"Yet."

"It's he-said-she-said."

"Not to a cop." Riordan leaned forward to explain, "Means, motive, and opportunity. He had the means. Put it in a bag, and walk out the service door. The motive is money. He was working in the apartment so he had the opportunity. Unfortunately, I can't talk to him without his union representative and lawyer present. But how much more do you need? Means . . . motive . . . opportunity. It's all right there."

"What about logic?"

"Logic?"

"Yes, logic," Belasco said. "Mr. Vela worked here for five years, and there has never been a problem. He's a carpenter. A maintenance guy. He's always had the means and the opportunity to steal anything he wanted, whenever he wanted . . ."

"But now, this time," Riordan noted, "he had a motive."

"What motive?"

"Pick one from the usual menu. Debt. Drugs. Gambling. Wife problems. Girlfriend problems. Boyfriend problems. Family problems. Want more?"

"I want something that makes sense," Belasco insisted. "I'd be willing to bet that there are tens of million dollars in cash hidden all over the Tower. I suspect there are more safes in this building than there are residents. If Mr. Vela was going to steal something, why wouldn't he go for Mrs. Essenbach's cash? Look under the bed? In the back of a desk drawer? In a shoebox in the closet? He had plenty of time, but the police said nothing in the apartment was disturbed."

"He looked," Riordan said, "couldn't find anything, and was careful enough not to make it appear as if he looked."

"Then how about her jewelry?"

"He couldn't find any."

"Come on . . . that woman puts on jewelry to brush her teeth. If he couldn't find any, it's because he wasn't looking."

"I'm not buying it," Riordan said.

"There are two maids and a chef working in the apartment. If he was crawling around searching through her things, wouldn't they have asked him what he was doing?"

"The chef was off, the first maid was out, and the second one says she was too busy to babysit a maintenance guy."

"Did he know that the chef was off and that the other maid was out? It's a big apartment. He didn't know who else might be there, so why not take something that's easy, that's right there, that fits into his pockets? She's got silver and gold all over the place. You saw her apartment. The woman owns six Fabergé eggs, including one of the great Easter eggs. If Mr. Vela stole that, he could afford to move into the Tower. She also has a couple of hundred gold snuffboxes. He could have walked away with a handful of snuffboxes, and she might not have realized they were missing for months."

"Vela comes from the projects. What does he know from Fabergé eggs and snuffboxes?"

"What does he know from a vicuna coat?"

"He knows he can wear it or pawn it."

"Wear it? Where? To his local bodega?" Belasco shook his head. "And how do you pawn a vicuna coat? Who would want it, anyway?"

Riordan sneered, "Ever been to the NBA?"

"You're out of line," Belasco said.

Riordan held up two hands. "Excuse me for stating the obvious."

"The question is moot," Antonia cut in. "The fact is that Mrs. Essenbach went to DJT and said she wanted the man fired."

"You mean, Mr. Trump," Belasco said.

Ignoring him, she went on. "DJT has told us, repeatedly, anyone who's been accused, or even suspected, of a crime jeopardizes the trust of the residents vis-à-vis the entire staff. Residents talk."

"So do the staff," Belasco said. "What does it say to them if we fire someone unjustly?"

"Bill's absolutely right." She looked at the former detective. "Means, motive, and opportunity? I'll bet in the old days you would have already had a confession."

He nodded, "Give me a few minutes alone with Vela . . . "

"Unfortunately," Belasco said, "we've got no budget for rubber hoses."

The others laughed.

Riordan didn't. "I could always borrow one."

Antonia didn't laugh, either. "If you don't want to fire him, I will."

"To begin with," Belasco pointed out, "you don't have the power to hire or fire anyone."

"My boss does."

"But you don't. And he won't because I am dealing with this."

"I'll be sure to let him know how you feel."

"I invite you to do that," he said. "What's more, you asked to be at these meetings as an observer. I agreed. As an observer." He pointed to "Big Sam," the building engineer who oversaw all of the maintenance functions. "Please. Go."

The man nodded. "Boiler one is up again. But I've got three guys off sick this week, so we're a little backed up. And if Vela's gone permanently . . . "

"I understand," Belasco said. "I'll let you know as soon as a final decision is made. If Mr. Vela is not coming back, you'll be authorized to hire someone in his place." Now he turned to Riordan, "Did you see that we've added Tommy Seasons to the Chapman List?"

"I've forwarded his name and photo to everyone."

"Tommy Seasons?" Antonia asked. "The actor? What's he done?"

Belasco told her, "He's been banned from the Tower at the request of a tenant."

"Which tenant?"

"That's unimportant," he said, then looked at the others. "Anyone else?"

Antonia was determined to find out. "I haven't seen anything about this coming across my boss' desk. Does DJT know?"

"You mean, does Mr. Trump know?" He answered her sternly, "At the moment this is a matter for my tenant, for Riordan and his staff, and for me. It will be noted in my weekly report to Mr. Trump. That report gets copied to the director of operations. So, yes, Mr. Trump will be informed of this and, yes, your boss will also be informed. Anything else?"

"Is the tenant's name some sort of national secret?"

"The tenant's name," he repeated, "is unimportant."

She looked away, not hiding her annoyance with Belasco's tone.

"Anything else? If not, thank you." He stood up, so did everyone else, and they all left the room.

Except Antonia.

She sat where she was, mumbling to one of the avocado plants.

BELASCO ASKED Brenda to ring Mrs. Essenbach to say that he would like to stop up.

While he was waiting at her desk, Riordan whispered in his ear, "If I was a cynic, I'd say El Bitcho is after your job."

He looked at Riordan, "You . . . a cynic?"

"I'd hate to be the boyfriend . . . if there is a boyfriend. Get my drift?" He patted Belasco on the back and walked away.

"No problem," Brenda said, hanging up. "Mrs. Essenbach said to tell you, Monsieur Belasco is always welcome, any time." She made a face. "Lucky you."

"Thank you." Heading out of the offices, he walked past the bank of elevators that serviced the ten floors of offices, turned right, and went down the long hall to the residents' elevators.

Twenty-four is the only floor in Trump Tower where you can cross to either set of elevators.

Riordan was waiting for an elevator.

"What I can't figure out," he said to Belasco, "is how the hell she got her job."

"Antonia? Her grandfather was one of Fred Trump's earliest backers," Belasco explained. "So grandpa phoned the boss and said, 'I stood by your old man, now my granddaughter is looking for a job.' The boss is a loyal guy and hired her."

"Is she qualified?"

"She has a background in hotels."

"I'll rephrase that. Is she qualified to steal your job?"

The elevator door opened and Alicia Melendez stepped out with a towel draped around her neck.

The tall Cuban American brunette, statuesque with high cheekbones and café-au-lait skin, was wearing a dark green leotard that was cut very high at her hips. "Hi Belasco," she said, then nodded at Riordan.

"Miss Melendez."

She waved and walked down the hall, obviously on her way to the health club on the northeast corner of the floor.

Riordan watched her walk away. "I know how she got her job."

Belasco disregarded the remark and stepped into the elevator. "Forty-two, please."

Miguel, the elevator operator, looked at Belasco.

He shook his head.

And the doors closed before Riordan had a chance to turn around.

4

Alicia stepped onto the treadmill, Alejandro set the speed, she started running, and he walked away.

At this hour, the big room with row after row of machines—and floor-to-ceiling windows that overlooked Fifth Avenue and Central Park—was empty. She had no trouble getting the machine in the far corner, the one she liked best because it had such great views.

"Very early or very late," she'd advised Carson, who also liked that machine.

"Very early to beat the before-the-market-opens crowd, or very late to beat the ladies who lunch."

Carson, a six-foot-three, mahogany-skinned former tennis player, eventually found that he could get that machine at 5:15. But Alicia didn't have to be at NBC until 11, which meant that now, at 9:30 a.m., she usually had the place to herself.

Herself and Alejandro.

He was a good-looking, sleepy-eyed kid from Costa Rica who was always helpful and friendly but showed no interest in her. He was the same with Cyndi. So Alicia and Cyndi decided Alejandro must be gay.

When Carson said, "Impossible," the two women set out to prove him wrong. Not that it mattered to them if Alejandro liked girls or boys. It was a game to play and they called it "Alejandro In or Out?"

One day, Alicia showed up in her coffee-with-cream-colored Lycra outfit, the one that Carson absolutely forbid her to wear in public because it made her look totally nude.

Cyndi was dying to know, "What happened?"

Alicia told her, "Nothing."

The day after that, Cyndi wore a tiny two-piece training set that was so tight there was absolutely nothing left for Alejandro to imagine.

Alicia asked, "What happened?"

Cyndi answered, "Nothing."

Finally, Carson decided it was up to him to make the winning move. "I'm going to ask."

"You can't do that," Cyndi said.

"Why not?" And he did. "My wife says you're gay. Are you gay?"

"Me?" Alejandro started laughing, not the nervous laugh of someone caught in a lie, but the real laugh of someone who is truly amused. "Me? I am right now currently having it with four different ladies in the Tower. Almost every day. Each one. Quatro. Four. I like *las mujeres* very much."

He warned Alejandro, "Not Alicia. And not Cyndi."

"Your señora? Your *mujer*? And her friend? No," he said, "only *las pumas*."

"*Las pumas?*"

Alejandro tried to find the word, "You know . . . *pumas, mujeres pumas* . . . cougars?"

"Old ladies?"

He nodded several times. "*Cincuenta. Cincuenta y cinco. Sesenta.*" Fifty. Fifty-five. Sixty.

"I win," Carson reported back to Alicia and Cyndi. "You guys are much too young for him."

Immediately, Alicia and Cyndi started making a list of the older women they spotted training with Alejandro. And within days, they were up to twenty.

"He told me four," Carson said.

"No way," Alicia said. "At least fourteen."

"Twenty-four," Cyndi said.

Carson eventually gave up and let the women play a new game they called, "Alejandro In or Out," but added the words, "of Who?"

Now, alone in the corner of the gym, running steadily on the machine with two clear views, Alicia stopped thinking about Alejandro and his *pumas*, and started thinking about Donald Trump, Fay Wray, Michael Jackson, Johnny Carson, Liberace, and Sophia Loren.

TWO WEEKS BEFORE, just as she'd come out of the afternoon story meeting, one of the college students who worked as a research assistant in the newsroom announced, "Some agent-man called and left a voice mail."

"Some agent-man?"

"He said he was an agent and he was a man, hence . . . "

"Agent-man," Alicia nodded. "Thanks," and went to listen to the message.

It was from Mel Berger at William Morris Endeavor. "We've got a project that might interest you. Will you give me a call, please?"

She dialed the number he had left, and when a man answered, she announced, "It's Alicia Melendez calling for . . . "

Before she could say, "Mr. Berger," he himself asked, "How would you like to write a book?"

"A book? Me? What about?"

"Let's meet."

"Give me a hint."

"No," he said, "because I may have to talk you into it and I won't be able to do that over the phone."

Intrigued, she agreed to stop by his office that evening after she got off the air.

"There's not a lot of money in it," Berger explained, sitting her down at the big, round table he used as his desk in the middle of the book-lined room. "But you're the perfect person to write it."

He had a friendly face, a big smile, and seemed pretty hip. She thought he looked a little like a blue-eyed, younger version of Al Pacino.

"Do I get to find out what I'm writing about before I write it?"

"Biggest tourist attraction in New York."

She said, "The Empire State Building."

"Good guess, no cigar."

"The Statue of Liberty?"

"Bigger. You need a boat to get to the statue. Your place, you don't need a boat."

"My place? NBC? Thirty Rock?"

He shook his head. "Trump Tower."

She didn't understand. "Trump Tower is the biggest tourist attraction in New York?"

"More tourists . . . more foot traffic . . . go through Trump Tower than anywhere else in New York. Iconic building. Big name brand. Free admission. No boat needed. The thirtieth anniversary is coming up. You live there, right?"

She nodded.

"Coffee table book. Gorgeous photographs. Twenty-five thousand words max. History of the building and some stories of the famous people who've lived there."

She was hesitant. "I don't think the people who live there necessarily want to find their names in a book . . . "

"Donald Trump?"

"Okay, yeah," she nodded. "But the others . . . "

"Fay Wray?"

"She's dead, so she probably won't mind."

"Michael Jackson?"

"That's three, but . . . "

"Johnny Carson?"

"Four."

"Liberace?"

"He lived there?"

"Sophia Loren?"

"She lived there too?"

"But not with Liberace," Berger smiled. "Steven Spielberg?"

"Ah . . . he will mind. At least, I think he will."

"Mikey Glass?"

"You sure he lives there? I thought he lives in LA. I mean, he's still doing that sitcom, right?"

"When they can't get Charlie Sheen, they get him. Except when they anger Ashton Kutcher. Mikey's wife and kids live in the Tower . . . sometimes. And he stays there too when he's in New York."

"Well . . . if he's stoned or drunk or both he won't mind. And, from what the papers say about him, if he isn't yet stoned or drunk or both, he's too busy working on it. So, okay, he won't mind."

"Andrew Lloyd Webber?"

"Oh, I suspect that he will mind."

"Cyndi Benson?"

"This one I know for sure," Alicia grinned. "Nothing fazes Cyndi. Absolutely nothing at all. But the others . . . "

"Edmond Greenwich?"

She pondered that. "If Andrew Lloyd Webber is in and Edmond's not, he'll mind a lot. Composers are very competitive. If Andrew Lloyd Webber is not in and Edmond is, Edmond might buy a lot of extra copies. But then . . . Andrew will scream bloody murder."

"Zeke Gimbel?"

She conceded, "He might actually sue if he's *not* in."

"The Holy Ghost?"

She was surprised. "Somebody from the Bible lives in Trump Tower?"

"The Yankee's Holy Ghost."

"Oh . . . him. Roberto Santos. Ah . . . I don't know. No one ever sees him. I mean, I've never seen him."

"Ricky Lips?"

She started laughing. "You mean, Richard Lipschitz of Ealing Broadway, West London, England Fucking UK?"

He looked at her. "What?"

"Lyrics to one of their songs. I take it you're not a big Still Fools fan."

"I prefer Jacques Brel. But he never lived in Trump Tower."

"And I've never written a book before."

"Most people haven't. But you may be the only person living in Trump Tower who can."

She thought about that for a moment, then went back to what he'd said about money. "How much is not a lot?"

"You live in Trump Tower so you obviously don't need the money . . . "

She immediately corrected him. "You wouldn't say that if you lived there. Maybe no one who lives there actually needs the money, but everyone who lives there can always actually use the money."

"Twenty-five thousand words . . . I can get you forty grand."

She confessed, "That will buy a few pairs of shoes."

"It works out to a dollar-sixty a word."

She wondered, "A buck-sixty for 'the' and 'and' and 'of' and 'holy ghost'?"

Now he corrected her. "Holy Ghost gets you three-twenty."

"SEÑORA?"

She was going at a pretty good pace now.

"Señora?" It was Alejandro signaling to her. "Señora?" He slowed down the machine. "Enough for today."

She stayed on the machine, at a walking pace, warming down before he stopped it completely and she stepped off.

"Wow," she said, putting her hands on her knees and trying to catch her breath. "Did I do all five miles? It felt like more." She looked at the number on the digital display. "Six and a half? No way. Really? Wow."

"See you Monday, Señora," Alejandro said.

She stood up and was about to wave goodbye when she noticed two older women coming into the gym.

One of them was the wrinkly old wife of some retired German business-man. The other, Alicia seemed to think, was married to a jeweler. She made a mental note to tell Cyndi there were two more candidates for the Alejandro list.

Back in her apartment, Alicia took a shower and got dressed. On the way out of the Tower, the concierge handed her an envelope that had been biked over. Inside were several dozen printed pages and a note from Mel Berger. "Sign all three copies and send them back to me. You are about to become a published author."

Smiling, she read the contract as she walked.

Arriving in the newsroom, she went to her desk and signed the contracts.

"What's that?" her editor, Howie, wanted to know.

"I'm writing a book," she said.

"Good for you," he said. "I hope you have the time."

"Why wouldn't I have the time?"

"You didn't hear this from me," he whispered. "They may or may not want you to know yet. And if you are supposed to know, they'll want to tell you themselves upstairs. But . . . substitute anchor at *Nightly*? You made the short list."

5

Zeke Gimbel, a smallish forty-five-year-old with a three-day growth of beard, thinning hair and a craggy but smiling face, looked at his tiny, white-haired, seventy-seven-year-old mother, Hattie, shook his head, turned to his lawyer, silent partner and oldest friend from childhood, Bobby Lerner, and sighed, "You talk to her. She always liked you best, anyway."

"Not true," the tall, heavy-set, nearly bald Lerner replied. "She likes me bet-ter, but not best. First, she likes her grandchildren."

Hattie cut in, "If I'd known better, I would have had them first."

"See?" Bobby continued, "Then comes your sister, your brother and me.

You come in a distant twelfth, after my wonderful, adorable and loving wife, your sister's idiot husband, your brother's have-you-seen-my-new-boobs-yet wife, your first wife, and Jay Leno."

Hattie closed her eyes and turned away. "At least Jay Leno wouldn't steal money from his mother."

"No one is stealing anything from you." Zeke took a deep breath, "Here we go again."

They were sitting at a table, under an umbrella by the huge swimming pool at Mar-A-Lago in Palm Beach, Florida.

Once the seventeen-acre private estate of Marjorie Merriweather Post—daughter of the man whose Post Toasties became the cornflakes staple of his cereal empire—when the house was completed in 1927, it had 115 rooms and its own nine-hole golf course. Then said to be the fifth-largest private residence in the country, today it is officially classified as a national historic landmark.

It sits on what might be the most unique and prime piece of property in all of south Florida, running from the Atlantic Ocean beachfront all the way to Lake Worth on the other side. In fact, the estate is so large that one night, after one of Merriweather Post's famously lavish dinner parties, there was enough room on the property for the entire Ringling Brothers and Barnum and Bailey Circus to entertain.

Heir to her father's fortune, which included cereals and other foods, plus oil-rich land in Texas, she married four times—husband number two was Wall Street financier E. F. Hutton, and their daughter, Nedenia Marjorie Hutton, grew up to be the actress Dina Merrill—and bequeathed Mar-A-Lago to the US government. Her idea was that it should be used as a guesthouse for foreign dignitaries and a winter White House for the president. Although no president ever lived there, the Kennedy family compound is down the beach, and JFK himself knew the house well.

When it became too expensive for the government to maintain, the estate was returned to the Merriweather Post family. Donald Trump bought it from them in 1985, modernized everything, and turned it into one of the most exclusive private clubs in the country.

Zeke Gimbel left Creative Artists Agency in 1999 to start his own agency, "Z." He joined Mar-A-Lago five years later.

"The United States Senate is the most exclusive club in the country," he once told the *Los Angeles Times*, "after Mar-A-Lago."

By then he'd bought out two smaller firms, had orchestrated an audacious takeover of the much bigger, much more powerful First National Artists, and followed that by purchasing another two smaller firms.

Suddenly, he found himself fourth in the Hollywood agency pecking order, after International Creative Management, William Morris Endeavor and CAA.

Now, he was looking to become an even bigger player.

"You want me out of your company?" His mother was still not looking at him. "This is how you show your appreciation?"

He tried, yet again, to reason with her. "I need you to sign these papers because if you don't and something goes wrong . . . I am showing you my appreciation . . . and my love . . . by telling you up front that your money is not going to be safe in the company because of the way Bobby and I have structured this deal and . . . "

"And, you want me out."

"And . . . yes . . . I want you out."

She turned back but looked at Bobby. "Did you ever hear of such a thing? A son throwing his own mother out of the family business?"

"Hattie . . . that's not what this is."

She shook her head. "His brother the doctor wouldn't do this to his mother."

Zeke told her, "My brother the doctor is too busy to phone his mother every day."

"Of course, he's busy. He runs that whole department, and he has a wonderful practice and two gorgeous, gorgeous children."

"And a wife you can't always stand."

Hattie shrugged, "Maybe not my cup of tea two or three days a week, but she's been a good mother to those gorgeous little children."

"Who are not so little and, frankly, not necessarily so gorgeous."

"They're still my grandchildren."

"So are Zoey and Max," he reminded her. "But my brother's children can do no wrong. And my sister's children are royalty."

"I never said anything of the kind. But when was the last time your children came to stay with their grandmother? In fact, when was the last time you came to stay with your mother?"

"I'm here with you now."

"No, you're in some fancy place and you schlep me over to see you. Could it hurt to come and see me?"

He sighed in exasperation. "Mother, we can't keep going round and round with this. Right now, your money . . . your shares in the company . . . are not safe. If I blow this deal, you could lose a lot of money. We both could. So we're putting your shares, your money, into another company. I'm protecting you." He begged, "Mother, please, sign the damn papers."

She gave him an angry look, then said to Bobby, "Give me a pen," and showed her total disdain by mumbling as she signed.

"Thank you." Zeke leaned over and tried to kiss his mother.

She moved away. "So now what? I live on my social security?"

Bobby put his hand on Hattie's arm. "I promise you, everything is the same. Nothing has changed. You have nothing to worry about."

"Of course not." She stood up. "Because my daughter and her husband and my other son will always look after me, no matter what."

"You're right, mother." He stood up too, and signaled to a valet standing on the verandah that his mother needed her car. "As long as your daughter and her husband and your other son . . . the doctor . . . if they can remember your phone number, I'm sure they'll do what they can for you."

She started walking toward the main house.

Zeke hurried up to her and took her arm. They walked like that, not speaking, through the house and out to the front driveway.

A Mercedes was already there with a chauffeur holding open the rear door.

Zeke leaned over and kissed her. "I love you. I'll talk to you tomorrow. And . . . I love you."

She nodded and got into the car.

He gave her a little wave.

Just as the chauffeur was closing the door, she reminded him, "Jay Leno would never do this to his mother."

Bobby walked up to Zeke and waved at Hattie as the car pulled away. "Call your sister. Maybe your mother will believe her."

"I refuse to cater to her bullshit. I've got to go. Thanks for handling this."

"That's what lawyers are for."

"I wish she'd understand."

"Mothers don't understand. They accept."

Zeke sighed and nodded. "Speaking of accepting . . . when do we hear back on the Sovereign Shields buyout?"

"It's only now about numbers. They're close."

"I hope it doesn't get in the way of this other thing. Deals coming from two different directions meet in the middle and . . . boom."

"Stop worrying."

"I'm my mother's son."

Sometime after Zeke and Bobby started putting together the complex deal that could take Z from being just another big agency into the stratosphere as a global entertainment industry powerhouse, Zeke had been in negotiations to buy the Sovereign Shields Sports Agency, the last vestige of the once-famous Gerald Shields' sports empire.

Forty years ago, Shields had been a visionary, much like Mark McCormack, in realizing the marketing potential of athletes. Unlike McCormack, however, whose commercial success, beginning in the 1960s with golfer Jack Nicklaus, really paved the way for the Federers, Beckhams and Woods of the modern era, Shields left the already-established pros to McCormack and waded into the amateur pools, looking for future stars.

He crisscrossed the country, sitting through thousands of high school and college basketball games, and football games, and baseball games, and track meets, and lacrosse practice, and inner-city gyms, and inner-city basketball courts, and even Saturday morning suburban soccer games in search of the next Tom Seaver, Edwin Moses, Joe Namath, Walt Frazier and Sugar Ray Leonard.

After two years of nonstop traveling, he'd discovered—and locked into iron-clad contracts—budding superstars like the Lakers' point guard Le-Vaughan Sylvester, Dodgers reliever Jovani San Pedro Santiago, Miami Dolphins all-pro receiver Longman Watt, Yankee second baseman Devontae "Crawfish" Perkins and world welterweight champion Filiberto "Kid" Cabrera.

Over the next ten years, any athlete not on McCormack's roster belonged—lock, stock and barrel—to Gerald Shields.

But by the time Tom Cruise came along as Jerry McGuire, and Cuba Gooding Jr. screamed, "Show me the money," sports agents were running all over the country, in colleges and high schools and drilling down deep into junior highs in search of the next big name.

Suddenly there was Don Meehan and Drew Rosenhaus, Tom Condon and Arn Tellem, and of course Scott Boras. And they were into everything, not just working the three big ball sports, and golf, tennis, boxing and ice hockey, but motor racing, horse racing, wrestling, soccer, lacrosse, rugby, track, field, gymnastics, even cricket and bowling.

Wherever there were athletes who could sell something, there were agents trying to sell athletes.

Gerald Shields sold out to the Truman brothers—Alan and Adam—two lawyers from the Cincinnati suburbs, but the cutthroat nature of the business became too much for them. They had a few big stars, but mostly they had young athletes whose careers were stalled.

Now Zeke Gimbel wanted to enter the fray.

"As soon as they sign," Zeke explained, "we hand the keys to the door to Perry and Monica." They were two young hotshot lawyers who worked for Z in LA. "We move them into new offices and keep them ring-fenced so that nothing that happens there can affect anything else. If that goes wrong, I don't want it bringing us down. If our deal goes wrong, the sports side may be all we have left."

"Compared to you," Bobby said, "Hattie is an optimist."

"Murphy's Law?" He looked at his old friend. "And it was Murphy who was the optimist."

"I still have doubts about the deadwood."

"Why?

"Because you think you can trade your way into a profitable business. Why would some other agency want the athletes you can't sell?"

"They're jocks, they get traded all the time. What's the difference if they go from Z to IMG, or from the Padres to the Cubs? Why do the Bears buy someone the Cowboys don't want?"

"Mr. Gimbel?" Giorgio, the resident manager, stepped outside. "You look well."

"Hi there. You too." He shook Giorgio's hand. "I got in last night . . . leaving today, right now, in fact."

"Back to Los Angeles?"

"No. New York for a party. LA tomorrow."

"Mr. Lerner?" Giorgio said, "Everything is arranged."

"I'll just go upstairs and grab my bag," Zeke said. Then he asked Bobby, "What's arranged?"

Giorgio held up his hand to show Zeke there was no need to go upstairs. "I'll have it brought down. And your car . . . to PBI?"

"The airport, yeah, thank you."

Giorgio stepped back inside the house.

"What's arranged?" Zeke asked again, as he took his cell phone and speed-dialed his pilot's cell. "See you in half an hour."

"Ready when you are," the pilot told him.

Zeke hung up and looked at Bobby. "You want to come to New York?"

"Sorry. Everything's arranged."

"Everything . . . what?"

Giorgio came back, said to Zeke, "Your bag will be right down." Then he looked at Bobby, "Is there anything else I can do?"

"Time out," Zeke gestured with both hands. "What are you guys talking about?"

"Being your friend is a hardship," Bobby explained. "In fact, the only benefit is that, when I told Mr. Giorgio I'd be here with you, he got me a tee-off time at Trump National. In an hour."

Zeke assured Giorgio, "I never saw him before."

"That's all right, sir, I'll vouch for Mr. Lerner. He's welcome any time."

"You're a gentleman and a scholar," Bobby patted Giorgio on his shoulder, then told Zeke, "He's even putting the green fee on your bill."

"A pleasure," Giorgio said, shook Zeke's hand and added, "Have a safe trip, sir. We look forward to seeing you again soon."

When they were alone again, Zeke put his arms around Bobby and hugged him. "I'm forty-five years old. I'm worth a hundred million dollars. I try to do the right thing for my mother, and she treats me like I'm twelve."

Bobby hugged him back. "If we can pull all this stuff off, you're going to be worth ten times as much and . . . you know what?"

"What?"

"Hattie is still going to treat you like you're twelve."

6

He played the conversation over again in his head.
Is she qualified?
She has a background in hotels.
I mean, is she qualified to steal your job?
It was a question Belasco had never even contemplated.

"If you can handle Frank Sinatra," Donald Trump had said to Belasco in Monte Carlo all those years ago, "you should be running a business for me."

"Thank you, but I'm not looking for a job, sir," he'd responded. "I already have the best job in the world."

"You only think so because you haven't yet heard my offer. I want you to run Trump Tower."

"Thank you anyway, sir." He'd said it as diplomatically as he could, "But leaving here is the farthest thing in my mind right now. I'm in the hotel business. It's what I do. It's who I am."

Although, Belasco had to admit to himself, if his first job as a sixteen-year-old assistant luggage porter at the Grand Hotel du Golf in his native ski resort village of Crans Montana, Switzerland, was one end of the spectrum, running Trump Tower was definitely the other.

He'd taken the porter job because he'd not been happy in school. His mother saw it as demeaning. He assured her it was just the first rung on the ladder. And, within six months, he'd maneuvered himself to the front desk as a receptionist.

A year after that, he was hired as a receptionist at the prestigious Baur au Lac Hotel in Zurich.

Three years later, when the assistant manager there left to become manager of the Hassler in Rome, he brought Belasco with him to be assistant manager for guest relations.

Three years after that, Belasco was recruited to become the youngest-ever food and beverage manager at the Danieli in Venice. He stayed there another three years, then moved on to be the assistant manager at the Crillon in Paris.

It was another three years when, at the age of twenty-nine, he was hired as the youngest-ever general manager at the legendary Raffles Hotel in Singapore.

From there he moved to London to run the ultra-stuffy Connaught Hotel and two years later, in 1991, he was hired by the Société des Bains de Mer in Monaco to be general manager for group hotels.

Overseeing the Hôtel de Paris, the Hermitage and the splendid Old Beach, Belasco worked out of a mezzanine office off the lobby of the Hôtel de Paris.

That's where Frank Sinatra changed his life.

During the five years that Belasco was there, Sinatra and his wife were frequent guests. There had been occasional incidents where Sinatra showed his displeasure with one thing or another—usually the paparazzi—but there'd hardly ever been anything like that Saturday night in 1996.

The Sinatras were having dinner in the big, ornate Louis XV restaurant on the ground floor with Roger Moore and his wife. Donald Trump was in Monaco at the same time and he'd joined them.

The bodyguards were at a nearby table.

Over dinner, Barbara Sinatra said something—no one remembers exactly what it was, except that it seemed harmless at the time—but it set off Sinatra's temper, and he started yelling and shouting at her.

Moore tried to calm him down, which did no good, while Trump tried to pretend it wasn't happening by turning his chair halfway around toward Roger's wife and making small talk with her. "Is your dish good? How's the wine? Isn't the bread wonderful? What do you think we should have for dessert?"

Sinatra's tirade went on to everyone's great embarrassment—especially Barbara Sinatra's—until, just like that, he went back to eating. He looked at the others, "Eat, *mangiate*, it's going to get cold." But before the five of them got to dessert, Sinatra announced, "Let's go shoot craps," got up and left.

The others decided not to stay at the table, so they followed him out to the lobby.

The bodyguards dropped their knives and forks and rushed out too.

Sinatra led the march to the front of the lobby where, in the right corner, there is a glass door.

Hidden behind it is an elevator.

The five of them crammed in and rode it down to a secret tunnel. The bodyguards arrived on the next elevator. But just as they all started making their way through the well-lit underground passageway, heading for the elevator at the far end that would bring them up inside the casino, a young couple in evening dress approached from the other direction.

The man, holding hands with a pretty woman, stopped. "Excuse me, Mr. Sinatra, my new wife and I, we just got married and we're on our honeymoon, and I want you to know how many romantic evenings we've had to your music. May I take a picture of you with my wife?" He pulled a little camera out of his pocket.

He might as well have waved a red flag in front of a bull.

Sinatra suddenly got furious, leaned back, and smacked the young man in the head, then screamed, "How the fuck dare you put your hand in my face?"

The young man fell to the ground.

His bride yelled.

The bodyguards rushed forward as Sinatra kicked the young man.

One of the guards grabbed Sinatra and pulled him away. The others got him into the elevator and to the Hôtel de Paris lobby, at which time Sinatra calmly announced, "The evening is over. Good night," and went up to his suite.

The young man, who had one black eye and several sore ribs, reported the incident to the night manager. Acting strictly by the book, the night manager alerted the general manager and the general manager alerted Belasco.

Immediately, Belasco arranged for a doctor to come to the hotel to treat the young man, then comped the honeymooning couple's entire stay. He insisted that there would be no bill and invited them to enjoy all of SBM's facilities as his guest.

The bride and groom said the only thing they wanted to do was go home.

Belasco moved them into a big suite on the top floor and sat with them for several hours, eventually persuading them to stay so that he could arrange fabulous day trips with chauffeured limousines, helicopter rides, a day on a private yacht, several romantic meals, a private jet to Paris and Concorde tickets back to the States.

On Sunday morning, Belasco told room service that he wanted to be notified as soon as the Sinatras ordered breakfast. He then went to speak to Moore and Trump about the incident. Both men admitted it might have been the most embarrassing night of their lives.

He'd just finished with them when a room service order was placed for the Sinatra suite. Belasco hurried down to the florist, picked up a bouquet of thirty-six long-stemmed red roses and personally wheeled the breakfast cart into the suite.

"Those for me?" Sinatra said, wearing a silk dressing gown. "I don't usually get roses from guys."

Belasco smiled. "Do you mind if I give them to Madame, instead?"

"Good idea, pal." Sinatra said, "Maybe she'll talk to you." He walked into the hallway and shouted toward one of the suite's two bedrooms, "How about breakfast and roses?"

The door was shut and there was no answer.

"I'll put them in a vase," Belasco said, then asked, "Dining room? Living room? Terrace?"

While Belasco filled a vase with water and carefully placed the roses in it, Sinatra walked out onto the big terrace, which overlooked the harbor. "Weather's great. Let's eat out here."

"Have a seat, I'll be right there."

He finished with the flowers, placed the vase in the living room with a note to Mrs. Sinatra that simply said, "We honor your presence—Pierre Belasco," and brought a tray out to the terrace.

"Grab a cup yourself," Sinatra said. "You're probably the only guy in town who's still talking to me."

Belasco laid out Sinatra's breakfast on a table next to his chair—the hotel specialized in fresh-baked mini-*croissants* and mini-*pains au chocolate*—poured coffee for him, and handed him a glass of fresh-squeezed orange juice.

"Where's your coffee?" he said. "Come on, sit down."

Belasco poured a cup for himself and sat down.

"Ever been over there?" Sinatra pointed to the palace. "I used to stay there when Grace was alive. Ever meet her?"

"I have been to the palace, yes . . . but unfortunately, I did not know the princess."

"Unfortunately is right. She was one classy dame, let me tell you. When we did that picture together, *High Society*, she was already engaged to Ray. We knew that after we finished, she was going off to get married, so we gave her an early wedding present. Guess what it was?"

"What's that?"

"A roulette wheel." Sinatra laughed. "What else? And in that picture, you know she's supposed to be engaged to get married, so she's wearing a big ring. That's actually the ring Ray gave her. It's real. No paste on her finger. Yeah," he said, taking his orange juice, "one classy dame."

"She certainly is missed," Belasco said. "I saw that as soon as I arrived here."

"What's it now . . . fourteen, fifteen years? Something like that." He finished his juice. "Speaking of rings . . . is Van Cleef and Arpels open today?"

"Sunday? I'm afraid not."

"Too bad. Especially because she'll know those roses are from you, not me."

Belasco understood what Sinatra was thinking. "If you'd like, I might be able to ring someone and make arrangements, not at the store, but for a visit here."

"Yeah," Sinatra nodded several times. "Good. Tell them big. I want a whole selection. Diamonds. You can do that?"

"I'm sure I can," Belasco said.

"Good . . . good." He took a *croissant* and ate it whole, followed it with some coffee and then ate a *pain au chocolate*. "How's the kid," he asked while chewing, not looking at Belasco. "I guess I duked him too good, huh?"

"I moved him and his bride into a big suite, and we're arranging some special trips and meals for the rest of their stay. I'm also flying them home on the Concorde."

"How bad was he hurt?"

"Black eye . . . and his ribs are tender."

"Is he really on his honeymoon?"

"Yes."

Sinatra stayed silent for the longest time. "Yeah . . . Van Cleef . . . I need them."

Belasco pointed toward the telephone in the living room. "May I?"

"Yeah."

Going to the phone, he called the switchboard and asked a woman there to locate the manager of the local Van Cleef's.

She managed it quickly.

When he got the man on the phone, Belasco explained that Mr. Sinatra wanted to make a purchase and the man agreed to come to the hotel.

Hanging up with him, Belasco walked back onto the terrace. "Is an hour good for you?"

Sinatra leaned over and patted Belasco on the face. "I love you, baby. Thank you."

When the Van Cleef and Arpels' manager arrived carrying a large case— with two bodyguards in tow—Belasco accompanied him up to the suite.

The roses were where he'd put them in the living room and Mrs. Sinatra was nowhere to be seen.

He introduced the man to Sinatra, the bodyguards withdrew to the hallway, and Belasco left them alone.

That evening, the young bride and groom asked to see Belasco. He went up to their suite and they seemed very confused.

"Look," the young man showed Belasco a diamond-studded broach. "He gives me a black eye and thinks he can buy off my wife with this."

Belasco hadn't realized that Sinatra was including them on his shopping list. "I'm sure it is meant as an apology."

"Then why didn't he apologize? No note. No nothing. Just this delivered in a box by some jewelry store guy who said this is from Frank Sinatra."

"It is very beautiful."

"We don't want it."

"You don't?"

"No. I'm not going to give that asshole the satisfaction of thinking he can just waltz in . . . "

His bride reluctantly agreed. "My husband is right."

Belasco suggested, "I'm sure that if you wanted to exchange it for something else . . . "

"No," the groom said. "We're returning it." Then he had a second thought. "And we'll keep the cash."

Belasco almost smiled. "If that's what you want, sir, I will make the suitable arrangements for you."

"That's exactly what we want," the groom said, looking at his bride, who put her hand on his black eye, and nodded. "We want the money."

On Monday morning, at Belasco's request, the man from Van Cleef and Arpels handed the young couple a check for $62,500.

Later that morning, Mrs. Sinatra came to Belasco's office to thank him for the roses. She was wearing a brand new diamond ring which, Belasco eventually learned, had cost her husband $5 million.

Then Sinatra himself showed up. "You're my guy, Pierre. Thank you for taking care of everything." He handed Belasco a small gift-wrapped package.

"I couldn't possibly, sir."

"The hell you can't," Sinatra grinned. "Turn me down, and I'll give you a black eye too."

Belasco thanked Sinatra. "This is very generous. Shall I open it now?"

"What the hell pal you going to wait for Chanukah?"

Inside was a pair of gold- and diamond-studded cuff links.

"These are magnificent. Thank you, very much."

He patted the side of Belasco's face and without saying anything more, walked away.

The Van Cleef manager confided in Belasco that Sinatra had paid $30,000 for the cuff links.

Unlike the groom and his bride, Belasco kept his gift.

An hour after Sinatra handed him the cuff links, Donald Trump appeared in Belasco's office.

"Frank tells me you're the greatest thing since sliced bread. Who the hell did you have to murder to make him so happy?"

"Just doing my job, sir."

"If you can handle Frank Sinatra," Trump said, "you should be running a business for me."

"Thank you, but I'm not looking for a job, sir. I already have the best job in the world."

"You only think so because you haven't yet heard my offer. I want you to run Trump Tower."

"Thank you, anyway, sir. But leaving here is the farthest thing in my mind right now. I'm in the hotel business. It's what I do. It's who I am."

"That's why I need you." Trump explained, "Until now, I've always had real estate people running Trump Tower. I need a hotel guy. But not just any hotel guy. I need you. And I want to do a deal with you right now."

"But sir . . . "

"I'm a deal guy." Trump leaned across Belasco's antique French desk, took a piece of paper and a pencil, and wrote down a number. "That's for openers."

He shoved the piece of paper in front of Belasco.

"There are also benefits and profit sharing. With various performance bonuses built into the deal, you could easily double that."

Belasco looked at the number and then at Trump. "You are serious about this."

He pointed to the paper. "That's a serious number. I'm back in New York next weekend. I'll FedEx a contract. Budget and personnel go through my director of operations. But you don't. You report directly to me. We'll move you from here and find you a great apartment somewhere in the Tower. I don't know what's available, but we'll find something you'll love."

"No, sir."

"What?" Trump couldn't believe it. "This is the greatest job in the world."

Belasco stared at the number on the piece of paper. "In this business, it's always better if the general manager doesn't live in. Perhaps . . . something suitable downtown?"

"Mr. Belasco?"

Trump extended his hand. "You're my guy."

"Mr. Belasco, sir?"

He snapped back to the moment. "Yes?"

"Forty-two, sir." Miguel the elevator operator said. "Your floor, sir."

"Oh . . . " He stepped out of the elevator. "Yes, Mrs. Essenbach's floor . . . thank you."

Is she qualified?

She has a background in hotels.

I mean, is she qualified to steal your job?

The elevator doors closed and Pierre Belasco said out loud, "Not in this lifetime."

7

C arson Haynes didn't mind getting up at five because, that way, he could get the running machine in the corner with the best views. And he always left the gym at 5:35 to go back to his apartment on the fifty-second floor to shower, dress and be at his office by six—First Ace Capital on the twenty-third floor—because, that way, he got there before anyone else.

Past the big door with the tennis ball logo, there was a small reception area and behind that an open-plan office for two secretaries. To the right was a small trading room with terminals and huge screens—the four traders who worked First Ace's little hedge fund usually staggered in by 6:30—and on the left of the open plan was a conference room, a bathroom, and a small kitchen.

Two private offices—tiny by Wall Street executive standards—ran along the Fifty-Sixth Street side of the building and weren't particularly private. Both had a glass wall looking back into the open plan. There was just enough room in each of those offices for a desk and a couch. But the day they moved in, Tommy Arcarro hung a framed sign on his glass door that read, "Size only matters if you don't know what you're doing."

His office was on the left. He handled their institutional customers and the hedge fund.

Carson's office was on the right. He dealt with their four private clients and was rainmaker-in-chief.

As always, the moment he stepped into his office, Carson turned on his computer, then went to make a latte on the espresso machine in the kitchen. By that time, the kid from the Greek's place over on Fifty-Ninth Street was there with his daily breakfast order—fresh papaya juice and a buttered bialy—which he took back to his office.

He then went through his double-wink ritual.

First, he winked at Rod Laver.

While Tommy used what little wall space he had to hang framed photos of himself playing tennis, Carson hung a large LeRoy Neiman oil painting of his hero winning the 1969 US Open at Forest Hills.

Then he winked at Alicia.

He'd taken that photo of her one morning on the deck of the beach house they'd rented in Aruba while the sun was coming up and her hair was blowing in the dawn breeze.

The photo always made him smile.

It sat on the window ledge, right next to his all-time favorite tennis trophy—fourteen large sterling silver letters on a black Belgian marble base, spelling out "Bragging Rights."

The trophy always made him proud.

Settling in to study his overnight e-mails, he sipped his juice until he spotted one that read, "I'm up."

Without checking the others, he speed-dialed Ken Warring in Omaha, and when Warring picked up, Carson wanted to know, "Why?"

"'Cause when I was your age," he said, "I was coming in at this hour, and now, at my age, when you're going out, I'm going to bed." But that was the extent of his morning small talk. "You see his e-mail yet?"

Putting down his juice, Carson quickly ran through his in-box until he found it.

I will not agree to your terms, but I will agree to meet.

"I see it," Carson said. "What do you think it means?"

"It means that," Warring said, "he thinks we're fools. We stay home, the deal is over, he wins. We go to Japan, the deal is still over, he still wins."

Warring had bought into a Japanese conglomerate, Shigetada Industries, after a chance meeting with the man who founded it, Chokichi Shigetada. They'd bumped into each other in 1993 in South Africa, where they'd both been the guest of Nelson Mandela at a gala party to celebrate his Nobel Peace Prize. Both of them had done business in South Africa, and both of them had been vocal Mandela supporters.

During the gala dinner, Shigetada mentioned to Warring that he was looking for private equity. Three weeks later, Warring became Shigetada's largest minority shareholder.

Everything worked fine, as far as Warring was concerned, until old man Shigetada passed away and Shigetada's eldest son, Daitaro—who was already in his sixties—took over.

Junior didn't have his father's business skills or, as far as Warring was concerned, his father's deeply ingrained culture.

They'd had no dealings at all while the old man was alive, but the moment Junior took over, he did not hide his resentment toward Warring for having ignored him. They clashed over business and they clashed personally, until Warring decided he wanted out. He liked the business enough to put an offer on the table to buy it. And he disliked Daitaro Shigetada enough to come up with a number for which Warring would sell his holding.

But Warring's price for buying was too low and his price for selling was too high to suit Shigetada, who now accused Warring of deliberately undermining him.

"How do you want to play it?" Carson asked.

"For keeps," Warring answered.

"We go?"

"No, you go."

"Let me think for a moment," Carson said, wanting the time to tear off a small piece of bialy and pop it into his mouth. "He's got fifty-one percent of the shares. We're second with twenty-two. So there's still twenty-seven out there. We know eighteen are with the institutions. That leaves nine somewhere. He knows the institutions aren't sellers and that if we picked up all of the remaining nine, we'd have to declare any intention to bid. It does us no good."

"Tell me something I don't know," Warring growled.

"How about something he doesn't know . . . that we're holding a lot of his paper."

"And?"

"And how about we threaten to call it in?"

"Then what?"

"Only some of the company's debt is secured. We threaten to pull the bottom out, half the institutions sell, half of the remaining nine sell, we drop our shares onto the market, and his paper goes down the toilet. He's out of business. We buy it all back at fire-sale prices."

"I like it," Warring said. "Except . . . that could put us out of business, too."

"Probably would, if we actually do it. It's called poker."

"And if he sees us and goes all in . . . it's called hara-kiri."

Carson checked the time. "It's quarter after eight at night in Japan. Nothing's going to happen now until Monday morning, Tokyo time. Let me keep thinking, and I'll get back to you."

When they hung up, Carson e-mailed Shigetada that he would come to Tokyo and asked if they could meet next Friday.

Much to Carson's surprise, an e-mail came back from Shigetada himself saying, "Come now. I will see you tomorrow."

"Sorry, dude," Carson said to his screen and e-mailed back, "I will be in Tokyo next Friday."

Shigetada responded, "I won't be."

"Then there is nothing more to discuss," Carson wrote, held his breath, and sent the e-mail.

This time, there was no immediate answer.

Carson stared at his screen for nearly fifteen minutes.

Nothing came back from Tokyo.

WARRING'S WIFE, Anita, had been dying of breast cancer when, in 2001, he set up a charity called "Play for a Cure."

He hosted, and personally funded, an annual, all-Omaha tennis tournament, handing out prizes for every possible category of entry, from school children and young couples all the way up to "Over 80s" and handicapped players.

The culmination of the weeklong event was an invitation-only, all-day Sunday, pro-celebrity, round-robin doubles event that saw six teams playing each other, vying for the "Bragging Rights" trophy.

Carson had vaguely heard about it from some of the guys on the tour—they said it was a terrific weekend—but he never gave it any thought until, out of the blue, a few months after he quit the pro circuit, Warring phoned to invite him to play.

Carson told Alicia he wasn't interested.

She asked him, "Why? You got something better to do?"

In fact, he didn't.

He'd been earning good money playing tennis since before he graduated from Miami in 1998 with a BA in business. That meant weekends in Tallahassee and Mobile, Macon and Shreveport, Palm Beach and Orlando, but he paid off his student loans that way and earned pocket money hustling games at private tennis clubs around south Florida.

Within a year of graduation, he'd been runner-up four times on the Futures Tour, won twice—in Hilton Head and Cape Cod—and soon accumulated enough ranking points to move up to the Challengers Tour.

He won there too—in Brazil, Chile, Tunisia and Australia—and was quickly promoted again, now given access to all the ATP World Tour events, including the nine masters.

His first year on that tour he played in thirty events and actually won two—Qatar and Johannesburg—but failed to qualify for any of the big four majors.

The next year he won three—Acapulco, Calgary and Helsinki—but failed to get to Wimbledon and lost handily in the first round in Australia. He did, however, make it into the second round in both the French and US Opens.

The year after that, he won four tournaments around the world—Salt Lake City, Quito, Mumbai and Johannesburg for the second time—but still couldn't progress past the second rounds of any of the big four.

But by now, traveling fifty weeks a year was taking its toll.

When he was beaten in the first round at Wimbledon in 2004 by Roger Federer—6–3, 6–3, 6–0—he shook the Swiss star's hand at the net and said, "I think I've had enough."

In the locker room, Federer asked what he meant by that.

"I'm tired," Carson said. "Not of playing tennis, but of the circuit. I'm tired of bad hotel rooms, I'm tired of bad food, I'm tired of airports, I'm tired of bimbos looking to score their first black guy, I'm tired of promising my girlfriend that I will make it big someday and that when I do, we'll have a great life together . . . because it's just not going to happen."

"You going to quit?" Federer asked it as if he couldn't imagine having any other life. "What are you going to do?"

"I've made enough money and still have most of it, so I can live okay. But I don't think I want this."

"What do you want?"

"Not what, who," he answered. "The girl back home."

Federer stared at him, as if the answer was obvious. "So what are you waiting for?"

Carson stared at him, "You're right," patted Federer on the arm, "Have a good life, *mon ami*," reached for his cell phone and dialed Miami.

As soon as Alicia answered he said, "Warm up the coffee, mama, I'm coming home."

She said sympathetically, "You lost already?"

"I did but you didn't."

"You did but I didn't . . . what?"

"I lost, you won."

"What did I win?"

"Me."

He flew back to Miami the next morning, and the two of them were married a week later in a small church in Little Havana.

The wedding made the front page of the *Miami Herald*.

Alicia had cohosted the biggest local morning show in Miami, *Today in South Florida*, on the NBC station since 2000.

Born and raised there—her father was a lawyer and her mother was a doctor—there wasn't anybody in Little Havana she didn't know, and there wasn't any Cuban in the entire state who she couldn't get to.

In 2000 she led the country on the coverage of the immigration and custody battle for the young Cuban refugee Elián González. Two years later she made headlines around the world covering the hunt for and capture of Miami's most powerful crack cocaine dealer, Ernesto "Machito" Faz.

Tipped off that the DEA was going to raid his heavily fortified house at the end of a dead-end street off West Flagler, Alicia had talked her way inside his house, with a camera crew, before the DEA arrived with a SWAT team from Miami-Dade Police. She'd wound up trapped there with Machito during a two-day standoff, all the time broadcasting regular reports that made it onto the network. The standoff had ended when Alicia convinced Machito to surrender. She walked him out and handed him over to the DEA.

She was a star.

But being Mr. Alicia Melendez was not what Carson wanted. And just two months into their marriage he confessed to her, "I really don't know what I want to do when I grow up."

That's when, out of the blue, Warring phoned. "I saw you play once in Palm Springs."

Carson told him, "I lost."

"And I saw you play in Vegas."

"I lost there, too."

"I saw you win in Punta del Este."

"See how far we both had to travel for a runner-up cut-glass vase?"

"I'll offer you a better trophy, and it's a lot closer. Come play in Omaha."

"Whoever you are, you're too late because I've hung up my Keds."

"It's a charity event," Warring said. "Last year I raised three mil. This year I'm gonna raise four. Give me an address, and I'll FedEx you all the bumf. Also, I read somewhere that you just got married. I'll send you a pair of first-class tickets. Maybe Omaha isn't much of a honeymoon destination, but I promise you'll have a good time."

The next day when a FedEx envelope arrived from Warring, Alicia Googled him, read several entries about him, and announced to Carson, "He's known as the other one."

"The other one what?"

"The other one other one," she said. "There are two in Omaha, and he's the other one."

"What are you talking about?"

"Gazillionaires. There's Warren Buffett, and there's Kenneth Warring."

Carson didn't want to know. "Just another rich guy."

"No," she insisted, "an extremely, very rich, rich guy . . . who likes you enough to invite us to Omaha for the weekend."

"He can't like me that much because he's inviting us to Omaha."

"You ever been there?"

"I have. And it was closed."

"I think we should go."

"Except you can't get there from here."

"He said he was sending us tickets . . . "

"What he didn't say was that we'll have to change planes nine times."

A week later, when Alicia opened the next FedEx from Warring, she told Carson, "He booked us on a direct flight."

"There is no direct flight from Miami to Omaha."

"On his airline there is." She said Warring was sending his plane for them, and hoped they could be there for lunch on Saturday.

Carson still wasn't sure. So Alicia mentioned on-air that she and Carson were going to the event and promised to report back on Monday's program.

That settled it and on that Saturday, Warring's G-5 whisked them off to Omaha.

Expecting a chauffeured limo to meet them, they were surprised to find Warring himself waiting for them, driving his own car.

Somewhere in his late sixties, he was short and robust, with a smallish head, large shoulders, no waist, a big grin and surprisingly large hands.

He brought them to a spectacular twelve-bedroom, 1930s mock Tudor home sitting on four acres in northeast Omaha, backing onto Carter Lake. Right away, he took them upstairs to introduce them to his third wife, Anita, who was in the final stages of the disease.

Alicia spent most of the weekend upstairs with her.

However, Anita did come down for lunch, so they were five. The other guest for lunch was Warren Buffett.

At dinner that night, under a huge marquee, everyone who was anyone in Omaha attended. So did a bunch of people Warring called "Non-Omers," including tennis greats Jimmy Connors and Ilie Nastase, boxer Smokin' Joe Frazier, actresses Morgan Fairchild and Rue McClanahan, actors Dick Van Dyke and John Spencer from the *West Wing*—it was just a year before he died—NBA star Karl Malone, Daunte Culpepper from the Minnesota Vikings and the inimitable Willie Nelson.

Warring got up at the end of the meal and announced that at this year's event, they'd raised $5.2 million.

Everyone stood up and applauded him, while he blew kisses to Anita.

Then Willie stood up.

Just like that, unplanned and unannounced, he walked to the front of the marquee, borrowed a guitar from a guy in the band, said, "Anita darlin', this is for you," and sang "On the Road Again," "Mamas Don't Let Your Babies Grow Up to Be Cowboys," and ended with "Blue Eyes Crying in the Rain."

The place went wild.

Before he sat down, he asked the audience, "Anyone know what the last thing is that a woman who sleeps with Willie Nelson wants to hear the next morning?" He said right away, "I'm not Willie Nelson."

On Sunday, Carson and Warring paired as a team and won the tournament. At the awards' presentation, Warring whispered to Carson he could only take the trophy home if he agreed to defend it next year.

Alicia and Carson have been back every year since. And Carson has won it two more times.

By now the charity tops $10 million a year.

But Warring has since changed the name of it. He calls it, "Anita's Play for a Cure."

She passed away ten days after Carson first played there.

As soon as they heard the news, Alicia and Carson rushed back to Omaha—"I don't care if we have to change planes fifty times," Carson said—to stand with Warring, holding his hand at Anita's funeral.

Three months later, Carson received a call from a woman at Goldman Sachs, asking if he could come to New York to meet with Mr. Green.

"Who's Mr. Green and why does he want to meet me?"

The woman was very vague and simply said she was relaying a message.

"From who?"

"From Mr. Green."

"But what does he want?"

"He wants to meet you."

"To do what? Play tennis? Sorry," he said, "I'm not interested."

The next thing Carson knew, Green himself was on the phone. "Please come to see me. I will explain everything when you get here."

When he got there, Carson was ushered into Gerald Green's huge corner office, where the sign on the door read, Vice Chairman. "We want you to come to work for us," Green said.

"Why?" Carson admitted, "I'm a has-been tennis player who doesn't know anything about finance, stocks, shares or the markets."

Green said, "You can learn."

Carson asked, "To do what? Be your corporate doubles partner?"

"That's not what this is all about."

"What is it all about?"

"It's about making money." Green said, "That's what we do. And one of our major private investors wants you on his investment team. He wants you to help us help him make money."

"Who?"

"Kenneth Warring."

That afternoon Carson phoned Warring to say thanks, "But what do I know from private investing?"

"You're going to learn," Warring said. "Because I have plans."

"For me?"

"For us."

"I appreciate it. But that world . . . "

"You have a degree in business."

"I have a piece of parchment that says I showed up and handed in enough term papers. Anyway . . . I can't take a job in New York. Alicia's show is doing really good. I'm not going to leave without her, and I can't ask her to give that up for me."

"Hang tight," Warring said. "I'm working on it. The difficult I can do right away. The impossible takes a day or two."

In fact, it was seven days later when Alicia received an offer she couldn't refuse from NBC—to anchor the flagship six o'clock news at their local New York affiliate, WNBC Channel 4.

Carson phoned Warring again. "How did you manage that?"

All he'd say was, "Sorry it took so long."

So the two of them moved to New York. Alicia established herself as a media personality, while Carson worked hard to learn the world of Wall Street.

Although he wasn't sure he'd figured it out enough by 2008, when the world's financial markets went into meltdown, other people believed that Carson knew what he was doing because he was asked to join Goldman's "Internal Team," the secret collective of traders, managers, gurus and strategists whose job it was to save the company from going broke.

After eight months of nonstop planning, convincing, conniving, buying, selling and restructuring—without any time off and hardly ever more than a couple of hours sleep a night—the sinking ship had been righted and was no longer taking on water.

That's when Warring told him, "Remember my plans for us? Now's as good a time as any. You and I are going out on our own."

"I am? We are?"

"Set up shop. I'll back us. Everybody's selling, so we're buying. Let's have some fun."

Carson went to see Warring in Puerto Vallarta where he was on his honeymoon with wife number four, Ellen Corley DeSoto, a blonde from Toronto who was a foot taller than him and at least thirty years younger.

She told Carson that she'd met Ken in Brazil, where she was living with her second husband, a racecar driver. According to Ellen, Warring had walked up to her at a party, said let's go, took her to his plane and flew her to Paris for a dirty weekend that turned into marriage.

But Warring said that he'd met Ellen in Monte Carlo on the arm of some British corporate raider and that he'd won her from the Brit after a long night in the private casino playing *chemin de fer*.

The truth, Carson decided, was probably somewhere between neither story and both.

Over the two days Carson was on their honeymoon with them, Warring drew up a business plan for a boutique operation that he decided should be called First Ace.

Carson's contribution was to add the word Capital.

Back in New York, Carson found office space downstairs in the Tower, called his old tennis pal Tommy Arcarro—who'd been on Wall Street much longer than him—and within two years they were flying higher than Carson ever imagined he would.

ALL OF A SUDDEN an e-mail arrived from Tokyo. "Friday, breakfast."

"You are not going to win," Carson said out loud to his screen, and e-mailed back, "Friday lunch. Omaha time. Or there is nothing more to discuss."

"You're correct," Shigetada wrote, "there is nothing more to discuss."

Now Carson took a deep breath, pumped himself up by saying, "Time to play for keeps," and e-mailed, "We're calling in your paper."

Half an hour later Shigetada answered, "Friday lunch, Omaha time."

8

The office of the director of operations was not in Trump Tower; it was at One Central Park West, on Columbus Circle, in the Trump International Hotel and Tower, which is the old Gulf and Western Building that Trump converted in 1997 into 176 hotel rooms and 158 condominium apartments.

Usually, whenever Antonia had to go between her second-floor office on the hotel side to any other Trump property, she took taxis.

Antonia has an expense account, she would remind herself. *Antonia is entitled.*

But she didn't use her entitlement this time.

She rode the elevator down from the staff meeting, all the time mumbling to herself, oblivious to the other people in there with her.

When it stopped on the ground floor, she pushed her way out first, hurried out of the atrium onto Fifth Avenue, turned right, rushed past Tiffany's to Fifty-Seventh Street, crossed there and headed west.

He embarrassed Antonia, she told herself.

She was walking faster than anyone else on the street.

That's what he did. He embarrassed Antonia.

People approaching in the opposite direction spotted her and stepped aside to get out of her way.

He embarrassed Antonia . . .

Now she started saying it loud enough for people on the street to hear.

" . . . and Antonia doesn't like to be embarrassed. Antonia doesn't like that. Antonia doesn't like Pierre."

9

He rang the bell, and one of Katarina Essenbach's two maids let him in. "Madame is in the library," she said, and walked him through the ornate, gold Louis XVI living room into the wood-paneled, book-filled study where Mrs. Essenbach was sitting on a leather couch, wearing a flowing gold lamé dressing gown.

"Cher Monsieur Belasco," she extended her hand but did not get up.

He went to her, took her hand, bowed and almost kissed it but not quite, which is the proper way to kiss a lady's hand.

"Madame," he said, "how nice to see you."

She opened her eyes very wide, licked her upper lip and smiled at him. "I assure you, it is my pleasure." She motioned, "Please, come sit by me."

He did.

"Coffee? Tea? Champagne? It is never too early for champagne, as I'm sure you know. Or perhaps something . . . " she paused and then said, smiling . . . "hard?"

"Nothing, thank you."

With a wave of her hand she dismissed the maid, who left and shut the door.

Said to have been one of the all-time great Hungarian beauties, rumor had it that in 1968, at the age of eighteen, Katarina Laszlo—as she was then known—so dazzled the conductor Herbert von Karajan, who was sixty at the time, that he brought her to Berlin as his mistress and maintained her for two years in a huge suite on the top floor of the Hotel Kempinsky on the Kurfürstendamn. She supposedly left him for the sixty-five-year-old Italian tenor Gian Carlo di Pasquale, with whom she lived in one of the last private villas off the Spanish Steps in Rome for three years.

She came to America, thanks to a remote family connection to Vilmos Gabor—father of Zsa Zsa, Eva and Magda—where she was introduced to the seventy-year-old exiled Hungarian film director Gergely Bartok, with whom she lived for five years. The couple divided their time between a home on Bellagio Road in Bel Air that had once been owned by Alfred Hitchcock, and a home in the south of France, on Cap Ferrat, right next door to the Grand Hotel. Because neither of them cooked, she arranged to have the hotel cater all their meals, including room-service breakfast, delivered to her bedroom— they had separate rooms—by white-gloved hotel waiters.

As none of her live-in lovers left her anything in their wills, after Bartok's death, the then-twenty-eight-year-old Katarina had to fend for herself.

So she embarked on a series of marriages, going from rich to richer, ending with Kurt Essenbach, an Austrian industrialist whom she married when he was eighty-one. Much to her often-admitted great relief, he died on their honeymoon, leaving her the entirety of his $200 million fortune.

Not surprisingly, Kurt's seven children from four previous marriages contested the will, but only managed to claw back half of his estate. And even though they tried to get the Trump Tower apartment too, when he bought it for her as an engagement love nest, she insisted that he put it in her name.

These days, money was the least of her problems. Top of the list was her rotten luck with plastic surgeons. A tummy tuck had gone wrong and, according to the press reports that Belasco had seen, her navel ended up two inches off-center. She successfully sued for $5 million, but never managed to get her belly button back to where it should be.

Then a facelift went wrong, distorting her mouth.

After another successful lawsuit—this time she won $8 million—a second facelift, to correct the first one, stretched her skin so tight that it seemed amazing she could smile.

More than a few people in the Tower commented—of course, behind her back—that the once-great beauty now had a mouth worthy of a Halloween mask.

"I should be hearing any day now on my construction permission," she said, crossing her legs and letting the gown slip just a bit, revealing some thigh.

Belasco smiled politely and averted his eyes, spotting an odd snapshot sitting on the coffee table. It showed Katarina Essenbach in a black leotard with her arms cozily around a bare-chested Alejandro, the trainer from the gym.

"A mere child," she said, reaching for the photo and turning it over. "Hardly the man you are."

"Yes," he said, then realized that she might think he was referring to her comparison with Alejandro. He quickly added, "Yes, I heard that your planning permission was coming up for consideration."

"I purchased the necessary space on the floor below more than a year ago. Why should this take so long? I presume you've seen the plans."

"I have," he said, and remembered thinking when he first saw them that these were the most extravagant use of indoor space he'd ever heard of.

Essenbach intended to turn her half of the forty-first floor into a tropical rain forest.

The Brazilian designer Yarah—she only used one name—had already created five of these private rain forests. The first was for the Italian industrialist Giacomo Amaducci. She built a glass-enclosed conservatory measuring seventy thousand square feet—about the size of a New York City block—on the oceanfront grounds of his estate on the Costa Smeralda in Sardinia. She stocked it with an elaborate irrigation system and machinery to keep the temperature range from 80 to 91 degrees Fahrenheit and to provide 140 to 150 inches of artificial rain annually.

Inside were more than fifteen hundred different plants, trees, and flora, plus four hundred different species of insects and animals from Brazil's own rain forest, including three types of monkeys—Spider, Squirrel, and Golden Lion Tamarins—baby sloths, baby anteaters, toucans, macaws, Anaconda snakes, Amazon turtles, Poison Arrow frogs, Piranha and Capybara, which are the biggest rodents on earth.

The "Amaducci Yarah," as this first installation came to be known, cost $19 million.

No sooner had she completed that when Tatyana Batukhtina, whose murdered husband, Taras, was one of the original Russian Oligarchs, installed a freestanding ninety thousand–square foot "Yarah" next to her Black Sea home. This one held more than two thousand trees, plants and flora varieties, in addition to six hundred different species of animals and insects.

Since then, Yarah had "installed" three more—for the Shanghai billionaire Yu Kwong Ni, who spent $13 million; for an oil baron in Brunei named Laclaclac Badawi, who paid $14 million; and for the wife of an Indian shipping magnate Vajra Chopra, whose was the biggest to date, and cost a whopping $21 million.

The "Essenbach Yarah" would be the first non-free-standing private rain forest, as it was going to be installed inside an apartment. It would also be the smallest. Although it would be the only Yarah that did not come stocked with any wildlife, as Trump Tower had a no-pets policy, it was still going to cost Mrs. Essenbach $15.4 million because temperature, humidity and ventilation were a nightmare. On top of that, Yarah was going to charge her $65,000 a month to maintain the installation.

"You know that we'll have to rip out the fourth bedroom and the Regency sitting room," she went on. "But I won't miss either. When it is installed, you will come to the party, won't you?"

He responded politely, "I look forward to your *vernissage*."

"And what an opening night it shall be, considering that there are no other tropical rain forests in the building, in the city, in the state, in the entire country." She opened her eyes wide again. "Or, perhaps, you might prefer it if the party was particularly small? Perhaps just the two of us?"

He disliked the way she made him feel uncomfortable. "I would have thought you'd prefer to celebrate with grandeur."

"Does that mean I must invite my neighbors? They're all so pitifully jealous." She pointed to the floor below. "Them?" Referring to the Advanis. "Don't get me started. They're returning just to oppose my request. He sits on the Residents' Board, hasn't been to a meeting in years, but he's coming all the way back from . . . wherever it is those people spend their time . . . just to annoy me."

"Yes, they're due back at the weekend, but I can't imagine . . . "

"You don't know how . . . those people . . . think," she said. "Not like us."

This was not a discussion he wanted to have, so he changed the subject. "Madame, I need to speak to you about Carlos Vela . . . "

She continued, "Can you imagine how they leave their chaste little daughter all alone for so many months at a time?"

"Amvi?" He said. "I assure you, she is well looked after."

Prakash Advani provided for round-the-clock bodyguards—after all, Amvi was the teenage daughter of one of the wealthiest men in the subcontinent, and there had been kidnap threats—plus a very strict Austrian governess, not to mention a full live-in household staff.

"I'm sure she misses her parents, but . . . "

She scowled, "If only they knew."

"If only they knew what?"

"You of all people . . . you don't know?"

He looked at her to show her he didn't. "About . . . what?"

"Chaste and proper little Amvi," she said. "Are her parents ever in for a surprise."

"I'm sorry . . . I don't."

"That English musician's son . . . the Jewish one who changed his name . . . "

"Mr. Lips?"

"Lips? You mean, Lipschitz."

"What about him?"

"Not him, his idiot son. And Amvi."

"I'm sorry," Belasco said, hiding his surprise. "I don't know anything about . . . "

"Have you fired him yet?"

"Fired him? Who?"

"Vela. Donald said to me that . . . "

"Oh, yes," he realized she'd changed subjects. "I know that you and Mr. Trump discussed it, but I must tell you . . . "

"Pierre, darling . . . " she reached for his hand and put hers on top of his, "you're not going to make excuses for this pathetic little thief . . . "

"I'm certainly not going to make excuses for anyone," he said smiling, then carefully moved his hand from under hers. "But there seems to be some doubt as to whether or not he's the one who actually stole . . . "

"Oh please," she snapped. "What doubt?"

"The police are not charging him."

She reached for his hand again, and this time took it in both of hers. "You know, dear Pierre, that I am very close to Donald."

Forcing a smile, he simply said, "It is always nice to see you, Madame. Let me discuss the situation concerning Mr. Vela again with Mr. Trump . . . "

"And with that Advani fellow," she said, not moving. "About my rain forest. I know that you don't have a formal vote on the Residents' Board, but you certainly have influence and . . . " She leaned back on the couch in what she obviously thought was a seductive pose. "I would be very grateful for your help. You know, of course, that I think about you often, Pierre."

"Thank you, Madame. I will indeed speak with Mr. Advani."

"I know I can count on you," she smiled. "And, Pierre . . . my husband need not know anything about this."

He looked at her, hoping not to give away his surprise. "Your husband, Madame?"

"There is no reason for him to know anything at all about . . . us."

"No," he assured her. "Of course not." He bowed. "Madame, I will let you know about both of these matters as soon as possible."

She nodded. "I will look forward to that."

He let himself out of the library and one of the maids let him out of the apartment.

Now, in the hallway, he took a deep breath. "Her husband?" He said to himself, "What husband?"

DOWNSTAIRS on the nineteenth floor, next to the hand-painted logo that said "Scarpe Pietrasanta," there was a small sign that read, "Please ring the bell." But the door was already open. So Belasco poked his head in and said, "Good morning?"

No one answered.

Stepping inside the small suite of offices on the east side of the Tower, he tried again, "Good morning? Anyone home?"

Still no one.

There was a reception area and behind that a showroom filled with displays of designer shoes. Off to one side was a large conference room with a built-in stainless steel kitchen and a very long table surrounded by a dozen chairs. On the other side, there were three small offices.

The doors to the first two were open, and Belasco could see they were empty.

But the door to the third office was shut. "Hello? Anyone home?" He knocked softly on it. "Hello?"

"Oh," a woman said inside and opened the door, surprised to find someone there. "I'm sorry . . . excuse me . . . may I help you?"

He guessed she was in her early- to mid-forties. She had a pleasant face and short auburn hair that had been lightened just a bit. He thought that she looked a little like the British actress Emma Thompson.

But her eyes were red.

"I'm Pierre Belasco," he held out his hand and smiled, "general manager of Trump Tower."

That's when he realized she'd been crying.

"Are you all right?"

She shook his hand quickly. "Rebecca Battelli."

It took him a few seconds. "Mr. Battelli's wife. My deepest condolences. I was shocked when I heard that your husband . . . "

"Me too," she said, and walked back into the small office.

He followed her in. "Of course, if there is anything I can do for you . . . "

She fell into the high-backed chair behind a desk covered in folders and papers piled high. "Can you give my husband back to me?"

He stood there. "If only I could, Madame . . . "

"Rebecca," she said. "I guess . . . I mean, as of two weeks ago . . . I'm no longer Madame anybody." Tears now poured out of her eyes.

He stood there, feeling helpless. "Perhaps this is not the best time . . . "

"Please," she motioned that he should sit down in one of the two chairs facing the desk, and took a tissue to dry her face. "I'm sorry, it's just . . . this is very new to me."

"I understand." He did not sit down. "Perhaps if I could get you some water or coffee or tea . . . anything?"

She shook her head. "It comes and goes. The first few days I couldn't stop. By the second week I was only crying twenty-three hours a day. Now . . . " she tried to smile . . . "now I'm only crying when I'm awake."

He motioned toward the empty showroom. "When do you expect everyone to come back to work?"

"I don't."

"You don't?"

"My husband's cousin . . . the business was started by my husband's grandfather," she explained. "He was a shoemaker in Italy. He left the business to his two sons. They left the business to their two sons. A few years ago my husband, Mark . . . Marco was his real name . . . he bought out half his cousin's share, so he controlled it. But Mark allowed his cousin . . . his name is Johnny . . . to work here. Johnny is now saying that the business should be his, and he wants to take it back. The staff . . . they don't think I can run it and are siding with him. They've left and gone away."

Belasco stared at her, then sat down. "Are you going to run it?"

She sighed, "I don't know if I can. I don't know anything about the business, except what Mark told me. I don't even know if there's any money left in it. Johnny might have already stolen everything out of it."

"Stolen it?"

"I don't know."

He took a deep breath. "I think the first thing you need is to get someone in here who can look at the books and tell you what's what."

Her eyes welled up again. "Be my guest."

"No, not me . . . " He leaned forward, "Who's your accountant?"

"I don't know. I presume we have one, but . . . "

"There must be records somewhere. Isn't there anybody who works here . . . or used to . . . you can trust?"

"Mark kept everything to himself. I was never a part of . . . " Now she started to cry again.

"Please . . . " He wanted to make her understand, "It's going to be all right."

"I feel like . . . " Tears poured down her cheeks . . . "I feel like a bird with a broken wing."

He hesitated, then slowly reached over and put his hand on hers.

She pulled it away and started crying again.

After a while he said, quietly, "I wish there was something I could do."

She stared at him with big, red eyes and repeated what she'd said to him earlier. "Can you give my husband back to me?"

HE TOOK the elevator up to twenty-four—*a bird with a broken wing,* he kept hearing her say—and crossed over to the residents' elevator.

The door opened, the elevator operator Alex said, "Hello, sir," and Belasco stepped in to find Odette.

"Monsieur Belasco," the elegantly dressed ninety-three-year-old said, "*Quel plaisir de vous voir.*" What a pleasure to see you.

He smiled at her, took her right hand and almost kissed it. "You are earlier than usual this morning," he said in French.

"It's Friday," she continued in French, "my busiest morning." Now she leaned forward and, so that Alex did not hear, asked quietly, "Did you hear the news?"

"What news, Madame?"

She whispered, "Michael Jackson is dead."

"Ah yes . . . I heard," Belasco said.

"I used to see him here all the time."

He didn't have the heart to tell her that Jackson was dead quite a while now. "He lived on sixty-six. Next door to Mr. Trump."

"Poor Michael." She shook her head. "How did he stand the noise?"

"Mr. Jackson?"

"No, Mr. Trump. Do you know how many times he told me, 'I like you so much'?"

"Mr. Trump?"

"No, poor Michael. He said he'd seen my movies. He said he thought I was the most beautiful star in the French cinema."

"I agree."

"You know," she nodded proudly, "he used to let me ride up in the service lift with him. I was the only one. He hated anyone seeing him bandaged like that. His face and all. But whenever he saw me, he would say, *would you like to ride with me?* He even learned to say it in French. I was the only one."

The elevator doors opened on the ground floor and Alex turned to Odette. "Madame."

"I was the only one," she said in French to Belasco. Then, in English, she asked Alex, "Please don't tell anyone about Michael Jackson." She got out.

"I won't," Alex promised.

Belasco followed her out of the elevator.

Odette walked into the residents' lobby and pointed to the small, unmarked door next to the concierge's desk. "May I?"

"Yes, of course," Belasco opened the door for her, then helped her down some steps into the tiny fire control office. He said, "Excuse us, please" to the man sitting there watching a bank of monitors, then opened another small door, this one leading into the atrium.

Odette stepped out, looked at the Trump Grill to her right, then spotted some tourists standing nearby taking photos. She walked straight up to them and greeted them, as if they should have recognized her.

Belasco returned to his office, took his Rolodex, found the card he was looking for and dialed the number.

A woman answered, "Ronald Rose and Company, how may I direct your call?"

"Is Ronnie there, please, it's Pierre Belasco."

She put him through.

"Pierre?" Rose said, "Audit or refund?"

"Neither," Belasco said. "A favor. Have you got a junior person in the office who could run through some books and figure out where a company stands?"

"Trump?"

"No. There's a company in the Tower . . . the owner died, and the widow is up to her neck in problems. I thought if someone could stop by . . . "

"When?"

"Monday? After lunch? Say, three?"

"Yep," Rose said. "I'll have someone there at three."

"Thank you."

"Who do we bill?"

"For the time being . . . me."

"Still pretending to be the Red Cross?"

"Just trying to help a little bird fly again."

"What?"

"Nothing," he said. "Thanks," and hung up.

He addressed a handwritten note to Mrs. Battelli. "I have arranged for my personal accountant to send someone by Monday at 3. I hope he will be able to help you make sense of your books." He signed it, "Pierre," looked at that for a long time, then added, "Belasco."

He asked one of the concierges to take it up to the nineteenth floor.

When a note came back that simply said, "Thank you. Rebecca," he asked himself why she hadn't signed it with her last name.

That's when he realized he'd completely forgotten to mention to her that Scarpe Pietrasanta was behind in the rent.

10

It was one of those unforgettable evenings.

Antoine de Maisonneuve, the interior designer whose fortieth birthday had been celebrated with cover stories this month in *Vogue, Vanity Fair* and *Harper's Bazaar*, was having his party.

His long-time partner, Bobby Baldwyn, who'd once been called the great black hope of American ballet, rented the Beacon Theater on Broadway at West Seventy-Fourth Street, removed all the seats, leveled the floor so that it didn't slope and put in tables for 250 people.

Alain Ducas created the appetizers and Joel Robuchon cooked the meal.

A floor-to-ceiling ice sculpture portrait of de Maisonneuve sat in the middle of the wonderful Art Deco room, where everyone who has ever been anybody in the world of rock has played. From the Stones, Jerry Garcia and Aerosmith, to Michael Jackson, James Taylor, Radiohead and Queen—they all appeared on the Beacon stage. So has Bill Clinton. So has the Dalai Lama.

Now the stage was set with forty chairs and forty music stands to accommodate the string section of the New York Philharmonic Orchestra. In front of that was a grand piano where, for seventy-five minutes, Elton John played his heart out. The music ended with "Happy Birthday," a duet by Elton and Madonna, who wheeled out a twelve-layer black currant mousse and marzipan cake created by Anne-Marie Pradel-Besson, who'd been flown in from Paris just for this.

"I could not eat another thing," Tina Lee Cove said to Donatella Versace. Karl Lagerfeld blew them both kisses and went to say goodnight to the birthday boy, who was telling Wendi Murdoch, Rupert's wife, that she looked more beautiful than ever. Charlize Theron held on to Mike Bloomberg's arm as he asked Corice Arman if she'd had enough to eat. "Anyone for a late night snack?" the mayor joked.

Diane Kruger groaned at the thought of more food, but Sarah Jessica Parker pointed to her husband, Matthew Broderick. "He does killer Eggs Benedict. Anyone up for breakfast?"

Elton kissed Lizzy Tisch, who was talking to Brian Williams and Alicia Melendez, while Daphne Guinness was chatting with Dylan Lauren.

Marc Jacobs was saying goodbye to Christina Hendricks, who was kissing Spike Lee goodbye, while David Beckham was telling a dirty joke to Kate Moss.

Across the room, Victoria Beckham never took her eyes off her husband, all the time assuring Neil Patrick Harris that he was better looking than Nacho Figeras, who happened to be standing right there, insisting that she was wrong.

Zeke Gimbel was explaining to Katie Couric how he was putting together a mega studio deal and bragged that he would soon own the world.

"Why do you want to own the world?" Couric asked.

"That's what Trump wanted to know when I mentioned the deal to him. You know what I told him?"

"What?"

"I said, 'Donald, when you own the world, you get laid a lot.'"

Couric looked at him askance.

"And you know what he said to me?" Zeke nodded several times, "He said that when he was single and running around with some of the most beautiful women on the planet, absolutely gorgeous girls, he used to get laid all the time. He said, 'Zeke, I didn't have to own the world.' And I said to him, 'Donald, of course not, because you already owned the air rights.'"

Couric smiled politely.

Not far away, Carson Haynes asked David Cove, "Need a ride home?"

"Nah," David, dressed all in black and wearing his square black sunglasses, grinned proudly, "I got us Trump's Phantom."

"Trump's Phantom?"

"Big white mother."

He had to know, "How'd you arrange that?"

"Out-putted him yesterday at Pebble Beach. That's why he's not here tonight. He's playing a charity thing with Tiger."

"You beat him out of his Rolls Royce?"

"For the night. But y'all gotta know I'll have it forever as long as he's willing to give me four strokes."

"What?"

"Damn right."

"You have the nerve to take four strokes from him?" Carson reminded David, "You play scratch . . . Trump's a two."

"Y'all have a problem with that?"

Carson mimicked David's accent, "Y'all got any friends left?"

David laughed, "At four, only Trump. At five? Not a one."

Carson shook his head in amazement, patted David on the shoulder, and went to find Alicia, who was suddenly standing too close to the French soccer star Thierry Henry.

Before long, David motioned to Tina, and the two of them made their exit. Just as they did, the white Rolls pulled up to the curb. David signaled to Harold, the driver, to stay put and opened the back door himself for Tina. She got in, and he got in, and Harold asked, "Home?"

"Home," David said, then sat all the way back and smiled at Tina. "Y'all gotta say that was a reasonable evening."

Harold pulled into traffic.

"Alicia is such a bitch," she said, taking her iPhone out of her bag. "Did you see the way she was looking at that polo player from Argentina?"

"You mean that Figeras kid?"

"Not him. The other polo player from Argentina."

"What other polo player from Argentina?" He pulled his own iPhone out of his pocket and turned it on.

"The one screwing Felipa."

"Who's Felipa?"

"Felipa Guillermo? The one who inherited her mother's estate? Two billion bucks worth? She's forty-one, and her polo player is twenty-two."

He shook his head, as if to say he didn't know who she was talking about.

She looked at him. "Red Chanel dress with those plastic things hanging out?"

"Oh. They're from Argentina?"

"No, they're from Dr. Howard Rosenberg of Hartsdale." Tina's e-mails clicked in and began downloading. "Marlboros?"

Now his e-mails also clicked in. "Nah." He scrolled down. "Felipa what?" Then he asked, "Copper wire?"

"Guillermo," she said. "No copper. How about iPads?"

"iPads?" He looked down his list of e-mails. "Ah . . . Malaysia? They're fake."

"Just like Felipa's."

"How 'bout some Chianti?"

She continued scrawling through her e-mails. "Italy or Chile?"

"Doesn't say." He read through the note. "Looks like a thousand pallets,

forty-eight cases to a pallet." It only took him a few seconds to do the calculations in his head. "Two-point-three million and change. Four and a quarter a
bottle. Four-twenty. Something like that."

"The Turk?"

"Himself. So it must be Chile. Distressed in Gib."

She checked her watch. "The sun's already up over the Bosphorus."

David nodded and speed-dialed a number in Istanbul.

On the other end a phone rang three times before a man with a gruff voice
asked, in Turkish, "Who is it?"

"Asil?" David said, putting his phone on speaker. "Tina and I have decided
we're thirsty."

He answered in good English, "How thirsty?"

"What can we do at . . . say, three-ninety a bottle?"

"Get thirstier. I'm looking for four-twenty-two."

"It's Chile, right?"

"It's Chile, right . . . except that everything is labeled product of Italy."

David looked at Tina. "Three-ninety-two."

Asil said, "Four-twenty-five."

"Y'all just said four-twenty-two."

"So now you have to come up to four-twenty-five."

"How about you come down to three-ninety-two?"

"For the beautiful Tina? All right, my friend, for her I'll come down to four-
twenty-two."

Tina leaned toward the phone. "The beautiful Tina used to love you."

He answered, "If the beautiful Tina will leave cowboy David for Asil, a man
of infinite intrigue, I will come down to four-fifteen. But that's my best best."

"Intrigue means what, in Turkish," David wanted to know, "bullshit?"

"I will disregard him," Asil said. "But tell me this, how much does good Italian Chianti sell for in New York? Fifteen dollars a bottle? Maybe twenty?"

"Good Italian Chianti that isn't from Italy?" David said, "That's why I'm
thinking three-ninety-three."

"I'll go down to four-eleven, but the offer is only open for fifteen minutes."

"I'm in a car."

"I'm in the bath."

"Give me thirty."

"Ten."

"Okay, fifteen."

"Drive carefully."

"Y'all don't forget to use soap."

As soon as David opened the door to their forty-fifth-floor duplex, Tina
kicked off her three-inch spike Louboutin heels—"My feet are numb"—and let

her black lamé dress fall to the floor. David took off his dinner jacket, dropped it on top of Tina's dress, then kicked off his shoes and took off his pants too.

She walked down the hall, wearing only a black lace half-bra, a black silk thong and her mother's pearls.

He followed her in his black dress shirt, black underpants and black socks.

In the corner room that looked toward Central Park and Fifth Avenue—the one they used as an office—Tina snapped on one of their four laptops, lit up the ninety-six-inch flat-screen hanging on the far wall, but left the rest of the lights off.

New York beyond the windows was still wide awake.

Somewhere not far away, an ambulance raced by with its siren blazing.

She logged on to three of the intranet sites they used, saw several bulletin boards come up in various sections of the huge screen, sat down and started sending e-mails.

David checked his watch and was about to dial Istanbul when Tina announced, "Three-ninety."

He said. "Keep fishing."

She highlighted every bulletin board. "There's nothing . . . he's the only one . . ."

Going over the various sections of the screens, David hoped to find someone who would be interested in taking this distressed cargo from them for a few cents more per bottle than they had to pay Asil for it. But no one seemed to be out there.

"Where's Shithead in LA?" He asked.

She reminded him, "He's never around after eight or nine at night."

"No one in Italy? Look for France. Spain? Try Germany."

"No one." She kept typing messages and sending them to all of their contacts around the world.

"Where's Boris, or whatever his name is, in the Ukraine who took the cigarettes last time?"

She typed a few lines on her keyboard, looked up at the big screen, waited for a moment, then said, "No one's home."

David shook his head, "Well . . . it was worth a shot," and put the call through to Istanbul.

The line rang once before Asil answered it. "You're late."

"We're trying to off-load this paint thinner for y'all, but even at four . . ."

Suddenly Tina grabbed his shoulder and pointed to the screen. Someone in Brazil was willing to pay $3.94.

David told Asil, "I mean . . . three-ninety is really where the market is," and motioned to Tina to get the Brazilian to bid higher.

"Four-ten," Asil said. "No way I can go lower."

Tina sent the message to Brazil, then grabbed David's shoulder again. Someone in France was coming in at $3.95.

"I got no room," David said to Asil, then pointed to the big screen where a new player, this one in Venezuela, was now bidding $3.97.

Asil sighed, "No problem, my friend, I will find someone else. . . ."

David poked Tina to get all the bidders up fast, and as she messaged them, he said to Asil, "I'm taking on your risk. If I can't unload this stuff . . . "

"You can unload anything," Asil assured him. "Four-seven."

Tina signaled that the Frenchman was up to $3.98, that the Venezuelan had gone away, but that there was somebody in Denmark offering $3.99.

"Best I can do . . . " he said, . . . "y'all call it three-ninety-three. Honestly, there's nothing out there. Nobody wants this stuff. I'm telling you straight. Nobody." And with that he motioned to Tina, higher.

"And I'm telling you straight, at four-six I'm a dead man."

All of a sudden Tina grabbed a phone, dialed a number—David saw a phone number in Seoul, South Korea, come up on the screen—and started talking in a whisper. She motioned to David to stall Asil.

"How long have y'all been shopping this stuff?"

Asil assured him, "You got it first."

"Because absolutely no one's interested . . . " David motioned to Tina to do something.

She mouthed the words, "Keep talking."

" . . . not even at three-ninety-four . . . "

Now Tina tugged at his hand and signaled with her fingers, four-two.

"I mean . . . there's zero . . . nobody . . . but because it's you . . . the very best . . . I mean, this is all I've got and believe me . . . "

"Of course I believe you," Asil cut in.

"Believe me . . . " David looked at Tina and then up at the screen where the Frenchman now offered four-four. "Believe me . . . three-ninety-six . . . "

Then the Brazilian came back with four-five and Tina motioned that South Korea was in with four-six.

" . . . and even that's kinda high 'cause I'm thinking that . . . " David lied again to Asil . . . "maybe I would just buy ten cases for myself and if y'all want four-two . . . "

"Since when do I do split loads?"

"Since the last time, when y'all were flogging microchips."

"That was technology," Asil insisted, "these are perishables."

David reminded him, "Good Chianti is supposed to get better with age."

"Like I said, these are perishables."

Tina indicated that South Korea was up to four-seven but was stopping there and that both Brazil and France had dropped out and that Denmark was no longer anywhere to be seen.

"Final offer," David said, "three-ninety-eight. Honestly, there isn't another penny in it."

"Honestly, final offer," Asil mimicked him. "Four-four."

David looked at Tina, as if to ask, is there anyone else out there—anywhere. She shook her head no.

"Y'all killing me pal. Three-ninety-nine. Final, final."

"Four-three," Asil said.

Tina nodded.

David said, "Sold."

Tina typed a message to Seoul and the deal was done.

There was still paperwork to arrange, but after David hung up with Asil, and after Tina hung up with Seoul, he reached for her bra and unhooked it. "Dr. Rosenberg, eat your heart out."

In the course of twenty minutes, they'd bought and sold 576,000 bottles of Chilean plonk disguised as Italian Chianti, squeezing out four cents per bottle in the middle for themselves, to make around $23,000.

"How much for the panties?"

"Twenty-five grand." She crossed her arms, hiding her breasts, "Sorry GI, maybe next time."

Now he moved in front of her. "My shirt and underpants are only twenty-two-five. I'll throw the socks in too."

"Sold." She reached for him. "Mind if I eat at my desk?"

SATURDAY

11

Pierre Belasco jumped out of the cab and hurried through the double set of glass doors into the residents' lobby.

Jorge, the night doorman, rushed up to him. "Sir?"

"At this hour?" Carlo, the night concierge, was genuinely surprised to see him. "I'd say good morning but it's still the middle of the night."

"Technically," Belasco said, "somewhere it is always morning." He walked through the lobby to his office.

"Good morning," Paolo, the night elevator operator, half-saluted. "A little early, no?"

"A lot early, yes." Belasco stepped into his office and turned on the light.

Carlo followed him in. "Is everything all right?"

"No. Our friend Mikey Glass has been involved in an incident."

"Mr. Glass . . . who lives here?"

He nodded. "He had a hotel room he decided to trash."

"Why would he have a room there when he lives here?"

"Wife here, nonstop party there," Belasco explained. "It's called separation of church and state."

Carlo smiled.

Jorge asked, "You want coffee? We have coffee."

"Yes, thank you," Belasco said.

Carlo and Jorge both went to fetch a cup for him.

Belasco now reached for his phone and dialed an extension.

A man answered, "Timmins."

"I received a call at home half an hour ago that Mikey Glass destroyed a room around the corner at the new Commodore Hotel on Central Park South. He'd been out at a restaurant and bumped into some circus performers."

"Bumped into . . . who?"

"Circus performers. Acrobats. Jugglers. People in clown costumes. I don't know. He told them he loved the circus, took them back to the hotel and they all started doing circus acts."

"Circus acts?"

"Juggling the furniture. Trampolining on the bed. Tumbling . . . lion taming . . . jumping through hoops of fire naked . . . they totally destroyed the room."

"Circus acts," he mumbled. "I wish I could say I'm surprised."

"The police are there now."

"Okay." Timmins didn't have to ask what Belasco wanted him to do because he knew. "I'll call for the cavalry."

"Thank you." Hanging up, Belasco looked around his office, took off his suit jacket and tossed it onto the couch. He thought about loosening his tie but he was in the office and couldn't bring himself to do that. Instead, he went to his desk, fell into his chair and waited for his coffee to arrive.

Belasco often came into the office on Saturday and had planned on being there that morning anyway. The Advanis were returning from India, and he wanted to welcome them home. But he never had to be in the office on Saturday at 3:15 a.m.

It was Carlo who appeared with the coffee. "Half and half, no sugar."

"Thank you." Belasco took the cup and then a sip. "What time did Mr. Glass leave last night?"

"He hasn't been here for a week. I checked because I knew you'd ask. His wife and the children are in the apartment. But we haven't seen him."

He nodded and stared but said nothing.

Carlo took the hint and went back to the concierge desk.

Alone, Belasco reached for his Rolodex, found a card for his old friend Antoine Cau, who was the general manager of the Commodore, and dialed the number.

A very sleepy man responded. "Hullo?"

"I know what time it is," Belasco said in French. "It's Pierre . . . and I apologize for waking you. Please forgive me."

Cau responded in French. "Pierre? What's wrong?"

"One of our residents . . . Mikey Glass . . . "

"The actor?"

" . . . he just destroyed one of your rooms. Apparently there are eight or ten circus performers involved as well. The police are there . . . "

"Circus performers?"

"It's a long story."

"Circus performers? You mean, people dressed like clowns . . . "

"And jugglers and lion tamers and tightrope walkers and ladies riding barebacked and, apparently, some of them not dressed at all. The police are there now. I've made arrangements to get him out of there. The cavalry is on the way."

"Who?"

"Someone we use. I wanted to give you a heads-up."

"Thanks. But how come the people who live at your place don't sleep at your place?"

"I'm afraid this had nothing to do with sleeping. Wrong verb."

There was a long pause before Cau said, "I'll find out what's happening. You at home?"

"I'm in the office."

"I hope Trump pays you by the hour." Cau hung up.

Now there was nothing to do but wait.

Belasco sipped more coffee, turned on the flat-screen television he had sitting in the middle of a bookshelf, clicked several channels, but gave up quickly when there wasn't anything he wanted to see. So he opened the laptop on his desk, logged on and started checking his e-mails.

He'd worked his way through a dozen or so e-mails when he heard someone in the lobby say much too loudly, "Fuck you, mate! I live here too."

Getting up, he left his office to find Ricky Lips' eighteen-year-old son, Joey, hands on his hips, defiantly glaring at Carlo.

Sporting a goatee that had finally grown in, so that he no longer looked like a teenager needing a shave, Joey was dressed in black, with an open-neck black shirt and a black fedora hat. The young woman with him was extremely thin and very tall—at least six inches taller than Joey—and, Belasco guessed, couldn't weigh more than 105 pounds.

She was dressed in white, with her blouse open to her navel, which did nothing to hide her small breasts.

Both Joey and the young woman had a glazed-over look in their eyes.

"We are going upstairs," Joey insisted.

"Good morning, sir," Belasco said.

"Oh, yeah," Joey pointed at him, said to the young woman. "He's the bloke in charge," then said to Belasco, "We're going upstairs."

"Yes, of course." He nodded to Carlo that it was all right. "Have you got a key, sir?"

"Who needs a key? My old man's there. I mean, where the bloody hell else do you think he is? Poor bastard can't leave, can he?" He looked at the young woman, "They won't let him leave."

Belasco said to Carlo, "Would you please take Mr. Lips and his companion upstairs . . . "

"I don't need no babysitter," Joey waved him off.

"It's our pleasure, sir," Belasco motioned for Carlo to escort them.

Joey grabbed the young woman's arm and went with Carlo. Paolo stepped aside to let them into the elevator. But now Joey came back into the hallway to whisper to Belasco, "Don't say nothing about this bird, will you mate? You-know-who would never understand."

Belasco asked, "Who in particular is that, sir, who would never understand?"

Joey mouthed the name, "Pocahontas."

Belasco stared at Joey. "Pocahontas?"

He answered, as if it was obvious. "Like in the cartoon. The Indian bird. Didn't you ever see that movie?"

"I'm afraid I might have missed that one."

"Pocahontas. It's really good. So that's what I call her."

"Call whom?"

"Amvi," he said. "I call her Pocahontas. She likes that. But she wouldn't understand."

"And what exactly is it that Miss Advani would not understand?"

"About this bird and me. She's too young to understand . . . you know . . . this sort of thing."

"Yes, sir," he nodded, "Miss Advani is certainly too young to understand." He motioned toward Paolo, who was waiting for him at the elevator, and Joey walked away.

Belasco went back to his office and shuddered at the thought of "this sort of thing."

At four o'clock Timmins phoned. "Cavalry's there . . . negotiating a settlement as we speak. He wants to know if there are any photographers out front. Central Park South is crawling with them."

"Hold on." Belasco got up, went to his door, and looked through the lobby to the street.

An attractive, young, dark-haired woman wearing semirectangular glasses was leaning against a parked car with two cameras over her shoulder.

Belasco came back to the phone. "One," he said, "and I know her."

"Should I make arrangements for the IBM?"

"Yes, please do that." He hung up, took his jacket from the couch, put it on, and walked through the lobby to the street.

Jorge started to follow him, but Belasco motioned for him to stay inside.

The young woman standing there with the two cameras smiled broadly—in fact, her whole pretty face lit up—when he appeared. "Mr. Belasco. How nice to see you. I presume we're both here at this hour for the same reason."

"Good morning, Dani . . . we have coffee, if you'd like."

"It would only keep me awake," she joked. "What time do you expect our friend to arrive? Or has he been arrested?"

"I honestly don't know. But I would have thought it's all happening at the Commodore. Isn't everyone else there?"

"That's why I'm here."

Just then, two men lugging big camera bags came down the street from Fifth Avenue. "Guess we've got the right idea," one of them said loudly.

Dani looked at them. "What are you guys doing here?"

"Same as you," the first one said.

The second photographer asked Belasco, "You the night manager or the concierge at this joint?"

"Something like that," Belasco said.

"He back here yet?" The first man asked Dani.

She told him no.

"'Cause he's not being arrested," the second man said. "Cops said they're going to hand him over to someone who's taking him somewhere to sleep it off."

"Perhaps another hotel," Belasco suggested to the second man. "Or perhaps they're simply going to let him stay there, in another room, without his circus performer friends. I can't imagine he'd come back here."

"Everybody lies," the second man said. "They tell us he's going one place and he shows up someplace else. Who are you, anyway?"

Dani cut in. "Night manager and concierge. He does both jobs."

Belasco smiled.

"We'll wait," the first man said.

"Anyone besides me care for a snort?" The second man produced a hip flask from his camera bag. "Keeps me away from caffeine," he bragged. "Anyone?"

The first photographer took a swig, but Dani and Belasco both said no.

That's when someone's cell phone rang. All four reached for theirs, but the call was for the second photographer. He listened to the person on the other end, then hung up. "He's left the hotel."

A Cadillac Escalade now turned onto Fifty-Sixth Street from Fifth Avenue and headed slowly down the block.

The three photographers grabbed their cameras and positioned themselves in the street so they could get pictures through the car's tinted windows as soon as it pulled to the curb.

The driver of the car flashed his high beams to warn the photographers to get out of his way.

The two men made ready with their cameras.

Dani quickly moved to the corner of the garage entrance, which would force the driver to stop if he went there.

Except the driver didn't pull up to the curb or turn into the Trump Tower garage. He continued slowly down the street, past the Tower, and into the garage at the IBM building.

When the car was gone, Belasco suggested, "I still think your best bet is the hospital."

Dani stared at Belasco.

"Maybe he's right," the first photographer said. "After all, it's only around the corner. If he was coming here, he'd be here by now."

The two men put their cameras back in their bags and left.

Belasco looked at Dani. "Not going to the hospital?"

She smiled, "He was right," referring to the second photographer, "everybody lies."

"Bends the truth, sometimes, perhaps." He motioned to Jorge who hurried out. "Whatever the lady needs. Coffee. Bathroom. Caffeine-free beverages?"

Jorge said, "Yes, of course, sir."

Dani said, "Thank you, anyway," and leaned back on the car again.

"You can sit in the lobby if you'd prefer."

"This feels more like a stakeout."

Belasco smiled, "You've seen too many episodes of *The Wire*," and went inside.

Walking past his office and the elevators, he went through the small door on the left and along the dark hallway to the service elevator. He rode it down to the sub-basement.

The Cadillac Esplanade was already there.

During the design phase of the Tower, Donald Trump himself personally decided there might be times when certain people—those kinds of people who needed to avoid the gazing eyes of other people—would welcome an ultradiscreet way into the building. So he built a secret tunnel entrance that connects underground with the sub-basement garage of the IBM building, halfway down the block toward Madison Avenue. It wasn't used often, but Belasco made a mental note to tell the boss that it had come in handy tonight.

There's a loading dock in the sub-basement where vans can deliver and pick up furniture and belongings for tenants moving in and out. Back in the corner is where Trump's private fleet of nine cars is always parked.

Belasco went up to the stocky, balding Jimmy Timmins, who was standing next to the Escalade, and shook his hand.

As he did, a tall, thin man with a mustache, wearing a dark-green bomber jacket and a University of West Virginia baseball cap stepped out of the Cadillac. He looked at Timmins, "Hey Timmy," then looked at Belasco. "How you doing, pal?"

He knew the man simply as Forbes—always assumed that was his last name—but didn't know anything more about him. He didn't know his first name or where he was from or even how to get in touch with him directly. He always had to go through Timmins.

But whenever Forbes showed up, things got done.

"Thank you for this," Belasco said.

"All in a day's work." He motioned to the car, "Your boy's in bad shape," and opened the back door.

A heavy-set, puffy-faced, dark-haired Mikey Glass, wearing a loose-fitting jogging suit and a Buster Keaton porkpie hat, was lying across the rear seat asleep.

"We'll take him upstairs," Timmins said.

Belasco nodded okay, and watched while Forbes woke Mikey.

"What the hell are you guys doing?" Mikey growled. "Who the fuck are you? Where are the midgets in the clown costumes? Where am I?"

They helped the groggy television star out of the car.

Mikey looked around, yanked his arms away from Forbes, and fell back against the car. "Whoa . . . this ship is moving." He started singing, "Anchors aweigh my boy . . . " then spotted Belasco. "You on this cruise, too? How's it hanging, admiral? Be on the lookout for submarines. U-boats are everywhere." He took one step forward and nearly fell again. "Christ . . . we've been torpedoed."

"Mr. Glass," Belasco said. "Apparently you've had quite a night. But you're home now."

"Home?"

"This is home."

"I live in a garage?"

"Not yet," Belasco said. "These gentlemen will help you upstairs to your apartment."

"My apartment?" His eyes opened wide. "Oh my God . . . my apartment . . . that's where my wife lives. She lives in my apartment. Or is it her apartment? She'll kill me. You've got to hide me somewhere. If she finds me, she'll murder me."

"Yes sir," Belasco agreed. "I expect she will. I'm afraid though, as you can see, there is no place to hide."

"I need to hide somewhere." He looked around. "You've got to have a hiding place. How about . . . " He pointed to the cars parked in the corner . . . "there. Those Trump's? Good. I'll hide under one of Trump's cars."

Belasco assured him, "It's the first place Mr. Trump always looks."

"As I suspected." He nodded several times. "Trump's in cahoots with my wife. Is he planning to kill me before she does or after she does?"

"I suspect he will leave that privilege to your wife."

"What a gentleman," Mikey proclaimed. "How about Los Angeles?"

"What about Los Angeles?"

"I live there too. Can I hide there? Trump will never think of looking for me there. He'll be too busy checking under all of his cars." He turned to get back into the Cadillac. "I'm going to hide in Los Angeles. Who's driving? Let's go. We have to leave fast."

"Have a good night, sir." Belasco motioned for Timmins and Forbes to take Mikey upstairs. "I'm certain if you ask your wife nicely, she will let you sleep for a few hours before she murders you."

"You don't know my wife," Mikey said. "But thank you, Belasco, you always have good ideas. I will ask. And I will ask nicely. I promise. I will say, please don't murder me until I've had some sleep . . . please." He saluted Belasco, . . . "Count on me . . . " then looked at Timmins and Forbes and held out his arms. "Gentlemen . . . shall we dance?"

They helped him upstairs.

BELASCO TOSSED his suit jacket back onto his office couch, asked Carlo for a fresh cup of coffee and sat down to go through a pile of reports that, otherwise, could have waited until Monday.

Then Timmins phoned. "He may not be out of the woods. A cop pal of mine at Midtown North called to say the circus performers may want to press charges. Apparently something about a trained seal and a mermaid and our Mr. Glass insisted she play the mermaid topless . . . "

"Has his wife killed him yet?"

"It's only a matter of time."

"The would-be mermaid's vengeance may yet be the softer option."

"If she presses charges it will be for sexual harassment and they'll have to arrest him," Timmins said.

Belasco knew how that would play out in the papers. Mikey Glass frog-marched out the front door of the residents' entrance with handcuffs on. Dozens of photographers shooting thousands of pictures with lenses purposely wide enough to get Mikey, the cops and the Trump Tower name into the same shot. Headlines would read, "Tower of Power Walk of Shame."

"Not what we need," Belasco said.

"If you want the cavalry, shout."

"Let me think about it."

AT SIX, Carlo, Jorge and Paolo went off duty. They all stopped by to say goodnight. Felicity and Pierro took over the front desk, Roberto took over the front door and three operators now manned the elevators.

Belasco chatted with the morning crew briefly until an Indian woman of a certain age, wearing a multicolored sari arrived, struggling with several packages.

Roberto and Pierro rushed to help her.

Belasco smiled, "Good morning, Kajjili."

"Mr. Belasco," she said, "I would say you are here very early this morning." She was head housekeeper for the Advanis.

"I know they're due in this morning."

"Yes," she said, "they are coming home today. I am planning that they will be here sometime after two and before three."

"Two to three?" He forced a smile, not wanting to show her that he didn't want to be stuck in the office all day. "I will be here to welcome them back."

The staff put her packages into the elevator.

"How is Miss Amvi? I haven't seen her in a few days."

"As fresh and as sweet as ever," Kajjili said. "She will be very pleased to have her parents home."

"I am sure she will," Belasco said.

Pierro escorted Kajjili up to the fortieth floor. The Advanis owned that entire floor and half of the forty-first as well.

"Belasco?" Someone said behind him, "What brings you to Disneyland at this hour?"

He turned. "I should ask you . . . it's just gone six . . . I never suppose anyone in Hollywood functions before lunch."

"Toto, I've a feeling we're not in Hollywood anymore," Zeke Gimbel said.

Belasco and Gimbel both said at the same time, "Thank God."

Gimbel was wearing jeans, a pair of beat-up Nikes, a sweatshirt with the agency's logo—a Zorro-like Z—and a Chicago Cubs baseball cap. But on his shoulder was a gorgeous custom-made, dark red leather Tumi laptop and carry-on bag.

Belasco couldn't help but stare.

He knew it was custom-made because he'd bought the exact same bag in the Tumi store on Madison Avenue, where the manager had assured him several times that the bag came in a choice of black or black.

"I didn't realize you were in," Belasco said.

"Came in for a party last night. Got to be back on the coast this afternoon. We're trying to put Cameron and Ang into a picture with Sean and Johnny, but scheduling is a nightmare . . . "

Belasco had no idea who he was talking about.

"Speaking of which," Gimbel continued, "you know I can always find a part for you if you ever want to become a movie star."

"I'm afraid . . . Mr. Gable has already played all the worthwhile parts."

"Offer is open," Gimbel extended his hand to shake Belasco's. "See you in a few days," he said and headed for the door.

A limo was waiting at the curb.

Roberto moved into place. "Is that your car, sir?" The glass doors opened.

"Yes," Gimbel said, on his way out.

Suddenly Belasco blurted out, "Mr. Gimbel? Please forgive me for being presumptuous . . . "

Gimbel turned around to look at Belasco.

" . . . but I don't suppose you're flying commercial."

He made a face. "Heaven forbid."

"So . . . again, please forgive me for being presumptuous . . . but . . . might you have room . . . "

"On the plane? For you? Sure. Come on. Don't bother packing a bag, you can get everything you need in LA."

"No. Not for me. There's someone who . . . " He hesitated, "Mikey Glass got into some trouble last night and it might be best for him if he was not in New York later this morning."

"Mikey? Got into trouble? So what else is new?"

"If you have room on the plane . . . "

"Mikey is wonderful company," Gimbel said, "but only when he's unconscious."

"There's a possibility that, if he's still in New York in a few hours, he might be arrested."

Gimbel stared at Belasco. "I'm a lawyer by training and trade. And I'm still a member of several bar associations. I am therefore an officer of several courts, including those in the state of New York. Are you really asking me to aid and abet the criminal flight of a fugitive from justice?"

Belasco nodded, "As long as you put it that way . . . actually . . . I am."

He said right away, "Sure. But only as a favor to you."

"I do appreciate it."

Then Gimbel warned, "Mikey can't get drunk on the plane. And he can't try to slip his hand under the stewardess' dress. And he can't touch the pilots or try to play with their steering wheel . . . "

"What time are you due to take off?"

"It's an on-time airline because I make up the time."

"Give me five minutes," Belasco said.

Gimbel agreed. "I'll be in the car."

Belasco escorted him outside and found Dani still there. "Do you know Dani? She's the nicest of the pack."

Gimbel extended his hand to say hello.

"Last time I photographed you," she said, "was at Fashion Week when you and Mrs. Gimbel . . . "

He grimaced. "The black dress?"

"The black dress," she nodded.

"Do you know how much a yard and a half of black silk mousseline tied into a bow costs?"

"Sorry," she shook her head, "they don't sell that at Urban Outfitters."

Gimbel handed his shoulder bag to the chauffeur, then asked Dani, "That's the new Canon, right?"

"Just bought it." She handed it to him.

"I love this."

Belasco left them cooing about her camera, went back inside and rushed upstairs to the Glass apartment on thirty-one. He rang the bell twice, then knocked on the door several times, trying not to knock too loud.

Mikey's wife Karen eventually opened it, looking pretty rough, as though they'd been fighting nonstop. "If you've come to help me throw him out . . . "

"Actually, I have."

When Mikey finally emerged, still dressed in his sweatpants, sweatshirt, and porkpie hat, he clung to Belasco's arm and they came downstairs.

"You are a prince among men," Mikey assured him. "You are saving my life, and all I can give you in return is . . . Belasco . . . name your reward. Anything. Anything at all. If you want to marry Karen and adopt my children as your own, please be my guest. You can adopt me too."

Belasco brought Mikey outside.

Dani took the camera back from Gimbel and moved into position.

"Wait a second," Belasco said to her, not wanting to appear in the photo.

Now Mikey spotted Gimbel. "As I live and breathe."

"If you call that living," Gimbel said. "You coming with me?"

"Where to?"

"I'm going to Los Angeles."

"I've already been there. Many times. Do I have to go to Los Angeles?" He looked at Gimbel, then at Dani, then at Belasco. "I understand that Bora Bora is wonderful this time of year."

"You can drop me in LA . . . it's on the way." Gimbel motioned to him, "Get in the car."

The chauffeur stepped up to help Mikey. Belasco quickly moved out of the shot and whispered to Dani, "Be my guest."

"No bags, sir?" The chauffeur asked Mikey as Dani shot pictures.

"I travel light," Mikey answered, then turned to Dani. "Want to come with us? We're going to Bora Bora."

"Thank you, but I have to work," she said, running off picture after picture.

"No, you don't. Marry me. I'm very rich." He thought about that, then pointed to Gimbel. "Not as rich as him. No one is. But I'm rich enough that we'll live happily ever after. You're beautiful. We can go native. I'll climb trees and bring you coconuts."

"I think I'll stick with Josh," she said.

"Who's Josh?"

"My boyfriend."

"Does he like coconuts? What the hell, bring him along. I've got a whole plane . . . "

"Actually," Gimbel cut in, "I'm the one who's got a whole plane and, Mikey, if you don't get into the car right now . . . "

Mikey pointed to Gimbel and told Dani, "He acts like I was married to him," then got into the car.

Dani kept taking pictures.

Gimbel jumped in, the chauffeur shut the door and then climbed behind the wheel. As they pulled away, Mikey yelled at Dani through the window, "To Bora Bora and beyond!"

Now she turned to Belasco, "Wow. Paper will love this. Thank you."

"My pleasure," he smiled. "Good night."

She corrected him, "Good morning."

"Technically," he said, "somewhere it is always night."

12

Before she'd agreed to the book project with Mel Berger, Alicia had decided that she needed to get NBC's official blessing.

Even if her boss' permission wasn't contractually required, politically, she and Carson had agreed that it was a good idea. So she'd written to her immediate bosses at WNBC, and had also written to Steve Capus, who was president of NBC News and, within two days, word came back from all of them that she was more than welcome to write the book.

Next, she'd wondered, *what about Donald Trump?*

Berger had assured her that Trump had already approved the project but agreed that, here, too, it might be politically correct if she dropped Trump a note to say she was doing it.

Clearly, Trump thought Alicia was a great choice because he'd phoned her in the newsroom to say, "I'm thrilled that you're doing it."

That night Carson said, "Looks like you're good to go."

But she still wasn't sure. "I think I need to send a note to everyone in the building and ask if anyone objects to being named."

So Alicia wrote to the Residents' Board, which had circulated her letter to all 209 of the stakeholders.

Lucy Greenwich had written back that before she and Edmond decided whether or not they'd cooperate, they wanted to know what Andrew Lloyd Webber was going to do.

Zeke Gimbel had mentioned that he would personally arrange for Lucca Ortelli—the fashion photographer whose signed, unique, 1975 photo of Queen Elizabeth in deep conversation with Keith Richards had been sold at

Sotheby's for a record $235,000—to photograph him with his art collection for the book.

There were a few people who'd asked whether or not their privacy would be protected if they allowed their apartment to be photographed without their names appearing.

The only out-and-out no was from the chairman of the Trade and Industry Banking Corporation of China, the government's official commercial investment bank.

The letter, written and signed by his legal adviser, was terse. "Thank you for your invitation to participate in your forthcoming project. But the chairman has asked me to advise you that, under no circumstances whatsoever, does he wish to be, or would he tolerate being, included."

It was noted at the bottom that a copy of this had been sent to both Mr. P. Belasco and to Mr. D. J. Trump.

Belasco had then written to Alicia, "I will gladly discuss this on your behalf with the chairman."

Trump's answer had been slightly less diplomatic. "Screw him!"

And then there'd been the response from Katarina Essenbach.

She'd written that, as hers was the best apartment in the building and would soon include Trump Tower's only indoor tropical rain forest, she could understand why Alicia was insisting that photographs of it be included. However, Essenbach warned, she would not cooperate unless the book contained a recipe—"No one else in the entire tower has a chef who can compete with mine"—and had suggested that the featured dish be *venison en croute*.

Now, on Saturday morning, barefoot and wearing a bright yellow tracksuit, Alicia installed herself at her dining room table, setting up her laptop and spreading out everything she already had about the book project.

"No rest for the weary," Carson said, dropping his overnight bag and six tennis rackets at the front door, then coming back into the dining room.

"You think Hemingway, Fitzgerald, Shakespeare and Martí took the weekend off?" She got up to kiss him goodbye. "Have a good weekend."

"Who's Marty?"

"Not Marty . . . Martí."

"He must have taken weekends off because I never heard of Marty or Marti."

"He's Cuba's most famous writer. José Julián Martí Pérez."

"We know for sure that no one in Cuba works on weekends. Anyway, I never heard of Pérez either." He kissed her and walked back to the door. "I'll call you when we land. Be a good girl."

"And you be a good boy," she said, following him.

He was meeting up with Tommy Arcarro and the two of them were off to the Greenbriar, in White Sulphur Springs, West Virginia, for one of their money-tennis weekends.

This time they'd hooked Lee-Jay Wesley Elkins III, possibly the richest twenty-five-year-old in the state. He was heir to his grandfather's mining fortune and couldn't care less about dropping fifty grand over a weekend of tennis because he loved playing with pros and former pros more than he cared about money.

Carson grabbed his rackets and bag. "I love you."

"As much as *venison en croute*? It's the recipe that the Dragon Lady wants to put in the book."

"Yes, I love you more than I love *venison en croute*," he assured her. "Are you really going to include a recipe?"

"No."

"Just as well. Dragon Lady probably serves it with her own homemade arsenic glaze? Good luck with this."

She put her hands on her head. "What have I gotten myself into?"

"How many people in the building? And every single one of them is convinced that he or she has the best apartment."

"Except we do."

"And the best view?"

"We don't, but we tell people we do."

"And the best chef?"

"Can we have a chef?"

"What would we do with a chef?"

"He would chef for us."

"Why do we need a chef?" Carson asked. "We bring food in. It's like having nine thousand chefs all over New York."

"You're probably right," she conceded. "Especially because if we had a chef, whenever you woke me in the middle of the night, I'd have to ask, is that a tuna fish sandwich in your pajamas or are you just happy to see me?"

"In case you haven't noticed, I don't wear pajamas."

"I have noticed," she said, pushing him out the door, "and that ain't no tuna."

ALICIA SPENT the rest of the morning going through every Internet mention of Trump Tower that she could find.

And there were thousands.

She pulled up references to the usual battles for planning permission and stories about other buildings that once stood on the same site, most notably, the famous old New York store Bonwit Teller.

Next, she went through references that brought up dozens of new names associated with Trump Tower, people who'd supposedly lived there for a period of time, adding to her list Pia Zadora, Dick Clark, Paul Anka, Martina Navratilova and Susan St. James.

Moving from Google to the very extensive news archives at NBC, which she could access from home, she continued listing names and facts and other leads to track down.

That's when her phone rang.

"Are we ladies who lunch?" It was Cyndi.

"No," Alicia said.

"Yes we are."

"We are?"

"When Donato calls, we are."

"Donato called?"

"Just now."

"I thought you two were having one of your every-other-month feuds."

"We are. I mean, we were. He wants to kiss and make up. Well, not exactly kiss because he doesn't do tongue with girls . . . But making up is good. He said, come to lunch and bring Alicia."

"He said, bring Alicia?"

"Not exactly. He said come to lunch, and I said I'll bring Alicia, and he said I love Alicia."

"What time's lunch?"

"I've called for a car. Meet you in the lobby in thirty minutes."

"How wonderful."

"Ladies who lunch," Cyndi said.

"This time," Alicia suggested, "let's try to keep our clothes on."

Donato Firenzi had been Donatella Versace's number two for many years before going out on his own to design women's lingerie. But his wasn't merely some up-market Italian version of Victoria's Secret. Firenzi actually made Victoria seem celibate.

As Firenzi himself described it once to Carson, "I create underwear for the whore that every man prays his mistress might become."

Alicia had been to these private lunches before. There were only six invited guests, but there was enough champagne for twice as many and the food was to die for. And even though Firenzi had the most gorgeous models in the world showing off his goods—more often than not, theirs, too—it wasn't unheard of that one or two of the women who'd been invited for lunch wound up on the catwalk as well.

He did these lunches once a month and invitations were always very last minute. All of the lingerie on show was, of course, for sale. But Firenzi never spoke about that. However, anyone who didn't buy never got a second invitation.

Alicia hurried back to the table to finish up.

Her laptop screen had a dozen open pages and she needed to rush through them before she jumped into the shower.

She bookmarked the pages she wanted to come back to and made a few extra notes on her pad. She closed out of Google and was about to sign off the NBC News archive site when she spotted a very small reference on the bottom of one page.

It read, "A mysterious buyer, believed to represent L. Arthur Farmer, has become the first residential tenant in Donald Trump's Tower."

That's all.

The date was 1979, the year construction began on the Tower.

Of course she knew who Farmer was. Everybody in the country had, at some point, heard of him, much the same way everybody in the forties, fifties, sixties and seventies had heard of Howard Hughes.

In fact, since Hughes' death in 1976, Farmer had taken on the mantle of America's most famous recluse. Google and Bing had thousands of references to him—Where is he? Is he alive or dead? How much is he worth?

A man whose business interests were wide and varied, he held significant positions through various companies in electronics, aviation, insurance, oil and mining. However, the heart of his empire, where he made his fortune before World War II, was food staples. He grew, processed, manufactured and/or distributed wheat, barley, rye, maize, tea, bananas, pineapples, olive oil, coconut oil and sugar.

But even those businesses paled in comparison to his hold on the planet's most important staple, the one at the heart of the diet for a huge portion of the human population—rice.

L. Arthur Farmer controlled nearly 20 percent of the world's rice.

Accordingly, his Wikipedia entry cited *Fortune* magazine, "He may be richer than Bill Gates and Warren Buffet. No one knows for sure. The only certainty is that he is not significantly poorer than either of them."

Alicia went back to the NBC query page and did a fast search for L. Arthur Farmer and Trump Tower. Only that single line reference appeared. She also tried Google and Bing, which brought no responses at all.

Now she really had to get ready. She shut down her computer, jumped into the shower, threw on a Versace pantsuit—being invited to this luncheon meant dressing the part—and was downstairs at the same time as Cyndi.

On the way to Firenzi, Alicia asked Cyndi, "Did you know that L. Arthur Farmer lived in our building?"

Cyndi shrugged, "Who?"

DONATO FIRENZI had a huge loft way downtown, on Washington Street, a block away from his former lover, Antoine de Maisonneuve.

Alicia and Cyndi were the first to arrive.

Security at the door checked off both their names before they were allowed upstairs.

Firenzi himself greeted them as soon as the elevator brought them up to the top floor.

Wearing tight, white leather pants and a bright green silk shirt open to his navel—with a large gold- and ruby-encrusted cross dangling from a heavy gold chain around his neck—he fawned all over Cyndi, kissed and hugged Alicia, then kissed and hugged Cyndi again.

"*Cara mia . . .*"

He was tall and thin, with dark eyes and a beautifully molded face. "We mustn't fight, *cara mia*," he said to Cyndi, playing up his accent as he brought the two women into the room where one large table at the very end of the cat-walk was set for seven. "*Cara mia . . . I* love you so much. *Ti amo.*"

Cyndi played her role to the hilt. "I love you too, so much so that there are times when I wish you had real balls."

"Darling," he laughed and hugged Alicia. "Isn't she wonderful? I love Cyndi."

"We all do," Alicia said, looking at Cyndi and mouthing the words, "Real balls?"

The elevator went down to the ground floor, then came back. Two more women arrived. And Firenzi moved away to greet his guests.

A gorgeous young woman wearing nothing but a white silk bra, white silk panties and a garter belt with stockings—some of Firenzi's tamer designs—walked over to Alicia and Cyndi, carrying a tray with champagne.

They both took a glass and waited for Firenzi to bring over the two women who'd just arrived.

One was Michelle Chevalier, who had modeled briefly for Dior in Paris when Cyndi was the face of Dior. She'd left the business to marry the French rock star, Percy Priest—his real name was Jean Marie Hubert, but on his first trip to Nashville, someone took him to the local lake with the same name and he decided that was a better name for a French rock star than his own—and now she spent most of her time traveling between homes in Paris, the Riviera and Nashville.

Michelle greeted Cyndi not like an old friend, because they weren't that, but like an old acquaintance who was too old to bother with the petty jealousies of youth.

Cyndi introduced Michelle to Alicia, and then Michelle introduced both of them to the young woman accompanying her, Sophie Gosselin.

She was the gorgeous nineteen-year-old who'd won this year's Cesar—the French equivalent of the Oscar—as Best Actress for her role as the seventeenth-century writer and consort to King Louis XIV, Françoise d'Aubigne de Maintenon.

Alicia politely said hello, and so did Cyndi, but when Sophie realized that Cyndi was Cyndi, she screamed with childish joy and hugged her. "I can't believe I'm meeting you. I grew up wanting to be you. I can't believe it."

Cyndi did her best to calm her down, while Michelle quickly turned her back and walked away to get some champagne.

The last two women to arrive were Amy Jane Hadley, whom Alicia knew because she was an up-and-coming television reporter at ABC-News, and her mother Melissa Hadley Jakes, who was the queen of Broadway press agents.

"You bring your mother to Firenzi's strip club?" Cyndi said much too loudly to Amy Jane.

Melissa heard that from where she was getting a second glass of champagne, turned around and said across the room to Cyndi, "Darling, you never know what a woman has under her jeans."

Champagne and canapés, served by young women in underwear, continued until Firenzi announced it was time for lunch.

The six women sat down at the table set with Royal Worcester's fruit pattern service and sterling utensils. Firenzi sat in between Cyndi and Sophie—who was still in awe of Cyndi—and the young women in underwear proceeded to serve a fabulous three-course lunch. They started with a duck mousse on a bed of *frisée* salad, proceeded to red snapper filets with a citron and garlic sauce on a bed of angel hair pasta, and finished with mini cannoli alongside homemade guava gelato.

There was still plenty of champagne, but now Firenzi brought out a bottle of homemade grappa, and after he poured seven little glasses, he announced, "Now ladies . . . the ladies."

The lights went dim and music came on, then a spotlight appeared and, one by one, Firenzi's models arrived on the catwalk, wearing less and less.

The bras and panties got smaller and smaller and, as the prices got higher and higher, the six women checked off what they wanted in little notebooks.

The catwalk show lasted half an hour, until Firenzi turned to his guests and asked, "Who would like to present the honeymoon ensemble?"

Cyndi whispered to Alicia. "Care to be naked in front of your new friends?"

Alicia shook her head, "Been there, done that."

Michelle suggested, "I nominate Cyndi."

"I have a better idea," Cyndi said and pointed to Melissa Hadley Jakes. "Speaking of what a woman has under her jeans . . ."

The oldest woman at the table—she was in her early forties—looked at the others and, in her deepest, sexiest voice said, "Nothing under my jeans, darling."

The women laughed.

Cyndi turned to the slightly embarrassed Amy Jane. "You know how lucky you are? My mother didn't even have a pussy."

Now everyone laughed, while Firenzi poured more grappa and, in the midst of that laughter, Sophie stood up. "I'll do it."

Before she could change her mind, one of the models took her back stage, and the next thing anyone knew, Sophie reappeared on the catwalk, unable to hide her nervousness, wearing a see-through gown, totally open at the front, with so little else that Cyndi remarked, "Obviously she's not my mother."

Packages of newly purchased underwear and a fresh bottle of champagne accompanied each of the women downstairs to their waiting cars.

"Let's drink to your health," Alicia started to sing the Cole Porter song from *High Society* as they rode uptown, all the while swigging champagne.

"Nah," Cyndi joined in, "let's drink to your—boobs." She took a long swig from her bottle.

"That's not in the song," Alicia said. "You like Sigmund Romberg?"

"I never met him."

Alicia started singing, "Drink, drink, drink . . ."

"What's that?" Cyndi wanted to know.

"*The Student Prince*. Sigmund Romberg."

Cyndi leaned over to Alicia. "You know what? I've done students. And I've done princes. But my life's work is not complete. I've never done a Sigmund."

Now Alicia broke into Julio Iglesias. "To all the men we've loved before . . ."

They sang and drank straight out of their bottles up to the front door, on the sidewalk, inside the residents' lobby and into the elevator.

Still laughing at everything, they went to Alicia's bedroom to try on what they'd bought.

Alicia put on an undercupped bra that left her breasts totally bare, and a G-string that had pieces of candy in the front where material should be.

Cyndi put on a garter belt, stockings and nothing else. "I'll be your serving wench. Champagne?"

The two women admired each other's choice of clothes, then Alicia asked, "That's your champagne. Where did I put my champagne?"

"Here," Cyndi started to hand her the bottle, "the drinks are on me." But then she decided to take a swig and noticed, "It's empty."

"More in the fridge," Alicia announced and walked through her apartment in her new underwear to get another bottle. She opened it, took a sip and started back to her bedroom.

She found Cyndi sprawled across her bed, fast asleep.

"Ah." Alicia stared at Cyndi for a long time, then pulled the duvet from under her and covered her with it.

She took another sip of champagne.

"You ever hear of L. Arthur Farmer?" She climbed into bed. "Did I already tell you he might have lived here?" She cuddled the bottle of champagne with one arm, "I'm going to tell you all about him," put her other arm around Cyndi, "except nobody knows anything about him," and promptly fell asleep too.

13

David was out of the apartment at the crack of dawn to drive sixty-five miles up the Hudson to Hopewell Junction, where he had an 8:10 tee-off time at the Trump National course there.

He took the Ferrari 612 again.

It was his monthly $1,000-a-hole skins game with the recently retired Eagles running back Lamar Duarte, the Detroit Red Wings left winger "Razor" Roland Guillaume and the Knick's inimitable but aging power forward Jamal "The Poison" Sumac.

All four of them played scratch golf, so for David this was the real thing. Last month he'd walked away losing six grand and considered himself unlucky because Razor and Poison both shot unbelievable four-under rounds. They couldn't miss a putt. This time he picked up two grand and considered himself lucky because he couldn't make a putt, blaming himself for leaving his Scott Cameron Tour Titleist triple black on the plane.

Back at Trump Tower by three, he found Tina only just getting up.

"You hungry?" He kissed her hello. "Where's Luisa?"

She was wearing his old Texas Tech football shirt and, even though it came down past her knees, he could see she had nothing else under it.

"Probably downstairs doing the laundry." She was still wiping the sleep out of her eyes. "You want breakfast?"

"I'll send out."

"We in tonight?"

"Wasn't there supposed to be something at the museum?"

"What museum?"

"Natural History."

"Oh . . . shit. I forgot all about that."

"Wanna go? We can still . . . "

"No. What do we care about dinosaurs? I'll send them a check."

"I like dinosaurs," he said.

"Then you send them a check."

"When's the Bulgari party?"

"Next week."

"So . . . we're in tonight?"

"Yeah," she said. "Chinese? Get the usual. I'll call it breakfast and you make it last for supper." She padded into the kitchen and went to her coffee machine.

They each had their own.

They'd started married life with an all-digital De Longhi Magnifica espresso machine that could be programmed weeks in advance to grind, tamp, brew and add frothy milk for a great cup of coffee. But one day David decided it was overly complicated—he could never get it to have fresh coffee waiting when he got up in the morning—and came home with a single-serve espresso machine, the kind that takes premeasured pods. "Only two hundred bucks," he told Tina. "It was on sale."

What he didn't tell Tina was that he'd also bought a year's supply—$900 worth—of different flavored coffee pods.

It turned out that he liked them all, but she wasn't crazy about any of the pods and, by that time, it was too late to go back to the De Longhi because David had given it to Luisa.

So she went out and bought herself a huge, chrome Jura Capresso Impressa Z5.

"It's the coffee machine equivalent of your Ferrari," she bragged.

"Can I drive it?" he asked.

"Sure," she said, "when you let me drive the Ferrari."

Every morning, he made his coffee pod espresso, and she made her Jura Capresso espresso, and the possibility of her driving his Ferrari was never discussed again.

"It's the Coves," David said when Keung answered the phone at the Autumn Moon on Third Avenue. This was one of the only Chinese restaurants in New York that did not deliver—except to some people. "Will you send up the usual, please?"

"Cove?" Keung said.

"Yes, Cove."

"Usual?"

"Yes, usual."

"Address for usual?"

He shook his head, "The usual address."

"Cove?"

"That's right."

"Twenty-five minute," Keung said and hung up.

"How long?" Tina asked, watching the coffee come from the machine into her cup.

"If there's no traffic, sometime next month."

The phone rang. David answered it. And a man with an odd accent said, "I'm looking for Mr. Cove."

"Who wants him?"

"My name is Vasyl Zhadanov. And I'm ringing on the advice of Asil Özgür in Istanbul. Is this Mr. Cove?"

"If Asil said to call, yeah, it is. What can I do for you?"

"I was hoping I might be able to do something for you. I'm an attorney here in New York. Is there a possibility we could meet this afternoon? The matter is rather urgent. My office? Your office? Neutral ground? Whatever is convenient for you. I assure you it will be worth your time."

"Where's your office?"

"I'm at Forty-Second and Fifth, right opposite the library. But I'll tell you what, instead of you coming downtown, why don't I come up? It's easier for you and no problem for me. You're at Trump Tower, right? So how about a glass of bubbly across the street from you at the Plaza?"

"When?"

"Fifteen minutes?"

"Lobby?"

"Champagne bar."

"Sure." David hung up and explained to Tina, "Lawyer friend of Asil's. I'm going to run across the street and find out what he wants."

"Lawyer friend of Asil's?"

"That's what he said."

"You going to call Asil and check?"

He looked at his watch. "I could. What time is it in Istanbul?" Then he decided, "But if I do and something comes of this, the son of a bitch will ask for a finder's fee. Remember the guy with the four cigarette boats in Orlando? Asil stuck us up for seventy grand."

"But Asil was the one who helped put that deal together."

"That's not what you said at the time."

"Do what you want." She took the first sip of her coffee. "But don't forget, he's a friend of Asil's, so after you shake hands, count your fingers."

As soon as David walked into the Champagne Bar—a high-ceilinged room with gorgeous chandeliers and floor-to-ceiling windows—a man walked up to him and extended his hand.

"I'm Vasyl Zhadanov. Thank you so much for agreeing to meet with me."

He brought David to a table in the corner and handed him his card, which read, "Vasyl Zhadanov, Attorney at Law." It gave his address as Suite 6501, 500 Fifth Avenue, New York 10110. Below it were phone numbers for the New York office, plus offices in Geneva and London.

David read it, then put the card in his pocket.

Zhadanov was somewhere in his midfifties, stout, with a weathered face, stubby hands, and dandruff from his black hair all over the shoulders of his off-the-rack blue suit. "What would you like?" he asked, signaling for a waiter.

"Mr. Zhadanov? Good afternoon," the waiter said. "Nice to see you again. What can I get you?"

David said, "Glass of champagne will do fine."

"Two," Zhadanov said. "Not the house stuff . . . the usual."

"Yes, sir." The waiter left them alone.

"I'd been meaning to get in touch with you for about a week now," Zhadanov began. "And when I spoke to Asil a few days ago . . . by the way, he asked to be remembered to you and your lovely wife, Tina . . . it reminded me that I had not yet made contact."

Smiling to be polite, David thought to himself, *how come Asil didn't tell me this guy was going to call?* "What's this all about?"

"Some clients of mine are looking to place some money, a rather large sum, that will have to be handled with the utmost discretion."

David wanted to know, "Who are your clients?"

"There will be time to talk about that."

"American?"

"No."

"So who . . . "

"You will meet them."

"And their money? Where's it all coming from?"

He looked at David. "Shall we call it investment money?"

"I didn't ask where it's going. I asked where it's coming from."

There was another long pause. "When you buy and sell a distressed cargo, you guarantee the purchase or sale with a line of bank credit, yes?"

"Yes."

"How big a line do you now run?"

He didn't like that question. "What's it to you?"

"Please . . . " Zhadanov held up both hands. "I do not mean to pry. But I wanted to give you an example of what my clients are thinking. If, say, you run a line of . . . pick a figure . . . two million dollars . . . "

"We'd be broke," David interjected.

"Then, say, five million."

David shook his head. "Flat ass out of business."

"Perhaps I should have done my homework," Zhadanov went on. "Shall we say, twenty million?"

"Still too low."

"What I'm trying to say is . . . what kind of business could you do if you had a line of, say, one hundred million?"

David conceded, "Pretty damn big."

"Then how would you like to be a pretty damn big player?"

The waiter arrived with two champagne flutes and six small verines. There were two tiny glasses, each with avocado mousse and smoked salmon, fois gras with ravioli, and crabmeat with pink grapefruit. "Your usual, sir," he said.

Zhadanov thanked him, picked up his champagne, and toasted David, "Your health."

David raised his glass, nodded, took a sip then. "Your client wants to sink a hundred mil into my business?"

"Let's say . . . " Zhadanov paused as if he needed to phrase this delicately . . . "my clients wish to extend your credit by sizable amounts. How much, for how long, and what we do about points against trading profits for the use of the credit line are mere details. The important thing is to see if you're the right person for my clients and, at the same time, if my clients are the right people for you."

"Where's this credit line going to be managed?"

"My client account, you name the bank."

"My bank?"

"You choose."

David needed to get this straight. "You're going to open an account at my bank and make that money available to me to secure credit . . . "

"What could be simpler?"

"And your clients are . . . who?"

"My clients are," Zhadanov paused, then admitted, "Colombians."

"Fuck me, pal. A hundred mil in drug cash? I don't think so."

"I don't, either. Because that's not what this is." He asked calmly, "What do you know about money laundering?"

"Enough to know I can wind up in jail for twenty years."

"Federal statutes dictate . . . that's right . . . twenty years per count. But that's for laundering money."

"Drug money."

"Any kind of money. The crime is laundering. In very general terms, that's defined as an act to conceal or obscure the origin, destination or beneficial owners of monies obtained illegally. But if the money is legitimate . . . "

"There is no such thing as legitimate Colombian money."

"Just because they're Colombians, it doesn't mean they're drug traffickers."

"Let me guess . . . they're dentists."

"No. They're . . . currency brokers. But they only broker dollars and Colombian pesos. And you don't have to worry about that. Once you meet them and they meet you, if you both get along, then that's the last you'll have anything to do with them. You'll be dealing with me."

David hesitated. "It's still Colombian money."

"Which you never actually touch. Your line of credit comes through your bank. This money merely secures it . . . big time."

In the back of his mind, David replayed a conversation with Tina.

Airplane parts.

Way out of our league.

Big money in that shit.

Big downside because we could never cover it.

Maybe someday when we grow up and get really rich.

He looked at Zhadanov for a long time. "This account you're going to open . . . "

"A lawyer's client account is protected by client-attorney privilege."

"When my bank guy asks . . . "

"He won't because he knows that the names behind the account and the source of the funds are protected."

"So it *is* drug money."

"It's money being brokered." Zhadanov insisted, "Meet these people. If you think they're traffickers, I'll get up and walk away with you. But when you meet them and realize they are who I say they are . . . we're talking a hundred million dollars. This is a game changer for you."

David stared at Zhadanov for the longest time.

Maybe someday when we grow up and get really rich.

"If they're drug traffickers, I'm walking out."

Tina had the fourteen cartons from Autumn Moon spread out all over the kitchen table.

"What did the lawyer want?"

David sat down, looked for the *mu shu* pork, took the carton, rolled some pancakes, and started eating.

"Made us an offer to extend our line of credit to a hundred mil."

"Who do we have to kill?"

"I'm meeting with his clients first thing Monday morning."

"Who are they?"

He paused, then told her, "A consortium of brokers."

"Wall Street?"

"Bunch of foreign guys."

"Tell me more."

"Not much to tell until I see the whites of their eyes. I'll fly down tomorrow . . . "

"Fly down to where?"

"They're at some sort of meeting in Curaçao."

"You're going all the way to Curaçao?"

"If I don't like them, I'm turning around and coming straight home. But if I do like them . . . Tina, this could be huge."

"I'm scheduled at T'ien tomorrow. I'll cancel and come with you."

"No. It's an initial meeting. You go ahead and do your thing. Anyway, I'm playing golf tomorrow morning, and I'll go straight to the plane from there."

"And this lawyer guy?" She asked, "How come Asil never mentioned him?"

David showed her both his hands. "Look, I came away with all my fingers."

14

"**O**y!"

Someone was banging hard on Ricky Lips' front door.

"Oy," he shouted again, "I'm on the way."

He came out of his bedroom, where he'd been watching a British snooker tournament on cable, wearing a pair of baggy, green Bermuda shorts, a well-worn gray Doors T-shirt that said, "Hello I Love You," his Ugg boots and, of course, his ankle bracelet.

Someone banged a third time on the door.

"Oy."

He maneuvered through the mess that was his living room, got to the door and yanked it open.

"Oy."

Neville Manley Jones, whose claim to fame was that he once played bass with his schoolboy chum Bob Marley, was standing there with a fierce-looking older black woman.

"Why didn't you ring up?" Ricky asked.

"I did ring up," Neville said in his island lilt.

"They're supposed to announce you at the front desk downstairs."

"They did."

"Who answered the phone?"

"How do I know?" Neville said. "Meet Mrs. Whelan. I told you about her."

"When?"

"When I said I'd bring Mrs. Whelan up to meet you."

Ricky looked at her, then at Neville, because he didn't know what Neville was talking about, then looked past them both to the hallway where Miguel, the elevator operator, was standing waiting to make sure that he would let them in.

"It's okay," Ricky waved to Miguel, then asked Neville, "Who's this?"

"It's Mrs. Whelan," he said, motioning to Ricky to move aside so that they could come in. "She comes recommended by Bono."

"Wayne Punch Webber," she corrected him.

"You told me Bono," Neville said.

"I told you Wayne Punch Webber."

Ricky wanted to know, "Who the fuck is Wayne Punch Webber?" Then asked Mrs. Whelan, "You sure it wasn't Bono?"

She glared at him.

He told her, "That's all right. I don't like you any less," and stepped aside to let them in.

Mrs. Whalen only got as far as the entrance to the living room and stopped right there. "What in the good Lord's name . . . "

"She also comes recommended by Rod Stewart," Neville said.

"Leon Boss Sherman," she corrected him again.

Ricky had to ask, "Who?"

"This place is a disaster," Mrs. Whelan said. "One big, awful, horrible disaster."

"Yeah," Ricky agreed, then asked Neville, "Who's Leon Boss Sherman?"

"Don't you ever straighten up?" she asked.

He admitted, "No."

Neville said, "Drummer?"

"How can you live like this?" Mrs. Whelan pointed to food cartons on the floor—most of them empty but a few half-full—ashtrays filled with cigarettes, and beer cans and soda bottles scattered everywhere.

He held out his hands in defeat, "Easy," then said to Neville, "Big, bald-headed bloke?"

She reached for an empty vodka bottle. "Aren't you an alcoholic?"

"I go to meetings," he said, then stopped. "Well, I can't exactly go to meetings because I can't exactly go anywhere, not with this . . . " He raised his leg to show her the ankle bracelet. "But it's coming off in a couple of weeks and then we're going on tour. Until then, the meetings come to me."

Neville looked at Mrs. Whelan. "They're going on tour."

"Who?" She asked, incredulously. "Still Fools?"

"Sorry luv," Ricky said, "me too, I was hoping for the Beatles."

"And that . . . device?"

"It's coming off in . . . I got this countdown clock from NASA . . . I can show you exactly how many hours, minutes . . . "

"You and your cocaine" she said scornfully. "I read all about it in the *Post*."

"They got it totally wrong," he protested. "Honestly, they did. They busted me for eight ounces. Not true. Six months house arrest for eight ounces. Unbelievable. Especially because it was a kilo and a half." He looked at Neville, "Can't believe anything you read in the papers, these days."

Mrs. Whelan put the bottle down on a small table and turned to Neville, "You expect me to work in a pigsty like this?"

"Baldheaded bloke. That's him," Neville said to Ricky, then told Mrs. Whelan, "I don't. He does."

"You have a housekeeper?" she asked Ricky.

"Yeah. Absolutely." He nodded. "I think so. I mean, I used to. Maybe I still do."

"Where is she?"

"Not a clue, luv."

"What's going on?" Ricky's son Joey appeared from the third bedroom.

"Our new housekeeper," Ricky said.

Joey nodded. "Pleased to make your acquaintance."

He asked Mrs. Whelan, "Can you live here when we go on tour?"

"No," she said right away.

"As soon as this damn thing comes off . . . and if you want to step into my bedroom I could tell you exactly when it's coming off . . . then we're going to Toronto for three weeks to rehearse and then going on tour for six months."

Joey looked at Mrs. Whelan, "Better not do my room yet 'cause my bird is naked and tied to the bed, and I came to get a pair of scissors to cut her loose."

Mrs. Whelan stared at him, shook her head, then dared to step, cautiously, through the living room. When she got to the master bedroom door, she opened it and looked inside. "Not any better in here," she said, closed the door, and continued her tour.

"Where are the scissors?" Joey asked.

"Beats me, mate," his father said.

"What am I supposed to do?"

His father repeated, "Beats me, mate," and kept watching Mrs. Whelan's every move.

"Oh, bloody hell," Joey said and went into the kitchen.

Mrs. Whelan made her way down the hallway to the second bedroom, opened the door, screamed, and shut the door. "There's a couple in there . . . "

"Really?" Ricky moved past her and opened the door. "Oh, yeah. Them."

Bugs and Shari were naked in bed, with sheets and pillows all over the floor, still going at it.

"Oy," Ricky said to them. "Checkout time is noon."

"No problem," Bugs said. "Finishing our shag now."

Ricky shut the door. "They're finishing their shag now," he repeated to Mrs. Whelan with some solemnity. "Won't be much longer."

Mrs. Whelan took a deep breath. "Dare I ask if you have a kitchen?"

"Sure, you dare," Ricky said. "You'll love it. Almost like new. Hardly ever used."

She approached the kitchen just as Joey came out carrying a meat cleaver.

"My God," Mrs. Whelan jumped in fright.

"Got to cut me bird loose," Joey said and walked back into the third bedroom.

"See?" Ricky pointed to dishes piled high in the sink. "That's the kitchen."

"Good Lord in heaven."

"Oh, if you're looking for toilet paper, we keep it in the oven. Lots of space there."

She opened the double doors of the huge fridge, but the moment she did an odor came out that was so pungent, she slammed the doors shut without ever seeing what was inside.

"None of this is mine," Ricky said. "Honestly. And I can prove it. I mean, I don't cook."

A phone started ringing.

"Can you get that?" Ricky said to Neville.

"Yeah, right," Neville said, trying to follow the sound of the ringing. It led him into the living room. "Where's the phone?"

"Wherever it's ringing," Ricky said.

"But where . . . " He looked behind the couch and got on his knees to search the floor, and then it stopped.

"Who is it?" Ricky asked.

"Couldn't find the phone," Neville said.

"Bloody hell." Ricky came into the living room and looked around until he saw an empty pizza box on the floor in the corner. He picked it up and found a BlackBerry. "Here it is." He handed it to Neville. "Check to see who called, will you?"

Neville fumbled with the phone. "There's a number here . . . "

"Ring it."

"You want me to press call?"

"Here." Ricky grabbed the phone and dialed the last number that had called him.

A woman answered, "Concierge, this is Felicity."

"Who?"

"This is Felicity."

"Oy," he said, "it's Ricky upstairs." He looked at Neville, "Bird down at the front desk." Then said to Felicity, "How are you, luv?"

"Mr. Lips? That you? I rang your apartment. You have some guests."

"Yeah, sure," he said. "Send them up. But . . . do I know them?"

"It's Mr. Windsor, sir."

"The King himself," Ricky said. "Send them up." He hung up and announced, "We have guests."

Immediately, he bent down and picked up an empty pizza box, looked around, didn't know where to hide it, and tossed it on top of another empty pizza box.

"Perhaps the couch," Mrs. Whelan suggested, took the cushions, and put them in place. Then she went to the empty pizza boxes and picked them up.

"Not too much," he said. "These are friends. It's not as if we've got a bunch of strangers coming up."

Mrs. Whelan glared at Neville. "Have you told him what this is going to cost?"

"Oh, yeah," Neville said to Ricky. "Mrs. Whelan gets forty-five dollars an hour, with an eight-hour minimum per day."

"In advance," she added.

"Sure," Ricky said. "That's fine. When do you want to start?"

Someone knocked on the door.

"Oy," Ricky shouted and went to open it.

King Windsor, lead singer with Weekend Fling was there—wearing his traditional skin-tight leather pants and an open silk shirt, except there was now a lot of belly hanging out—alongside a very tall, very young, very busty blonde who was carrying a large carton.

"This is Tyne," King said, "meet me old mate Ricky."

"Pleasure," she said.

Ricky hugged King and gave Tyne a wet kiss on the mouth. "Come on in." He brought them into the living room. "You know Neville . . . and you're . . . Time?" He looked at her, "Like time marches on?" He pointed to Mrs. Whelan. "And this is my new housekeeper . . . this is King and Time . . . "

"Tyne," she said, handing the box to him. "Like the river."

"Which river?" Ricky said to her, then explained to King, "Mrs. Whelan also works for Bono." He took the box. "For me?" But something inside moved. "Jeezus . . . what's in there?"

"Open it," King said. "We found it in the neighborhood. A stray. And I figured with you all shut up in here like this . . . "

Ricky tore the box open and inside was a kitten. "Precisely what every guy needs . . . a little pussy."

He lifted it up and took it out to show everyone.

The cream-colored cat was not so small—probably already weighed a couple of pounds—had very big eyes, pointed ears, and lots of light reddish-brown squares on its white body that almost looked like stripes.

"I love it," Ricky said, showing it to them. "Look at that . . . " He turned it over and decided, "A little boy." He showed them that, too. "What shall we name him?"

"Mr. Lips?" Mrs. Whelan was shaking her head and moving slowly toward the door.

"How about Felix?" Tyne suggested. "He was a boy cat."

"Nah," King said, "got to give it a real bloke's name. Let's call him Mike Tyson."

"Mr. Lips?" Mrs. Whelan tried again, now from the hallway.

Just then Bugs and Shari appeared from the second bedroom. They were dressed, but disheveled. "We'll be off now Ricky," Bugs said.

"Oh look," Shari went to pet the animal. "A little pussy."

"That's what I said when I saw you," Ricky gave her one of his big wet kisses on the mouth.

"What's its name?" she asked.

King answered, "Mike Tyson."

Bugs wondered, "Shouldn't it be something English? Like . . . Noel Gallagher?"

Ricky shook his head. "Remember me parrot that died? That was his name."

"Oh, sorry to hear about your loss," Bugs bowed his head.

"You want real English?" King suggested, "How about Freddie Mercury? You and him always got along good."

Ricky glared at his old friend. "Freddie was a poofter."

"Mr. Lips?" Mrs. Whelan was very anxious to get his attention.

Tyne piped up. "Then why not Queen?"

Ricky couldn't believe she'd said that. "'Cause the cat's a bloke and the Queen's a bird."

"I've got it," Neville volunteered. "Real English. William the Shakespeare."

"I like it," Ricky agreed, and put his hand on the animal's head. "I dub thee, Bill the Shakespeare."

"Mr. Lips?" Mrs. Whelan spoke loud and forcefully. "Mr. Lips, I cannot and will not work here."

He turned and, for the first time, realized she was halfway out the door. "Why?"

"That." She pointed to the animal.

"Bill?" He held it up. "You allergic to cats, or something?"

"That . . . " she turned and started out the door . . . "is not a cat. It's an ocelot."

15

It was 6:30 that night when everyone started gathering in front of the residents' entrance.

Pierre Belasco, who'd been in the building since three-something in the morning, stepped out of his office.

Three maids, all in saris, were waiting at the curb with bouquets of flowers. Kajjili was standing off to the side with a bowl of rose petals.

No sooner were they in place when Amvi arrived—tall and thin with her long, black hair demurely tied into a ponytail—wearing a gorgeous blue and green silk sari, surrounded by three very bulky bodyguards, all armed, and with wires in their ears. She was also accompanied by her governess, the inimitable Mrs. Churchward, a robust, rigidly stern woman in her early fifties.

Gossip around the Tower had it that she'd been governess to all of Mick Jagger's children, both of Prince Andrew's daughters, all of the various Redgrave grandchildren, the offspring of the most popular British socialites in the Caribbean, Lord and Lady Montagu-Wind—even though they were, famously, childless—and had even been the first governess of HRH Prince Charles, despite the fact that the prince was at least a dozen years older than Mrs. Churchward.

That was typical, Belasco understood, of the nonstop gossip that circulates wildly about everything and everyone at Trump Tower. "Don't believe half of what you hear," he would say to the staff, trying to encourage them not to feed the fires, "and doubt one hundred percent of the rest. It is a historical fact that gossip was invented in Trump Tower."

Belasco also seriously doubted the "Mrs." part of Churchward's name. She was not, in his mind, anyone who anyone else would ever want to marry.

Donald Trump didn't think so, either. "Can you imagine the old battle-ax on her honeymoon?" He'd once confided in Belasco, "She shows up naked except for a pair of white gloves. The eager Mr. Churchward is waiting for her in bed and says, 'My darling, why the white gloves?' And the blushing bride responds, 'In case I have to touch the nasty thing.'"

"Good evening," he greeted Mrs. Churchward and Amvi as they moved through the lobby with the bodyguards.

The woman turned and nodded. "Mr. Belasco."

The bodyguards made only enough room for him to shake her hand, then extend his hand to Amvi.

"And how are you, Miss Amvi?"

The girl lowered her head slightly and looked at him through the top of her big, dark eyes. "*Bon jour, monsieur*," she said shaking his hand. She continued in French, "I'm very pleased that my parents are returning today. You know, they've been away for so long and . . . " She glanced and smiled at Mrs. Churchward, who clearly did not understand French, "I am sick and tired of this miserable old cow."

"I understand fully," he answered in French, trying not to smile. Then he turned to Mrs. Churchward and said in English, "Miss Amvi's French is absolutely perfect."

"Brearley has a very strong program," she noted, referring to the private school where Amvi was a junior. "Of course, she is an A student. One would expect nothing less."

"Only one year left after this one," Belasco said to Amvi, in English. "Have you given any thought to what you want to do next?"

Mrs. Churchward answered for her. "We're considering both Harvard and Yale, of course, although given the state of New Haven, Connecticut, we feel that Harvard would be more suitable."

"So Harvard it shall be," Amvi said in English, then reverted to French. "Unless I run away and join the Navy first."

"I'm sure," he said in English, smiling at her to show he appreciated her sense of humor, "that you will find . . . a sea of opportunities."

She grinned at him, then looked at Mrs. Churchward to reassure herself that the woman didn't understand a word of what they were saying.

One of the bodyguards put his hand up to his earpiece, then announced, "The eagle is landing."

"Places," Mrs. Churchward said.

Belasco nodded toward Jaime, the afternoon doorman, who held the double doors open as the group hurried out to the curb. Then Belasco motioned to Gilbert, the temporary concierge, to come and hold the other doors open when the Advanis arrived.

Now, three black four-door Mercedes E-Class sedans pulled up quickly, followed by a black Mercedes SUV.

Immediately, two bodyguards jumped out of the first sedan. The chauffeur of the second jumped out equally as fast and went to open the rear door.

Mr. Advani's personal assistant, a sickly young man named Chakor, rushed out of the third car, followed immediately by Mrs. Advani's secretary, a plump, young woman named Miss Rangarajan.

Then Mrs. Advani—a beautiful woman in her early forties with long, shiny black hair—got out wearing a dark charcoal Armani pantsuit with Gucci boots, small heeled so that she wouldn't look too much taller than her husband.

Amvi ran up to her mother and kissed her and held her and started crying.

From the other side, one of the bodyguards helped Prakash Advani get out.

He was in his midsixties, heavy set and nearly bald, with dark-dyed hair on the sides, and wearing a perfectly fitted navy blue suit with a white shirt and paisley blue tie.

Kajjili started throwing rose petals where the Advanis were about to walk.

Mr. Advani came around to greet his daughter—she let go of her mother long enough to hug and kiss him—then held onto her mother again.

Belasco could see that Mrs. Advani was crying too.

Mr. Advani stepped forward and shook Belasco's hand. "How nice to see you again."

"Welcome home, sir. I trust you've had a good trip."

"Good, yes, but I might add, very long." With that he moved away to greet Kajjili and Mrs. Churchward. He also greeted the three maids, each of whom presented him with flowers.

He showed them to his wife, then handed them off to Miss Rangarajan, who took them and nodded to the maids to follow her quickly upstairs.

Mr. Advani went back to whisper something to his daughter, who looked at him and smiled. Then he put his arm around Amvi and his wife and said, "Let's go home."

Behind them, the chauffeurs were unloading luggage.

Seeing how many pieces they had, Belasco whispered to Jaime, "Close down one of the elevators and please help deal with the luggage."

"I will," Jaime said, motioning to Gilbert to take the door.

Belasco nodded to Jaime and watched as Gilbert moved into place.

Then, suddenly, Joey Lips and his girlfriend stepped out of an elevator and, with his arm around her, started toward the lobby.

Amvi was still clinging to her mother.

Mrs. Churchward was hovering close behind.

Mr. Advani was trying to herd his wife and daughter inside.

Belasco had no idea what might happen if Amvi and Joey saw each other—maybe nothing at all—but after Joey's comment early this morning, he decided to err on the side of caution. He whispered in Gilbert's ear, "Quick, get Mr. Lips and his lady friend into my office. And close the door."

Gilbert nodded and went to do that.

Now Belasco manned the door but did not open it all the way.

Mr. Advani had to stop right there.

"The luggage will be up shortly," Belasco said, watching Gilbert out of the corner of his eye, speaking with Joey.

That's when Amvi and her mother turned toward the door.

Joey was still in the lobby.

"Please," Belasco said, stepping in the way of Mr. Advani, "Oh, excuse me, sir," to open the door for Amvi and her mother.

Mr. Advani moved aside to let his wife and daughter go through the doors first.

Mrs. Advani smiled.

Now Joey seemed to be arguing with Gilbert.

Belasco quickly reached for Mrs. Advani's hand, bowed, and almost kissed it. "Madame, welcome home."

"Thank you," the woman said, and was about to go inside when Belasco reached for Amvi's hand.

Mrs. Advani stopped.

"Mademoiselle," Belasco said, almost kissing her hand, "I bid you pleasant evening."

Amvi curtsied politely.

"You know, Madame," he said to Mrs. Advani, "her French is excellent. You should be very proud."

Mrs. Advani said, "Thank you Mr. Belasco, I assure you that my husband and I are extremely proud of Amvi."

He smiled at her, then at Amvi, then said to Mr. Advani, "Very proud."

"Yes," he responded, "we are indeed."

Mrs. Advani took her daughter's hand, and there was nothing else Belasco could do but allow Amvi and her mother to walk through the double doors.

But now, Joey and his girlfriend were nowhere to be seen.

Belasco stepped aside for Mr. Advani. "Sir . . . welcome home again, and good evening."

Kajjili followed him, with Mrs. Churchward close behind.

Mr. and Mrs. Advani stopped briefly at the concierge desk where Schaune was waiting—actually standing in front of the desk—to bow and shake their hands and say, "Welcome home."

While Schaune was greeting the Advanis, the three bodyguards hurried inside, leaving the two outside at the curb to protect the luggage.

The Advanis, with their bodyguards next to them, walked straight into the waiting elevator.

The chauffeurs began unloading what turned out to be sixteen pieces of luggage.

Taking a deep breath, Belasco went to his office where Jaime was explaining to a rather annoyed Joey, "He wants a word . . . oh, here he is . . . Mr. Belasco?"

"What's going on?" Joey wanted to know.

Belasco bowed slightly toward the skinny young woman, still wearing the open white dress, and to Joey, who was dressed in ripped jeans and a T-shirt but still wearing the black fedora. "I wanted to apologize for any inconvenience."

Joey gave him an odd look. "What inconvenience?"

He nodded to Joey, "Yes, sir, exactly. In any case, I wish you and Mademoiselle a pleasant evening."

Joey stared at him, "Whatever," and motioned to his girlfriend, "Let's go."

As soon as they were gone, Belasco announced to his staff in the lobby, "I think my work here is done. Have a good evening." And he too turned to leave.

"Sir?" Jaime followed him.

Belasco stopped at the double doors to let a chauffeur in with luggage.

The rose petals on the sidewalk were now well trampled.

"Sir?" Jaime asked again, "Inconvenience?"

Belasco headed home. "What inconvenience?"

16

Zeke's flight home with Mikey Glass was, for the most part, uneventful. Mikey quickly fell asleep and stayed that way until they were somewhere over Nevada. When he finally stirred and the stewardess brought him some coffee, he asked Zeke, "You going home?"

"LA," Zeke answered, knowing that Mikey was looking for a lift to Malibu, where his house was only six doors down from Zeke's beach place.

"Yeah, okay," Mikey responded. "Actually . . . I think I left my car at the airport."

"You don't know?"

"Who can remember? It was three days ago. Well, maybe four. How time flies when you're having fun."

Zeke stared at him. "You really don't know if you left your car at the airport?"

"No problem. I'll call the limo service and when I get home if the car isn't there, then I'll know it's at the airport. Or . . . somewhere else. Good thing I have a lot of cars." He started listing them. "Let's see, I have a Porsche and a Mercedes and another Mercedes and a Porsche . . . I said that already . . . maybe I have two Porsches. I wonder where the second one is?"

When they landed, Zeke put Mikey in a limo, then drove himself home to Tower Road, off Benedict Canyon Drive in Beverly Hills, the house where Spencer Tracy had once lived.

Built in 1942 on a little over two acres, it was a two-story, twenty-two-room house hidden from the road by huge trees and shrubs, and protected by a large, electronic gate. The driveway wound up a slight incline to the right, leading to a large parking area and a four-car garage.

A set of heavy wooden double doors opens into a marble vestibule, with living rooms off to each side and a formal dining room straight ahead at the back, looking out onto a manicured garden and a blue, heart-shaped swimming pool.

Zeke dropped his keys on the table in the vestibule and found a note there from Birgitta, saying that she was playing tennis. He called out for their maid, Maria, but she didn't answer. He found his sixteen-year-old son, Max, upstairs in his room. However, Max was much too engrossed in some NBA video game, and the music blaring from his headset was so loud that Zeke could hear it at the door.

He went back downstairs.

Knowing that Max would surface when he wanted food, and figuring that Birgitta would come home when she was ready, Zeke went out through the kitchen door to the pool house he used as an office.

He picked up his iPad and a phone and reached into the fridge for a copper-bottled Samuel Adams Utopia.

Now on the deck, facing the pool, he pulled one of the six large, yellow-and-blue cushioned chairs over to a glass table, sat down and, surrounded by trees and shrubs, cracked open the beer and started making calls.

He wanted to be certain that everything was ready for Monday.

He found Lenny Silverberg on the golf course in East Hampton, on Long Island. "I still don't know why we're not doing this in New York," Silverberg said.

"So that you have the excuse to shack up at the Bel Air with the singer from Mexico City."

"Oh, yeah," he said, "sounds like a plan. See you Monday."

Then he found Bing O'Leary on his boat off the coast of Catalina. "Everything's ready to go," he assured Zeke. "My father-in-law says he's in if you still have room."

"For Harry, there is always room."

After that, he called Carl Kravitz at his weekend home in Cabo San Lucas, Mexico. "I'm flying in very early Monday morning. I'll come straight to Malibu from the airport."

"What about the other guy?"

"His name is Isbister."

"What kind of a name is that?"

"Apparently Scottish."

"How's he getting here?"

"I don't know him. Never met him. He said he would find us."

Before Zeke could make another call, his phone rang, and caller ID said it was Bobby Lerner. "You get home all right?"

"Yeah. You back yet?"

"No, I'm in Chicago, but I'm home tomorrow night."

"Looks like everybody is ready to go."

"See you Monday."

Now Zeke phoned the last man on the list, Ken Warring in Omaha.

"We're all set for Monday morning," Zeke told him.

"Only problem is," Warring said, "I've got to be in Dallas Monday night. I'm out of your place right after lunch."

"No problem," Zeke assured him, then thought to himself . . . lunch. The idea of food hadn't even dawned on him. So he phoned Olinda, his house-keeper in Malibu, and said they'd be eight for lunch on Monday.

She asked him what he wanted her to prepare.

"Call Nobu. Tell them I want a big selection for ten." Then he changed his mind. "No . . . portions are too small . . . tell them for fifteen. But no waiters. They deliver, but they don't come inside. You serve. Okay?"

Hanging up with her, he took a long pull of his beer, ran through his e-mails, and spotted a note from Caroline Tremblay.

"Sorry I missed speaking to you while you were in New York," she wrote. "I'm on my mobile all weekend."

"Shit." He got her on the phone and apologized. "I meant to call, really."

"It's all right. You will be at the sale, won't you? Otherwise . . . "

"I'll be there."

"Good. I'll meet you in the room, say nine forty-five? It starts at ten."

"Yes, I will be there. And . . . what kind of interest is there?"

"The market is soft," she warned.

"Doesn't sound encouraging."

"It really depends if you're buying or selling."

He reminded her, "Both."

"Then we'll have to see."

"Thanks. See you Wednesday." He hung up and said out loud, "Optimism is not the woman's strong suit."

He took another pull of his beer, said out loud, "Speaking of optimism . . . " and dialed his first wife, Miriam.

She'd been his high school sweetheart back in Chicago. "My mother asked for you. She might even have sent her love. But with her it's always hard to tell."

"Of course, she sent her love. She says it all the time. I speak to her twice a week."

"You do?"

"Why not? I've known her as long as I've known you, and she is the grandmother of my children."

"But she likes her other grandchildren better."

"Actually, she doesn't," Miriam insisted. "However, I know for a fact that she likes me better than any of your other wives. And she tells me she likes me better than she likes you."

"I'm not surprised."

"You could be nicer to her."

"I'm wonderful to her."

"That's not her version of events. What's this about you taking money away from her?"

"She tell you that?" He groaned loudly to show her that he was annoyed. "It's too complicated. Believe me when I say I'm not taking anything away from her."

"Your brother and sister don't believe you. But I will, if you really need someone to."

"My brother and sister? You talk to them too?"

"Yes," she said. "I've got to go. Goodbye."

She hung up before he could ask if Zoey was there.

Shaking his head, he dialed Zoey's cell but got voice mail. "This is your father who loves you, even if you are screening calls, which I suspect you do because I only ever get voice mail."

Putting the phone down and going back to his beer, he wondered for a moment what life would be like if he and Miriam had stayed together. They were good together in high school before they started having sex, and really good together at Northwestern, when sex was all they ever seemed to do. They got married, and while he went through University of Chicago Law, she taught at an inner-city elementary school.

They had Zoey, and then they had Max, and then they moved to LA, which is where everything changed. He made money and she started calling herself Miri because, she said, "Miriam Greenberg Gimbel sounds too East Coast."

He reminded her, "We're not from the East Coast, we're from Chicagoland, that's the Midwest, and the nickname for Miriam is Mimi, not Miri."

"This is LA," she insisted, "where if I want to be Miri, I can be Miri."

Maybe, he thought, *I was too busy to understand why being Miriam Greenberg Gimbel was not who she wanted to be anymore. Or maybe she was fooling herself into thinking she was someone else. Or maybe that's what LA does to you if you're not ready for LA.* Whatever it was, their marriage went steadily downhill until the day she decided it was over. They were living in Brentwood and had gone out to dinner at a local Italian place. A few glasses of wine and he was thinking the mood was right to wind up making love all night when she announced over dessert, "I want a divorce."

Two years after he moved out of the house, leaving Miriam there with the kids, he married a long-legged brunette dancer whose name was Savannah Galleria.

Except it wasn't.

"Did your mother name you after a shopping center somewhere?" He'd asked her on their first date, which turned into a weekend shacked up in Las Vegas.

"No," she said, "my mother named me Savannah because that's where I was born, and the family name is Boots. But Savannah Boots sounded too silly for an actress, so I changed it. I named myself after a shopping mall. Cool, no?"

That marriage barely lasted six months.

She wasn't getting work as an actress, and he said that booking her through his agency would be a conflict of interest—by which he really meant that it conflicted with the agency's interest in only having clients who were good enough to get jobs—so she decided to leave the agency, to leave him and to leave town.

They'd gone out to dinner, to Celestine's—they'd been on the waiting list for nearly two months because, in those days, it was the toughest restaurant in southern California to get reservations—and had eaten and drunk their way through an exquisite meal when the dessert menu arrived. He asked Savannah if she wanted the chocolate mousse cake or the apricot soufflé, and she said, "Actually, I want a divorce."

"Lucky for me we've got a pre-nup," he muttered as they were walking out of Celestine's. "Otherwise I wouldn't have been able to afford this place."

A year later, he met a blonde, Swedish, bathing-suit designer named Birgitta Mathias. She'd been in LA for nearly ten years and had already gone through two marriages herself.

As they got to know each other, Birgitta told Zeke she was done with the

LA party scene and wanted to settle down. That sounded good to him, so after five months of dating, they got married, at which time she stopped designing bathing suits and turned herself into a kind of reality-show LA housewife. She shopped and played tennis and lunched and otherwise hung out with a bunch of other women who shopped and played tennis and lunched. She and her gal-pals were seen at all the best restaurants. And at all the best parties. And at all the fanciest plastic surgeons in Beverly Hills.

It wasn't the lifestyle Zeke had in mind, but he didn't have to play any of her games, and she pretty much stayed out of his life, except every night when she insisted that, before they fall asleep, they must have some kind of sex.

"An orgasm is better for me than Ambien," she liked to say while they un-dressed each other.

He'd help her out of her clothes and whisper in her ear, "Tonight, do you want the brand name or the generic?"

Now she called to him from the kitchen, "When did you get home?"

He looked up and saw her there, still in her tennis clothes. "About an hour ago? Forty-five minutes ago. Half an hour ago. Something like that."

She stepped out of the house and started taking off her clothes.

He watched as she pulled off her top and let her shorts fall to the patio floor.

"What are you doing?" he asked.

"If we had music, it would be called a striptease." She unsnapped her bra, twirled it over her head, and tossed it aside.

Zeke had to admit she was the best-looking woman he'd ever slept with. And he loved it when she was naked. He loved it, too, that she often walked around the house like that. But now he had to warn her, "Max is home."

She pulled off her thong . . . "Won't be the first time he's caught me like this . . . " did a little wiggle, then dove into the pool.

"What do you mean? Not the first time? When . . . "

But she didn't hear him start the question because she was under water, and she didn't hear him try to finish the question because she was doing laps.

He watched her swim, throwing one arm out, and then the other, and kick-ing with her feet, gliding perfectly through the water. He especially liked the way the way the water ran over her backside.

"How do I want my Swedish women?" He asked himself out loud, then an-swered his own question. "Wet."

She swam to the pool house deck where he was watching her and pulled herself out of the water.

Standing naked, she ran her hands through her hair.

Zeke inspected her, nodding approvingly.

"Jesus, Daddy, get a room."

He looked past her and saw Zoey standing in the kitchen door.

Birgitta turned, waved, and went into the pool house to find a towel.

"If you guys can't wear clothes," Zoey said, "I'm not coming home."

"I am wearing clothes," Zeke told his daughter, then noticed a curtain in an upstairs bedroom move.

Max had been watching Birgitta.

"I phoned just now," Zeke said. "You get my voice mail?"

"I don't do voice mail," she said walking up to him and kissing the side of his face. "You've got to learn to text."

He smiled at his daughter, dark haired and a bit on the plump side, looking exactly like Miriam at that age. "That's why you never return my calls?"

Birgitta came back out, rubbing her hair with the towel, but still naked.

"You know," Zoey said to her, "my brother watches you like that all the time."

Birgitta shrugged. "It's only a human body."

"To a sixteen-year-old boy?" Zoey said. "It's boobs and booty."

"Nice mouth," Zeke snapped. "Where did you learn to talk like that?"

"If I told you you'd only get angry."

"I *am* angry," he said, then turned to Birgitta. "Do me a favor please . . . wrap the towel around yourself."

"Fancy you telling me that," she said, still drying her hair.

"Hi." It was Max walking out of the house.

Birgitta reluctantly put the towel around herself.

"When did you get home?" he asked his father.

"Little while ago."

He nodded at his sister and at Birgitta. "I'm hungry. Where's Maria?"

Birgitta answered, "I gave her the afternoon off."

"What am I supposed to do?" Max wondered.

"I know it's a hardship," Zeke said, "but you may have to open the fridge door yourself."

"Never mind . . . it's easier to send out."

Zoey shook her head disapprovingly. "I've got work to do for school. And I don't have a date for tonight. Can we go out to dinner?"

"Yeah, okay," Zeke said, looking at Zoey, then Birgitta, then Max. "Anywhere special?"

Zoey headed back to the house. "I like Spago."

"I'm sure you do," Zeke said.

"That's fine with me," Max waved and followed his sister inside.

"Why not," Birgitta agreed, unwrapping the towel and drying her hair again.

Zeke looked at his naked wife, then reached for his beer and said softly, "Spago it is."

For most people, getting a table at Spago this late on a Saturday would be impossible. But Zeke had a special unlisted number for last-minute reservations—a number that was handed out to fewer than one hundred of the restaurant's best customers and friends—so when Zeke asked, "Tonight, table for four?" the answer was, "What time?"

A lot of people who eat there regularly like the front tables because they want to be seen. Or they like the patio because it's a pleasant place to have dinner. But Zeke always took a table at the back because he liked walking through the place and seeing who else was there.

They arrived at quarter to seven, which is early even for LA, and there were still empty tables. But Orlando Bloom was there with friends and happy to introduce Zeke to them, and Eddie Murphy hugged Zeke, and Julia Roberts said she couldn't get over how grown up Zoey and Max were.

Then Max spotted Kareem Abdul-Jabbar sitting with a small group of people.

Tugging at his father's arm, Max nodded toward the basketball great. His father looked over and decided Kareem was too busy talking to the people at his table.

"Aw, come on," Max pleaded.

"No," Zeke said. "You know the rules."

Just then, Kareem looked up, spotted Zeke, and waved. Zeke waved back, and Max took that as a sign of approval. He hurried over to Kareem's table to shake hands and get an autograph.

Courteney Cox, who'd followed Zeke in with three other adults and half a dozen kids, was seated at the next table. She made a point of telling the maître d', "We'll have whatever Mr. Gimbel and his family are having, and be sure to put it on Mr. Gimbel's bill."

Zeke sent her and her friends a bottle of wine.

Max came back, proudly showing everyone the autographed napkin.

The waiter took their order, and as a way of saying thanks, Zeke also sent a bottle of wine to Kareem's table.

Zeke, Birgitta, Zoey, and Max all started with the hamachi and sashimi. Zeke and Birgitta had the steamed loup de mer, Zoey had the rack of lamb, and Max had the spicy beef goulash. Zeke ordered a bottle of French Gewürztraminer for Birgitta and himself and offered some to both his kids, but Zoey insisted she couldn't possibly drink white wine with lamb, and Max said he'd prefer a Coke, which his father refused to order because, "Coke doesn't go with anything in restaurants that don't have drive-through windows."

Zoey and Max had to settle for sparkling water.

After their main course, the waiter brought the dessert menu.

The four of them were studying it when Zeke wondered, "Who's having the peach dessert?"

Birgitta announced, "No dessert for me. But I want a divorce."

SUNDAY

17

Alicia stirred, looked over to the other side of the bed for Carson . . . and found Cyndi.

At the same time, Cyndi turned from one side to the other, opened her eyes, and saw Alicia. "What happened?" she said groggily.

"Firenzi," Alicia reminded her.

"What time is it?"

Alicia glanced at her clock radio. "Nine fifteen."

"Want to go to a movie? We can still catch . . . "

"In the morning."

Cyndi's eyes opened wide. "In the morning? I hate Firenzi," she said, lifting the sheets to look at herself and then at Alicia. "I don't even leave these things on all night when I'm with a guy."

Alicia laughed. "Want breakfast?"

Cyndi pointed to Alicia's thong. "Those really candies?"

Alicia told her, "I was thinking, something more like coffee and toast."

"Nine fifteen in the morning?" Suddenly, Cyndi jumped out of bed. "Oh my God!" She raced around to the side of it to fetch her clothes. "I've got to be someplace at ten."

"Where?"

"I have two dates." Cyndi pulled on her jeans over her garter belt and stockings.

"Two?"

"At ten and eleven."

"With who?"

"You know."

"No, I don't."

"Yes, you do."

"For breakfast?"

"For . . . you know."

Alicia assured her, "No, I don't."

Throwing on her top, she headed out the door. "Bye. It's been lovely sleeping with you." Cyndi stopped, came back to grab her packages from Firenzi, leaned over and kissed Alicia. "I promise to call you, darlin', if I'm ever in town again."

TINA OPENED her eyes, saw the other side of her bed was empty, smiled and wrapped her arms around one of her many pillows.

The best thing about mornings, she thought, is waking up alone.

Second best, she decided, is going back to sleep alone.

She hadn't always thought this way. When she was in school, and even when she started working, she loved waking up with some guy wrapped around her, turning him on, then climbing on top of him.

Those were, as she called them, her better-than-cornflakes mornings.

And in the beginning with David, who was always ready whenever she was, mornings suited her. When he wasn't around, if she wanted to, it was easy to find someone else. That suited her too.

But now, being older and wiser than she was when she was younger and just as eager—and with a lot more miles on the clock—waking up alone, then going back to sleep, and waking up alone again, was the new better-than-cornflakes.

THERE WERE plenty of other churches downtown, but he particularly liked Most Precious Blood, which backed onto Mulberry Street in Little Italy, because it reminded him of the churches he'd known in Europe.

The priest's voice rang out in prayer. And the congregation answered in unison.

Every Sunday morning, early, Pierre Belasco would walk there, no matter what the weather was like, and get there before mass so that he could light two candles. He would then take a seat in the back of the large room with the gorgeous altar and sit there alone with his eyes closed, breathing in the incense and thinking about what might have been.

CARSON STOOD on the baseline, tossed the ball high into the air, reached and jumped to get it, slamming his racket through the ball, and watched as it screamed across the net to land inside the box on the other side, clipping the line.

The young black boy standing at the net said, "Great serve."

"Strike one." Carson picked up another ball, readied himself by bouncing it several times, got set, tossed it in the air and slammed it across the net in exactly the same place.

"Wow," the boy said.

"Strike two," Carson nodded. Then he did it a third time, placing the ball within an inch of where the other two had landed.

"Awesome."

"Strike three." Carson pointed to the boy. "And that is how it's done."

"But . . . come on, those were fast balls. Anyone can serve fastballs. How's your curve?"

"Okay," Carson said. "Go stand at the corner of the box. Inside the service area . . . there at the corner of the baseline."

The boy rushed to the other side of the net and stood where Carson told him.

"Now," Carson said bouncing the ball, "don't move."

"Why?"

"'Cause I'm aiming for your feet."

The boy nodded.

Carson bounced the ball a few more times, looked at the boy's feet, threw the ball high in the air, leaped into his serve, and sent the ball heading directly for the boy's feet, but as it crossed the net it began to curve away and wound up hitting inside the service area, but on the other side.

"Wow," the boy screamed, "did you see that damn thing curve?"

"You like that?"

The boy fetched the several dozen balls Carson had served during his practice session and put them back in the wire basket. "How fast do you reckon?"

Carson put his racket in the sleeve and zipped it up. "Not as fast as I used to be." He walked to the other side of the net and took a twenty-dollar bill out of his pocket. "Thanks."

The boy took the money and smiled, "Thank you. I mean, that curve you put on it . . . where'd you ever learn . . . "

"Takes a lot of practice," Carson said. "I think we're on Court Two in an hour. You want to work the game?"

"Yeah, I can do that," the boy said, then added, "Hey, Mr. Haynes? Will you sign a ball for me?"

"Sure. Got a pen?"

"No. You got one?"

"No."

"Promise you'll do it later?"

"Promise." He looked at the boy. "You play?"

"I'm trying. They let us warm up if we get here real early, you know, before the members and guests."

"How old are you?"

"Fourteen."

"Where's your racket?"

The boy explained, "I got my brother's old racket at home, and if no one's around, I can usually borrow one from the locker room . . . "

"Here." Carson handed him the racket he'd been using. "Go on over there. Let's see what you can do."

"Really?"

"Really." Carson took out another racket, and for the next hour—until Tony Arcarro and Lee-Jay Wesley Elkins showed up with Elkins' partner in tow—Carson volleyed with the boy, shouting at him from across the net, "Plant your feet first . . . keep your head down . . . arm straight . . . go for the passing shot . . . swing through the ball . . . quick, come into the net . . . great shot . . . don't stand still . . . move, quick, move . . . "

"So now you're a teaching pro," Arcarro called to him.

Carson had worked up a little sweat. "Come on in," he said to the boy, and walked over to where Arcarro was standing with the two other men. "Doing my good deed."

Arcarro told the others, "Carson is the oldest Boy Scout in America."

"Hey, thanks," the boy said. "That was great." He handed the racket back to Carson.

"Keep it."

The boy's eyes opened very wide. "Keep it?"

"Yeah."

"Really?"

"Really."

"I can keep the racket?" The boy kept saying, "Thank you . . . thank you . . . this is awesome . . . wow . . . thank you . . . "

"You ready?" Arcarro asked Carson.

"I still have time for breakfast?"

"Nope," Elkins said. "Maybe now I'll stand half a chance."

Carson said, "Maybe."

But the fourteen-year-old boy, still standing there admiring his gift, mumbled, "No way."

And he was right.

DAVID PLANTED his feet firmly in the grass, looked again at the green some eighty yards away, wiggled his pitching wedge, steadied himself, brought the club back slowly, and swung through the ball, sending it high into the air.

"That's good," his caddy said.

"Y'all better believe it," David said, watching the ball hit the green about nine feet past the pin, bounce, then spin back, rolling nearly five feet toward the hole before finally stopping. "Better believe it." He handed the caddy his club, who exchanged it for a putter.

"Ah . . . horseshit," David said when he saw it.

"What?" the caddy asked.

"Damn. I'll never make the putt with this thing. I left my good putter on the plane. Damn."

He missed the putt to the right by two inches.

TINA STAYED in bed all morning.

When she heard Luisa downstairs, she picked up the phone and dialed the kitchen. "Good morning," she said. "Coffee and maybe some melba toast, please. That's all I want."

"Yes, Señora," Luisa said.

But by the time she'd brought up the tray, Tina was fast asleep again.

CYNDI RACED into her bathroom and filled the huge tub for a bath.

She got undressed, left her cell phone on the upholstered chair next to the tub and, when the tub was nearly full, tossed in one of those flavored bubble-bath bombs.

It exploded with foam in the water, filled the tub with bubbles, and suddenly her bathroom smelled of vanilla and peach.

Slipping into the water, she lay back and, with vanilla and peach flavored bubbles up to her neck, she waited.

At exactly ten o'clock, her phone rang.

"What time is it in Italy?" she asked.

The count's gravelly voice responded, "It is four in the afternoon."

"And where are you?"

"I am in Rome . . . in my study watching football. Where are you?"

"I am in my bathtub, the way you asked."

"Naked in your bathtub?"

"No," she joked. "I'm wearing one of those wetsuits that surfers wear, with a mask and swim fins . . . "

He laughed. "I wish I could see you . . . "

"I think you prefer football."

"No. I prefer you."

"Then you should get someone to make your computer work and I would show you . . . "

The two of them talked for a long time—mostly about Cyndi being naked in the bathtub—until the Count said, quietly, "I must go."

"Until next week," she said and hung up.

By now the water was getting cold, so she flicked the hot button with the big toe on her right foot—the tub was custom-made and didn't work with a normal tap—and hot water started to pour into the tub.

She used the big toe on her left foot to push the little button marked "Drain" so that as more hot water came in, the colder water on the bottom drained out, until the water was hot enough.

Then she closed the drain and turned off the hot water and lay back to wait.

At exactly eleven o'clock, her phone rang again.

The Sheikh demanded, "Where are you?"

"If you really must know . . . I am naked in my bathtub."

"Ah . . . this is very good."

"What time is it in Kuwait?"

"I am in Doha."

"Okay, what time is it in Doha?"

"Early evening."

"And what are you doing?"

"I am alone in my suite. I have been working all day, and I am going out to dinner in a little while. What are you doing?"

"I am in my bathtub, naked, the way you asked."

"Are you alone?"

"No," she giggled, "I'm here with Ali Baba and thirty-seven of the forty thieves. The other three are waiting in the hallway. They didn't have tickets."

She thought that was funny.

He didn't. "Never joke with me about that. I need to know you are alone."

She assured him, "Yes, I am alone."

"Good," he said. "Now tell me what you look like and what you are doing . . . "

She talked to him—mostly about being naked in the bathtub—until the Sheikh said, "This is very good. I will go now."

As soon as she hung up with him, she put her big toe on "Drain" and lay there until all the water was out of the tub.

She stood up, got out, and stepped into the large shower on the other side of the bathroom, where she washed off the bubbles.

Drying herself, she went to her bedroom and, still naked, climbed into bed. She closed her eyes.

And as she fell asleep, she thought to herself, "What some girls have to do to pay the rent . . . *oy vey!*"

ALICIA PULLED herself out of bed, got into the shower, threw on some sweats, made coffee, and sat down at the dining room table to go through her notes from yesterday.

"L. Arthur Farmer," she said. "Did you live here? Are you alive? Where are you?"

She randomly scanned a couple of hundred Google entries on him but couldn't find anything that answered any of those questions.

Except, perhaps, for the *where are you* part. Farmer's main business had an address and listed a phone number, not in Trump Tower, but in Saginaw, Michigan.

As far as Google was concerned, the last public sighting of Farmer had been in 1972 at a political fund-raiser in Florida for Richard Nixon. But there were almost as many entries suggesting that the sighting had not actually happened.

She found a reference to a more recent sighting that claimed Farmer had made an appearance in Federal District Court in San Francisco to testify in an antitrust suit against a consortium of freight shippers who were trying to take over the port. But when she looked into it further, instead of actually appearing in court, he'd consented to being deposed in a lawyer's office.

Other than that, there really wasn't anything in the way of sightings, or even recent facts about him. And though there were tens of thousands of Google hits with his name, nothing showed up anywhere—except the NBC archives—that satisfied the search terms, "L. Arthur Farmer" and "Trump Tower."

Then she stumbled across something that struck her as downright bizarre.

It was a reference to a hearing that had apparently taken place in the Michigan Senate in 1974 that was entitled, "The Influence of Finfolkmen over the In-State Business Affairs of L. Arthur Farmer."

The influence of what? She read it again, then Googled "Finfolkmen." Up came several thousand references to a religious sect that hailed originally from Scotland and had settled in the eighteenth century in Michigan's Upper Peninsula.

She clicked on a few of the links, read a couple of brief histories, and decided these people sounded very strange.

Next, she Googled "Finfolkmen" and "L. Arthur Farmer." Sure enough, several hundred references appeared. From what she read, it looked to her like this religious sect had worked its way into Farmer's life.

Going deeper, she found a *Detroit Free Press* reference to the Michigan Senate hearing. "Amidst rumors that a religious group based in the Upper Peninsula has effectively taken control of all access to Farmer, State Senator John Penrose Selkirk (R-38th) tabled an adjournment motion before the committee that was accepted, effectively ending the inquiry before it even began."

Now she queried "Finfolkmen" and "Trump."

Nothing came up.

She read the NBC database reference again. "A mysterious buyer, believed to represent L. Arthur Farmer, has become the first residential tenant in Donald Trump's Tower."

Alicia didn't understand why that reference should be the only one. Maybe, she rationalized, because it was 1979. Pre-Internet. That was the only thing that made sense to her. Or maybe, she thought, he never lived here and that's why there's nothing anywhere else.

Then she looked again at the *Free Press* blurb again. " . . . has effectively taken control of all access to Farmer."

The phone rang.

Finfolkmen?

It rang again. "Hello?"

Tina said, "Hey . . . meet you downstairs in half an hour?"

Alicia saw that it was already 12:15. "Oh my God . . . I didn't know it was this late. I'll be there."

Hanging up, she bookmarked all the pages she wanted to save, shut down her laptop, and went to get ready, still asking herself, *L. Arthur Farmer, where are you?*

18

Tina told the driver, "T'ien," and he asked, just to be sure, "That's . . . what . . . Ninety-Second between Madison and Park?"

"Yes," she said, "that's right," and sat back.

"I've been looking forward to this all week," Alicia said.

"Me, too." Then Tina leaned close to Alicia and whispered, so that the driver couldn't hear, "Apparently . . . Felipa . . . now this is the rumor . . . Felipa claims there actually is one masseur at T'ien."

"No way."

"Way."

"Really?"

"Apparently. I've never seen him, and no one ever mentions him, except Felipa, who says that he's there to do . . . you know . . . the full-body thing."

"Get out."

"That's the rumor."

"You heard this from Felipa Guillermo?"

"At the party the other night."

"I thought all she did was the entire Argentine polo team . . . and their horses . . . "

Tina laughed.

Alicia wanted to know, "This masseur have a name?"

"I asked the same question," Tina confessed. "Alas."

When they arrived at the beautiful white stone, five-story townhouse, Tina told the driver, "Four hours."

There were no signs out front to say this was T'ien—in Cantonese it means "heaven"—but then heaven is not the sort of place that has to advertise.

The women who need to know where T'ien is and how to get an appointment, know.

A young Chinese woman greeted them at the door. "Miss Lee, Miss Melendez, it is so nice to see you both again." She introduced herself as Huan and brought them into a small lobby area, where there was a low couch and a red bamboo desk. Huan checked their appointment times and took their credit cards. "I will return them to you at the end of your visit," she said. "You are very welcome here," then escorted Tina and Alicia to the elevator.

Bringing them up to the second floor, Huan showed Alicia into one of the private changing rooms, and showed Tina into the changing room next to it.

Inside was a bamboo table with a leather box, slippers, a very thick, very heavy terrycloth robe and a large bamboo basket.

Both women undressed completely, put their jewelry in the leather box, and folded their clothes into the bamboo basket.

Alicia had remembered to leave most of her jewelry at home. She was only wearing her small Piaget watch. But Tina was wearing a Bulgari sapphire ring and a Cartier watch, plus the gold Tiffany ankle bracelet that her father gave her for her twenty-first birthday. She took them off and left them sitting right there on the table.

Both women came out, wearing nothing but the terrycloth robes.

That's when Tina remembered her gold and diamond navel piercing, excused herself, went back to the changing room, and left it there with the rest of her jewelry.

Huan locked the changing rooms and accompanied Tina and Alicia to the third floor.

She brought them into a softly lit room with two chaise lounge beds and a small table with a teapot. Soft Chinese music was playing on hidden speakers. After motioning to Tina and Alicia to lie down, Huan poured them each a small cup of herbal tea, then left them there to sip their tea.

Ten minutes later, Huan returned to take them to the sauna. She helped them out of their robes and, now naked, Alicia and Tina stepped into the first of their four saunas.

"Wow," Alicia said. "I forgot how hot this is."

A typical rock sauna, it smelled of chamomile.

"Is it me," Tina asked, sitting down on the lower of the two benches, "or do you think they put something in that tea?"

They stayed there for nearly fifteen minutes before Huan invited them to come out, handed them each another cup of that herbal tea, then took them into another sauna, this one more like a steam bath.

"Where's David?" Alicia asked.

"Where else?" Tina answered. "He loves to tell me that golf is like sex. He says, 'When it's good, it's great, when it's bad, it's still pretty good.'"

"Only a man would say that."

"Trust me," Tina confided, "there are times when even I'd rather be playing golf."

"I didn't know you played golf."

"I don't."

Before they knew it, Huan was back to give them more tea and take them into the third sauna, which was very dry and felt much hotter than the previous two.

It smelled of eucalyptus.

"Where's Carson?" Tina asked.

"One of his tennis weekends. He's got a list of people who are willing to pay a lot of money to play with an ex-tour pro. A lot of the guys do it when they quit the tour."

"And it gives you the weekend off."

"Except I like having him around. He keeps my feet warm."

"Always a good idea to start at the feet," Tina smiled.

"Anyway, now with the book . . . I'm starting it . . . so having the weekend alone to think . . . "

"Or to spend with anyone else you want to."

Alicia smiled, "I've been trying to spend the weekend with L. Arthur Farmer, but I can't find him."

"Farmer? The rice guy? He's got to be two hundred years old. Or dead. Or both. Why him?"

"For the book," Alicia said. "I found a reference in one of the archives that he might have once lived in Trump Tower."

"I thought he lived in Las Vegas."

"Apparently he's lived in lot of places. There are references to him in the islands, and in Florida and in California. And there's a reference I found, but only one, that he lived at Trump Tower."

"I never heard that."

"It was back in 1979."

"I thought the Tower was built in 1983."

"That's when it opened. But this reference . . . it was in the NBC database . . . this reference said that he was the first to buy into Trump Tower."

Tina shook her head, "In 1979? I don't think it was called Trump Tower back then."

"It wasn't?"

"I heard that somewhere from someone."

Huan returned with more tea and then delivered them into a very small room with wood walls like a sauna. But it wasn't hot. And there was no bench to sit on. Instead, there were two very large wooden stools, side by side.

Neither Tina nor Alicia had ever been in this room before.

"Very new," Huan motioned to the stools. "Keep your robes on if you wish . . . but sit there, please . . . "

Tina pointed to the stools, which were open at the bottom.

"What's this?" Alicia asked, bending down to study the small copper pot under each stool.

Steam was rising out of the pot and going up through the hole in the stool.

Huan answered, "We put you together. You are friends, yes? You don't mind?"

"Mind what?" Tina wanted to know.

"Please . . . sit."

Alicia and Tina looked at each other and then back at the stools.

"But what is that?" Tina wanted to know.

"Very new. Your first time? It is mugwort and wormwood. For there." Huan pointed to Tina's crotch.

Tina looked at Alicia, "What the fuck is a mugwort?"

Staring at the hole in the stool, Alicia decided, "I don't think I want any wood worms up there."

"Not wood worms," Tina started giggling. "Wormwood. Still . . . " Tina pointed to the stool and asked Huan, "We're supposed to sit on that?"

"Reduce stress," Huan said. "More energy. Relax blood vessels. Make you very fertile."

Alicia put her hand over the hole in the stool to feel the heat.

Tina did the same.

Alicia asked, "Why does this feel like we're doing something naughty?"

Tina kept giggling. "Like being eight years old and playing doctor." She made a face and offered, "I will if you will."

"Like being sixteen years old and playing doctor," Alicia agreed.

Pulling their robes aside, the two women sat down—cautiously— positioning themselves on the stool so that the steam came up between their open legs.

"Whoa," Alicia's eyes opened wide. "That will wake you up."

"Kind of hot but . . . hello . . . " Tina squirmed a bit.

Huan bowed and said she would return shortly.

"Something tells me," Tina grinned, "a guy invented this."

"Absolutely not," Alicia laughed, "because if a guy had invented this, there would be moving parts."

Tina's giggle turned into a laugh.

And the more she laughed, the more Alicia laughed too.

"What do you think this really does?" Tina asked.

"Makes you squirm good," Alicia made a face, and the two of them kept laughing.

"I love a good squirm," Tina said.

Alicia laughed, "Mugwort and squirm-good."

Tina managed to say, "How do we explain this if anyone asks?"

Alicia only just managed to answer, "Asks what? Did you sit on a bowl of steaming mugwort?"

That sent them into gales of laughter.

Tina said, "This is really very . . . "

Alicia asked, "Warm and wet?"

"I love warm and wet."

"Maybe a guy did invent this after all."

They kept laughing.

Alicia suggested, "It's kind of like a facial."

Tina couldn't control her laughter. "Hey, that ain't my face down there."

Alicia said, "I was thinking of Carson and David."

And the two of them didn't stop laughing until Huan came back and escorted them out of there.

"Here's to mugwort," Tina said, sipping some tea.

"And to wormwood squirm-good," Alicia toasted.

That set them off again, laughing.

Huan now led them into a shower area, where two young women doused them with a fairly strong spray, soaped them with huge sponges—Alicia and Tina were quickly covered in a thick foam that smelled of rose—then used that strong spray again to wash off all the foam.

Two other young women dried them off before Huan brought Tina and Alicia into a room for a pedicure.

After that they went to a second room for a facial.

Then they went to a third room for Brazil wax.

After that, Huan escorted the two women to the fourth floor for their massage.

She brought Alicia into a small room where the massage table was covered in a white cotton sheet and introduced her to Meili, a very tiny woman who bowed and smiled and invited Alicia to take off her robe and lie down on the table.

Stepping back into the hall, Huan motioned to Tina to follow her.

But Tina stopped to ask, in Mandarin, "Mrs. Guillermo . . . she comes here often . . . "

Huan smiled politely but didn't say anything.

" . . . because she is my good friend." Tina went on, "I would like the same masseur that she has."

Nodding several times, Huan showed Tina into her massage room and said something quietly to the masseuse. Those two both smiled demurely, bowed, and left. Tina took off her robe and lay down on her stomach.

A few minutes later, a tall, well-built young Chinese man in white slacks and an open white shirt, with dark shoulder-length hair and a big smile, walked into the room.

He shut the door, then stood there for a moment running his eyes over her nude body.

Tina watched him as he inspected her.

He bowed.

She nodded, "Yes."

Four hours after the driver had left them at T'ien, he was double-parked on Ninety-Second Street, in front of the five-story townhouse waiting for them.

Alicia took her credit card back, glanced at the charge—$2,000—smiled at Huan and said thank you.

Tina took her card, also said thank you, but put the card and receipt away quickly, before Alicia could see that hers read, "$2,500."

19

David Cove's pilots, Barry and Gavin, had to fight strong crosswinds landing at Curaçao International, which is on the beach along the northern side of the island. It was very bumpy coming down, and the lawyer, Vasyl Zhadanov, was visibly upset.

"I don't like small planes," he kept saying. "I really don't. Why can't the pilots do a better job? How well trained are they? This is terrible. I will probably not come back to New York with you."

By this point, David could not have cared less.

Zhadanov was late getting to Teterboro, which meant, for David, the trip started on a sour note. He wanted to leave when he wanted to leave, and standing around waiting for someone else always annoyed him.

As soon as they took off, Zhadanov began drinking heavily. He complained that the vodka was Grey Goose and not Stolichnaya—"How can you drink French vodka? Vodka is Russian. I only ever drink Stolichnaya. I only ever drink Russian vodka."—though that didn't stop him from going through half the bottle.

Two hours into the flight, the man asked Wendy, the stewardess, "How much would you want to be topless right now?" which upset her so much that David had to tell Zhadanov, "Don't talk to her again. If you want anything from the galley, y'all have to fetch it yourself."

Now the man was moaning about the landing. "I have never flown with pilots as bad as this. Seriously, this is like we're going to crash. I will not come back to New York with you."

David didn't hide his displeasure. "Y'all got that right, pal."

While they were still taxiing, Zhadanov dialed a number on his BlackBerry. David checked his e-mails on his iPhone and wondered, *what the hell am I doing here.*

"Did you remember to make reservations for us?" David asked as he scrolled through his in-box. "You said there's a Hyatt and a Hilton . . . "

Zhadanov held up his hand, to remind David that he was on the phone.

"I gotta make arrangements for the crew," David said.

But Zhadanov was too busy, speaking very quietly to the person on the other end—David thought, *it's almost as if he doesn't want me to hear*—then hung up and turned to David. "I'm afraid there's been a change of plans."

CARSON AND TONY cracked a bottle of Champagne as soon as they took off for New York, congratulating themselves on a successful West Virginia weekend.

They'd separated Lee-Jay Wesley Elkins and his friends from nearly $38,000 in cash.

It was 4:25 when they landed back at Teterboro. Tony had his car and offered to drop Carson in the City, but Carson said that was crazy because Tony lived in Connecticut, and anyway, Carson had a limo waiting.

As soon as the driver left the airport, he took his phone, found the number for Maryse, and when she answered, he told her, "I'm on my way."

"If the door is locked when you get here," she said, "call me and I'll come down to open it."

"You are magic," he said.

"Oh," Maryse sighed, "what might have been."

Hanging up, Carson sat back and said to the driver, "If we don't hit traffic, we'll be okay."

The driver assured him, "I'll get you there."

But they did hit Sunday evening traffic going into the tunnel, then hit traffic again on the West Side Highway. It was 5:45 when the limo finally pulled up to the southeast corner of Fifth Avenue and Fifty-Seventh Street.

Carson jumped out, thanked the driver, grabbed his overnight bag and rackets from the trunk, slammed the trunk shut, and rushed up to Tiffany's door.

It was locked.

A guard inside waved his finger to show him they were closed.

Carson took his cell and dialed Maryse. "I'm here."

He waited on the street until a large, black woman in her sixties, with white hair and half glasses perched on her nose, arrived at the door and nodded to the guard to open it.

He stepped inside.

"Where have you been?" She took his hand and led him to the elevators and up to the second floor.

"I was in West Virginia."

"I don't mean now. I mean since you last came to see this old lady. You only live next door. It's not as if you have to even cross the street."

"I'm seeing you before I even see my wife. Isn't that enough?"

"Nope." Still holding his hand, she led him into a private room with a small table, two chairs and a large metal cabinet. "Got it right here," she said, taking some keys out of her pocket and unlocking the cabinet. "How did Alicia like the earrings?"

"Loved them. And she wears the bracelet all the time."

Maryse brought out a Tiffany blue box with a tag attached to it where she'd written, "Mr. C. Haynes."

Inside was a gold and deep pink sapphire necklace—the pink was almost red enough to be a ruby—and a large ring with an equally beautiful stone.

"Yeah," he said, "we'll do the necklace now and the ring next time."

"Shall I wrap it?"

"You think I'm going to wear it out?"

"Be right back," she said, and left the room.

He sat there looking at the ring.

When Maryse returned, she was carrying a Tiffany box tied with a bow, and the necessary paperwork.

He looked at the bill, reached into his pocket, took out a large wad of cash, and handed her $16,460.

She said, "I'll bring you your change," left the room again and when she returned, she handed him $1.48.

He stared at it. "Can't even buy myself a subway ticket with this."

She had to know, "When was the last time your poor butt sat on a subway train?" She put the box with the ring in it back in the cabinet and locked it. "For next time." Then she looked at him and shook her head. "Oh what could have been . . . if only I was forty years younger or you were ten years younger."

He laughed, "Thanks for keeping the place open. You make me feel like the Queen of England at Harrods," and started to leave.

"Where do you think you're going?"

"Home."

"This place is locked-down shut. There's no way you, or the Queen of England, could get out of here alive without me."

Downstairs, she hugged him, said "Love to Alicia," and the guard let him out. He strolled the few dozen yards along Fifth Avenue to Fifty-Sixth Street, turned left, went into the residents' lobby and then upstairs.

"How did you do?" Alicia kissed him hello.

"Funny you should ask," he said. "How did you do?"

"I did good . . . I'm doing good . . . working on the book. Why's it funny I should ask?"

"'Cause I did so good . . . " He handed her the Tiffany box.

She broke out into a huge smile, opened the box, and right away said, "Oh my God . . . Carson . . . I love it." She kissed him. "I love this and I love you." She quickly put it on and went to check it in the hallway mirror. "Carson . . . oh I love you." She kissed him again. "And . . . come to think of it, I have a present for you."

"Really?"

"Yes, wait here."

"Where?"

"Right here. Don't move." She raced into her bedroom, threw off all her clothes, and stepped into the tiny thong she'd bought at Firenzi. "You ready?" she called to him.

"I am."

She headed out the bedroom door wearing nothing but the necklace and the thong. "Care for a piece of candy before dinner?"

"WHAT THE HELL do you mean?" David barked at Zhadanov. "What kind of change of plans?"

"My contacts, the men we were supposed to meet tomorrow . . . they insist that we meet tonight."

He checked his watch. "Nine thirty on a Sunday night?"

"They have given me an address . . . "

"Y'all said they're businessmen. I thought we were going to someone's office tomorrow morning."

"They have changed the plans. I told them it's all right. We will need a car to take us. I don't know if you want to spend the night here or go back to New York later."

David stared at him. "Y'all got us rooms at which hotel?"

Zhadanov hesitated. "Sometimes they do this . . . change plans at the last minute . . . "

"You mean there are no reservations? What kind of shit is this? I come all the way down here, and now you tell me . . . "

Barry cut off the engines and Gavin shouted back to Wendy, "Good to go."

She got out of her jump seat and opened the front door. No sooner did she have the steps down when a customs officer and an immigration officer came into the plane, saluted, and the immigration officer said, "Welcome to the Netherland Antilles. Passports please."

They went through the usual formalities—David couldn't tell from the fleeting glance he had of Zhadanov's passport which country it was from, except it clearly wasn't a US passport—and while Zhadanov went to find a car, David asked Barry, "What's the deal with turn-around and crew rest and all that stuff? Can we go back tonight? This asshole is screwing with my head."

Barry checked his watch and did a fast calculation. "We can hold here . . . maybe four more hours, then we're probably illegal. But what the hell, boss, if you want . . . "

"No," David said. "You guys go get rooms. There's got to be a hotel around the airport. Go to sleep but stick by your cell. If we're staying, we're staying. If not, I'll phone. Four hours? Call it two in the morning?"

"We'll be fueled and ready to go."

"Thanks," David said and left the plane.

Zhadanov was waiting with a taxi. "It's a house about thirty minutes from here."

The two climbed in the backseat, and the driver left the airport. There wasn't a lot of conversation during the ride. Zhadanov tried to make small talk, but David wasn't interested.

The driver headed up the beach on dark, empty roads until he came to a sharp turn and stopped, almost in the middle of the road. "This is it," he said.

David looked around but couldn't see anything. "Where?" There were no houselights. There was nothing.

"Down there," the driver pointed.

Zhadanov opened his window and spotted a small footpath leading to the beach. "This is it, yes, this is it."

David decided, "I'm not getting out of the car."

"What do you mean? We're here." Zhadanov demanded, "You must get out. The house is down there at the water's edge."

"I'm not going down there. You tell them to come up."

"What do you mean?"

He didn't like the change of plans, and he didn't like the fact that they were in the middle of nowhere. "What don't you understand? Either they come up or I'm on my way back to New York."

"Why are you being like this? I have arranged . . . "

"'Cause you're fucking with my head." David tapped the driver on the shoulder, "We're outta here. Back to the airport, pal."

"Wait, wait," Zhadanov reached for his phone, got out of the car and dialed a number.

David tried to listen through the open window but couldn't tell what Zhadanov was saying.

Zhadanov soon stuck his head inside the car. "The man himself will come up to greet you. It may take a while, but he will come to you."

"Two minutes," David said and sat back to wait.

Several minutes passed.

He listened to the waves on the beach and all the usual night noises. "Where is he?" David asked.

"He said he'd come up," Zhadanov insisted. "Please . . . hang on . . . "

Several more minutes passed.

"What the hell is taking so long?"

Zhadanov reassured him, "The man himself will be here . . . "

"No, no," David finally decided, "I'm gone. There's something wrong about this . . . " He leaned forward to tell the driver, "Let's go. Back to the airport." Then he told Zhadanov, "Y'all gotta make your own way home."

"Wait," Zhadanov begged, "here he is. He's here now."

David looked and saw flashlight beams coming up what appeared to be a steep set of stairs. He watched as the beams got closer . . . there were three flashlights . . . getting closer, but very slowly.

"Thank you," Zhadanov said loudly, "Don Pepe. Thank you so much for coming to greet us."

The three light beams were at the top of the steps now.

Zhadanov hugged the dark shadow of a small man.

Getting out of the car, David cautiously came around the back to find two very large men carrying flashlights—shining their beams at him, which meant he couldn't see them—but then he heard a voice say, "Mr. Cove, thank you very much for coming all this way."

David raised his hands to show everyone that the light was in his eyes, and when the men moved the beams down to his chest, he found himself standing face to face with a small man in his late seventies or early eighties.

"This is Señor Forero," Zhadanov said.

"Please . . . " Forero extended his hand with a smile. "My friends call me Pepe."

"David." He said, and they shook hands.

The man had white hair, a pleasant face, with a nice smile and warm eyes.

He was wearing a black silk shirt, not tucked in, and white pants. But then David noticed, he was leaning on a crutch. And when David looked down, he saw that this man only had one leg.

Suddenly he felt terrible, having made a crippled man walk up all those stairs. "I'm sorry if I have inconvenienced you . . . I didn't know . . . "

Forero waved him off. "You have come a long way. It is the least I can do to greet you here. Please," he motioned toward the steps. "I have put food on my table for you, and there is plenty to drink. I hope you will do me the honor of joining me in my home."

David didn't know what he was expecting, but a nice old man with one leg wasn't it. "Yeah . . . sure," he said, "my pleasure."

Zhadanov ordered the driver to wait. "We'll be a few hours."

All five men now made their way slowly down the steps to the house.

They came into the living room, which David thought must have been seventy-five feet long and opened onto a wonderful deck. There were several couches, facing the sea—which he could hear but it was pitch-black in the night—and a huge wooden table laid out exquisitely with plates of fruit and fish and several bottles of liquor and wine.

The two large men who'd accompanied Forero up the steps stayed back at the side of the living room, out of the way.

Obviously bodyguards, David decided.

Then two more men appeared. Both of them were closer to Forero's age than David's, and both of them shook his hand.

"Call me Juan Felipe," the first man said. "Very nice to meet you."

"And my name is Javier. Thank you for coming all this way to meet with us."

He shook their hands, "David," he said to each of them, then watched as they hugged Zhadanov, showing David that they knew him.

Forero suggested they all have something to eat first, so David took a plate of cold grouper with rice and fruit, and an Amstel beer. The others followed him, sitting on various couches with plates on their laps.

Except for Forero. He motioned to one of the large men at the side of the living room who left and came back with a wheelchair. Forero sat in it, and the man pushed the wheelchair right in front of where David was sitting.

That's when David noticed the man was carrying a gun under his shirt.

Looking around, David spotted two other men sitting on the deck in the dark, and from the outline he could tell that one of them was carrying a big, automatic weapon.

"Tell me Señor Forero . . . " David had to know.

"Pepe," the man corrected him.

"Okay . . . Pepe . . . why are you surrounded by men with guns?"

The old man smiled, "Juan Felipe . . . Javier and I . . . we come from a country where kidnapping is a common occurrence. Unfortunately, we are forced to take such precautions."

"But . . . we're not in Colombia now."

"Do the terrorists attack Americans only in America?" He smiled, "In my country, if they can kidnap you outside the country and force your family to pay a ransom, then they can kill you outside the country and the Colombian authorities can do nothing. It is a sad fact of life that we live with." He pointed to his missing leg. "I know what I'm speaking about."

David wasn't sure he understood. "They cut off your leg?"

"I was kidnapped nearly ten years ago in Aruba. By the FARC. The *Fuerzas Armadas Revolucionarias de Colombia*. You have heard of them? They are a Marxist-Leninist terrorist organization. They didn't cut my leg off, they . . . " He paused for a moment . . . "They sent a live video back to my family, demanding ransom. When my family hesitated, they shot me in the leg so badly that . . . they left me to die."

David asked, "And your family didn't pay?"

"Of course, they paid. And the FARC still left me to die."

"Nice guys," David muttered.

"Extremely," Forero agreed. "But let's speak of more pleasant things. Doing business with you. Has our good friend Vasyl explained what it is we want?"

David looked at Zhadanov—he'd found an expensive-looking bottle of *genever*, which is Dutch gin, and was drinking it straight—then back at Forero. "He said you were looking to put some serious money through my business."

"In a nutshell, yes."

"But . . . " David tried to say this gently, "seeing as how you're all from Colombia . . . you know . . . "

"Drug money," Forero cut in. "We understand your concern."

"I'm not going to get involved with anything . . . " David started to say.

And Forero finished it, " . . . like money laundering."

"Exactly."

"I don't blame you," Forero said. "But then, look at Juan Felipe and Javier, and look at me. Do you see Pablo Escobar?"

David forced a smile.

"We are businessmen," Forero went on, "who have access to large amounts of money in the United States."

"Drug money?" David blurted out.

"Tax evasion," Forero claimed. "There is a large market in brokering dollars and Colombian pesos . . . and although Juan Felipe is a travel agent by profession, and Javier is a jeweler and I am an industrialist . . . all of us from Bogota . . . we make substantial amounts of money brokering dollars and pesos."

David wanted to know, "How does tax evasion . . ."

Forero smiled. "There are people who believe that football . . . soccer to you . . . is the national sport of Colombia. Those are people who don't know my country. The national sport is tax evasion. No one looks down on anyone who cheats the government in Colombia because everybody cheats . . . especially people in the government. But the problem with tax evasion is that if you have money that should have gone to the tax department, you cannot spend it in Colombia. If you do, they will know. So the entire country wants dollars in America. They have pesos, we have dollars, and we move money back and forth. You understand?"

David confessed, "Not exactly."

"If you have five million dollars in pesos," Forero went on, "and you buy yourself a nice *hacienda*, the government will ask where you got the money. But if that money is not in Colombia, if it is in America, then there are all sorts of ways that you can spend it there, or enjoy it outside Colombia, or even buy things and send them back to Colombia."

"And you want to put that money into my business."

"No," Forero said. "We want to make that money available to you to guarantee your line of credit against your trading. You never see the money. You never see us. It is bedded down in several business accounts."

Zhadanov piped up for the first time, "All of which comes through my attorney-client account."

Forero continued, "Security for your line of credit. You deal with your bankers, not us. We put up the money so that your bankers can deal with you."

On the surface, it sounded to David like a foolproof scheme. "What kind of money are we talking about?"

"Twenty? Fifty? A hundred? What kind of money do you need?"

A hundred million dollars, David thought, in addition to the line of credit he was already working, that would make him and Tina major players. There wouldn't be a cargo anywhere in the world they couldn't buy. They could even afford to sit on a cargo for a few days if they had to before unloading it. Airplane parts. Metals. Oil. Nothing would be out of their reach.

But then David had seen foolproof schemes before. "So what's in it for you?"

"Twenty-five points on your profit . . . "

"A quarter's a big cut."

"And paperwork."

"What kind of paperwork?"

"To justify the twenty-five points."

David thought about that. "You want me to doctor up paperwork . . . "

"No," Forero said. "We need the paperwork from your bank to show the trading profit and our share. The principal stays in Vasyl's client account, always in the name of a business. That secures your line of credit, while the profits that come back to us get used to buy something like farm equipment. That then is shipped back to Colombia as part of a business plan. The farm equipment or television sets or cars, whatever, gets sold in Colombia. We get our pesos back to spend, and after a lot of transactional deductions, the tax gets paid at a much, much lower rate."

David tried to take it all in. "So what I'm really doing is . . . facilitating income tax fraud."

"Please understand that you are not committing any crime, whatsoever," Forero insisted. "To begin with, if we don't pay our taxes in Colombia, that's not a crime in the United States, and that has nothing to do with you. In any case, you never touch any of our money."

"I'm trading with it."

"No, you're trading with your money and your bank's money. Our money is never anything more than a guarantee to your bank. Not to you. Only to your bank. Please . . . " he motioned toward the table . . . "help yourself to another plate."

David wasn't yet totally convinced, but the more they ate, and the more they drank, the more he realized this could make him the biggest player in the game.

By the time the sun came up—lighting the white sand beach and the gorgeous turquoise sea and turning the sky from bright red and orange into deep blue—the deal was sounding very sweet.

MONDAY

20

The first thing Antonia did when she got up on Monday morning was walk into her living room and look out the window for baseball caps.

From her bedroom, all she could see was another apartment building, but from the living room she had a view of West Eighty-Eighth Street and, by leaning forward a bit, then craning her neck to the left, she could see the northwest corner at Broadway.

If she saw people bundled up or carrying umbrellas, she'd have to make a six-minute dash to Eighty-Sixth Street for the six-minute subway ride to Columbus Circle. But if she spotted men in suits and women wearing dresses with running shoes wearing baseball caps, that meant it was walking weather.

And this morning, there were plenty of baseball caps.

She showered and dressed, put on her running shoes, stuffed her heels into a shopping bag, looked around the apartment one last time—decided no, after spending the entire weekend moving furniture around, she still didn't like the arrangement in the living room—and headed out the door.

Walking fast down Broadway, the way New Yorkers do, she peeled off after four blocks into Le Macaron D'Or, a tiny French pastry shop, where she bought two *croissants* and a cup of French roast chicory coffee to go.

This was what she liked best about walking to work, and what she liked best about work was being in New York.

She'd grown up in New Jersey, staring at a city that was calling to her from across the river. It was where everyone she knew aspired to be. It was where she knew she had to wind up.

There are two types of people in New Jersey—she and her friends had convinced themselves ever since they were old enough to know where New York was—those who stay and those who leave. But her road to New York had taken her around the world. All the hotels she'd worked in, all the exotic locations she'd come to know, as far as she was concerned, it was those roads that led here.

"It doesn't get better than New York," she said out loud, arriving at Columbus Circle at the same time that she finished her first *croissant*, "Someday . . . Antonia is going to have the Big Apple by the balls."

Upstairs, in her tiny second-floor office just before eight o'clock—her boss usually never wandered in until 8:30—she ran through the reports she needed to see, but stopped when she came to Pierre Belasco's report on Carlos Vela.

It amazed her how careful he was to avoid saying that Vela was guilty of anything.

She checked her watch—by now it was 8:16—and knew she was cutting it close but decided there was enough time. So she left her coffee and second *croissant* on her desk, stepped out of her office, looked around to see that no one else was in yet, and went into Anthony Gallicano's office.

The man responsible for all the Trump Organization properties in the greater New York area had a big corner room with views south past Columbus Circle, and east along Central Park South.

Antonia had long ago cracked his code—his wife's initials and her birthday—so now she turned on his computer and, when it was ready, typed in "MAG616."

It brought her straight into his inbox.

Running down his list of unread e-mails, she saw nothing of any consequence. But there were several e-mails in the draft box. And one of them was a memo to Trump himself. The subject was "Carlos Vela."

The memo was very brief. "Concerning the employee in question, Carlos Vela, Belasco reports there is insufficient evidence for dismissal. The resident is adamant. Your call."

She didn't know why it hadn't been sent. Maybe Gallicano was waiting to attach something. In any case, she erased the first two letters of the word "insufficient," then she pushed send.

A copy appeared in the sent file, which she immediately erased. She then searched through the other e-mails in the sent file and noticed one from Gallicano to all department heads. It said that the Broadway actor, Tommy Seasons—and there were several photos attached, including some taken of him by the CCTV cameras in Trump Tower—was to be considered *persona non grata* throughout the group properties. Gallicano wrote, "Sightings of him should be reported immediately."

Also attached was a one-page Word document, written by the Tower security guy, Bill Riordan, explaining the nature of the complaint against Tommy, along with some background.

Antonia read it and saw that Tommy Seasons had been involved with Cyndi Benson.

"Hah!" She said out loud, forwarded the report to herself—not to her office e-mail address, but to her secret *jerseyhot1983@gmail.com* account—then erased that sent copy, so that Gallicano could never see she'd done it.

Logging out of her boss' computer, she hurried back to her office.

A few minutes later, Gallicano walked past her open door and waved, "How come you always beat me to work?"

Finishing her second *croissant*, she waved back. "Worms."

He stopped short. "Did you say . . . worms?"

"As in, what the early bird gets."

"Oh . . . yeah, of course. Any good worms this morning?"

She raised her paper cup and toasted him with the rest of her coffee. "A couple."

21

Carson was up at his usual hour, but when he came out of the bathroom and started looking for his gym clothes, he noticed that Alicia was also awake.

"Go back to sleep."

"I can't."

"Why not?"

"I'm thinking."

"You can think later," he said pulling on his shorts. "You have all day to think. Right now, you should sleep."

"Do I really want a coffee table book to be my first book?"

"What?"

She said it again. "Do I really want a coffee table book to be my first book?"

"That's what you're losing sleep about?"

"Yes."

"Why?"

"Because it's a coffee table book."

"Think of it as something to do while you're working on *War and Peace*."

She swung her feet onto the floor and sat up. "Somewhere in my mind I saw myself one day writing a book about . . . I don't know . . . women in broadcasting. Or glass ceilings in the media. Something more substantial than a coffee table book."

He stared at her sitting there, wearing nothing, with the sheet half covering her, and the other half falling onto the floor. "I'm thinking of writing a book, too."

"What about?"

"The substantial adventures of Cuban-American-girl-journalist-turned-TV-anchor and black-boy-tennis-player-turned-whiz-kid, on a balcony at the Hermitage Hotel in Monte Carlo during the Grand Prix?"

She raised her eyebrows, "Whiz kid?"

He made a sound like racecars speeding by. "We should return to that balcony every year. Make it our annual pilgrimage. Like Lourdes."

"Lourdes?"

"Sure healed what ailed me."

"Don't push your luck, whiz kid."

"Luck? What luck? That was skill. That's why it was . . . so very amusing."

"I beg your pardon? So very amusing?"

"If I remember correctly, you were so very amused . . . several times."

"Well . . . " She smiled as if she was remembering it. "Maybe you did . . . amuse me."

"Only maybe?"

"If life was like television news, you know, where you can go back to the tape, I'd be willing to run it again to check the facts."

"Just the facts, ma'am," he said moving close to her, pulling the sheet away. "We don't have a balcony, and there are no racecars down there, and even if there's no whipped cream and chocolate sauce in the fridge . . . "

"I thought you were going to the gym."

"There you go, thinking again."

"This time, it's not about my book." She pulled down his shorts.

He knelt down in front of her, moving his mouth from her face to her neck and down to her chest. "How about if Cuban girl and whiz kid write a chapter for my new book?"

"What's your new book called?"

"Multiple Amused."

GETTING TO the office later than usual, Carson winked at Rod Laver, then winked at Alicia, and then breakfast arrived. He paid the delivery kid for the papaya juice and buttered bialy, took it with his latte back to his desk and started making plans for Japan.

His first thought was that he should leave Tuesday night, because that would give him a day to recover from the fourteen-hour flight.

But then he checked his calendar and realized he'd forgotten the Clinton Foundation's "New York Loves—written with a heart—Haiti" party at the Metropolitan Museum.

So he booked himself a first-class ticket on the flight that left JFK at 11:35

Wednesday morning, which would bring him into Tokyo at 3:35 Thursday afternoon, local time.

Next, he sorted through his phone's address book until he found the number for the Peninsula Hotel. The name he'd put there was Hattori. So he dialed the number and asked for Mr. Hattori. It was only when a woman came on saying that she was Miss Hattori that he decided he'd confused her with the reservations manager at the Peninsula in Bangkok, whose name was . . .

He couldn't remember.

Adding "Miss" to the Tokyo listing, he booked the suite he liked, overlooking Hibiya Park and the Imperial Palace Gardens.

"We look forward to seeing you again," Miss Hattori said. "Have a good flight."

"Thank you," he said, then remembered, "One other thing. When I arrive on Thursday, I need to meet with a *feng shui* expert. Can you set up an appointment at the hotel for me, please?"

"*Feng shui*?"

"Yes."

"*Feng shui*," she said, "is Chinese."

"Oh. Ah . . . okay . . . but surely there must be someone in Tokyo . . . "

"In Japan we have *kaso*."

"*Kaso*? That's the same as feng shui?"

"Very similar. *Ka* is house and *So* is . . . something like phase or season. Then there is also *fuusui*."

"What's that?"

"It means wind and water."

"How about one of each?"

"I will check with the concierge and make an appointment for you. Not to worry."

He thanked her and hung up.

Kaso, fuusui, house, season, wind, and some water on the side. And with the Clinton party Tuesday night still on his mind, he wondered if he should also throw in some good old-fashioned Haitian voodoo.

OKAY, IT'S JUST *a coffee table book*, Alicia kept telling herself as she flicked through the links she'd bookmarked on L. Arthur Farmer and that religious sect. *But if the man who controls twenty percent of the world's rice, regardless of whether or not he ever lived in Trump Tower, is still alive . . . and if he really is surrounded by this religious sect . . . that's not just a coffee-table-book kind of story.*

The NBC database had some fascinating stuff on these Finfolkmen, and she also found several references to the senator in Michigan. There was even a phone number for him.

Then she saw that he'd died in 1984.

Undaunted, she located the number for Farmer's business in Saginaw.

A switchboard operator answered, "Corporate."

Alicia tried, "Mr. Farmer's office, please."

The operator said, "No one here by that name," and hung up.

CARSON WENT OVER the numbers he'd already discussed with Warring, then drew up a small chart.

Shigetada's got fifty-one percent. He confirmed that. We're second with twenty-two. He confirmed that.

As the traders came into the office, they called out to him, "Hey" and "What's happening" and "You ever go home?"

We know eighteen are with the institutions. That leaves nine somewhere.

He spotted Mesumi disappearing into the kitchen, then caught her on the way out with a coffee. "You got a minute?"

"Who are you fooling? With you, the word minute is never singular."

She was a super-smart, slightly plump Princeton grad who'd worked in the Tokyo markets for a couple of years before coming to Wall Street. Carson met her at Goldman, and she'd been his first hire.

"What's happening?" She sat down on his couch.

"Here's what we know . . . " He handed her the chart. "We need to figure out which institutions are holding the eighteen and where the nine are."

She studied it, handed it back, sipped her coffee, and shook her head. "This is what I get for being born in Kyoto."

"No, this is what you get for going to Princeton." He pointed to the conference room, "Let's work there."

They set up their laptops back-to-back across the table and went in search of the Shigetada shares.

When Tony Arcarro got to the office, he volunteered, "Mitsubishi is holding around two. Saw it on some Intel tip sheet last week. Shigetada makes something that goes into something else that Mitsubishi needs. A phrannaporsennon."

"A what?" Mesumi asked.

"Phrannaporsennon," Carson confirmed.

"What's a phrannaporsennon?"

Arcarro asked, "You know what a widget is? Well, a widget and a phrannaporsennon . . . they're actually two entirely different things."

"Oh . . . " Mesumi got it. "Is it true they only come in yellow or blue?"

Arcarro pointed at Mesumi and reminded Carson, "Princeton."

"Even at Princeton," Carson said, "eighteen minus two leaves sixteen."

"Got to be the usual suspects," Arcarro suggested. "Mizuho Bank. Daiwa Group. Dai-Ichi Kangyo."

"Japanese Industrial Bank." Mesumi added to the list.

"Nomura?" Carson looked at Mesumi. "Don't you have a friend there?"

"Ren? We went to school together."

"That school?"

"Yes . . . that school."

"You okay with giving her a call?"

"Sure. She's in their office at Thirty-Seventh and Park."

Carson reached for the phone on the conference table and pushed it across to her.

Mesumi found Ren's number on her cell, dialed it on the office line, and spoke to her in Japanese.

Carson picked up the words, *ohayo gozaimasu*, at the beginning of the call—it's the traditional way of saying good morning—and the word *sayonara* at the end of the call, which, of course, is the traditional way of saying goodbye.

When Mesumi hung up, he stared at her. "And?"

"And," she stood up, "I'm on my way to admire her new engagement ring."

"What's the traditional Japanese way of saying, congratulations?"

Mesumi assured him, "*Mazel tov.*"

ALICIA SAT through the morning story meeting, then started working on what, at least at this hour, looked like it would lead the show—the murder last night of a nurse who worked at an abortion clinic in Queens. They'd already sent a crew with a reporter to the crime scene and another to the police press conference downtown at three.

Once that was set, she put in a pitch for a sidebar story on violence at other abortion clinics around the city. Her editor, Greg Mandel, was all for it, but he was the only one.

That's when she got a call from Sandy Bridgeman at *Nightly*. "Alishe . . . I need to see you. Come on down."

She left her newsroom on the seventh floor and went down to the *Nightly* offices at Studio 3C.

Bridgeman, who was six-foot-six and heavyset, and looked more like a linebacker than a television news executive, was waiting for her in the hallway when she stepped out of the elevator. They chatted briefly, she hugged him, then came running back to her desk upstairs to call Carson.

He answered on the first ring. "Hi there."

"Guess what?"

"What?"

"You'll never guess."

"You've signed as a free agent with the Heat to play point guard?"

"Better than that."

"The Lakers?"

"How about a call from Sandy Bridgeman?"

"Who's that?"

"The man who decides."

"Decides what?"

"That it's official. I'm on the short list."

"That's great," he said. "I'm really glad someone finally made it official, especially since everybody unofficially knew it was official. So . . . good night from me and everybody here at *NBC Nightly News*."

"Not so fast. There are two other candidates."

"Who?"

She told him, "Clinton Fields. He's been bureau chief in Moscow for the past two years, and in Afghanistan for a couple of years before that. He wants to come home."

"And?"

"And JPO," she said referring to J. P. O'Malley. "He was in London and is now at the White House. His kids live in New York and he's looking for a move here."

"But . . . you win because you already live in New York."

"Except . . . Fields is the real deal, and JPO isn't to be sneezed at. They're already hooked into *Nightly*. They're on all the time, and both of these guys have been around a long time."

"Come on, you're a shoe-in." He reminded her, "Two white guys and a great-looking minority girl with perfect boobs? No contest."

"Maybe that gets me into Harvard, but if tomorrow Brian Williams moved to CBS . . . "

"Scott Pelley would be furious."

"Yes. And both these guys would make the short list for the big job. I wouldn't."

"Hey, the big job is the next step. Anyway, both these guys already have network day jobs. Just because they want to live in New York . . . "

"Right now, their cards look better to me than my cards. I need to compete on their level. They've worked overseas, I haven't. They've got national street cred, I don't. They've been around forever, I'm the new kid on the block."

"You've got two Emmys."

"Local. They've got seven between them. And two are nationals. I need the same kind of big-deal story that puts them on *Nightly*. I need to prove that I'm worthy."

"Build it and they will come."

"Call me if you find a vacant cornfield in Iowa."

"Maybe this is the encouragement you need to do the book."

"The book? Yes, I'm going to do it. I mean, I've been thinking about it all morning, and I decided, why wouldn't I? But it's still a coffee table book."

"It's still a book."

"But it's not a serious book. I need a big-deal book. Or, at least, a big-deal story."

"Like what?"

"Like my guy . . . L. Arthur Farmer."

22

Tina barely opened her eyes wide enough to look at the clock.

It said six.

She wondered why the radio hadn't clicked on.

Then the numbers jumped to 6:01 and the radio came on. " . . . all news all the time . . . you give us twenty-two minutes and we'll give you the world. Ten ten WINS time is six o'clock."

As she listened to the headlines, she fidgeted with the clock, moving the time back one minute. She also checked to see that the time was correct on the DVD player that sat on the big, Italian, carved wooden chest at the foot of their bed, in front of the wide-screen TV.

Throwing on a pair of San Francisco 49er sweats, she padded barefoot downstairs, made coffee in her coffeemaker, then carried the mug into the corner office and turned on all the screens.

She sat down, grabbed her iPhone, and began checking her e-mail.

There was nothing from David, so she texted him. "A) Ran away with Gwyneth Paltrow? B) Kidnapped by pirates? C) Gone native and found work on a banana plantation? D) Miss me so much that you can't get home fast enough?"

A few seconds later her phone rang.

"E," he said. "Got drunk, ate too much, did a deal with some strange guys . . . I'm talking real strange guys . . . and I'm getting on the plane now."

"But not D."

"And also D."

"How real strange?"

"That I can't get home fast enough? That's not strange . . . "

"No, idiot, how strange is real strange? These people you got drunk with and did a deal with?"

"Real strange," he said, "as in . . . seriously very real strange. I'll tell you all about them when I get home."

"You'd better," she warned.

When they hung up she looked at the screens and spotted $347,000 worth of Ralph Lauren men's bathing suits stuck in the port at Trujillo, Peru. She shrugged, "Why not," found the sellers in Singapore, bought the bathing suits for $207,000 and easily moved them to somebody in Dubai for $223,000.

Sixteen grand to the good, Tina picked up her mug and her coffee was still hot.

AT ONE POINT that night, Zhadanov changed his mind, saying that he would come back to New York with David. But because David didn't like that, he lied to Zhadanov that the pilots were expecting a lot of turbulence. Zhadanov decided to stay in Curaçao until he could get a commercial flight home.

Pepe Forero then asked David, would he mind if one of his guys hitched a ride with him to New York.

David didn't like that either, so he lied again, this time saying that he was planning on stopping first in Houston.

Forero decided that it would be better if his guy flew up to New York directly.

Zhadanov said, "He can come with me."

So that settled that.

Except it didn't.

As the sun was coming up, the bunch of them moved from the living room onto the deck to watch the sea change from dark blue to turquoise, at which time a very drunk David magnanimously invited all of the others to come back to New York with him.

Zhadanov said, okay, fine, and Forero's guy said okay, fine, and so did Juan Felipe the travel agent and Javier the jeweler.

David regretted the invitation immediately.

Juan Felipe started singing, "New York. New York," off-key, and the others joined in, and a few more bottles were opened, until David noticed that Javier wasn't singing, that he was snoring.

So David made his move. He got up and left. He climbed the steps from the house up to the street where the taxi was still waiting. The others didn't realize he was leaving or, if they did, they were too drunk to follow him. Either way, David told himself on the ride to the airport, *I've escaped.*

He slept for the entire flight home and showed up, looking worse for the wear, just after one o'clock.

"What happened to you?" Tina asked.

"Fucking Colombians."

"They are? Or, you were?"

He thought about that for a moment. "Huh?" Then he got it. "Oh, yeah . . . I mean, no. I wasn't. It's . . . they are."

"Colombians?"

"Yeah."

"David, what are you doing with Colombians?"

"A deal."

"No, David. Not with Colombians."

"Don't worry about them . . . honestly, they're not what y'all think."

"Not what I think? I think they're Colombians. David . . . does the word cocaine ring any bells?"

"They're not that. They're strange but they're not."

"Strange," she repeated what he'd said to her on the phone. "Seriously very real strange. Well, how strange is 'seriously very real strange'?"

"Strange because . . . they had guns."

"Are you out of your fucking mind?"

He insisted. "It's not what y'all think."

"You just said they had guns. It's not what I think? David, they're Colombians with guns."

"It's all about tax evasion."

"I don't care. We're not touching that money."

"We don't have to. That's the beauty of this. We never see their money."

"Then what's the point?"

"We get to use it. It gets put in that lawyer's client account. He takes that to our bank . . . where we have a line of credit . . . and we get a big expansion on that line because our credit is now secured by the Colombians' money."

"David . . . it's fucking cocaine!"

"No, Tina, it's fucking tax evasion. We never touch their money. We never even see their money."

"But we use their money."

"We use the bank's money."

"The answer is no, David. We are not going there."

"Listen to me . . . " He needed to make her understand. "With the kind of money they're talking, there isn't a deal we can't do. Airplane parts. Oil. All the really big stuff."

"There isn't a deal I'm going to do, not with their money."

"It's not their money, it's the bank's money."

"Count me out."

"How can I count you out?"

"You want to get involved with these sleazebags, then you open a separate trading account. My money stays out of it. Our joint money stays out of it. My name stays out of it."

"If that's the way you want it," he said, "fine."

"If you're fucking stupid enough to get involved with these guys . . . "

"Fine," he said.

"Fine," she said, and went back to the office.

He went upstairs to sleep.

Before the banks closed, he set up a separate trading account for himself, with a $30 million line of credit. That done, he texted Zhadanov, "You back in NYC yet? I'm ready to go."

"Me too." Zhadanov texted back, then asked for David's banking information.

David sent him what he needed.

Zhadanov assured him, "Money is there. Go for it."

Now for the first time since he'd gotten up from his sleep, David turned to Tina and said, "I'm on my way. Everything's good. I'm in and . . . y'all are completely locked out."

"Fine," she said, getting up from her desk and leaving the room.

"Fine," he said, and began looking everywhere for a really big cargo.

23

Pierre Belasco got out of his taxi at the Fifth Avenue entrance to Trump Tower, walked through the atrium—it was starting to get busy—stepped into the elevator, and hit the button for twenty-four.

He needed to speak to Bill Riordan.

But before the doors closed, he decided on a slight detour and hit the button for nineteen.

Getting out there, he walked down the hallway to the Scarpe Pietrasanta office.

The door was locked, and when he knocked on it, no one answered.

He took the next elevator up to twenty-four.

The security office had a windowless room with several banks of large monitors for the cameras positioned throughout Trump Tower and another windowless room with a bank of mainframe computers programmed to monitor everything that needed to be monitored.

Sitting directly in front of the doors to those rooms was a desk for the office secretary, and off that was a room with a view onto Fifty-Sixth Street, where Riordan worked.

"You got a minute?" Belasco asked.

Riordan looked up, "Sure," and motioned to Belasco to come in. "Usually I'm here by seven. But I met a couple of my buddies for breakfast, guys who are still on the job. You know, to keep my hand in."

Belasco smiled politely, sat in the chair facing Riordan's cluttered, folder-covered desk. "I'm still bothered about Carlos Vela."

"Moot," Riordan said. "You see the e-mail?"

"I haven't been downstairs yet."

"From the boss himself." He typed a few things on his computer keyboard, clicked his mouse, and turned the screen to face Belasco. "There."

Leaning forward, Belasco looked at the e-mail signed DJT, which was in response to an e-mail from Anthony Gallicano earlier this morning. It was cc'd Belasco and Riordan, and said simply, "Fire him."

Riordan announced, almost triumphantly, "Case closed."

Belasco took a deep breath and stood up. "Not the first time an innocent man gets hung."

"If he was innocent, okay. But he's not."

"You sure?"

"Positive."

"I'm not."

"Does it matter?" Riordan asked, pointing to the e-mail on the computer screen. "He is."

DOWNSTAIRS, Belasco found a copy of that e-mail waiting in his in-box. He didn't read it again—he didn't have to—because the boss' instructions were crystal clear.

With no choice, he rang Big Sam, the building engineer, and told him, "Decision's been made that Vela is gone. But I want to be the one who tells him. Can you have him, his union rep, and if he wants, his lawyer, in my office this morning at eleven? You can come along too."

Big Sam answered, "I'll get on it right now."

No sooner had he hung up when a young man he knew only as Gino knocked on his door and asked, "Can I see you for a moment?"

"Sure," he said. "What can I do for you?"

"It's her again." Gino worked in the food court, downstairs, at the coffee and pastry counter. "You wanted us to tell you if it ever happened again. And it has."

"Her?"

"The old lady. This time, it's four donuts."

"Oh . . . yes . . . okay." He pulled himself up from behind his desk and walked out with Gino, going through the fire safety office into the atrium.

"She's there," Gino pointed.

"Thank you," Belasco said. "I'll take it from here."

Gino headed for the escalators to go downstairs.

Belasco strolled to where Odette was leaning against a wall eating a donut, all the time careful not to let any crumbs fall on the polished marble floor.

"*Bonjour, Madame,*" he said. "*Bon appétit.*"

She answered in French, "Oh, Monsieur Belasco, will you join me for breakfast?"

"Thank you," he continued in French, "I've already eaten. But, you know, you should never eat standing up."

"Quite right," Odette said, still chewing. "Are you sure?" She extended a napkin with three other donuts wrapped inside. "Please, help yourself. And perhaps someday you will install tables and chairs here so I don't have to eat breakfast standing up."

"Perhaps . . . shall I hold those for you?"

"No," she answered sharply.

"You are up early, Madame. I don't usually see you until . . . "

"Monday is a busy day for me here," she said, "so many tourists on Monday morning . . . " Then she asked, "Is it true?"

"Is what true?"

"That Mr. Lips . . . you know who he is, that English musician?"

"Yes, I know Mr. Lips. But what about him?"

"Well . . . I heard . . . " She leaned forward to whisper, "that he fired his housekeeper all because she was allergic to cats."

"Really?"

She continued whispering. "Apparently, he and Mrs. Cove, you know the Chinese woman on forty-five? Well, she was seen leaving Mr. Lips's apartment on thirty-two."

Belasco smiled. "Perhaps she was visiting."

"She was," Odette assured him, "visiting. I should say so. All night. Quite a visit, no?"

"And you know this, Madame . . . how?"

Odette closed her eyes and shook her head as if to say, *I won't talk.*

"Of course." He nodded that he understood. "You seem to know quite a bit about Mr. Lips."

"Let's say," she wiped her hands with one napkin while still holding onto the donuts with another, "that I am very observant." Then she handed the napkin with the donuts to him. "Imagine . . . firing a housekeeper because she's allergic to cats in a building where cats are not permitted."

"Imagine that," he said looking at the donuts, then at her.

"It's always lovely speaking with you, monsieur, but the tourists are here. I must go. *Au revoir.*"

He watched her approach a small group of Japanese tourists and start talking to them.

Allergic to cats. Mr. Lips and Mrs. Cove.

He shook his head.

Cats weren't permitted in the Tower. Nor were any other animals. But of course, Belasco knew, there were plenty of cats and dogs, and there were certainly birds and fish. He'd even been led to believe that at least one resident had a pet boa constrictor. He'd never seen it, and when he mentioned it to the resident, the resident denied it. Yet one of the maintenance men swore he'd seen it.

As for Mr. Lips and Mrs. Cove, that didn't concern him any more than the dogs, fish, birds and cats did.

He carried the three donuts downstairs to the counter, where he tried to hand them back to Gino. "Sorry about that," he said.

Gino held up his hands to show Belasco that he didn't want them. "I can't take them back. Health regulations. They're no good to me once she's touched them."

"Of course." Belasco put them on the counter, then reached into his pocket for a five-dollar bill. "Here . . . will this do?"

The man took the money. "That's fine. They're only . . . "

"Never mind," Pierre said, taking the three wrapped donuts off the counter. "Thanks for letting me know."

He walked away, went back to the residents' reception and put the donuts on the concierge's desk.

"Compliments of Madame Odette," he said to Felicity, who was sorting mail, and to Pierro, who was going through undelivered newspapers.

"Thanks," Felicity said. "And this is for you."

She handed him a small box.

He saw the return address, "Ah . . . thank you . . . " brought it into his office, opened it, took what he wanted out of it, rewrapped the contents in a manila envelope, and added the note "Christmas is early this year." Sealing the envelope, he addressed it and walked it back to Felicity. "Run it upstairs, please."

She looked at it and nodded.

"Pierre?" Bill Riordan hurried out of the door at the end of the hallway, where the service elevator was. "Pierre, you need to see this."

"What is it?"

"You won't believe it." Motioning that they needed to speak privately, the two men went into Belasco's office and Riordan shut the door. "Have you got a DVD player?"

He pointed to the flat-screen television in the bookcase. "Under that."

Riordan put a DVD into the machine, took the remote from Belasco's desk and pushed play. The screen flickered, and the camera shot remained static on a large table for a long time.

"The boardroom," Riordan said. "The one the boss uses in the television show."

"*The Celebrity Apprentice* boardroom?"

"Yeah . . . watch."

Fast-forwarding the DVD, the time clock raced to 03:27. That's when Riordan slowed it down.

"Now, watch."

Two shadows stepped in front of the camera, then moved away and came into focus.

It was hard to see because the boardroom set was unlit. But Belasco watched as the two people went to the big table.

It was a man and a woman.

"Here you go," Riordan said.

The two looked around, then the man moved in on the woman, and they embraced. Then the man pulled down his pants, and pulled down the woman's pants, and within a minute she was lying on the table and he was lying on top of her.

"Can you believe that?" Riordan stopped the DVD.

"This was last night?"

"This morning . . . what did it say, three something in the morning."

"How did they get in there? I thought the set was locked when they aren't filming."

"Whole floor should be locked."

"Then how . . . "

"You mean, you didn't recognize our little Romeo?"

"No."

"Your boy Tomas."

"Tomas Tejeda?" Belasco was shocked. "My elevator operator?"

"We've got him on camera sneaking up the back stairs and onto the floor with some woman. What time does he come on?"

"He's on now."

"If you need any more proof than that . . . "

"The boss know?"

"You get a call from him yet?"

"No."

"Then there's your answer. Because you can bet your ass as soon as he . . . "

"Wait here," Belasco said, stepped outside, and saw that Jaquim's was the only elevator on the ground floor. "Which elevator is Tomas on?"

Jaquim answered, "Three."

Belasco stood there waiting.

When the third elevator door opened, Robert Gildenstein, an orthopedic surgeon, got out.

"Good morning, Pierre," he stopped to say hello. "I forget, do you go to the residents' board meetings?"

"Not usually."

"It's at our place, tonight. Should be interesting. You might want to pop up."

"Mrs. Essenbach's Brazilian jungle?"

Gildenstein whispered to Belasco, "Prakash . . . you know, Advani . . . he's been lobbying everybody. She doesn't stand a chance." He slapped Belasco on the back, "Eight thirty if you can make it."

"For all sorts of reasons, doctor, I think this time I'll keep my distance."

"Then come for drinks afterward."

"That might be a better idea."

"Around nine thirty? Have a good day."

"You too," Belasco said as he left, then turned to Tomas, who was standing outside his elevator. "In my office, please."

Tomas looked at Belasco, then at Jaquim, then walked into Belasco's office.

Immediately, Riordan barked, "How fucking stupid are you, pal?"

Belasco shut the door. "I would listen to an explanation if you had one."

Tomas shook his head, "No."

"I'm afraid that your dismissal is effective immediately," Belasco said. "Mr. Riordan will accompany you to the locker room where you will be permitted to take any personal belongings. But your ID card and everything that is property of Trump Tower will stay here."

"Who's the woman," Riordan demanded. "I want to know right now . . . "

"No," Belasco stopped him.

Riordan didn't like that. "It's important to find out who she is . . . if she works here . . . "

Belasco asked Tomas, "Does the woman work here?"

"No, Señor," he said quietly.

"Then you will go with Mr. Riordan now."

Riordan glared at Belasco. "You're going to take his word for it?" He turned to Tomas. "I want her name."

"No," Belasco said again.

"If she works here . . . "

Belasco ignored him and looked at Tomas. "Your union representative will explain that you are entitled to a lawyer, and I'm advising you now not to say anything to anyone about this without first consulting an attorney. I will make arrangements with accounting to send you whatever money is due, including vacation time. But you will not be permitted back in Trump Tower under any circumstances. And if asked by a future employer for a character reference, we will note that you were fired for conduct unbecoming an employee. Do you understand?"

Tomas nodded and said quietly, "Yes."

"Wait outside," Riordan ordered, watched as Tomas left, then berated Belasco, "How the hell can you let him walk without telling us who the woman was?"

"If she doesn't work here, it's none of our business."

"And if she does work here?"

"He said she didn't."

Riordan shook his head several times and started out of the office. "What a piece of cake you are, my friend."

"Don't ask him again who the woman was," Belasco warned. "It doesn't matter. And as for this . . . " He went to his DVD player, pulled out the disk, and snapped it in half. "One copy gets sent to the lawyers. All the others get shredded. This isn't for distribution."

"This clown and the other one, Vela . . . two sleazebags give you a song and dance . . . and you buy their stories, lock, stock and barrel. Just like that, you believe them both. These guys need to be nailed."

Belasco motioned to Riordan that the discussion was over. "I don't do crucifixions."

24

Ricky Lips was half-asleep, laying on his back, naked except for his ankle bracelet, with the bed covers spilling onto the floor, when he felt her move close to him.

Instinctively, he reached for her.

With his eyes shut, he felt her slide up his chest, and then she was on his face, so he opened his mouth and then . . . "Ahhhhhhh."

He screamed and sat up.

"Ahhhhhhh."

The woman next to him screamed.

"Ahhhhhhh."

The ocelot growled and hissed, clawed the woman, then jumped off Ricky's face to the floor and raced away from the bed.

"What the fuck . . . " He yelled, spitting the ocelot's taste off his tongue.

"Damn cat scratched me," she shouted.

"Pthew." He spit. "I licked it. Pthew."

The ocelot crouched in the corner of the room, growling and hissing.

"I'm bleeding," she screamed. "Fucking cat . . . I'm bleeding."

"Pthew." He looked at her. "You're bleeding."

"Fucking cat . . . "

"Pthew." He spit one more time, then reached for a pillow and tossed it at the ocelot.

The animal raced to the other side of the room, still hissing.

"Fuck me," Ricky said, getting out of bed and going into the bathroom.

"I'm bleeding," the woman yelled again. "Ricky, your fucking cat . . . "

"Hold on luv, I'm taking a whiz . . . " He stood at the toilet and peed, flushed, then came out carrying a towel. He tossed it to her. "Wrap it around your arm . . . ain't that bad anyway, just a little scratch . . . "

"Your fucking cat," she kept saying.

He stared at the ocelot that was staring intently at him. Then he started looking around the room. "What's that smell?"

The woman was too busy inspecting her scratch.

"You smell that?" He moved through the room slowly, watching the ocelot out of the corner of his eyes, then got down on his knees and smelled under the bed. "Ah fuck me . . . the fucking cat shit under the bed."

"Fuck you, Ricky . . . " The woman got out of bed nude—Ricky looked at her and nodded his approval—picked up a pillow to toss at the ocelot, then decided to toss it at Ricky. She grabbed her clothes, went into the bathroom and slammed the door.

"Fuck you," Ricky screamed at the ocelot. "You're supposed to shit in that fucking cat litter box we bought for you." He took the pillow the woman had thrown at him and threw it at the ocelot.

The animal leaped out of the way, raced across the room, and hissed at him.

"Fuck me," Ricky said, left his bedroom, and went straight to Joey's room.

Joey was asleep, and there was some woman asleep next to him. He had no idea who she was. "Oy . . . " He went to the side of the bed to wake his son. "Oy. The fucking cat. Oy . . . get up."

Joey didn't move, but the woman next to him opened her eyes, spotted Ricky standing there naked, and screamed.

"Oy." Ricky shoved Joey.

Now Joey sat up and saw his father there. "What the fuck?"

The woman next to him continued screaming.

"It's that cat," Ricky said. "He shit under me bed."

"Go put some clothes on," Joey ordered. "You're scaring me bird."

"Oh yeah." Ricky looked down at himself, then at the woman next to Joey. "Sorry luv . . . Little Ricky here . . . " He pointed to his crotch . . . "we didn't mean to frighten you."

"Get dressed," Joey shoved his father.

Back in his own bedroom, the woman he'd been sleeping with was gone. So was the ocelot.

Ricky stepped into a pair of shorts.

"Help." The woman screamed from somewhere in the apartment. "Ricky . . . help . . . "

He raced out of his bedroom and found her in the kitchen.

"Help," she screamed and pointed to the fridge door, which was open.

"What?" Ricky demanded.

"Your cat," she said. "I came here to get some orange juice . . . "

"Hey Ricky . . . " Bugs appeared.

Ricky stared at him. "You still here?"

A woman Ricky had never seen walked up behind Bugs and put her arms around him. "What's all the noise?"

Both of them were naked.

"The chicken," screamed the woman who'd been sleeping with Ricky.

Ricky inspected the naked woman next to Bugs. "What chicken?"

"The one in the fridge. I opened the door, it really stank in there, but that cat leaped in and grabbed it and . . . "

Bugs pointed under the kitchen table. "Look at that."

Ricky bent down and watched as the ocelot ripped apart what was left of a broiled chicken. "Bloody hell . . . "

"What's going on?" Joey came into the kitchen wearing a bathrobe. He saw the ocelot under the table eating the chicken. "Fuck me."

Ricky stood there shaking his head. "Where'd that chicken come from?"

25

Carson was desperate to find the missing 9 percent, when Arcarro stopped by to see how he was doing.

"It's tough," he told his partner, "because I don't know what I'm looking for and won't know until after I find it."

"Where are you looking?"

"Obviously, I started in Japan. But some of it could be anywhere. Hong Kong. Singapore. Malaysia. Maybe in the States. Maybe in Europe."

"Have you tried the moon?"

"That's probably not as much of a joke as you think it is."

"I'm not joking. I think you're going about it backward. You're looking for a single needle in a field of haystacks."

"Yeah?"

"Instead of trying to find the needle, try hiding one and see what the haystacks have to say."

Carson stared at his partner for several seconds, then began to smile. "EXIT-Strategies?"

"Great minds really do think alike," Arcarro said, and left Carson to get on with the hunt.

EXIT-Strategies was the invention of Milt McKeever who, like Carson, was also a Goldman Sachs refugee. But McKeever had gotten out back in 2000 when the getting was really good, took a bundle of cash with him and set up EXIT. It stood for Electronic Xchange and International Trading. McKeever's aim was to compete on a small scale with Goldman's Sigma X, Credit Suisse's CrossFinder, and all the other big guys like BNP Paribas, Citi, Deutsche Bank, Morgan Stanley and UBS that were swimming in "dark pools."

A hidden-from-public-view market for trading very large blocks of shares in one go, they're officially known as "dark pools of liquidity." Much the way a black hole in space absorbs everything within its reach, these unseen dark pools suck the liquidity out of the market until it completely disappears. The names of the sellers and the names of the buyers are not revealed before the trade or, necessarily, even after the trade. In fact, it's only after the trade that the price is disclosed.

Absolutely legal, and accounting for a very significant percentage of America's daily stock trading volume—some reports say 12 percent, some say 25 percent—it is the playground of speculators, traders, moguls and hedge fund managers who wish to move in and out of shares without tipping their hand to the general public, which might otherwise affect the big markets, like the NYSE and the NASDAQ, where everybody else has to play.

Because the blocks traded in these dark pools have to be large—minimums generally run anywhere from ten thousand shares to as high as one hundred thousand—this is not a market for the average investor.

Nor is it a market for the fainthearted. Tens of millions of dollars change hands and the time it takes is measured in milliseconds.

When Carson got McKeever on the phone and asked about Shigetada, McKeever said he didn't think anything was floating around at the moment. "Not a company we see a lot of. Like never."

"Where can I find some?"

"I'll look around for you. There are a few dark pools in Asia, mainly Hong Kong, but they're small and generally incestuous. You want GM or Citi or Exxon, no problem. Shigetada? Probably not. But if I find anything, we can handle the trade for you."

"I'd be grateful," Carson said.

Not five minutes later, McKeever was on the phone again. "There's a tiny operator in Hong Kong who's got three hundred thousand."

"Sounds promising."

"Nah . . . they've been sitting around for over a week. Looks like the price is forty-one and a half."

"We know who he is?"

"No. Then again, that's the point."

"I'll call you right back." Carson got off the line with him and dialed Ken Warring's cell. "You up yet?"

"Crack of dawn. What's happening?"

"It's late for you . . . " He checked the time. "It's six thirty your time."

"Except I'm in LA."

"Whoops." That meant it was 4:30 for Warring. "I'm really sorry about that."

"What's up?"

"We're looking around for our best friend's shares and I've found about half a percent's worth in Hong Kong."

"How much and who's selling?"

"Forty-one. And we don't know. It's been sitting in a dark pool for a week."

"Where did it close in Tokyo and what was the volume?"

"Hold on." He brought a screen up on his laptop. "Forty-four and change. And . . . nothing. None. Zip."

Warring decided, "If you can get it for under forty, go ahead. But put it offshore. If nothing else, we can always arbitrage it and make a few pennies."

"No one's buying at forty-four . . . and whoever this is can't sell at forty-one . . . we may have to rethink our numbers."

"When are you going out there?"

"Wednesday."

"I'm sure we'll talk again before the cows come home."

"Go back to sleep."

"Can't now."

"Why?"

"'Cause you woke me." Warring hung up.

Carson made a face, "Should have turned your phone off," then rang McKeever back. "We'll take it at thirty-eight."

"I'll try. First Ace?"

"No." He thought quickly. "Put it through . . . company's called Pennin Inc. It's Hong Kong."

"Pen and . . . ink?"

"Our little joke," he said. "Pennin." He spelled it. "Pennin Inc. Hong Kong Holdings."

"Call you back."

Off the phone with McKeever, Carson took a fast look at the Pennin account, which was held at HSBC in Hong Kong, to make certain there were sufficient funds. There were.

But when McKeever got back to him, he said, "No soap. Best is forty and a half."

"Pass," Carson said. "But keep an eye out, will you? We're buyers under forty." Then he remembered what Arcarro said about haystacks. "In fact, we're sellers, too. Can I move twenty-five thousand with you?"

"Yeah, we'll take it."

"All right, twenty-five at forty. Let's see if we can wake up the haystacks."

MESUMI walked back into the office after lunch.

"That was one helluva cup of coffee," Carson noted.

"Sorry," she said. "That took a little longer than I'd expected. Cost us lunch."

"Us?"

"You."

"What did I get for my sashimi?"

"Why do you immediately assume that when two Japanese American women get together for lunch, they have sashimi?"

"What did you have?"

She handed him the bill. "Happy now?"

He looked at it, smiled, took $30 from his pocket, and handed it to her. "Does that include the tip?"

The bill was for two pastramis on rye with Swiss cheese, coleslaw, pickles and . . .

"Cel-Ray Tonic?" He pointed to the bill. "Who drinks Cel-Ray Tonic?"

"I love it."

"Something else you learned at Princeton?"

"No. Princeton was during the week. Cel-Ray Tonic was sophomore year weekends in New York with Ethan Pearlman."

"Ethan Pearlman?" He was surprised. "Sammy Pearlman's son?"

"Why are you so surprised?"

"Ah . . . I don't know. I'm not surprised but . . . I would have thought that the kid . . . I mean, given that his father is one of the top-ten richest guys on Wall Street . . . "

"An acquired taste," she said.

"Ethan?"

"Cel-Ray Tonic." She shook her head. "Do you want to know what you got for your thirty bucks including the tip?"

"Besides the fact that we now have a way into Sammy Pearlman's shop? The kid works there, doesn't he?"

"Besides the fact that he dumped me bad and wound up marrying someone else, and I got even with him by posting a few inappropriate photos of him on the Net . . . "

"Wow . . . there's a whole side of you I never knew about."

"Which starts and ends with Cel-Ray Tonic," she said sternly. "Ren was helpful. What would you like to know about Chiba Investment Bank?"

"Small . . . family owned, I think. Why? Are they holding Shigetada?"

"What did you say . . . eighteen with the institutions? That left nine?"

"Right."

"Chiba has six of the nine."

"Oooh," his eyes opened wide. "This is good. But how come it doesn't show up anywhere?"

"Old man Shigetada . . . not the son, but the father . . . that's his brother's wife's family."

"Old man . . . brother's wife . . . " He tried to work that out. "Our guy . . . that would be his aunt's family?"

"His cousins. They're holding the shares in various trusts."

"Good work," he said. "Really good."

She nodded and started to walk away, then turned to him, "You ever tell anybody that I was sleeping with Ethan Pearlman . . . "

He grinned. "I promise not to mention it to more than nine people."

She didn't find that funny.

Carson went to his office to take a close look at the Chiba Investment Bank.

Except for the fact that they were holding 6 of the missing 9 percent, he didn't realize how valuable this information was going to be until he stumbled across a tiny blurb in one of the market tip sheets that referenced a lawsuit in Tokyo.

The Chiba cousins had sued Shigetada over a governance issue.

Carson immediately e-mailed his lawyers in Tokyo and asked them to send him whatever they could find, in English, on the matter.

Then he picked up the phone and rang Peter Mann's Wines on Madison Avenue. He got Peter on the line and told him, "That Burgundy you sent me last year . . . "

He thought for a moment. "Nineteen ninety Musigny from De Vogué?"

"That's it."

"I need another case."

"It's great, isn't it?"

"Can you get me a case?"

"I'm sure I can find one." But then he warned Carson, "The price has gone up. It's like nine hundred bucks a bottle."

"Whatever." Carson gave him Mesumi's home address. "Put in a card from me that reads, "Really good job. Thank you."

"Done," Peter said. "Anything else?"

"No . . . and thanks." But then he changed his mind. "Actually, yes. I don't know where you're going to find it, but if anyone can . . . with that order, send her three cases of Cel-Ray Tonic."

26

A white stretch limousine pulled up to the residents' entrance on Fifty-Sixth Street, and a tall man in his early sixties with very short, dark hair jumped out.

He was wearing tight, black leather pants, a black silk shirt with a gold silk scarf tied loosely around his neck, a lot of gold jewelry and sunglasses.

"Good morning, sir," Roberto opened the door for him and motioned toward the concierge desk.

The man went there and announced in a clipped British accent, "Miss Cyndi Benson, please."

Felicity smiled, "Yes sir, may I tell her who's calling?"

"Horace Belgrave," he announced. "Please tell her that her chariot awaits."

"Certainly sir." Felicity dialed Cyndi's apartment, and when she answered, Felicity announced, "Mr. Belgrave and your chariot await."

"Be right down," Cyndi said.

Felicity smiled at Horace, "She will be right down."

But it was another twenty-five minutes before Cyndi appeared.

Wearing no makeup, no jewelry, and with wet hair under a red mariner's flat cap, she was dressed in faded-blue Roberto Cavalli jeans torn at the knees, a simple red and black T-shirt, red trainers, and was carrying a really big red canvas shoulder bag with the words "Dirt Cheap" in black on the side.

"Darling . . . " Horace fell into her arms. "I have missed you terribly . . . "

She hugged and kissed him, waved at Felicity, took Horace's arm in hers, kissed him again, and started out the door.

Roberto tipped his hat. "Good morning, ma'am . . . sir."

"Hi," she said, then suddenly stopped. "Oh . . . is Mr. Belasco in?"

"I believe so," Robert said.

Cyndi said to Horace, "Wait here, darling, please, just a second," turned back and hurried to Belasco's office.

She poked her head in. "Merry Christmas to you, too." She opened her hands and put her palms together, as if they were handcuffed.

He looked up from his desk and smiled. "I kept the spare key, just in case."

"I'll think of you every time."

"That's probably not necessary . . . but nice of you to offer."

She blew him a kiss, "Thank you," waved and ran back to Horace. She kissed him yet again, took his arm, "I am so glad you're here," and the two of them left the Tower.

The limo driver was standing next to the rear door, holding it open. Cyndi got in and Horace climbed in next to her.

They'd known each other since her Chanel days. Once upon a long time ago, he'd been a theatrical hairdresser in London's West End. And, for a while, when he first moved to Paris, he oversaw makeup for several French houses. By the time Cyndi met him, he was dressing models and directing traffic backstage at all the major catwalk shows.

He treated the models like the benevolent headmaster of a school for wayward girls.

They all called him "Uncle Horace," but never to his face.

These days, retired and living in Arizona, he occasionally freelanced as a shoot supervisor, but only for those models he still liked. Most of them he didn't.

He'd always treated Cyndi like a daughter and somewhere in her mind, he was almost the father she never had. So when she phoned him and asked him to fly east for her, he got on the first plane.

They spoke on the phone all the time, but they hadn't seen each other for nearly three years.

"I'm so glad we're doing this," he swooned, pointing to a cooler and showing her that there was champagne.

She shook her head to say, *no champagne*, then told him, "Me too. Makes me feel like old times."

"I'll have yours, darling," and he poured himself a glass. "Speaking of old times . . . I've lined up everyone. Giancarlo will do hair with Inez on makeup. And, of course, the moment Gennaro heard you'd agreed to do this, he insisted on flying in from Paris. Cartier was thrilled beyond words, darling, absolutely thrilled beyond words. Now . . . don't be shocked when you see him because he walks with a cane, but even so . . . how I still wish he wasn't straight."

She gently patted the side of his face. "He was always much too old for you."

"We're the same age. But I know what you mean." Horace raised his eyebrows. "And do you remember Sienna? His toy-girl? She must have been, what, sixteen? Dirty old bugger that he is. Well, believe it or not, she's all grown up and they're still together. Now, instead of pretending that she's his children's nanny, she pretends that she's his assistant."

"Sounds like a party," she said.

"A sixth form reunion."

"Sixth form?"

"High school to you, my dear."

"I wasn't going to do it," she said. "When Arthur called to say he'd received a request . . . he didn't tell me who it was . . . well, I told him no. And even when he told me the fee . . . "

"Oh . . . yes . . . the fee." Horace said, "I heard. We've come a long way from the thousand French Franc days . . . haven't we just."

"Arthur told me the fee and even then I said no. Then he told me that Cartier would hire you, and when you said that you wanted to bring Gennaro . . . "

"One of those offers you couldn't refuse."

"What else would I do all day on a Monday? How's Roland?"

He paused for a second, then forced a smile. "Same old, same old," he said. "Mondays he plays tennis and I sit home and . . . bake."

She clasped his hands in hers. "Thank you for doing this for me." But something in his eyes had changed.

"Stop thanking me or we'll both start weeping."

She looked at him and for a brief second she wanted to ask him if everything was really all right.

But then he said, "You will never guess who I ran into in Palm Springs a few weeks ago . . . did I already tell you?"

And the moment passed. "Who?"

"Remember Isabella?"

"Isabella? With the cross-eyed nipples?"

He crossed his eyes and made a face.

As they rode downtown, Horace went through a long list of people they'd both known in Paris and gave her all the latest gossip.

Cartier's original idea was to shoot Cyndi in her own apartment, but then Gennaro bumped into Antoine de Maisonneuve in Paris, said that he was coming to New York for a shoot, and Antoine said, "You're welcome to use my place."

He and Bobby Baldwyn lived in a four-story, old pickle factory on Washington Street, a few blocks below Canal Street.

Architectural Digest had featured it in their top-ten list of best apartments in the world.

The limo pulled up to the front door, where three burly security men in dark suits were waiting with a strikingly beautiful redhead in a miniskirt.

"Sienna," Cyndi screamed and rushed into her arms. They hugged and kissed, and then Sienna kissed Horace, and after several minutes of that, Sienna brought them into the building.

There was a small lobby where Cyndi, Horace, Sienna and one of the security men stepped into a decorated elevator that was large enough for the four of them, and also for two rococo couches that were there in case someone wanted to sit.

When they got to the top floor, the door opened and Gennaro was waiting with Giancarlo and Inez.

The hugging and kissing started all over again.

"I can't believe it," Cyndi kept saying.

Giancarlo and Inez still looked pretty much the same, but she had to admit that Gennaro looked much older. Although he still had that wonderful head of hair that flopped in front of his handsome, weathered face.

"Nothing's changed," Cyndi lied, seeing him holding a cane, and kissing the three of them again.

The floor was loft style, wide open, decorated impeccably with museum-quality, signed-Deco furniture and major twentieth-century American art.

There was Picasso, Rothko, Rauschenberg, Lichtenstein, Warhol, Francis Bacon and the most recent addition to the collection, a huge Jasper Johns American Flag, which de Maisonneuve bought for himself at Christie's as a birthday present, paying a record price of $30.9 million.

For the shoot, Gennaro and Maisonneuve's "apartment manager"—a young man named Alain—had cleared away a corner of the room. The Johns hung on one wall, the other had huge windows looking out to the Hudson River and New Jersey beyond it.

In the middle of this empty space, Gennaro had placed an original, signed Emile-Jacques Ruhlmann chair—once part of Yves St. Laurent's personal Art Deco collection, for which Maisonneuve had also paid a record auction price of $393,000—and lit it.

That's all that was going to be in the shot—a corner of the Jasper Johns painting, a corner of the window with the Hudson and New Jersey, a large expanse of hardwood floor, the chair and Cyndi.

Maisonneuve's two Portuguese housekeepers now both appeared, reminding everyone that they'd set the dining table on the far side of the room with refreshments.

Alain was introduced to Cyndi—he gave her a slight kiss on both cheeks—then introduced her to an older woman named Karen. Next to her was a very burly young man wearing a shoulder holster.

Karen was carrying a large, silk-covered box. "This is them," she said.

Cyndi couldn't wait. "Can I see?"

Karen opened the box.

Inside was a magnificent double strand of eighty-eight natural pearls.

Each pearl, Karen explained, weighed 2.15 carats, was silvery white in color with overtones of pink and was of the highest quality of luster.

Not only was each pearl separated with a diamond, but there was a six-carat heart-shaped diamond pendant in the front.

"Oh my God . . . " Cyndi's eyes were wide open. "Wow."

Horace leaned over, inspected the necklace, and started singing softly, " . . . Woolworth's doesn't sell, baby . . . "

Now Gennaro whispered in Cyndi's ear, "If you brought your credit card, it's only three point four million."

She turned to him. "Think of all the airline miles."

Karen shut the box, nodded to her bodyguard and the two of them went back to the far side of the room.

Next, Alain escorted over a bunch of other people to meet Cyndi—five young men and four young women—who were introduced as being from the ad agency. They were eating and holding wine glasses while they shook hands with her. She smiled politely as they gushed on about how glad they were that she'd agreed to do this.

While they hovered around her, the security guard who'd come up in the elevator with her stood close by.

One of the young men pointed to the set. "That's all?"

Gennaro said, "That's all."

Not surprisingly, most of those young men and some of those women started making suggestions. "Maybe a plant . . . how about a bottle of champagne on the floor . . . why don't we wait until sundown and backlight her with the sunset and the river . . . "

Gennaro paid absolutely no attention to them.

Neither did Cyndi, who announced, "Hair and war paint, please, excuse me," and walked away.

Giancarlo and Inez took her down the back stairway to a dressing area off de Maisonneuve's bedroom, and Horace followed.

Having no one else to talk to, the group turned to Sienna, who said, "Excuse me," and got very busy with Gennaro.

Two hours later, once Cyndi's hair and makeup was done, Horace reappeared and said to the crowd of young men and young women—a few of whom were pretty tipsy by this point—"Thank you very much for coming along this morning, and now if you will all please excuse us . . . " He extended his arm to show them to the elevator.

"What do you think you're doing?" One of the young men demanded.

"I'm afraid this is a closed shoot," Horace said.

The man objected. "You got that wrong, friend."

Another man agreed. "We're the agency people who are . . . "

"I'm sure, as agency people, you've seen the rider," Horace said.

"What rider?" the second man wanted to know.

"Who are you anyway?" one of the women demanded.

Horace motioned to Sienna, who went to a notebook, found a sheet of paper, handed it to him and he then handed it to them.

It was the list of conditions for the shoot.

The first item read, "Closed Shoot. No ad agency personnel. No one except the photographer, his immediate team and Cyndi's immediate team, including one security guard and a matron, to be named by Cartier, for the safeguarding of the jewels."

One of the agency men grabbed the rider, crumpled it and tossed it back rudely at Horace. "You can shove this up your ass. It's worthless. We're staying."

Horace looked down at the crumpled paper on the floor, then up at the man who'd thrown it at him.

"Had you bothered to read it," he said with a touch of arrogance deliberately put on because he knew it would annoy the hell out of these people, "you would have seen that, if all of the demands in the rider are not met, Miss Benson is still entitled to her fee and expenses, and you are entitled to nothing more than a copy of that rider, suitable for framing."

"We'll see about this," another man said, taking his cell phone out. "Anyone know the lawyers' number?"

"Call my office," one of the women said, "Alice has it."

Horace now turned to the security guard nearby and the Cartier guard standing next to Karen. "Would you two gentlemen please show our guests out, as they may need some privacy for their many phone calls."

The first guard pushed the button for the elevator and the doors opened. "Ladies and gentlemen . . . this way please." There was a lot of moaning and groaning, and one man even challenged the guard, "You'll have to carry me out."

When the guard glared at him, "If that's what you want, sir," the defiant man backed down.

One by one they got into the elevator and, still cursing and threatening Horace, left the building accompanied by the first guard.

A few minutes later, that guard returned. "Our two men downstairs will stay on the street with them. They're angry, but I don't think they'll last long out there. One of them is already looking for a taxi."

"Thank you," Horace said.

Seeing a small key above the elevator's call button, Horace turned it, then pushed the call button. Nothing happened.

"It seems this locks the lift." And he left it locked at the top floor.

Sienna announced, "I think we're ready."

Gennaro agreed and turned on the lights. "Cyndi, where are you?"

Inez and Giancarlo brought Cyndi onto the set.

She was barefoot, wearing a paisley silk robe.

Gennaro pointed, "In front of the chair, please."

Cyndi and Inez went there.

"Pearls?" Gennaro called out.

Karen walked onto the set with the bodyguard next to her, handed the box to Inez and opened it. She lifted the pearls out very carefully, Cyndi opened her robe just enough and Karen placed them around her neck. When she had it right, she nodded.

Horace motioned to Karen and the bodyguard that they should stand at the back of the room as far out of the way as he could get them. He invited the second guard to stand there, too. Then he asked Alain and the two housekeepers to move there as well.

"Now . . . " Gennaro motioned to Sienna, "the single most important thing."

She walked over to Cyndi carrying a pile of CDs.

Cyndi looked through them, then suddenly broke out into a huge grin and pulled one out. "You remembered."

"Of course, I did," Gennaro smiled. "I wanted to see if you did."

She handed the CD to Sienna. "For old times' sake."

Sienna went to an enormous entertainment center that sat under a sixty-four-inch plasma-screen television, looked at all the equipment for a couple of minutes, then turned to Horace. "I don't know."

"I do," he said, took the CD from her, turned the player on, turned the speakers up to very loud and waited there.

Gennaro pointed to Cyndi. "If you please."

She dropped the robe.

Except for the pearls, she was completely nude.

Inez began touching up Cyndi's body makeup. Gennaro did another light check. Giancarlo put a tiny towel on the chair. And when Inez said, "*C'est bon*," Cyndi carefully sat down.

Giancarlo checked to make certain that none of the towel was showing.

Sienna adjusted the pearls, "A little to the left."

Inez and Giancarlo moved away.

Gennaro grabbed his big Hasselblad, clicked it a few times to make certain that the lights flashed, then said, "Ready?"

Cyndi wet her lips, crossed her legs, covered her breasts and said, "Ready."

Gennaro looked at Horace. "Ready?"

Horace said, "Ready."

Then Gennaro yelled, "Let's go."

Horace pushed the button, Madonna blasted through the room singing, "Like a Virgin," and Gennaro ran off picture after picture.

He moved to his left, bent down, moved to his right—moving like a man who didn't need a cane—while Cyndi stared straight into the camera and with every shot changed the tilt of her head, or changed her expression, or changed the way her eyes looked right through the lens.

Her legs stayed crossed, and her hands never revealed her breasts, but she became someone else with each shot. Her mouth opened. She played her lips across her tongue. She winked. She smiled. She pouted. She laughed. She cried. She hated. She loved.

And all the time Gennaro kept shooting.

And all the time the lights kept exploding on.

And all the time Madonna kept singing.

Without missing a beat, Gennaro handed the Hasselblad to Sienna, who gave him a Nikon, and he continued shooting pictures of Cyndi naked on the chair, surrounded by the Johns and the window and the hardwood floor.

She made love to his camera.

And he didn't stop her for nearly twenty minutes.

Then, suddenly, just like that, Gennaro leapt up and screamed, "Cyndi Benson . . . I love you."

And everyone in the room applauded.

Cyndi jumped up and hugged Gennaro, then hugged Inez and Giancarlo and Sienna, and finally—naked except for the string of pearls—she hugged Horace. "I love you."

"The magic is still there." His eyes filled up with tears. "It's still there. It's still there."

She held onto him for a moment, then kissed the side of his face, took the robe from Inez and let the woman from Cartier take the necklace from her.

Downstairs, Cyndi took a fast shower to get rid of the makeup and stepped back into her street clothes.

"You were unbelievable," Sienna said. "Wait till you see. It was twelve years ago, all over again. But better."

Now Cyndi pulled Sienna aside and whispered to her, "Horace . . . what's wrong?"

"Nothing," Sienna stared at her. "Why?"

"Tell me," Cyndi said. "Something's wrong. I can see it in his eyes. There is something. Tell me what it is."

"Cyndi," she shook her head, "nothing . . . really . . . "

"Don't lie. Tell me."

Sienna took a deep breath. "No one's supposed to know. Gennaro knows, but Horace made him promise not to tell anyone. Except he told me."

"What?"

"You must never let on . . . "

"I won't. Tell me . . . "

"Roland . . . he has terminal cancer."

"Oh God . . . " Cyndi's eyes got very red.

"Horace doesn't want anyone to know. It's Roland's pancreas. But you mustn't say anything or he will be furious at you and at me and at Gennaro . . . "

"How long?"

"They told him . . . a year."

"When?"

"Six months ago."

Now the tears poured out of her eyes.

Sienna put her arms around Cyndi and held her.

It only lasted a minute or so, until Cyndi took some deep breaths and stopped. She sniffled a few times. "You're right." She dried her eyes. "He must never know that I know."

"You'll be okay?"

"Yeah," she said. "Let's go upstairs and look at the pictures."

"Wait till you see . . . they're unbelievable."

Cyndi kissed Sienna, grabbed her big, red "Dirt Cheap" bag, threw her wet towel in there and went upstairs.

Alain and the two housekeepers had put the living room back to the way Maisonneuve had left it. Every piece of furniture was in its place.

"Come here and look at this." Horace motioned to Cyndi.

They hovered over Gennaro's laptop.

"The magic . . . the magic . . . " Gennaro clicked through shot by shot.

Cyndi looked at the photos of herself, showing nothing but a lot of skin and a fabulous set of pearls and diamonds.

The tagline for the photo, which would run in magazines and on billboards around the world would be, "All a woman really needs is her pearls."

Gennaro clicked through the more than one thousand shots he'd taken of Cyndi.

And all that time, Cyndi held Horace's hand.

They left the apartment and rode together in the stretch, emptying the first champagne bottle and opening another.

At P. J. Clarke's on Third Avenue, the six of them sat around a big table, eating and laughing about the Chanel days.

The party ended a little after five.

"We're on the nine o'clock to Paris," Gennaro said.

"And I'm on the eight fifteen to Phoenix," Horace said.

"Nothing's changed," Cyndi said, as they made their way back to the limo. "I get naked, everyone has food and then you all leave the country."

They dropped her off first.

She kissed them goodbye, hugged them, then kissed them again. Everyone promised to stay in touch.

Horace even said to her, "Don't wait another three years."

Smiling, she got out of the car and stood on the curb while they drove away.

Then the tears started again, and she rushed upstairs to her apartment.

It took a little longer this time to pull herself together. When she did, she phoned her agent. "Arthur, it was great."

"If you want to keep working . . . "

"Not a lot," she confessed. "But this time . . . thanks."

"Thank you," he said. "That's a pretty sizeable paycheck for a Monday morning."

She thought about that. "Horace threw the agency people out."

"Fuck 'em," Arthur said. "They weren't supposed to be there to begin with."

"And, hey, it wasn't only the morning, we were there until two."

He laughed, "For four hundred grand, some people would have stayed until six."

She thought about the money again. "Arthur . . . I need to call Sydney Feinberg. I love you."

He said, "I love you too. Good work today," and hung up.

Now she dialed her lawyer and his secretary put her straight through. "To what do I owe a phone call from my most gorgeous client?"

"Hi, Sydney, I need some advice."

"Of course."

"A very old friend of mine . . . his lover is dying. They live in Arizona. He doesn't know that I know and he must never find out. I don't know what their money situation is and I don't know what sort of treatment he can get . . . maybe none. But he must have whatever he can get. I'll e-mail you his name and address and phone number. I made some money today. Minus Arthur's commission . . . I'll wire you three hundred and forty thousand dollars tomorrow to pay for whatever they need. Buy them anything and everything they need or want. Whatever it takes. I don't care what it is or what it costs. If we run out, I'll send more. Tell them they won the lotto. Tell them it comes from a fund for experimental medicine. Tell them it's the Tooth Fairy. Tell them anything they'll believe. But they must never know that the money is from me."

"Wow, that old friend must mean a lot to you."

"He does."

She hung up, lay down on her bed, wrapped her arms around a pillow as if she was cuddling someone, and cried herself to sleep.

27

There was a lot of paperwork necessary to set in motion Tomas' permanent dismissal.

Belasco spent the rest of the morning dealing with that upstairs on the twenty-fourth floor, e-mailing several key people, sending a brief personal message to the entire Tower staff of 265, then sending a long, personal memo to both Donald Trump and Anthony Gallicano to explain what had taken place and how he'd handled it.

"When does Shannon come back?" He asked Brenda, the woman who dealt with the residence side of the towers.

"Next Monday," she said.

"Her temp replacement . . . "

"Gilbert," she nodded. "I've taken care of the goodbye gift . . . "

"Tell him that there's an opening on the elevators. I think we've promised to move Ricardo off weekends and nights, so we'll let Ricardo take over from

Tomas and Gilbert can fill Ricardo's place while he's waiting for something to open up at the concierge desk. How's that?"

"He'll jump at it," Brenda said. "I know he will."

"Good." Belasco headed for the door. "Oh . . . and tell him I said he can keep the going-away presents."

AT ELEVEN O'CLOCK, Bill Riordan walked into Belasco's office with Carlos Vela. It was just the two of them. No one was there from the union. There was no lawyer.

Short and in his midtwenties, Vela stood with his head down, staring at the carpet.

"This is not a pleasant task," Belasco said, standing in front of his desk.

"Mr. Riordan already informed me," Vela said in a soft voice.

Belasco glared at Riordan, then told Vela, "I want you to know that the decision was made above my head. I also want you to know that I believe you . . . that you did not steal the coat."

Vela looked up at Belasco, "I did not steal anything . . . "

"For Chrissake, Pierre," Riordan bellowed. "He's guilty. He's fired." He turned to Vela, "You're outta here."

Belasco gave Riordan one of his looks of disdain, then turned to Vela, "There's paperwork you'll need to fill out. Mr. Riordan will walk you through the procedure upstairs." He extended his hand, "I'm very sorry about this, and I wish you good luck."

Vela was now in tears. "I didn't steal that coat."

"I know you didn't," Belasco said.

"The hell he didn't," Riordan said loudly. "The hell he didn't," and escorted Vela out of the office.

Throwing himself in his chair, he shook his head, "Riordan, you're an idiot."

That's when an e-mail came in from Antonia. "Pierre, I'm following up on a couple of queries from Anthony. Can you confirm, please, that Carlos Vela has been dismissed? And about the overdue rent at Scarpe Pietrasanta. Can you confirm, please, that it's been dealt with?"

He started to reply with one word, "Yes," but didn't push send. Instead, he picked up his phone and dialed Anthony Gallicano.

"You were asking about Carlos Vela and the overdue rent for Scarpe Pietrasanta . . . "

"I was?" Gallicano said. "Who's Scarpe . . . "

"Scarpe Pietrasanta."

"Never heard of him."

"And Carlos Vela?"

"Yeah, I saw Trump's e-mail. He had to go."

"I thought you knew that Scarpe Pietrasanta . . . it's a shoe company on the nineteenth floor . . . it's in the report."

"If it is, I didn't pay attention. Sorry."

"The owner died and his widow . . . "

"Nope. It's not really my neighborhood. This is what the boss gives you the big bucks for."

Belasco hung up and looked again at Antonia's e-mail.

Following up on a couple of queries from Anthony.

He wasn't exactly sure why, but instead of erasing it, he saved it in his hold file.

"Mr. Belasco? A moment of your time, please?"

Mr. Advani was at his door.

"Sir," Belasco stood up and walked from behind his desk to greet the man. "Please . . . " He extended his hand to shake and then brought him into the office.

Dressed in a dark suit, Advani sat on the couch while Belasco pulled up a chair.

"It was most kind of you to be there when we arrived home on Saturday."

Out of the corner of his eyes, Belasco noticed that two of Advani's assistants and several bodyguards were waiting just outside the door.

"It was my pleasure, sir. I trust that you and Mrs. Advani are settling in all right."

"Yes, we are doing very well, considering the amount of flying time we have done in the past few months."

"It doesn't get any easier," Belasco said.

"No, it doesn't," Advani forced a polite smile, then got down to business. "This evening's residents' board meeting."

"Yes sir."

"Will you attend?"

"I don't normally, sir. This is the residents' condo committee and unless there is a matter . . . "

"There is," he said. "It concerns this fool-hearty proposal by Mrs. Essenbach to install a rain forest. Have you ever heard of anything this outlandish?"

The Advanis had all of the fortieth floor and half of the forty-first. Mrs. Essenbach lived above the Advanis on forty-two. A year ago, she'd somehow managed to purchase the other half of forty-one.

Advani was very bitter about losing it, as he himself had tried to top her offer.

"I am aware that this will be discussed," Belasco said.

"And vetoed," Advani insisted. "There is no way that this woman should be allowed to disrupt our lives with major construction . . . or should I say, reconstruction . . . in the building. As you are well aware, her plans affect me directly, as her rain forest will be immediately next door to my second floor. Can you imagine the humidity and moisture problems? And the animals? I know she's not permitted to bring animals into the building, but Brazilian jungle animals? Mark my words, she fully intends to sneak them in. Along with insects? This is lunacy."

Belasco confided in Advani, "I have serious doubts, sir, that this will ever happen."

"She simply must not be permitted to do this," Advani said. "A jungle immediately next door to me? I will not permit it. I am prepared to do whatever I must to see that she is stopped." He stood up, shook Belasco's hand. "I hope I can count on you . . . "

Pierre answered him diplomatically, "I'm here to do whatever I can for the residents."

"Thank you," he said, and left.

Returning to his desk, Belasco typed an e-mail to the boss, reminding him of the background in the matter. He ended the memo with, "Mr. Advani assures me he is prepared to do, whatever he must to see that she is stopped. This might present you with the chance to back away and let him play the bad guy."

An e-mail came back saying, "When it comes to Mrs. Essenbach, I don't need, nor do I want, anyone else to play the bad guy. It is my pleasure."

Belasco liked that.

Advani and the boss were both taking aim at Mrs. Essenbach. But then, if Dr. Gildenstein was right—and Belasco had every reason to think he was—everyone else on the board was taking aim at her, too.

That provided cover for him.

I get to play the good guy.

Taking his calendar, he jotted down, "Drinks after Board meeting. 9:30. Gildenstein."

Above that, he'd noted his three o'clock appointment with Rebecca Battelli and someone from his accountant's office.

He picked up his phone and dialed Scarpe Pietrasanta to remind her.

The number went straight to voice mail.

He hesitated, was about to hang up, but at the last minute left a message. "It's Pierre Belasco. Checking up on you. Bye bye," and he hung up.

Bye bye? He winced. *I never say bye bye.*

AT TEN to three, Ronnie Rose showed up.

"Accountant here. Delivery."

"You told me you were going to send one of the juniors."

"No, you told me to send someone junior. My wife says this company makes sensational shoes and gave me her size, just in case. I'm here at her orders."

Belasco took Rose outside, turned left on Fifty-Sixth Street, and then into the atrium entrance. On the way to the nineteenth floor, he briefed Rose on Rebecca.

But the door at Scarpe Pietrasanta was still locked.

No one answered when he knocked.

Again, voice mail picked up his call.

"It's Pierre Belasco. I'd promised to drop by at three with my accountant. If you get this message, would you phone me please?"

This time when he hung up he didn't say "bye bye."

And after waiting in Belasco's office for twenty minutes, Rose left.

28

Arriving home after dinner on Saturday night, Zeke had asked Birgitta what she wanted to do.

She'd answered, "I'm staying here for the time being. Until you and I settle terms and I can get myself someplace to live."

Still in shock that his marriage had evaporated so abruptly, he'd told Zoey and Max, "Not to worry," and had driven that night to Malibu.

His place was toward the end of Malibu Colony Road. But even as secluded as it was, with Mikey Glass just up the street—he warned himself, *no sense announcing I'm home 'cause he'll show up*—Zeke made sure to park in his garage.

Like all the houses along that stretch, Zeke's was perpendicular to the beach. The entrance from the street led into a big living room that ran the length of the house to a glass-enclosed patio where all three sides opened completely onto a mahogany deck. Outside, there were chaise lounges and chairs for a dozen people to sit in the sun or have a meal at the big, pink marble table next to the huge outdoor grill.

The beach was down a few steps.

On one side of the living room there was a large, open kitchen with a dining room next to it. On the garage side, stairs led up to four bedrooms.

The master bedroom overlooked the beach from a patio. There were bedrooms for Zoey and Max and one for a guest. Above the garage he'd built himself an office with a patio facing the beach.

He'd bought the house while he was still married to Miriam and she'd hired Caesar Dahl to decorate it. Everyone in Malibu was vying for him, but Zeke knew Dylan Tyke, the set designer who was Caesar's lover. After Zeke got Dylan a job working on two pictures with Sean Penn's company, Dylan returned the favor by putting the Gimbels on the top of Caesar's "to do" list.

Unfortunately for Caesar, though, right after he finished the Gimbel beach house—in seashell whites, sandy off-whites, and Malibu pale blue—he and Dylan had a fight while at their home in Rio. And Dylan shot him.

Dylan wound up with fifteen years for manslaughter and Zeke's house became famous for being, as the *New York Times Magazine* cover story put it, "The Ultimate Dahl House."

Savannah had hinted about making some changes, which Zeke refused to let her do. And when Birgitta insisted on decorating the bedrooms and turning his office into a gym for her, Zeke also said no. His excuse was, this is how Caesar Dahl wanted it. But deep down what he really meant was, *this is how Miriam and I liked it.*

MOST OF SUNDAY morning was spent on his office patio, talking on the phone to Bobby Lerner about Birgitta's divorce demands and going over the details of the Sovereign Shields deal.

"You have a chance to look through their client list?" Bobby asked.

"Yeah, I did. And I know a lot of these guys. Some pretty good athletes, very marketable. But the funny thing is, when I went back to see, you know, historically, who Shields had and who the Trumans had, I found one of my neighbors in New York."

"Who's that?"

"Tennis player named Carson Haynes. He signed with them in 2001 but got out of the game a few years later. I'll have to ask him if they ever found him any work."

"Nope," Bobby said. "Don't remember him."

"He's married to a gorgeous Cuban girl who does the news in New York."

"Maybe you should try to sign her."

"Not a bad idea," Zeke said. "I see them every now and then at parties. Maybe next time I'll ask."

When Max and Zoey showed up—"Why should we have to stay in LA alone with her?"—the three of them drove halfway back to Santa Monica along the Pacific Coast Highway for a late brunch at Duke's.

Zoey and Max then went home to Miriam's.

On Sunday night, Zeke called Birgitta, but there was no answer at the house and, by then, he was too tired to call her cell.

OLINDA CAME to work early Monday morning and was surprised to find Zeke already there.

"Is Madame with you?"

"No," he said, and changed the subject. "What time is Nobu delivering?"

"At eleven."

"We'll be eight and we'll eat outside."

Olinda began preparing the table while Zeke phoned the Colony's gate-house off the Malibu Road and gave the guards there the names of his guests.

Bobby Lerner was first to arrive. "I stopped by the office to check your pre-nup. Essentially, she gets nothing. A little bit of cash to tide her over, but not much else. Basically, nada."

"What does 'not much else' mean?"

"Her two cars. Any jewelry you bought her. Possibly the two Julian Schnabel paintings. But I'm not sure about them. Of course, she will ask for the Warhols, but they're safe."

"There are three Schnabels."

"Okay, three Schnabels. Her lawyers will make up a list. If she doesn't re-member the third one, we won't remind her."

"What will be on their list?"

"Everything they can think of. Same shit we went through with Savannah, but worse because Birgitta is smarter."

"And nastier."

Bobby assured him, "No matter what they put on their list, the pre-nup is what it is. Everything in New York is safe because it's an office. Out here, trust me, we're watertight."

"How much is a little bit of cash?"

"A lot to her but not a lot to you. What are you worried about?"

"How much?" Zeke demanded.

"No more than two and a half."

"Fuck me." Zeke shook his head. "My father earned twenty-eight grand a year. With that he sent me to law school, sent my brother to med school and sent my sister someplace where she could find a doctor husband. How much did your old man earn?"

"Not as much as yours," he confessed. "But I never had a sister who wouldn't settle for anything less than a doctor."

Zeke kept shaking his head. "Two and a half? Doesn't that strike you as be-ing obscene?"

"In Chicago, yes. In LA? Imagine life without the pre-nup."

Lenny Silverberg was the next to arrive.

Now seventy, tall with white hair and a permanent tan, he'd hung up his Wall Street boots more than twenty years ago to become a full-time "dabbler." He dabbled in film and he dabbled in television, but what he really liked most was to dabble in music. Instead of stocks and shares, he bought songs.

"All I have to do is ask my grandchildren what they're listening to." His music catalog, supposedly holding nearly seventy-eight thousand songs, was estimated to be the third most valuable in the world, right behind the old Michael Jackson catalog and Paul McCartney's. "Except for some Sammy Cahn and Jimmy Van Heusen hits, and maybe a little Cole Porter, I don't have to listen to anything I own."

"How's the Bel Air," Zeke asked, "and your Mexican singer, whose name I can never remember?"

Silverberg grinned. "Remember how Ronnie used to say, nothing is better for the inside of man than the outside of a horse?" He was referring to Ronald Reagan's love of riding. "Well, every time I come out here I think, nothing is better for the outside of Lenny Silverberg than the inside of Abrille Hidalgo."

Then Bing O'Leary walked in with his father-in-law, Harry Kahn. O'Leary was Zeke's age and Kahn was probably somewhere around eighty. Zeke didn't know for sure and Kahn never mentioned it.

What Zeke did know about Kahn was that he'd sunk money into just about every hit movie over the past thirty years.

He also knew that O'Leary had been first in his class at Notre Dame Law, and was clever enough to overcome every hurdle Kahn and his wife Ilsa threw at him when he wanted to marry their only daughter, Ilene. O'Leary even converted. For that, he was named head of Kahn's private investment vehicle, Goose Chase, which Zeke guessed was probably worth a couple of billion.

While Olinda served drinks on the deck and the men talked, the delivery from Nobu arrived. Because Zeke didn't want the delivery guys to see who was at his house, he and Bobby and Olinda intercepted the order at the front door.

No sooner had the Nobu van driven off, when Carl Kravitz walked in with Ken Warring.

"Look who I bumped into?" Kravitz said with his arm around Warring. "We landed last night at the same time."

"But I got a better parking space," Warring said.

"That's 'cause you've got a better plane," Kravitz suggested.

And Warring agreed. "Yes, I do."

Kravitz was sixty, a Hollywood lawyer who'd also turned to investing in film and television, but had been particularly smart in understanding that the future of the media was the Internet. At a time when the studios were fighting to keep films off the Net, Kravitz was developing libraries of films and television programs that could be downloaded onto computers around the world. A year ago he sold out for $3.6 billion.

The last to arrive was James Malcolm Isbister.

A man in his late forties with iron-straight posture, close-cropped dark hair, a drawn face and a slightly pasty complexion—he was the only one wearing a suit, a white shirt and a tie.

"I appreciate your letting me join you," Isbister shook Zeke's hand firmly. "It's very nice to meet you. I've heard a lot about you."

"You're very welcome," Zeke said, bringing him into the house through the living room and onto the deck, where he introduced Isbister to the others. "Would you like a drink? G and T? V and T? Bloody Mary? Beer?"

"I don't drink," Isbister said. "Pomegranate juice, if you have some. Otherwise water will be fine."

"Pomegranate juice?" Zeke gave Isbister a slightly embarrassed look. "I'm afraid that narrows down the choice to bubbles or no bubbles."

"No bubbles," he said. "Thank you."

Zeke poured him a glass of Vittel, while Kravitz, Kahn and Warring asked Isbister all sorts of questions.

"Do you come out to the coast often? . . . Have you people invested in films before? . . . Where in New York are you from? . . . Why don't you take your jacket and tie off, you'll be more comfortable because it can get hot out here."

Isbister sipped his water and, polite to a fault, never answered a single question with anything more than a vague response.

He kept his tie and jacket on.

When Olinda nodded that everything was ready, Zeke announced, "Lunch is served."

They sat down at the table and began the ritual of passing around dozens of plates.

There was akadashi, miso and spicy seafood soups; shiitake and kelp salads; chicken, seafood and tempura udon; beef, chicken and salmon with teriyaki sauce; a selection of sashimi, tempura and sushi that included bigeye tuna, bluefin toro, yellowtail, Japanese red snapper, Japanese eel, octopus, live scallops and sea urchin.

Then there was lobster salad with spicy lemon dressing, bigeye and bluefin toro tartar, moroheiya pasta salad with fresh lobster, king crab tempura with amazu ponzu, Chilean sea bass with black bean sauce and, finally, for dessert, mojito ice cream, fresh mango and green tea mousse.

"I hate to be Cinderella," Ken Warring said when he finally put his spoon down and pushed what little remained of the mojito ice cream out of the way, "but I'm due in Dallas tonight for dinner."

"For Chrissake, Kenny," Silverberg raised his hands in surrender, "how the hell can you think about dinner after a lunch like that?"

"I'm not thinking about dinner . . . "

"Ever again," Kahn said.

"I'm thinking about being in Dallas." He turned to Zeke. "So tell us, where are we?"

Zeke moved his chair slightly away from the table, crossed his legs and began. "We looked at Pinewood, Thames and Astor in London, and we're ready to move on Astor. Great facilities that need refurbishment and a huge back lot."

"How much?" Kravitz wanted to know.

"In the neighborhood of eighty-five. That's sterling. In dollars, call it one thirty-five and change. One forty. But that includes the back lot, and if this thing goes south, it's prime land for development. Our downside there is covered."

O'Leary asked, "Last time you were talking about Canada."

"Montreal," Zeke said. "Vancouver won't work and Toronto is way over-priced. But around the corner from the port of Montreal, there's a place called Nuns Island. It's mixed-use residential and commercial. We want to pick up the old Cine Quebec lot. Three big sound stages, small back lot, loads of space for production facilities."

"How much is that?" Kravitz asked.

"If we can keep this thing quiet, we're probably only looking at forty-five or fifty. If word leaks, put twenty-five percent on top of it."

"Downside?" Silverberg asked.

"Right now the area is zoned industrial. But we've got someone up there looking into what it will take to change it to residential. It's an island, people want to live there and no one's making any more land."

"Get it changed to residential," Warring proposed, "and let's not waste time making movies."

The others laughed.

"New York," O'Leary asked. "Silvercup? That's not going to be easy."

"That may not be necessary," Zeke said. "We could probably buy it if we really wanted. But then what? We'd wind up with facilities in Queens and have the same problem selling them that they have now. We want the West Side. We're looking at two piers. One or both would be great. We can connect to a lot in Jersey, across the river and a little south. That's what Dick Wolf did with his *Law and Order* franchise. Offices and studios in Manhattan. At Chelsea Piers. A whole city to shoot on the street. Then a sound stage in Jersey with permanent sets. We've found a disused oil terminal port in Jersey. We build a lot there and run our own ferry service back and forth."

"I hope that means you've given up on your dreams of the Bronx." Kahn shook his head. "I was born there and couldn't get out fast enough. You were born someplace else and wanted to go there willingly."

"It's six acres, Harry," Zeke said. "Big industrial zone. I thought if we created jobs, Albany would send us money."

"Albany's broke," Kahn pointed out.

"The city isn't. Bloomberg says it is, but we can deal with him. Except for Chelsea Piers, the others are falling into the Hudson. We take the one that's ripest for picking and redevelop and he'll make sure that things happen. Long lease. Tax breaks. Jersey is slightly different, but they're as broke as New York and the land is sitting there doing nothing. Call it twenty to buy and another forty to develop."

"Whatever happened to Brooklyn?" Kahn wanted to know.

Zeke told him, "Coney Island. Gone largely residential. Anyway, even if we could have gotten in there, it would have been another Silvercup. Except further away. Same reason we turned down Staten Island. Would have worked, except you can't get there from anywhere. The piers are our best bet."

"So far, so good." Warring tried to add up the totals. "Six hundred?"

"About that," Zeke agreed.

Now Kravitz said, "Last piece of the puzzle is LA."

Silverberg pointed out, "That means taking over one of the big guys. But do we really want to get in a fight with Sony?"

"No need," Zeke said, "I want to buy Polyscope."

"Polyscope?" Silverberg looked at him like he was crazy. "They haven't made a movie since Tom Mix."

"That's what you think," Zeke responded. "They're half-owned by Astor in the UK. They've done a bunch of indies in the past few years. Not a very good business. But then, they're not very good businessmen. What Polyscope offers us is something that none of the big kids on the block can. Our own airport."

"Airport?" O'Leary asked, "What the hell are you talking about?"

"Ever hear of Eddie Butch Bauer?" When no one had, Zeke continued, "Navy pilot. One of the original aces during World War Two. Killed in a dogfight over Wake Island after sinking a Japanese submarine. Flew a couple of hundred missions. Big deal hero."

"This a movie project?" Kravitz asked.

"No," Zeke smiled. "It's an abandoned Navy air training facility. Bauer Field. In Chino Hills. About an hour away. Bobby found the land on a government list. They own it. And guess who lives right next door? Polyscope."

Kahn asked, "What's there now?"

"Besides a handful of buildings owned by Polyscope? How about nine acres of concrete overrun with crabgrass."

"How much?" Silverberg said, "Because this sounds like one of those too-good-to-be-true deals."

Lerner explained, "Polyscope bought an option on the land from the government thirty years ago. I looked into it and, believe it or not, it's still good. Someone in the government screwed up, the option never timed out and Polyscope never had the money to exercise it. For all I know, they don't even remember that there is an option. We take Astor, that brings us into Polyscope, and Polyscope's long-forgotten option gives us the biggest and best lot in the business."

The men sitting around Zeke's table looked at each other and, one by one, started nodding.

Everybody . . . except James Malcolm Isbister. "What makes you think if you develop this property, anyone will use it?"

"You see my list of clients?" Zeke said, "We don't merely represent them, we package deals. Our writers, our directors, our stars . . . now, our studios."

"Antitrust," Isbister said right away.

"No way," Bobby shook his head.

Kravitz agreed. "Take over a studio and the government might look into it. Build your own . . . no problem."

"We're not talking forced labor," Bobby continued. "There are plenty of studios still standing that real competition is simply not an issue."

Isbister thought about that. "This is, obviously, not a business we know. The real estate side interests us, but I don't think we want to gamble on the motion picture side of this."

"We can structure a deal," Bobby offered, "so that you're only a real estate partner."

"That would be more to our liking," Isbister said. "How much are you looking for?"

Zeke added it up. "We're at six now. Polyscope, the option and redevelopment costs add, say, another six. Then we factor in an additional third for running costs. Total is in the ballpark of one point six billion."

"First year's return?" Isbister asked.

Zeke admitted, "Zero."

"Second year?"

"Zero."

Isbister didn't understand. "How long do you expect to be running a charity?"

"Five years out," Zeke said, "we're either bust or we own the world."

"Gentlemen . . . " Ken Warring stood up. "Off to Dallas. I'm in."

Harry Kahn and Bing O'Leary soon followed. "We're in."

Isbister announced that it was time he left, too. "I will study the numbers.

As I said, it's not a business we know, but if you . . . " He looked at Bobby Lerner . . . "if you will send me a real estate–only plan . . . the kind of money you're talking about is not beyond our means. Not at all."

"I will e-mail it to you tonight," Bobby promised.

"Thank you." Isbister handed him a card that had nothing but his name and e-mail address. He shook everyone's hands—"I will be in touch shortly"—and left.

Now Lenny Silverberg headed for the door. "I have something waiting for me at the Bel Air. Gentlemen, I'm sure you understand. Count me in."

Zeke looked at all the food left on the table. "Olinda . . . you take this home. Everything."

"Everything?" Olinda asked. "There is a lot . . . "

"Everything," Zeke said. "Except . . . maybe I'll pick and choose a little for the plane tonight."

"Where are you off to?" Kravitz asked.

"New York."

"You just came back from New York."

"Big party tomorrow night with Bill. And an appointment on Wednesday morning."

"Bill who?"

Zeke made a face.

"Oh," Kravitz said, "that Bill."

"I'm back Wednesday night."

"Listen, if you and Birgitta want to come down to Cabo in ten days, Arnie said he wants to come down, so it will just be the five of us."

"Arnie called me," Zeke said. "I like him. But how the hell do you book the ex-governator into a rom-com with Jennifer Aniston?" Then Zeke took a deep breath and confessed to Kravitz, "Birgitta and I are splitting up."

"Oh," Kravitz said. "I'm sorry to hear that. Is there someone . . . "

"No."

"Come alone if you want. Otherwise, take a rain check. You're always welcome." He patted Zeke on the shoulder. "What do you think of our new best friend, Mr. Isbister?"

"Strange man," Zeke said.

"Wouldn't even loosen his tie," Bobby added.

"Yeah, but . . . " Kravitz said, "when he heard the numbers, he didn't even blink."

"Hey," Zeke said, "you wouldn't blink either if your boss controlled twenty percent of the world's rice."

29

D r. Robert Gildenstein and his wife, Dr. Susan O'Malley, who were both orthopedic surgeons, lived in a large three-bedroom apartment on the thirty-seventh floor with their twin four-year-old daughters.

About a year ago, right after they'd moved in, *New York Magazine* ran a big feature story about them titled, "The Most Powerful Husband-Wife Doctor Team in the City."

According to the magazine, Susan and Robert had saved so many athletic careers that more than one hundred former patients had since been inducted into various Halls of Fame or won world records or owned World Cup medals.

"If you're an athlete whose career has been cut short by injury," the story concluded, "there is hope. But first you need to find their unlisted number, and then you'd better have a world-class athlete's salary because hope for those who enter the inner sanctum of their unmarked, very private, world-class clinic on Park Avenue comes at a very steep world-class price."

Pierre Belasco liked them because their taste level was also world class.

He admired their furniture. Most of it was George III, like the fall-front desk that lived in their study. It was a sister piece to one owned by Thomas Jefferson and on display in the South Square Room at Monticello.

He also liked their art. They owned two good Constables and a very respectable Turner, in addition to several small Whistler drawings.

But it was only when he arrived that night, after the residents' board meeting, that he discovered he also liked their food.

Serving board members a cup of coffee and some pound cake might be fine for other people, but the Gildensteins were offering six different minisized French pastries and ice-cold 2002 vintage Dom Perignon champagne.

"You cater a very good meeting," he told Susan when she insisted he have another glass of champagne.

The gathering had been called for 8:30, had adjourned by 9:20, and now, at five to ten, most of the board members had already left.

"Robert and I decided that if we don't set the standard," she said to Belasco, "then, at the next meeting, whoever hosts it will serve prunes wrapped in bacon and diet Dr. Pepper."

He grinned, "I don't believe that for a moment."

"Maybe . . . well, not quite . . . but almost. We live in a building where people don't cook. This is reheat city."

"Surely not everybody . . . "

"Pierre, I have visited perhaps three dozen apartments in this building, and in at least two out of every three of those, the kitchen has never been used. Not once. I notice these things."

"I suppose if people send out every night," Belasco nodded, "it's like room service."

"Remember when Robertos Santos first moved in?" She reminded him, "He was hurt and on the Yankees' disabled list for two months. I know because I operated on his knee. Well, he decided he wanted to be neighborly . . . not a lot but a little . . . so he invited us and half a dozen other people up to his place to watch the All-Star game. He said he was feeling sorry for himself, not playing, and wanted company."

"Sounds like a nice thing to do. But don't tell me you were expecting him to cook."

"Of course not. He catered the party . . . with hot dogs brought in from Yankee Stadium."

"Relish and sauerkraut? Beer in plastic cups? Sounds right for baseball. And all the more reason why you and Robert should be nicer to Mrs. Essenbach. She has her own chef and doesn't do ballpark hot dogs."

"After tonight . . . " She shook her head, " . . . any food she serves us will be laced with strychnine."

"That bad?"

"Unanimous against her."

Prakash Advani walked up to say hello to Belasco and goodnight to Susan. "Your desserts were splendid."

"Thank you. I was telling Pierre that Katarina Essenbach won't be a happy camper when she finds out."

"Unanimous," Advani said to Belasco. "Not even one abstention that might have otherwise been in her favor."

Belasco wondered, "Who gets to be the lucky one to tell her?"

"We write her," Susan said.

"If you like," Belasco volunteered, "I will break the news to her. She'll only hear about it anyway. And it might be better for everyone if she heard it from me."

Susan bowed. "You're a better man than I am, Gunga Din."

Advani looked at her in an odd way. "Gunga Din?"

"Sorry about that," she said. "Nothing personal. Care for more champagne?"

LEAVING THE Gildenstein's apartment, Belasco worried that ten o'clock might be too late but dialed Mrs. Essenbach's number, anyway. "I hope I haven't disturbed you."

"Pierre . . . " she gushed, "you never disturb me. How lovely to hear your voice this late in the evening. Where are you?"

"I'm in the Tower."

"Oh yes," she said, as if she wanted him to believe she'd forgotten, "the residents' board meeting."

"Indeed." He hesitated, "Would it be convenient if I stopped by?"

"It is never anything but convenient," she assured him, "to see you. Especially after hours."

"I'll be right there," he promised, rang for the lift, and when the doors opened, he told Ricardo, "Forty-two, please."

Her front door was already open.

Still, he rang the bell.

"Let yourself in," she called from deep inside the apartment.

He did.

"Keep walking, and you'll find me. A bit like hide and seek."

He didn't like that. "Mrs. Essenbach . . . unfortunately, I cannot stay long."

"Did you ever play hide and seek when you were a young boy, Pierre?"

"I'm afraid it's late . . . "

"All right then," she sighed. "I'm in the study."

He found her sprawled out across the couch, wearing a fur dressing gown. There was a bottle of champagne on the table in front of her.

"Good evening."

"You can pour us both a glass," she said.

"None for me, thank you." But he did pour one for her.

"Give me the news." She raised her glass, and motioned for him to sit down. "Tell me that God is in heaven and all is right with the world."

"I'm sure he is," Belasco said, still standing. "But I'm afraid the news is not good. The board voted no."

Her mood changed instantly. "How did that happen?"

"I don't know how or why, except that they voted no."

"How close was the vote?"

He could see her anger building up. "It was . . . not at all close."

"Who voted for me?"

He wanted her to know the truth. "No one."

"What about you?"

"I'm not on the board. I don't have a vote."

"This is Advani's doing. He's the instigator."

"Again, Madame, I don't know what was discussed, as I'm not privy to the meetings . . . "

She demanded, "Tell me how this happened? How could you let this happen."

"I assure you, Madame . . . "

"You already assured me. You assured me that you would see this through for me. Now you've turned your back on me . . . "

Without warning, she threw the champagne glass at him.

"Madame . . . "

It missed.

" . . . if you will excuse me, there is nothing more to discuss this evening."

"You let this happen . . . you gave me assurances . . . "

"I did nothing of the kind, Madame." He turned on his heels and started to leave. "Good evening."

She screamed at him, "You assured me that you would take care of this. You made promises to me."

BELASCO IMMEDIATELY returned to his office, shut his door, sat down at his desk, and wrote a very detailed two-page report of his confrontation with Mrs. Essenbach.

He e-mailed it to the boss and copied Anthony Gallicano, because he wanted them to hear it from him, first.

By the time he got home, Gallicano had answered. "I am forwarding this to the lawyers. It's important that, should the matter somehow escalate, although I don't think it will, we have something on the record from you. Don't worry about her. She has been a pain in the ass to everyone since day one. Good job and good night."

Half an hour later, an e-mail came in from Bill Riordan. "You've made my night. Us 1, Man in Underwear 0."

30

Alicia was in her double-sized, heated bathtub, up to her neck in bubbles, with her head on one of the two pillows at the end, holding several typed pages high out of the water to keep them dry, when Carson walked in.

"Excuse me, madam, I'm working my way through medical school, may I examine you."

She glared at him. "Is there no privacy anymore?"

He started pulling off his clothes. "Not when you're naked."

When he was, he got into the tub with her, sitting at the other end so that he could face her, spilling bubbles and soapy water all over the floor.

"As I was saying . . . " He leaned forward and moved his hand all the way up her leg.

Her eyes opened wide. "What do you think you're doing?"

"Say . . . ah."

"Hey," she squirmed, bent her left knee, picked up her foot and put her heel up against his groin. "Leave me alone or else . . . "

"You're so mean." He pulled back his hand.

She moved her foot so her toes were touching him there. "Really?"

He smiled. "Not really."

Then she moved her foot away.

"Yes, really. Put it back."

She shook her head, "Not really," and started to read to him from the typed pages she was holding out of the water. "Like the English pilgrims of the seventeenth century, the Finfolkmen left the Orkney Islands to escape religious persecution . . . "

"What?"

She repeated, "The Finfolkmen left the Orkney Islands . . . he's surrounded by them."

"Who is?"

"L. Arthur Farmer. They protect him."

"Who does?"

"The Finfolkmen."

"What the fuck are Finfolkmen?" He asked, then wondered, "And why does that sound like an answer on *Jeopardy*?"

"They're a mythical creature."

"From Finland?"

"No, from the Orkney Islands." She flicked through a few pages. "Here," and handed one to him.

He looked at it. "Finfolk kidnap fishermen and force them into servitude." Then he looked at her. "Huh?"

"Read on," she ordered.

"They are territorial and greedy. They have a special weakness for silver."

"See?"

"See what?"

"They have a special weakness for silver. L. Arthur Farmer's silver?"

"L. Arthur Farmer's silver? The rice guy? Does it say somewhere that they can't tell the difference between Chinese food and dimes?"

"This is for real," she said.

He shook his head. "Alicia, these are mythical creatures."

"Finfolk kidnap fishermen. What if they've kidnapped Farmer?"

"Mythical creatures can't kidnap anyone because they don't exist. That's why they're called . . . mythical."

"You don't understand anything."

"I understand some things . . . " He reached for her under the water again. "Did you say ah yet?"

"Hey." She moved his hand away, "Gimme . . . " and took the page back. "It says here . . . " She looked for the line she wanted to read . . . "they disguise themselves as sea animals, plants, or even floating clothes."

"Well then . . . " He took a deep breath and nodded, reassuringly, "The mystery is solved. All you have to do is find an old man being held captive by a geranium bush and pile of wet undershirts."

"Stop it. Listen to this." She read, "Worshipping the creature during the Middle Ages, the Finfolkmen . . . " She reminded him, "those are the religious people, not the mythical creature who are just Finfolk . . . " then continued reading, . . . "evolved a belief in the power of the sea and left the Orkney Islands, landing in northern New Brunswick, Canada, where they established a small religious colony. By the end of the following century, some of them had migrated west to establish a second religious colony on the shores of Lake Superior, along Michigan's Upper Peninsula."

Carson wasn't having it. "This mythical creature they worship . . . if they're not from Finland, why aren't they called Orkneyfolkmen?"

"You're impossible."

He crossed his eyes and stuck out his tongue. "But loveable."

"This is important to me."

"Okay. I'm all ears." He made that face again, but this time he pushed his ears forward.

Alicia disregarded him. "They don't worship mythical creatures. These are Christians who believe they are derived from a mythical creature and, accordingly, deny both the Roman and Episcopal glossary."

He stared at her. "What the hell does that mean?"

"It means . . . that's why they had to flee England."

"Sorry to be pedantic but . . . the Orkneys are part of Scotland. And Scotland isn't England."

"You are being pedantic."

"I already apologized for being pedantic. It's just that thinking Scotland and England are the same place can get you into big trouble in Thurso."

She scowled at him and put the heel of her foot back in his groin. "And thinking that you're not going to listen to what I have to say can get you into big trouble in little Mr. Carson-land."

He raised his arms. "I surrender."

"Wise move." She pulled her foot away, found another page and read, "They shun contacts with all but their own, maintaining a secretive and closed community dedicated to their own purist rendition of the bible, which predates King John. They believe in honoring God, country, hard toil, and their elders. Every young man is expected to serve in the military before returning to the community to marry and propagate."

"Ah . . . " Carson smiled, leaned forward, and reached under the water. "Speaking of propagating . . . "

She brought her knees up and moved as far away from him as she could get in the big tub. "Listen . . . "

"If I pretend to listen, then can we propagate?"

"You fake listening," she warned, "and I fake propagating."

"Deal." He sat back in the tub. "I'm listening."

She thumbed through several pages. "Here . . . Farmer, who was born in Grand Rapids, Michigan, is known to have spent summers in the Upper Peninsula as a child at his grandfather's cabin. As Farmer's people were themselves pilgrims from England, he would have earned a certain trust among the Finfolkmen."

"Say that again."

She did.

He repeated, "A certain trust among the Finfolkmen."

"That's what it says."

He thought about that, then wondered, "Like Howard Hughes and the Mormons?"

"Yes. Exactly. These guys have cut him off from everybody. They're holding him captive. He's their prisoner. They own him."

"Him and all his silver."

"Duh," she said, as if that was obvious.

"You are assuming that he's still alive. Which he probably isn't."

"Who knows?"

"The guy hasn't been seen by anyone who isn't a mythical creature since . . . "

"No one's seen him . . . except his Finfolkmen captors."

"If he's alive."

"Yes," she agreed, "if he's alive. Because they don't want anyone to see him. But does it really matter if he's alive or dead? They own his business."

"But if he's dead, which he probably is , . . "

" . . . and if they can make people think he's alive while they're running everything, then they've become him."

Carson decided, "So it's Howard Hughes meets the Wizard of Oz."

"Exactly," she agreed. "The Finfolkmen *are* the Wizard of Oz."

Now Carson shut one eye and stared at her with the other to show her he was thinking. "If the world knows Farmer is dead, his share price goes through the floor. As long as the markets think he's alive . . . "

"Now you are listening."

"If it quacks like a yellow brick road . . . "

"That's why I love you." She leaned out of the tub and tossed the papers on the floor, far enough away to stay dry. Then she brought her toes back to where they had been and started flicking them against him.

"Oh," he looked at her. "Just when I start getting interested. Don't you want to talk about Finfolkmen?"

She moved onto her knees, spilling more water onto the floor, and reached for him. "Let's finfuckman, instead."

TUESDAY

31

"**Y**ou are okay with this?" David asked. "Right?"

"No, I am not okay with this," Tina replied. "Wrong!"

"I'm only talking about the way I've got it set up now."

"No. You cannot convince me."

"Y'all said you wanted to stay separate."

"Separate, yes. 'Cause I know you're going to do it, no matter what I say. But I'm not okay with it, not any part of this."

"Listen to me . . . I'm ring-fenced. I keep telling you. There can't be any fallout to you."

"I don't know how many times I have to say it, and yet you insist on going ahead with this . . . "

He took a deep breath to show her he was exasperated with her. "I've listened to your opinion about this six times."

"And if you keep asking me, you're going to hear it six more times. Nothing's going to change."

"Y'all got that right. Nothing's gonna change. What I'm doing is fine. It's perfect. You're not at all involved. I'm a big boy. I got me a passport and I've had all my shots . . . "

"You're a big boy who's acting like a schmuck. What if all this goes wrong?"

"It can't."

"Other than that, Mrs. Lincoln, how did you enjoy the play?"

"Why can't y'all leave this alone?"

"Remember two weeks ago when you said the same thing about that cargo of Cuban mahogany that turned out to be maple or birch or some other kind of crap from Bangladesh?"

"Stop throwing that in my face. We'll get that money back."

"Yeah," she said, "when the cows come home."

"Shit happens," he said. "That's business."

She waved him off. "This time David, when shit happens, I'm not sticking around long enough to tell you I told you so."

He shook his head and went to the far side of the room to a spare desk, where he sat down at a terminal and began looking for some deals he could do.

She sat down on the other side of the room at her desk and started looking for some deals she could do.

TINA SPOTTED a small cargo of Sony DVD players in Honduras, about $40,000 worth, but couldn't get in fast enough and lost it.

David thought he found an oil tanker out of Lagos that was late coming into Montevideo with $28 million worth of crude, but after spending two hours trying to grab it, he discovered that Exxon had already diverted it to Port Elizabeth, South Africa.

Tina found $2.3 million worth of polycarbonate panels on their way to Dunedin, New Zealand. She bought the shipment from a trader in Cairo, sold it to another trader in Houston, and walked away with $22,400.

David spotted that trade come up on his screen and wanted to shout over to her, "Well done," but he knew if he did, she would think he was patronizing her, so he went back to looking for something big.

Tina now got on the phone, called Fabrice over on Madison Avenue and asked him, "Any chance Martine can come by for a fast wash and a manicure?"

Fabrice must have said no, but that he would squeeze her in if she came to the salon, because David heard her say, "All right, I understand, thanks Fabrice . . . I'll be right there."

She logged off and left without saying anything to him.

Just as well, he thought, and went back on the hunt.

He found a $112,000 shipment of ink stranded in Colombo, Sri Lanka, looked at it closely—it was a fast in-and-out deal, the kind that Tina liked—but decided to let it go.

Then he found a cargo of newsprint, about $400,000 worth, stuck in Masqat. He disliked shipments from that part of the world because getting from there to the rest of the world meant sailing through the western Indian Ocean. With Somalian pirates all over those waters grabbing whatever they could, insurance rates were sky high. Even if he found someone to take the cargo, he'd have to guarantee delivery—which other traders were insisting on because of the pirate threat—which meant his margins would be wiped out by the inflated insurance costs.

Some traders like Asil bragged about overinsuring, hoping that the pirates would seize the ship and its cargo, but that game took too much effort for too little return, and David wasn't interested.

He left the newsprint in Masqat, started looking for something else, then thought again about the ink in Colombo. "What the hell . . . "

He bought it for $229,000, sold it for an even $240,000, and put the trade through Tina's account.

"There y'all go," he looked at her empty desk. "That's eleven grand for doing nothing because I'm a real nice guy."

Except, deep down, he knew she would say, *Eleven grand is not enough of an apology for being a schmuck.*

That's when Uncle RD called. "What's happening?"

"Nothing. What's up?"

"Trying to get me into a swap deal with Azerbaijan and Belarus. The Venezuelans are doing it, but the State Department might be looking down its nose at us making money for that Commie-prick Chavez. So I reckon we could move it through Mexico. Y'all still got those contacts with the Rojas brothers down there?"

"Yeah, I do," David assured him. "No problem."

"I'll let you know when I need you to make that call. Also, might have a small deal on some low-sulfur number-two diesel fuel. Where's the best spot?"

David clicked onto a spot-oil trading screen and ran his eyes over the numbers. "LA is slightly better than New York."

"Gulf Coast?"

"Way distant third."

"I'll let you know about that, too."

"Everything all right?" David asked.

Uncle RD's voice changed. "Well . . . you tell me. I got a call from Tina. And don't you be telling her I told you, 'cause if you do, I'll whip your ass so bad . . . "

"I know what she's calling about," he said. "But she doesn't understand the deal."

"She said you're getting into bed with some Colombians."

"That's what I mean . . . she doesn't understand."

"Son, why don't y'all help me understand."

David took a deep breath and told RD the whole story, ending with, "We never touch their money. They said it's tax evasion . . . "

"You're not really that naïve, are you?"

"I believe them. But even if it is . . . "

"Drug money? Of course it's drug money."

"Even if it is, we never touch it. It's in a lawyer's client account, and he deals with the bank."

"Tina's worried."

"I know. But y'all gotta trust me when I say, she's protected. Everybody is."

"You?"

"Me too."

Uncle RD paused. "Y'all get your ass whipped on this, boy, and we're gonna leave you swinging in the wind."

"I know what I'm doing."

"Sounds to me like you're betting the ranch on that and, frankly, I wouldn't bet the ranch that tomorrow is Wednesday."

Sometimes his uncle really pissed him off, but he didn't dare remind him of that. "Let me know when you want me to call the Rojas brothers."

"Y'all keep your ass protected, and don't you dare tell Tina I called."

He promised, "I won't," hung up, mumbled to himself, "They don't understand that it's foolproof," and went right back to looking for that really big trade.

But the market was flat.

There were a bunch of small- to medium-sized deals floating around— porcelain, silk, cement, there was even another cargo of Cuban mahogany— but he didn't go near any of them, especially the Cuban mahogany, because he reckoned the time had come to prove Tina and Uncle RD wrong by putting all his eggs into one huge killer-deal basket.

32

The block was at a standstill, with cars stuck in the mess—mostly Yellow Cabs—and drivers showing their displeasure by honking their horns and shouting obscenities out their windows, as traffic also backed up along Fifth Avenue because no one could turn into Fifty-Sixth Street.

"It's us," David the relief doorman said as Pierre Belasco walked up to him.

"What's the problem?"

David pointed to a huge moving van that was half turned into the Tower's garage but unable to get inside because the door was still shut. "Same thing like six months ago."

Belasco walked over to the entrance and found Big Sam, the building engineer, yelling above the street noise into a walkie-talkie to someone who was obviously on the other side of the garage door. "Then go manual," he shouted. "Get the fucker open."

"Thought you said it was fixed," Belasco reminded Big Sam.

"It is," he said, as a static-filled answer came back over the walkie-talkie. "It's the lower lever that's jammed . . . we're trying to . . . "

Big Sam looked at Pierre. "Nothing like a little excitement to start the day."

The van driver was out of his cab, telling the small crowd that had gathered along the sidewalk, "I can't even back out . . . "

"Move your fucking truck," someone shouted from a stuck car, "you stupid prick of an idiot . . . "

The van driver turned to the man yelling at him. "The keys are in the van, asshole, you move it."

The man in the car opened his door and started to get out. "Fuck you . . . "

The van driver pulled himself up to his full height—he was tall and heavy-set—and shouted to the driver, "You got a problem asshole?"

"Yeah, I do," the driver said.

Belasco told the van driver, "Please get back into your truck, we'll take care of it," and then walked over to the man shouting from his car. "Sir, we're doing the best we can."

"Fuck you too," he shouted at Belasco and tried to open his door.

Belasco looked around, saw a cop hurrying down the block, and put his hand on the car door to stop the man from getting out.

"Take your fucking hands off my car," he shouted.

"Certainly, sir." But Belasco left them right where they were. "Officer," he called to the cop, "this gentleman is causing a scene."

The cop demanded to know, "What's going on here? You got the whole friggin' city tied up in gridlock." He looked at the man in the car. "And you, you stay right where you are. Get out of that car, and you're going to jail."

Belasco smiled at the man, took his hands off the car door, and walked away.

"Fuck you," the man shouted at Belasco.

But the cop thought he was shouting at him. "Say what? One more word out of you . . . "

The man in the car rolled up his window and sat there, cursing under his breath.

"Thank you, officer," Belasco said as horns kept honking. "We're trying to get this solved."

The cop turned to the drivers honking their horns and gestured for them to stop.

They didn't.

"Stop," he pointed to several cars.

A cabbie called to the cop, "Officer, don't just stand there, do something, get them to move the truck out of the way," and leaned on his horn for at least fifteen seconds.

"You'd better get that door open before World War Three breaks out," the cop warned Belasco, then walked over to the cabbie. "Sit there, shut up, and if you honk that horn again, you're going to jail."

"Got it," Big Sam shouted into the walkie-talkie, then turned to Belasco, "Got it."

The garage door opened.

The van driver started his engine, and within a minute he was inside the garage.

Fifty-Sixth Street was moving again.

"Fuck you," the driver who'd been cautioned by the cop shouted at Belasco as he drove down the block.

The cabbie who'd been warned about honking his horn leaned on his horn again as he drove away.

Belasco patted Big Sam on the back and smiled. "Please don't hesitate to ask if I can solve any other problems for you."

Inside, he found Shannon, the concierge who'd just had a baby, back on duty.

"I want to see the pictures." Belasco motioned to her to come into his office. "Bring them in."

She followed him in, pulled out her phone and showed him the photos of her baby.

"Looks like you," Belasco said, as she brought one photo after another up on the tiny screen. "He's beautiful."

She pointed, "That's the New York Yankee pajama set that Mr. and Mrs. Trump sent us. And here . . . " she changed the photo . . . "that's the crib from you. It's beautiful. Thank you, so much, again."

Now Timmins appeared at his door. "Got a minute?"

Motioning for him to come in, Belasco smiled at Shannon, "He really is a beautiful baby."

She said, "Thank you," nodded at Timmins and walked out of the office.

Belasco asked Timmins, "Aren't you off duty?"

"This is so good I couldn't go home without showing it to you." He waved a DVD, put it in the machine, and turned on the big screen.

The view was from a camera on the forty-second floor and showed the main hallway in front of the three elevators.

Belasco watched as nothing happened.

Then suddenly, he saw movement on the right side of the screen. It looked to him as if someone had come out of a door . . . Mrs. Essenbach's door . . . stumbled and fell. By the way that person was hurrying back to his feet, Belasco realized he'd been shoved.

"Here it comes," Timmins pointed to the screen.

A short, bald-headed man, probably in his late sixties, moved into view, and all he was wearing was a pair of briefs and a sleeveless undershirt.

"Who's that?"

Timmins replied, "Current husband."

"Until last week I didn't know that she had a current husband."

"She does . . . or did. She tossed him out in his underwear."

Belasco saw the time code and realized that this had only taken place seven or eight minutes after he'd stormed out of her apartment. "What happens to him?"

"Watch." Timmins fast-forwarded the DVD.

The view changed from the hallway on the forty-second floor to the residents' lobby.

Belasco saw the man in his underwear step out of an elevator, hurry through the lobby, and go out onto the street.

Timmins fast-forwarded yet again.

Now the shot was from the camera facing the curb.

The man in his underwear hailed a taxi. A cab pulled up, Jorge the doorman helped him in, and the cab pulled away.

Turning off the DVD, Timmins announced, "Elvis has left the building."

Belasco grinned, finally understanding Riordan's message—Us 1, Man in Underwear 0—and warned Timmins, "We have to be careful with that. The lawyers will need a copy."

"The boss saw it last night. I had to show it to him. He said he's having copies made to send out with his Christmas cards."

Belasco smiled. "I can see why. But before we start selling copies on eBay, I'll speak to him about it."

Pierro, the concierge on duty with Shannon, appeared at the door. "Sir . . . Mrs. Gooding for you."

Belasco said, "Thank you," to Timmins and followed him out.

A beautifully dressed elderly woman was standing in the lobby with her son and daughter-in-law.

"Mrs. Gooding," he extended his hand to her. "We're going to miss you."

She took his hand. "I always knew this day would come."

Belasco shook hands with her son and daughter-in-law, then smiled warmly at Mrs. Gooding, "Please . . . don't be a stranger."

"Thank you, Pierre." Her eyes got red. "Thank you for everything . . . for so many wonderful memories."

He went to her, put his arms around her, and she started crying.

Belasco held her as he said to her son, "Your father was a great man. And your mother is one of the truly great ladies."

Shannon motioned to Belasco and caught his eye. Belasco understood and nodded to her. She and Pierro came from behind the concierge desk carrying a dozen long-stemmed roses and handed them to Mrs. Gooding.

Now the woman was weeping. She took the flowers, hugged Shannon, hugged Pierro, and hugged Belasco again.

"Thank you," the son said, then reached for his mother. "Come on, mom, we have to go."

She looked up at Belasco and he kissed her on both cheeks. "Trump Tower won't be the same without you."

Stepping back, she let her son take her arm, waved at Shannon and Pierro, and walked out onto the street.

Belasco quickly turned back to his office.

He didn't want Shannon or Pierro to see that his eyes were red, too.

"Am I interrupting?" Rebecca Battelli was standing right there. "Do you have a moment?"

"No," he smiled at her. "You're not . . . I mean, yes . . . please. I'm happy to see you." He showed her into his office.

For an instant he thought about shutting his door so they wouldn't be disturbed, but he didn't.

"Please . . . " He motioned to the couch.

She sat there and he pulled up a chair for himself.

"Do you always get misty-eyed when someone leaves Trump Tower?"

He gave a little shrug. "The Goodings were here twenty-two years. He made his money in rubber. And when he passed away five months ago, his obituary in the *New York Times* noted that, over his lifetime, he and his wife had given away more than five hundred million dollars to various charities."

"That's a lot of money."

"You can live on that," he joked.

She smiled politely.

"They were always very nice people, especially to the staff." He said, "You know, we have people coming and going here every month. Sometimes . . . well, sometimes it's not always easy to say goodbye."

"It's even harder when you don't have the opportunity to say goodbye." He knew she was referring to her husband's death.

"You know those notices that other people put into the paper?" He said, "The ones that say the management and staff of some company regrets the loss of . . . whoever? When Mr. Gooding passed away, there were several hundred of them in the *Times*. They ran for more than a week."

She looked at Belasco sadly. "There were only two for my husband. And I paid for both of them."

He didn't know what to say—the little voice in the back of his head warned him, *just shut up*—so he said nothing.

She looked away, turning her eyes down to the floor. "I'm sorry about yesterday. I couldn't bring myself . . . "

"That's all right . . . "

"No, it's not. I'm not usually rude. Please have that accountant send me his bill."

"Don't worry about that. It's more important that we set a date for him to come back. This week, perhaps. Today, if you like. The sooner he can advise you . . . "

Still not looking at him, she started shaking her head. "I couldn't bring myself to come in yesterday. I couldn't bear the thought of finding out that the company is broke. I'm so confused. I don't know if I'm capable of running the business. And I don't want to be told that I have to close the business."

"I'm sure he can help you . . . "

She looked up at him and started to cry. "Pierre . . . I don't know what to do."

He hesitated, leaned forward to reach for her hands, and held them.

They stayed that way for a moment, her hands in his, then she slowly pulled away. "I'm being a silly little girl." She wiped her eyes.

He leaned back away from her, feeling clumsy and awkward. "I'll phone the accountant right now. I'll try to get him here today. This morning if he can. Otherwise, this afternoon."

She shook her head slowly. "My husband's family . . . actually his cousin . . . is insisting that I give him complete control of the business."

"He wants you to sell out?"

"No. He wants me to hand it to him and walk away."

"That doesn't seem fair."

"He's not a fair person. He says I can't run it, that I don't know what I'm doing, that I will ruin it. He says my husband never intended on leaving the business to me. Except he did."

He looked at her for a few moments, until he realized he was staring, then stood up. "Let's see about that." He got Ronnie Rose on the phone. "Mrs. Battelli wasn't available yesterday, but she's in my office now. Can we do something for her today?"

"The shoe lady?" his accountant said. "Let me tell you, Pierre, when I came home last night without any shoes . . . my wife can get very nasty when she needs to make a point."

Belasco tried not to laugh in front of Rebecca. "I really appreciate it. What time is good for you?"

Rose said, "Two?"

Belasco repeated it to Rebecca and she nodded.

He hung up with Rose, then escorted her to the elevator. He instructed Miguel, "Please take Mrs. Battelli to twenty-four," then said to her, "You know how to change elevators there, don't you?"

She said she did.

"I will see you with the accountant at two."

"Thank you." She extended her hand. He shook it gently, smiled, and she stepped into the elevator.

When the doors closed, he went back to his office.

A bird with a broken wing.

"Sir?" Pierro startled him. "Mrs. Essenbach is in the lobby . . . "

Coming around his desk, Belasco was at his door when she spotted him. "You betrayed me," she yelled. "I will never forgive you."

He went to her and extended his hand. "May we speak privately?"

"No . . . we may not."

Belasco could see out of the corner of his eyes that both Shannon and Pierro were pretending to look away, but that David was watching from the door and Jaquim was watching from in front of his elevator.

She said very loudly, "Your betrayal is unforgivable. You made me a promise."

"Madame, I did nothing of the kind. If you would please step into my office so that we can discuss this."

"I will expose you for the fraud that you are," she continued. "A lying, cheating fraud." She turned toward the concierge desk. "You will all know what a fraud he is. I will expose him."

With that, the woman stormed out of Trump Tower.

Both Shannon and Pierro shook their heads to show Belasco that they weren't going to believe anything that the woman said.

He looked at David and Jaquim, and now both of them turned away, as if to pretend that they hadn't witnessed this scene.

Saying nothing to any of them, Belasco returned to his office and rang Bill Riordan. "There's been an incident in the residents' lobby with Mrs. Essenbach."

"Star of our latest video," Riordan laughed. "You see it yet? It's going onto our 'Best Hits' reel."

"She was ranting and raving and making vague threats. She did it in front of my staff."

"Keep your powder dry, Pierre. I'll pull a copy of the lobby CCTV and send one to you."

"And one to the lawyers."

"Obviously, there's no sound . . . write it up the way it happened . . . you know . . . what she said and what you said . . . and add who was there to witness it. Then, maybe, you should meet with the lawyers to go over this. She's got enough money to make trouble for everyone if she wants to."

"Thanks." He hung up and rang Carole Ann Mendelsohn, the woman who ran the in-house legal team.

"It's Mrs. Essenbach," he told her.

"I've seen the DVD," Mendelsohn said. "Did you know she had a husband? I was surprised. I thought black widow spiders ate them."

He smiled. "We should talk about her. She's been ranting and raving in the lobby. Bill Riordan will send you a copy of the CCTV footage."

"How's two this afternoon?"

"Two thirty would be better."

"Done. See you then."

They hung up.

That's when Belasco's phone rang.

It was Rebecca Battelli and she was hysterical. "I've been robbed."

33

An e-mail was waiting in the office for Carson, with a large attachment from the lawyers in Tokyo. "As per your request. There was nothing in English, but we've done a fast translation of the summary. Let us know if you need more."

He e-mailed back, "Thank you. I'm in Tokyo this week. Can we meet Friday morning?"

Opening the attachment, he started to read it, then quickly got Ken Warring on the phone.

"If you're still in LA, then I'm waking you again."

"No," Warring said. "I'm in Dallas. And, yes, you're still waking me."

"Shigetada. Remember that we said there was nine percent missing? Yesterday we found six of the nine at a small, family-owned investment bank called Chiba. The managing partners are Shigetada's cousins."

"And?"

"And this morning I learned that they hate him."

"We love hate," Warring said. "You should meet with them."

"Not yet."

"Why wait?"

Carson explained, "We need to hold this card close. If the shit hits the fan, they'll be the first to bail out."

"Then we need to be there selling parachutes."

"What I don't understood," Carson confessed, "is why, if they hate him, are they still holding his shares?"

"Ask yourself the same question. Why would you?"

He pondered that. "The obvious thing is that I'd be looking to get more than they're worth now."

"Or?"

"Or . . . I could care less and put them away forever because it's a family thing."

"Unlikely. Emotion shouldn't enter into the equation."

"It often does."

"And when it does," Warring reminded him, "that's when you lose money."

"So . . . what else?"

"You're asking me to second-guess some Japanese guys I've never met before the day's first cup of coffee . . . but how about this? If you really hated some guy, wouldn't you want to hold onto his shares until you could use them to hurt him?"

Carson smiled. "Kind of like what we're thinking of doing to Shigetada."

"Kinda . . . exactly."

"Speaking of which," Carson said, "I never heard back on those three hundred thousand shares in the dark pool in Hong Kong, which means no movement there. And we put twenty-five thousand out at forty and haven't heard back about that, either. Have to presume no one is interested."

"Keep me informed," Warring said.

"How was LA?"

"Might be interesting. I'll let you know. Might be something you want to put some of your own money into."

"And how's Dallas?"

"I'm meeting with RD Cove this morning for breakfast."

"I think I've mentioned that his nephew David lives in Trump Tower."

Warring wasn't impressed. "I'll let you know if anything works out here."

"Go back to sleep."

"You keep waking me and then saying that."

"Sorry."

"FYI," Warring said, "I'm home tonight. Which means you can find me there tomorrow morning. In case you want to wake me three days in a row."

WHEN ALICIA got her first job in television, as a young woman fresh out of school in Miami, there was an old news editor named Cornelius O'Casey who, every time he sent her out on an assignment, never failed to remind her, "Start at the beginning."

She never forgot that, and this time, like every time, she started at the beginning.

Instead of going to the gym, she put together her clothes for that night—it was much too early to call Cyndi, so she made the decision herself, settling on a Dolce & Gabbana black strapless dress with satin ankle-strap heels—put everything in a garment bag, left it in the living room, then called for a car to take her downtown.

She was the first person to walk into the New York City Municipal Archives—across the street from city hall—when they opened their doors at exactly nine o'clock.

Some of the clerks working there recognized her, and one of them offered to help her. She said she wanted to find everything they might have on Trump Tower. He showed where she could locate a few documents, but there wasn't much.

Next door, at the New York City Hall library, she found a few additional records, but she didn't learn more than she already knew.

Across the park, at the Department of Buildings, a clerk walked her through the process of finding building plans. He even photocopied a few things for her.

She thumbed through the photocopies in the car back to Trump Tower, dumped them in the apartment, grabbed her garment bag and had the driver take her to 30 Rockefeller Center.

Leaving her dress hanging in the makeup room, which was a few doors down from the newsroom on the seventh floor, she went into the morning meeting. Greg, her editor, threw a bunch of story ideas around. A homeless man in Brooklyn who won $110,000 in the lottery. A three-alarm fire on Staten Island that the NYPD were calling arson. A Board of Education meeting planned for Wednesday where, according to leaked documents, school closures were going to be announced.

Then the party came up.

Alicia reminded him, "I'm a guest . . . a paid guest . . . not a working girl."

Greg looked at Alicia. "Just the president."

She shook her head. "Not fair."

"But then it's not fair that you get to go and I don't. So, as long as you're there . . . "

"We've been through this." She pointed to Meagan O'Donnell, who'd been hired one week ago as a local street reporter. "I'm conflicted. Anyway, you already told Meagan she could do a live feed."

"Yeah," Meagan said. "You promised me."

Greg shook his head. "Meagan gets everybody coming in. I'm talking about Clinton upstairs on the roof."

"I'll go to the roof," Meagan offered, anxiously. "I can do that. No big deal."

"Except it is a big deal. Except you don't have a roof pass. Except Alicia's already up there."

"Except," Alicia cut in, "I'm paying for my ticket and that makes it look like I'm paying for access. It's a conflict of interest. And, it's not fair to Meagan."

"If life were fair," he pointed out, "I'd be batting cleanup for the Yankees." He turned to one of his staff who was sorting out the rundown. "Meagan does a live feed from the museum steps at the opening . . . then we go back to her at the end, and at that point we'll run tape with whoever she's got."

"Thanks," Meagan nodded to Greg, then smiled at Alicia. "Thank you."

"If you can get Bill," Greg said to Meagan, then looked at Sammy Stevens, who was going to produce Meagan's feeds from the street, "If you get Bill, we'll run a short piece at six, then a longer piece at eleven. Maybe we can get him on the way out, too."

"Is he coming in the front door?" Stevens asked.

"Find out," Greg said.

"We'll cover all the bases," Stevens promised and nodded at Meagan.

Greg looked again at Alicia.

"Stop," she said.

When the meeting ended, Alicia sat down to start writing her intros to the stories that were, at least preliminarily, in the running order.

Then an e-mail arrived from Greg. "Dear Little Goody Two-Shoes, where's the killer instinct? Obviously you were never a Marine." He signed it, "Semper Fi."

She looked across the newsroom at him. He was staring at her, grinning, as if he was imploring her one more time to do the gig.

Smiling, she wrote back, "Obviously you never won a prize in the seventh grade for selling the most boxes of mint chocolate cookies." She signed it "Respect myself and others, respect authority, use resources wisely, make the world a better place, and be a sister to every Girl Scout. XXX"

CARSON HAD HOPED to spend the rest of the day preparing for Japan, but Tony Arcarro had other ideas. "I need you to help with the BNP Paribas deal."

That took several hours.

Then Mesumi came in gushing, "Thank you. Wow. You are the best. My doorman called to tell me about the delivery. I had him read me the note. Carson . . . thank you."

"You're welcome. Drink it in good health."

"The wine looks fabulous. But . . . three cases of Cel-Ray Tonic? I mean, I love it but . . . seriously, what am I supposed to do with so much?"

Carson suggested, "Hope Ethan Pearlman gets a divorce?"

Around lunchtime, he thought about going to the gym, but before he could get away, Milt McKeever called. "We hooked a fish with the twenty-five. Done at forty."

"Really? There's someone out there who wants Shigetada shares?"

"Yeah, but I don't know who yet. I'll call you as soon as I find out."

Carson informed Arcarro, "One of the haystacks turned up."

"Got a name?"

"Not yet. McKeever put twenty-five in a dark pool and it got took."

"Twenty-five." Arcarro thought out loud. "Small potatoes. That's a bottom feeder who's looking to acquire a stake. You find out who and you'll find more shares."

Carson asked his partner, "Be honest . . . isn't this more fun than working for a living?"

"Working for a living, yes. But we had better groupies in tennis."

34

"I'm gonna murder you . . . " he screamed over the music blaring on the fifteen speakers spread out all over the apartment.

The ocelot tore out of Ricky's bedroom.

" . . . bloody fucking cat . . . " He chased after it, racing into the living room, wearing nothing but his underpants and his ankle bracelet.

"Put that down," screamed a young woman he'd been sleeping with.

"Come here you fucking miserable cat . . . " He was carrying a meat cleaver.

"Can you turn down that fucking music?" Shouted some guy standing in the hallway, in front of the third bedroom, wearing nothing but an undershirt.

"That fucking music," Ricky yelled back at him, "pays the fucking bills. And who the fuck are you, anyway?"

"Gimme that." The young woman, who was wearing nothing but a pair of Ricky's underpants, tried to grab the meat cleaver.

"I'm Hughie . . . Nessie's bloke."

He demanded, "Who's Nessie? And where are your strides?"

Suddenly the ocelot darted out from behind one of the couches, jumped over a chair, and ran into the kitchen.

" . . . fucking gonna kill you," Ricky screamed at the animal.

"I said I'm Nessie's bloke."

"I heard you the first time." Ricky stopped in the middle of the living room where couch cushions were on the floor, ripped to shreds by the ocelot's claws. "So who the fuck is Nessie?"

"The Loch Ness fucking monster," he answered, went back into the bedroom and slammed the door shut.

"Give me that cleaver." The young woman grabbed at it again.

Ricky went into the kitchen.

Garbage was spilled all over the floor where the animal had been looking for food.

"Come here you miserable fucking . . . "

The animal jumped onto the sink, pushing dishes from the counter and sending them crashing to the floor.

Ricky screamed, "You're gonna be stuffed and turned into a couch pillow . . . "

The woman screamed, "Ricky, give me that cleaver."

Now the ocelot hissed at Ricky and bared its teeth, and when he stepped back, the animal darted off the counter, ran right through Ricky's legs and back into the living room.

"What's all the bloody noise?" Someone shouted. "Fuck me, it's a lion."

Ricky came out of the kitchen to find a young guy standing there, looking very much like the first guy, and also wearing nothing but an undershirt.

He demanded, "Who the fuck are you?"

"I'm Jules."

"Yeah, well," Ricky pointed, "your jewels are hanging kinda low."

The woman in the underpants stared.

Jules wasn't at all fazed. "Is that a baby tiger?"

"Where did it go?" Ricky wanted to know.

"I don't know. It ran past me . . . "

That's when there was a horrific scream from Joey's bedroom. A woman yelled, "Help . . . help . . . help . . . "

"Must have gone that way," Jules pointed toward the bedroom.

Ricky ran down the hall to Joey's bedroom, with the woman and Jules following, where they found a very chubby redhead standing nude on the bed, trembling with fright and screaming, "Help . . . help . . . "

"Oy," Ricky demanded, "who the fuck are you?"

Now someone was ringing the doorbell.

The chubby woman kept on screaming, "Help . . . help . . . help . . . "

"And who the fuck is that?" Ricky asked the woman he'd been sleeping with.

"How should I know?" she protested.

The bell rang again.

"Bloody hell," he said, staring at the chubby redhead.

"Ain't you gonna answer it?" Jules asked.

Ricky went to the door. "What?"

A very young woman was standing there.

Ricky had no idea who she was. "Who the fuck are you?"

The young woman stared at Ricky in his underpants, hoisting a meat cleaver, and seemed too shocked to say anything.

"Hullo?" He said to her, "Anyone home?"

Looking past him, she saw the woman wearing Ricky's underpants and nothing else, and Jules wearing an undershirt and nothing else.

Somehow she managed to say, "Joey . . . is Joey here?"

"Joey? Ah . . . " Ricky turned to ask the other two, "Anyone seen Joey?"

They said no, just as Hughie came into the living room, still wearing nothing but an undershirt. "If you can't turn the fucking music down, mate . . . "

Ricky stared at Hughie, then at Jules, then decided, "You're fucking twins."

Hughie answered, "And you're Sherlock fucking Holmes."

Turning back to the young woman in the doorway, Ricky said, "No, luv, sorry. Joey's not here." Then he wondered, "Can I tell him who's been looking for him?"

Suddenly, the ocelot shot out the door and into the hallway.

The young woman screamed in fright.

"Bugger me," Ricky yelled, then asked, "So who are you?"

She only just managed to say, "My name is Amvi."

35

"**W**ait till you see this," Tony Gallicano said.

"Oh . . . hi . . . good morning." Antonia was surprised to find her boss in this early and, instead of going into her own office, she walked straight into his. "See what?"

He was leaning back in his chair with his feet up on his desk, reading a report in a thick-bound notebook. He pointed to the wide-screen television hanging on the wall of his office, then pushed the clicker. "Watch the right side of the screen . . . there in the corner."

It was the CCTV footage of Katarina Essenbach throwing her husband out of the Tower in his underwear.

"Who is that?" Antonia stood there—her shoes in a plastic shopping bag in one hand, her coffee in the other—staring at the screen as the cameras followed the man in his underwear down the elevator, outside, and into a taxi.

"Apparently he's married to Mrs. Essenbach . . . you know . . . the woman in the Tower."

"Sheena of the jungle?"

"The wannabe jungle lady. Not going to happen."

Antonia remembered. "The meeting was last night."

"Residents voted no, as we always knew they would." He clicked off the television. "Unanimous. She never stood a chance. Pierre Belasco went to tell her that she'd been turned down, and she gave him hell. Then she gave her husband hell."

"Why?"

"Considering the number of husbands she's had, I suspect that's what she does?"

"No, I meant why Pierre? What's it got to do with him?"

"She claims he promised to get the residents to agree."

"He made her a promise?"

"Of course not. She's lying. But that doesn't change the fact that she could cause trouble. That's what liars usually do."

"That's terrible." She made a point of telling Gallicano, "I adore Pierre, and I'm on his side one hundred percent."

He pointed to some papers on his desk. "He was pretty upset and e-mailed his version of events late last night, right after she confronted him. The lawyers are handling it. You can read it if you want."

"The lawyers . . . " She put her coffee on his desk and reached for the papers. "Could I read this in my office? I'll get it back to you. I'd like to change out of my running shoes . . . "

"Sure," he said.

She reached for Belasco's report. "Sounds like Mrs. Essenbach is exactly the sort of person we need to avoid."

"The boss can't stand her. Never liked her since the day he met her. She's a troublemaker."

"How interesting." Antonia smiled politely. "How very interesting."

Gallicano went back to the file he was reading.

Antonia went to her office.

As she took off her running shoes, she read Belasco's e-mail. Then she put on her heels, saw that Gallicano was still engrossed in what he was reading, and quickly took the report down the hallway to make a photocopy. She dropped it on her desk, then returned the original to Gallicano.

"The woman sounds like a nutcase."

He nodded, "Certainly does," then went back to reading.

In her own office, she thought about shutting her door but decided that might look odd because no one on the floor ever closed their door. Instead, she angled her computer in such a way that no one coming into the room could see what she was looking at.

Googling "Katarina Essenbach," she sorted through a couple of dozen links, reading all the references, especially about the woman's various marriages and the lawsuits against her plastic surgeons.

Antonia sent the links she wanted to save to her *jerseyhot1983* address, quickly changed back to her homepage, and deleted her "browser history" files, so that nobody could see what she'd been Googling. She also deleted her sent e-mail files, in case someone looked to see where she'd been e-mailing.

She could study everything better at home tonight.

Now she wondered where else could she find out more about Mrs. Essenbach.

There was a specialist database the company used for top executive background checks, except she couldn't recall what the name of it was. It had something to do with dancing.

She knew that Tony would know, but she couldn't ask without him wondering why.

So she went back to Google and this time did searches for "background check" and "corporate intelligence" and "executive background intelligence." But none of the links that came up sounded familiar or had anything to do with dancing.

Short of asking Tony, she thought about logging into someone's classified personnel file—she guessed that the data mining service would be referenced there—but she worried that the log-in would pop up as an unauthorized access request, and someone like Bill Riordan would start asking questions.

Bill Riordan, she thought.

If Antonia beats around the bush with him, he'll suspect something. So why doesn't Antonia simply ask him outright?

She dialed his extension, got his voice mail and his beeper number, then dialed that. She left her number, and he rang back right away.

"Sorry to bother you but my sister phoned me . . . " She thought that sounded pretty good. "The company she works for is looking for one of those firms that does top-of-the-line background checks on senior executives. They're hiring, and she asked me if I knew of one, and I said I'd ask you who we used?"

Instead of giving her the name, he wanted to know, "Why are you asking me?"

"Because . . . she asked me and I figured you could recommend the best one."

"No," he said, "you didn't ask for the best, you asked for the one we use."

Once a cop always a cop. "Isn't that the same thing?"

"Why didn't you ask Tony?"

"'Cause my first thought was to ask you. I mean . . . what's the big secret?"

"Tell your sister she can find plenty of companies that do what she wants done on the Net."

"Thanks a million for your help."

"Anytime." He hung up.

"Asshole," she said out loud.

"Anybody I know?"

Antonia swung around to find Tony's secretary standing in the doorway.

"I was trying to do a favor for my sister and I asked . . . " she stopped and shook her head. "No one you know."

"I dropped by to say there's no hurry on the New Jersey property amortization calculations . . . "

She'd forgotten all about that. "I'm doing them now."

"He's had to run out," she pointed to Tony's office, "and won't be back for the rest of the day. So tomorrow's fine."

"Okay," Antonia said. "Thanks."

The woman backed away.

"My sister . . . " Antonia called to her. "My sister asked me which background check firm we used, because her company was looking to hire someone . . . you know, a senior executive . . . and all I could remember is that there was one we used, or once used, that had a name with the word . . . "

"You mean Thirty-Five Tango?"

Dancing! That was it. "Ah . . . " Antonia backtracked, just in case. "I've been checking the Net for the word . . . detective . . . too many online detectives, Internet detectives, private detectives, public detectives." She grinned, "Thanks, anyway."

The woman waved and walked away.

Fuck you, Bill Riordan. She went to her keyboard and started to type, "www.thirty . . . " then stopped.

She wondered if Riordan, or anyone else, could access what searches she did and what sites she visited. She knew that the company had fired employees in the past for using their office computer to pull up porn sites. And if you downloaded certain unauthorized software, even something that seemed as innocuous as a solitaire game, nasty e-mails arrived from IT noting that they'd automatically removed the software, and warning not to do it again.

Clearing her browser history again, she put her running shoes back on, stood up, and walked out of the office.

Outside on Columbus Circle, Antonia took her phone and did a map check for nearby Internet cafés. There was one a few blocks up Broadway, but that was too close. She didn't want someone from the office happening by and spotting her.

Fordham's Lincoln Center campus was nearby, and she figured they must have a library with public access computers, but she didn't know if she could talk her way into it.

Then she spotted a D-Luxor Internet Café on the map at Eighth Avenue near Eighteenth Street. It was more than far enough away, so she jumped into a taxi and went there.

The place was a hole in the wall that smelled of cigarettes and Clorox, where some fat Egyptian guy—"I'm from Luxor . . . delux . . . D-Luxor . . . get it?"—served bad coffee and stale pastries.

There were half a dozen computers upstairs near the window, most of them occupied. But the Egyptian fellow said there were another dozen machines downstairs. And that's where the printers were, too.

She paid up front for one hour and went downstairs.

The basement was damp and dingy. Not surprisingly, no one else was there. She sat down at a computer in the corner, logged on, and tried to get into the Thirty-Five Tango site by spelling out the word.

It didn't work. So she tried it with the number 35. Nothing. She typed the words with hyphens, then underscores, then used dot net instead of dot com, and then she tried dot org. Still nothing.

Frustrated, she Googled, "Thirty-Five Tango."

The first entry explained that the name signified an MOS, which is a "military occupational specialty" for intelligence officers. And reference after reference went into detail about intelligence officers. It wasn't until she got to the second page that she found the link, http://35tango.int.

Typing that into the browser, a page came up asking for her user's login and password. Obviously, she didn't have one. But at the bottom of that page, in the lower right-hand corner, there was a little arrow and the words, "to register." That brought her to a new-user page.

She almost typed in her name, then stopped because she wanted to know how much this was going to cost.

On the price page it said that a one-day pass to the site's basic background package—which provided open source information from federal, state and local databases, including complete address history, relatives and associates, previous marriages and divorces, a nationwide criminal records search, some financial information like credit bureau ratings, references to licenses and permits, and information on properties owned with sale date and prices—would set her back $275 plus tax.

That stopped her.

And this was the cheapest package. Others ranged from one week to one year and from five figures up to six. The corporate "Platinum Level," which was the one she assumed the company used, not only provided unlimited searches of all the open source databases throughout the world, but included private data mining around the world. The subscription price for that was based on the number of people employed by a company and the number of people who would have access to the database. Subscriptions started at $125,000 a year.

She had no idea if that was expensive or a bargain for a company as big as the Trump Organization, but $275 plus tax out of her pocket to find out about Katarina Essenbach . . .

Nearly three hundred bucks to find out . . . what?

Mrs. Essenbach isn't worth it, she decided. But then she wondered what information all these databases had on her. *Do they know about Antonia's secret life?*

At the sign-in page, she typed her name and address and provided her credit card information.

As if Antonia has a secret life.

A pop-up appeared, giving her a one-day password, with a little note at the bottom as a reminder that one-day meant twenty-four hours.

Even better. Antonia can play with this all night.

Her first search was herself and several dozen links came up. But they merely took her to information that she assumed would be there. Driver's license. School background. Various addresses where she'd lived. There was nothing of any particular interest, nothing she would care about if somebody else found out.

She ran a fast search on her parents and then on her sister, and nothing there seemed terribly fascinating either. Although she was shocked to see that the three-bedroom house with the finished basement where she'd grown up, which her parents had sold ten years ago for $235,000, was today worth four times that.

Now she typed "Katarina Essenbach" into the search form.

This time, several dozen pages popped up, containing more than a thousand links.

"Wow."

She chose one of the first links at random—addresses—and up came thirty different addresses for Katarina Essenbach, spanning as many years.

Five were listed as "still current." There was Trump Tower, then addresses in Las Vegas, London, Santiago and Antigua.

Another link noted that Mrs. Essenbach was claiming Las Vegas as her legal residence, which struck Antonia as odd because she knew that the woman lived most of the year in New York.

Now checking family links, she found loads of details about the woman's various marriages.

According to one of the databases, her current husband—the man in the underwear—was Julio de Garcia-Gutierrez, an exiled Chilean diplomat who'd been implicated by the Spanish government in the theft of several hundred million dollars. According to this, he'd been in cahoots with the former dictator General Augusto Pinochet.

Holy shit, Antonia . . . this game is getting really good.

From there she went to the links that described Essenbach's various lawsuits. There were documents and newspaper clippings and court reports
about how she'd sued her plastic surgeons for botched operations, and several
other people along the way as well, mostly for bad business deals. But then
Antonia found a file on how Mrs. Essenbach had sued her investment broker,
and a banker, and even her veterinarian when her dog Ma Jolie died on his operating table. It cost the vet $175,000.

Next, Antonia found newspaper clippings and court documents from Great
Britain where Mrs. Essenbach had sued two newspapers for libel.

They'd accused her of murder.

According to the *Daily Express* and the *Mail* on Sunday, Katarina had been
questioned by police in connection with the death of her last husband, Kurt
Essenbach.

The story made the British papers because, as it turned out, the late Mr. Essenbach had once been involved in a torrid and much-publicized love affair
with the queen's sister, Princess Margaret.

In this case, the papers noted, Kurt and Katarina were honeymooning on a
private yacht, sailing up the coast of Alaska, when he suddenly died. The
Alaskan State Police were suspicious, but the autopsy proved inconclusive,
and Katarina was allowed to leave with his body.

The British newspapers admitted that she's never been charged with any
crime but implied she should have been.

"Murder," Antonia said, closing her left eye, tilting her head, and trying to
sound like Inspector Columbo. "Oh . . . ah, I almost forgot . . . Mrs. Essenbach . . . excuse me for bothering you again, ma'am . . . one more thing . . . you
see, ma'am, I'm curious . . . I mean, forgive me ma'am for prying . . . but after
all those lawsuits and after killing your last husband . . . I'm trying to get this
straight in my own mind . . . what do you think of Pierre Belasco?"

She stared at the screen for a very long time, until a pop-up appeared saying
that there were only five minutes left on her prepaid hour.

That brought her back to the moment.

She quickly sent all the links she still had on the screen to her *jerseyhot1983*
account, then logged off the 35Tango site. There would be plenty of time to go
back there tonight. But before she shut down, she did a fast phone search, and
when she found the number she was looking for, she entered it into her cell
phone address book and left.

Stepping out onto Eighth Avenue, she looked around to get her bearings,
and realized she was a couple of blocks from Chelsea Market. That would be a
very good place to meet.

Now she took her phone and dialed that number, and when a man answered, Antonia asked, "Is Mrs. Essenbach there please."

36

"This is terrible," Belasco said as soon as he walked into the showroom. "Are you all right?"

Desk and file drawers were emptied, with papers and files strewn everywhere. Shelves were overturned. Furniture was upended, and some of it was destroyed. Shoes and shoeboxes were scattered all over the place.

"No." Rebecca was standing in the middle of the room, her hands holding her face, dazed and trembling. "No, I'm not."

He went to her and reached for her hands.

She quickly moved away. "What am I going to do?"

He hesitated, embarrassed that he'd been clumsy. "You need to call the police."

Taking his cell phone, he dialed Bill Riordan and got voice mail.

"Can you come to Scarpe Pietrasanta on the nineteenth floor, please, right away?" He pushed star, got back to the main menu, and this time left a numeric page.

"My security man is on his way," he told her. "We have cameras everywhere so I'm sure we'll be able to figure out who did this to you. Everything's going to be all right. I promise."

Rebecca closed her eyes and shook her head, and the two of them stood there, like that, for a very long time not speaking.

"What the hell . . . " Riordan appeared in the doorway.

Belasco motioned for him to come in. "Mrs. Battelli found this when she got here this morning. We haven't touched anything."

The first thing Riordan did was check the front door. "No sign of a forced entry. That means someone had a key."

Stepping into the showroom, and being careful where he walked, Riordan poked his head into the offices and into the tiny kitchen. Everything there was smashed and on the floor.

"Somebody's very angry at you," he said to Rebecca, then took his phone and called one of his team. "Harry, we've got a ten-twenty-one on nineteen. Scarpe Pietrasanta. Send someone down with a video camera. I want the scene documented. Then get on our cameras and go back . . . " He stopped and asked Rebecca, "When was the last time you were here?"

Belasco answered, "She was here Friday."

Riordan looked at Rebecca. "Is that correct? The last time you saw the office was Friday? And everything was all right?"

She nodded, "Yes."

He told Harry, "Go back to Thursday, close of business. Every elevator stop on nineteen. Check the stairwell, too. I want to identify everybody who's been on the floor since Thursday night." He hung up. "We'll find him. But we need to bring in the police."

Rebecca shook her head, "I don't know."

"You must," Belasco said.

"Mrs. Battelli . . . " Riordan spoke softly and slowly, "I can tell you from experience that whoever did this to you is very angry. I can tell you from experience that it was more than one person. Probably two."

"Please . . . " She tried to wave him off. "Maybe tomorrow . . . "

He continued. "I can tell you from experience that nothing will be missing, unless you had cash hidden somewhere and these people found it. And that if you don't let the police handle this . . . and we will work with them, and we will be here for you . . . but if you don't let the police handle this, these people will be back."

"No . . . please . . . " she begged "I think I want to go home now."

"They may not come here," Riordan wanted her to understand, "but they will strike again. They may come to your home. They may try to do you some physical harm. For your own safety . . . "

"Rebecca," Belasco said, "listen to him."

"No," she said. "I know who did it. He won't harm me. It's my husband's cousin. Johnny. All he wants is for me to give him this business."

Riordan was insistent. "Mrs. Battelli . . . a crime has been committed in Trump Tower. We have a responsibility to you. But we also have a responsibility to our other tenants. We need to protect you . . . and them. You say you know who did it, and whether or not you want to cooperate with the police is up to you . . . but we don't have a choice. If you don't want to bring the police in, that's your decision. We have to."

Folding her arms across her chest, she stepped over the debris on the floor and looked into her office . . . the one that had been her husband's.

The couch was turned upside down, and every desk drawer was spilled onto the floor. Shelves were tipped over. And there was glass on the floor.

Glass? She looked at the little bookcase sitting in front of the window. The top shelf was empty. In a panic, she started pushing furniture aside.

"Mrs. Battelli . . . " Riordan was right there. "Please don't touch anything. Don't disturb anything."

She ignored him and continued shoving things out of the way until she found a silver picture frame, crushed on the floor.

The photo was gone.

Frantically, she started looking everywhere for it.

She found the bottom half sitting in the feed of her shredder.

Someone had deliberately shredded the top half.

It was a photo from her honeymoon. She and Mark were in Italy, holding hands and smiling at each other, leaning to the left in front of the Leaning Tower of Pisa, which was tilted to the right.

It always made her laugh.

And there were no other copies of it.

"Bastard," she screamed, and turned to Riordan. "Call the police. Yes, please, call the police."

TWO OF Riordan's people showed up with a video camera and started filming. Then two uniformed NYPD officers arrived, followed by two detectives.

Belasco suggested that if the officers needed a place to talk to Mrs. Battelli, they were welcome to use his office. Riordan said no, it would be easier if they all sat down in the small conference room upstairs next to his office.

So while Riordan's two men documented the scene, and the two uniformed officers stayed there to protect it, Rebecca went with Riordan and the detectives upstairs.

They did not invite Belasco to come along.

IN HIS own office, he sat down to write an incident report, which he sent to Donald Trump and Anthony Gallicano and copied to his department heads.

A little while later, he remembered the appointment with his accountant and phoned Ronnie Rose to cancel. "We'll try again for later this week. Sorry about this, but . . . it's not a good time, right now."

He also postponed his appointment with the lawyer, Carole Ann Mendelsohn, to talk about Mrs. Essenbach. "Can we do this tomorrow, please. Something's come up."

Now what? He asked himself. And the only thing he really wanted to do was go upstairs to find Rebecca.

She was sitting in the CCTV monitoring room with Riordan, the detectives, and Riordan's guy Harry. They were running through the camera footage from the nineteenth floor. But now there was a young woman standing next to Rebecca, holding her hand.

"This is my daughter, Gabriella."

She was around twenty, dressed in jeans and a sweatshirt, with long hair. She looked like her mother.

"I'm very glad to meet you," Belasco said.

"We may have something," Riordan told Harry. "Run it back."

Gabriella nodded politely, shook Belasco's hand, then took her mother's hand again.

"There," Riordan pointed to a monitor.

The view was from one of the cameras in the Tower lobby. Two men walked in from Fifth Avenue—wearing raincoats—and went to the elevators. The security officer looked toward them, and one of the men appeared to flash him a pass.

"What's wrong with this picture?" Riordan asked, then answered his own question. "This is last night around eleven. They're wearing raincoats."

Belasco didn't get it. "So?"

"So?" Riordan said. "It didn't rain last night."

The two men stepped into the elevator.

The shot on the monitor changed to inside the elevator, where the two men, their faces now clearly visible, stood not speaking.

"It didn't rain at all yesterday," one of the detectives picked up on Riordan's explanation, "and the reason that's significant is because the raincoats are there to hide whatever it is they're carrying."

Belasco asked, "Like what?"

"Like burglar tools?" Riordan said. "Like weapons? Or, they're not carrying anything in, but expect to carry something out."

Belasco turned to Rebecca, "Do you recognize either of those men?"

The monitor showed them getting off the elevator on the nineteenth floor, then disappearing down the hall, out of the camera's range.

"No," she said. "I don't."

Harry sped up the playback, then slowed it down when the men reappeared.

"This is eighteen and a half minutes later," Riordan said.

The cameras followed the men into the elevator, down and out through the lobby to Fifth Avenue.

"So you've got your suspects," Belasco said.

"What we've got," the second detective decided, "are two persons of interest."

"Are you sure you don't know them?" Belasco asked Rebecca again.

She shook her head. "I'm sure."

"What about your husband's cousin? You said that . . . "

"Johnny Battelli," the detective said. "Florida. We checked. Been there all week."

Belasco thought out loud, "If it's not him . . . "

Riordan cut in, "Just because he isn't in town doesn't mean he isn't involved. Remember our little talk about means, motive and opportunity?"

"Except that he didn't have the opportunity. He's in Florida."

"According to Mrs. Battelli, he has a motive. And because they got into the building with a pass, and got into the office with a key, at least it looks like that, maybe he gifted them the opportunity."

"Does he have a building pass?"

Riordan leaned back to hand Belasco an index card–sized copy of a security pass. "Apparently he does."

"These two guys . . . " Belasco looked at the detectives. "You can find them, right?"

One of them answered, "How would you suggest we start?"

"You've got their faces."

"Then what?"

"Then . . . don't you check them against other people's faces? What do they say on television . . . find out if they're in the system."

"Let's say for the sake of argument," the other detective proposed, "that these two guys were hired to trash Mrs. Battelli's office. So go back to why they were wearing raincoats when it wasn't raining."

Belasco thought about that for a moment. "I suppose . . . as Bill said . . . to bring something into the building. Or to carry something out. They wore raincoats because they didn't want to be seen doing that."

"By who?" Riordan quizzed him. "Who are they hiding something from?"

"Your people . . . or anyone else."

"When you say, anyone else, you mean the CCTV cameras?"

"Okay," Belasco said, "the CCTV cameras."

Now the first detective asked, "If these guys are involved with this in some way, then how come they don't care who sees their faces? How come they don't care about the CCTV cameras?"

"Because . . . " Belasco offered, "they didn't know there are cameras?"

"Most criminals are dumb," the detective went on. "But very few are that dumb. They know there are CCTV cameras everywhere in a place like Trump Tower. The reason they don't care about their faces is because they know we won't recognize them."

"Why not?"

"They're not from here. They flew in on Monday afternoon and they flew out Monday night or Tuesday morning."

"What do they do when they leave Trump Tower?"

Riordan said, "Camera shows them walking out to Fifth Avenue, turning right, and disappearing up the block."

Belasco thought for a moment. "Okay, say they flew in . . . "

"Or came in by train," the detective said.

"Or by bus," Riordan said.

"Okay . . . by plane or train or bus. There are CCTV cameras at the airports and at Penn Station and at Grand Central and at the bus terminal."

"Sir?" The first detective stared at him. "Do you know how many people come into New York City every day?"

Belasco conceded, "I guess it's asking too much."

"Believe me," the detective said, "we're trying the best we can with what we've got."

"Have you got fingerprints?"

"They wore gloves."

"How do you know?"

"Sir," the detective leaned forward, "I don't know exactly what it is you do for a living, but this is what my partner and I do for a living. If they don't care about their faces it's because we won't recognize them. But they do care about what we can recognize, which is their fingerprints. I guarantee they wore gloves."

"There must be something you can do," Belasco said. "There must be some way of finding them."

"Pierre," Riordan shook his head. "You don't understand how these things work. No one's been hurt. There's been no physical violence. It may not even technically qualify as a burglary because unless we can identify something that was taken . . . "

The other detective chimed in, "As a favor to Lieutenant Riordan, we'll go ten yards beyond the extra ten yards. But the world you see on television, that's not the real world of the NYPD."

"They make a report," Riordan continued, "and the case stays open. Leads get followed up if there are leads. But right now . . . "

"Of course, we'll try to find out if anyone knows those two guys," the first detective promised. "We'll get Mrs. Battelli's cousin-in-law on the phone and talk to him at length. If we need to, when he comes back up north, we'll sit down with him, face to face. And, yeah, we'll put out the pictures of these two . . . " he motioned toward the monitors . . . "as persons of interest. Maybe we'll get lucky."

"Your best shot is luck?" Belasco was dismayed.

"In this case," the detective agreed, "'fraid so."

Belasco looked at Rebecca who was still looking away. "May I speak to Mrs. Battelli and her daughter for a moment, please . . . alone?"

Riordan said, "Be my guest."

The three of them walked out of the monitor room and into the conference room. Belasco shut the door. "I'm really sorry they're not being more helpful."

Rebecca shook her head. "I suppose they're doing the best they can."

"What do you want to do?"

"Go home," she said. "Go away. Fall off the face of the earth."

"You've got to stop it," Gabriella said to her mother, then said to Belasco, "I want her to fight back."

"What for?" Rebecca asked.

"For everything my father tried to build. For us. For him."

"Where do I even begin?" Rebecca wanted to know. "You see the mess they left? That's the mess they've made in my life . . . in our lives."

Gabriella said, "Then we begin by cleaning up the mess."

"If you need help . . . " Belasco offered.

"Yes," Gabriella said, "we need help. We need to hire people to help us clean up that mess, and we need help to stay in business. This was my father's business. And his father's business . . . "

"And Johnny's business," Rebecca cut in.

Gabriella was having none of it. "I refuse to let you walk away."

Rebecca sighed, "She's too young to realize . . . "

"I am not," Gabriella said sharply. She turned to Pierre. "I graduate next year. I'm at Sarah Lawrence. I'm half an hour away. I will do what I can until then. I've got this summer to help. I'll be here for her. But we need help."

Pierre thought for a moment. "You're insured, right?"

"I suppose," Rebecca said.

"You'll have to check your insurance, but you should be covered, at least for a lot of it. I'll find someone to help you clean up the place and put everything back together. My accountant will come in to go over the books . . . he was going to come in today . . . "

"I forgot again, I'm sorry . . . "

"That's all right. We'll put the place back together, go over the books, and I'll also see what I can do about keeping the detectives on the case."

"Thank you," Gabriella said.

For the first time, Rebecca looked at him, reached out, and took his hands in hers. "Thank you."

He smiled at her, waited until she let go, then said, "I'll be right back."

Outside the conference room he asked Riordan and the detectives, "Are you finished with Mrs. Battelli?"

"Yeah," Riordan said, then looked at the detectives to check. Both of them nodded. "At least for the time being." He added, "She doesn't understand."

Belasco admitted, "Neither do I."

He asked Riordan to make a copy of the CCTV footage of the two men in raincoats, and to let him also have a copy of the videotape his people made in Rebecca's office. Then he went to find Little Sam, his human resources supervisor. He asked to see a personnel file, took a piece of paper, copied down a phone number from the file, wrote a name next to the number, and returned to the conference room, where he handed the piece of paper to Gabriella.

"Call this fellow. Tell him I said it's all right. Tell him if he has any questions, he can call me. Tell him that I suggested you hire him to help you clean up the place. He needs a job, and he's a very good worker."

Gabriella looked at the paper. "Carlos Vela?"

Belasco nodded. "I'll vouch for him."

DOWNSTAIRS in his own office, Belasco dialed a number and waited for someone to answer.

A man picked up the call on the fourth ring, and sounded still asleep. "Hello?"

"Did I wake you? It's Pierre Belasco."

"Yeah . . . that's okay, what's up?"

"We had a break-in late last night. On the nineteenth floor. The police are here, but they're . . . "

"Not very helpful?"

"Not much to go on, apparently."

"What do you want me to do?" Timmins asked.

Belasco answered, "Call the cavalry."

37

"**G**o get Billy," Ricky pointed down the hall. "Quick. The cat. Go get him."

Amvi was too frightened to move. "What is it?"

Hughie and Jules and the woman in Ricky's underpants all ran to the door. "Where'd it go?"

"Fucking music is too loud."

"Go get the cat."

"Turn down that fucking music."

And all the time, the chubby redhead was still screaming, "Help . . . help . . . help . . . "

"Go on, go on," Ricky begged Amvi, then poked his head out the door and called to the animal. "Here Billy . . . here Billy . . . " He looked at Amvi again, "Go on then, get the cat and bring it back."

"It's not a cat." She didn't budge.

"I can't, luv," he pointed to the ankle bracelet. "If I leave it goes off. I'll get arrested again. But you can . . . go on . . . "

She repeated, "It's not a cat."

He looked up and down the hall. "Bloody hell. Where is it?" He turned to Hughie and Jules, "Go on, get the fucking cat."

Just then, a completely naked woman walked out of the second bedroom and into the living room, saw the commotion, said, "Pardon me . . . didn't know you had company," turned around, and went back inside.

"Who was that?" Ricky asked.

Hughie said, "Shari."

"Who's Shari?"

"Bugs' girlfriend."

"Who's Bugs?"

"The other bloke banging Shari."

By now Amvi was shaking. "I must go. I must leave. Please . . . "

"Wait till we find Billy . . . "

That's when the elevator door opened, and Joey stepped out with a very short redhead. "What's going . . . " He spotted Amvi. "Pocahontas?"

The ocelot darted into the elevator.

"Hey," Miguel, the elevator operator yelled, "Get out . . . "

"Wait!" Ricky screamed. "Don't leave with my cat . . . "

Joey picked up the ocelot and asked, "Pocahontas . . . what are you doing here?"

"Nice cat," the redhead said.

"Who's she?" Amvi asked Joey.

"Who's Pocahontas," the redhead wanted to know.

Amvi shouted, "Wait Miguel," jumped into the elevator and the doors shut.

38

The moment she spotted Mrs. Essenbach getting out of her chauffeur-driven Jaguar, Antonia understood why this woman had sued several plastic surgeons. Her face was so tightly pulled back, Antonia worried what might happen if she tried to laugh.

"Mrs. Essenbach?" Antonia went to the curb to greet her.

"Miss Lawrence." The woman stepped out of the backseat with some help from her chauffeur, then extended her hand to Antonia. "You must be . . . "

"Yes, ma'am." They shook hands. "I'm very pleased to meet you, and thank you for coming to see me."

She was dressed in a beige pantsuit and was wearing a flowery Hermès scarf around her neck. "I confess to being intrigued."

"Shall we go inside?" Antonia motioned toward the doors.

The two of them walked through Chelsea Market.

"Isn't this wonderful?" Antonia tried to engage Mrs. Essenbach in conversation.

But the woman was having none of it. "This place smells of fish."

They went into a snack bar and ordered coffee—Antonia made a point of paying—then sat at a table as far away from the other customers as they could.

"How quaint," Mrs. Essenbach said, "paper cups."

Antonia didn't know what to say, so she tried, "Do you ever shop here?"

"Shop?" Mrs. Essenbach looked surprised. "I haven't been inside a supermarket in . . . I can't even remember. Maybe, twenty years. Do you shop?"

"Here?"

"Anywhere."

"Yes."

"And what do you buy when you shop?"

She thought to herself, *what kind of a question is that?* "I buy . . . I guess I buy the usual things."

"Usual for who?"

"Usual . . . for me."

"Which is?"

"Milk? I don't know . . . eggs, coffee, butter . . . toast?" She shrugged, "The same things everyone else buys."

"Hardly."

"Don't you buy milk and eggs?"

"That's why I have help. Frankly, I don't know what they buy."

Antonia tried to make a joke. "Besides champagne and caviar."

From Mrs. Essenbach's expression, it was clear that she didn't find that amusing. "You said you could help me."

"I said I'd like to try."

"Is that not the same thing?"

"Well . . . it could be. I work in the Trump Organization. My boss reports directly to Mr. Trump himself. So let's say that I have certain access . . . "

"I understand. Now tell me, how are you going to try to help me? You, and your . . . certain access?"

Antonia forced a smile. "When I was informed that Mr. Belasco made you promises . . . well, Mrs. Essenbach, we're a business that keeps our promises. Our word is our bond."

"One would not have thought so from the meeting last night. I was hung out to dry." She shook her head. "I repeat . . . how are you going to try to help me?"

"I, for one, find Mr. Belasco's behavior despicable."

"Clearly your Mr. Trump doesn't because like all the others, he voted against me. And from what I've learned this morning from several people, it seems everyone is standing by Mr. Belasco. At least, I haven't heard anything to the contrary. Still, that doesn't answer my question."

"The board members were clearly following Mr. Belasco's lead."

"He assured me that he had no influence."

Antonia stoked the fire. "That's what he said?"

"He did. But more important than that is his . . . let's call it what it is . . . his betrayal. We were very close."

That surprised Antonia. "Very close?"

She slowly smiled. "On a personal basis."

"You and Mr. Belasco?"

"You can see why his betrayal is twice as difficult for me."

Antonia didn't believe it. Not with this woman. And anyway, she'd always assumed that Belasco was gay. She'd never seen him with a woman. She didn't even know if he had a personal life. But that didn't really matter. If Mrs. Essenbach was saying . . .

"You seem surprised."

"Not surprised that Mr. Belasco would find you . . . " She looked for the right words and the only thing she could think of was, "exotic and irresistible."

"He is . . . I'm sure you will agree . . . a very attractive man."

"Absolutely," Antonia nodded. "And he is, particularly, discreet. I mean, none of us who work closely with him even suspected . . . we never knew . . . "

"Extremely discreet," Mrs. Essenbach agreed.

There's no way that anything ever happened, Antonia said to herself. *But if she keeps saying it did and other people start to believe it . . .* "I'm shocked that a man like Mr. Belasco could, under those circumstances . . . I mean, if he told you. . . "

"He did tell me," she insisted.

" . . . yes, of course . . . I meant, the fact that he told you he would make it happen and then . . . " She paused for effect. "I'm shocked beyond words."

"How do you think I feel? A man like that . . . under those circumstances . . . indeed."

"This needs to be made right." She looked straight into Mrs. Essenbach's eyes. "What do you suppose would happen if Mr. Belasco was forced to admit or, for that matter, forced to deny that you and he were . . . close? Or that he made you a promise?"

"You tell me."

She thought to herself, *you would murder him the same way you murdered your husband.* "It would be much too embarrassing."

"For me?"

"For him. At the same time, it would put pressure on your neighbors, the very people on the residents' board who voted against you."

"Why would they care who Pierre . . . well, you know."

"They'll care because they're very private people. They live in Trump Tower, as you do, because it affords them real privacy. If Mr. Belasco was forced to make an admission in public . . . say, if he was forced to testify . . . Mrs. Essenbach, can you imagine any of your neighbors being willing to expose themselves to public ridicule and the press simply to save Mr. Belasco's job?"

She thought about that.

"Then what you need to do is call Mr. Belasco's bluff," Antonia said. "Your neighbors will not stand by him. Put him on the defensive, and they will desert him. Rather than expose himself to public ridicule, he will walk away from Trump Tower. At that point, whoever takes over from him will give you what you want in order to restore confidence in the building management."

It was as if a light suddenly went on in Mrs. Essenbach's head. She started to grin. "And who do you suppose might take over if Mr. Belasco were to leave?"

Antonia gestured, "I wouldn't know."

"Much," Mrs. Essenbach said.

"Much," Antonia nodded, reached for her coffee, picked it up, and toasted. "To your health."

The woman picked up her coffee cup, too. "And to yours."

39

Cyndi spent part of the day at T'ien.

When she was done there and in the car on her way back to Trump Tower, a text message arrived on her phone. "You will always be one of my life's great loves. Alas. George."

Alas? She wondered, why alas?

The only Georges she thought she knew were George Timothy Daniels and George Masterson. But Daniels always signed his texts Timmy, and Masterson always signed his texts Bat, after the cowboy.

She hadn't seen Daniels for a year or so, although he texted every now and then to joke, "We'll always have the Lincoln Bedroom," referring to the most famous sleepover spot in Washington, DC.

Except, they'd never been to the White House together. It stemmed from a chance meeting in Lincoln, Nebraska, when they found themselves at the same hotel. They were both doing publicity tours—him for a space shuttle flight, Cyndi for her "À Poil" cosmetics line—and every time they tried to sneak off together, one of the people traveling with them got in the way.

Come to think of it, she decided, she hadn't seen George Masterson in quite a while, either. Not since he'd bought the racing rights to the name Bugatti, had built himself a car he called the Bugatti Fangio Nero—named after the great Argentine driver, Juan Manuel Fangio—and had started competing in Formula One.

They'd known each other since Masterson's racing years with McLaren. He hardly ever texted, but every month a dozen long-stemmed roses arrived for her with the same note, "Always and forever. Bat."

So if it isn't Timmy and it isn't Bat—she reread the text for the umpteenth time—*who's George?*

She didn't have a clue.

And the sender's number was hidden, so she couldn't even reply, "Please, give me one more chance."

That made her laugh.

Back at Trump Tower, she walked into the lobby to find that Fabrice and his assistant Joelle were already there. She kissed them on the sides of their faces twice and motioned to them to follow her. They carried their two cases—with all their hairdressing equipment—to the elevator, where Miguel was waiting.

But before Cyndi got in, she said, "Hold on a sec," and went to Belasco's office. He was sitting at his desk writing something.

"*Bonjour*," she said.

He looked up, smiled broadly . . . "Miss Benson . . . " then stood up and walked to the door to shake her hand. "Are you well?"

"Confused," she said.

"Confused?"

"Do you ever sign your texts George?"

"My texts?"

"Text messages. From your phone. Do you ever sign them George?"

"No." He stared at her. "Now I'm confused."

"Don't be." She blew him a kiss. "*Au revoir*."

She went back to Fabrice and Joelle in the elevator, grinned at Miguel, "*Vamanos, caballero*," and went home to have her hair done.

40

A young, dark-haired twenty-year-old woman in an NBC page uniform arrived at Alicia's desk in the newsroom. "Miss Melendez?"

Alicia looked up from her computer screen, then grinned. "Suzy?"

The young woman in the uniform nodded. "I wanted you to see what I look like." She did a quick pirouette. "How cool is this? Suzy Timmins, NBC guest relations . . . " she curtsied . . . "at your service."

"You look terrific."

"My father and my mother and me . . . " She put a small, wrapped box down on Alicia's desk. "Thank you. I hope you like Godiva chocolates. My dad said everybody likes . . . "

"I love them," Alicia held Suzy's hands. "That's very sweet of you. And I was delighted to help."

"MTA is going to announce another fare hike," Greg shouted from across the newsroom. "We'll go with the MTA right after Meagan live."

Alicia waved at Greg, then said to Suzy, "Now that you're part of the family, if you want to stick around and see how we make magic . . . "

"I can't," she said. "I have to go. But thank you. Really . . . to you and Mr. Haynes . . . "

"Mr. Haynes had absolutely nothing to do with it," she assured Suzy. "I did it all on my own. And I'm not, repeat not, sharing my chocolates with him."

Suzy giggled, then waved and walked away.

She'd hardly known Suzy's father, but when he dropped her a note and introduced himself as the night security supervisor at Trump Tower and asked for her help, Carson told her, "You never know when you might need a favor from him."

"Like what?"

"Like . . . when I'm away and you need him to destroy the CCTV footage of you coming home with . . . "

She suggested, "Johnny Depp?"

"For example."

She shook her head. "Forget it. That's CCTV footage I'm keeping."

Her phone rang.

"Do him the favor, anyway," Carson said.

And she did. She got his daughter an interview for a page job—they were very tough to get—then put in a good word for Suzy at Guest Relations. It worked, and Alicia was glad that it had.

Her phone rang again.

"So if you're keeping the footage with Johnny Depp . . . "

"Sometimes a girl wants to brag."

"Why him?"

"You said you were away."

"I think I'll stop traveling." He nodded, then announced, "Cameron Diaz."

"You?" She looked at him, "You manage that and, trust me, I'll let you keep the tape."

Her phone rang again.

"Alicia," she said grabbing it.

"Alishe . . . Sandy at *Nightly*. You got a minute?"

"Sure."

"Come on down."

As soon as she walked into the newsroom there, Sandy Bridgeman spotted her, came over to greet her, took her hand, and pulled her off to the side of the big newsroom where they could talk privately.

"We need a favor," he said, towering over her. "Bill."

"Bill?"

"We've been given the go for a camera on the roof of the museum tonight."

"Oh . . . that Bill."

"Yeah . . . that Bill. We've got a producer, everything's ready, and Bill's agreed. We need you to do ten to twelve minutes with him for a package tomorrow night."

Wow, she thought, a piece on *Nightly*. "What about Brian?" She looked around and spotted him on the other side of the newsroom in a meeting. "He's going."

Sandy paused. "Yeah . . . well . . . Brian's going as a paid guest and, you know, his neutrality thing. He felt there was a conflict . . . paying his way in and getting the interview . . . "

"I'm paying my way in."

"It's different."

She wanted to know, "How?"

"Because he's the *Nightly* anchor and you're not."

She gave him a nasty look.

Picking up on that, Sandy added the word, "Yet."

She smiled. "If he's conflicted, then I'm conflicted."

"You've been given Papal dispensation. I've already spoken to Steve," he said, referring to the president of NBC News. "He adores you, so he's okay with it. Brian adores you, so he's also okay with it. And I love you unabashedly, so I'm okay with it."

Alicia took a deep breath. "I don't know."

"What don't you know? Alishe, this is an exclusive one-on-one with the former president of the United States talking to you on network television about his work for Haiti."

"I'd love to do it but . . . " She confessed . . . "I already told Greg Mandel I wouldn't."

"So? Tell him you will."

"It's not that easy. I am conflicted. I'm a paying guest at the party. Anyway, we've got a young reporter named Meagan O'Donnell on the steps tonight in front of the museum. We're leading with her at six, then coming back to her with a tape insert at the bottom of the show. She's looking to get Clinton, and anyone else."

He stared at Alicia for a very long time. "We're talking about a package on *Nightly* . . ."

"I know but . . . it's a conflict exactly like Brian's."

"It's not the same thing."

"It is . . . except, maybe, a little different."

He took a deep breath, then said, "Hold on," and left her there to go across the newsroom to speak with Brian Williams.

The two men talked for a couple of minutes before Sandy came back smiling. "Alishe . . . Brian says, good for you."

"Really?"

"Yes, really."

Alicia looked at Brian, and he gave her a thumbs up.

She smiled and waved.

"But he wants me to call Greg Mandel and strike a deal. We'll offer him two minutes of your interview for his eleven o'clock. But he'll have to trailer us. You know, something like, see the full interview tomorrow night on *NBC Nightly*. We can work that out."

She looked at Sandy. "Now Carson will kill me."

"Why?"

"Because it's a party, and I'm not supposed to be working."

"If he does," Sandy promised, "we'll lead with the murder tomorrow on *Nightly*, then headline the package as your final interview. Should be great for the ratings."

NEWS FOUR NEW YORK opened with Alicia going to a live feed from Fifth Avenue, where Meagan was standing on the steps of the Metropolitan Museum. The two women talked about the evening. That done, Meagan fed back to Alicia, who promised they'd return to Meagan at the museum at the end of the broadcast.

From there, Alicia went straight into the MTA fare hike story.

She followed that with the package on a new redevelopment plan for Coney Island, and then a live feed from the site of the arson in Staten Island.

Three more local stories came up before she went to the weather and then to sports.

Alicia was about to go into a package on broken windows in New York City schools, when Greg called into her earpiece from the booth that they needed extra time with Meagan at the museum. So the broken windows story got pulled, and Alicia went back to Meagan.

From the steps of the museum, Meagan did a quick "on the red carpet" with Jay-Z—he reminded viewers how important it was that they all send money to the Clinton Haiti fund—got a hello from Donald and Melania Trump, another hello from Jon Stewart, a fast fifteen seconds with Nina Danielle Sklar, then went into a taped forty-five seconds with the Haitian singer and political activist Wyclef Jean.

After that, it was back to Meagan, live again, now holding onto the great old character actor Harry Lustig, who was there with his wife, the actress Dorothy Dall, their son Greg—he was just about to open on Broadway in a revival of *Pajama Game*—and Greg's wife, the singer-songwriter Christine Spane.

"New Yorkers love Haiti," Harry said in his characteristic Brooklyn growl.

"Christine is from Allentown, Pennsylvania," Greg reminded his dad.

"Don't argue with your father," Dorothy warned her son.

"I'm not arguing," Greg insisted.

"Stop arguing," Christine said.

Then the four of them chimed in, together to camera, "New Yorkers love Haiti, and so does everyone from Allentown."

Meagan, who had obviously arranged this, was grinning from ear to ear. "More from here at eleven. Now back to you, Alicia."

"Thank you, Meagan, and thanks to the Lustig quartet," she said. "*NBC Nightly News* with Brian Williams is next. From all of us here at *News Four New York*, good night."

She smiled at the camera, then looked down at her script on the desk.

Over the studio speaker she heard Michael Douglas' introduction to *Nightly*, and then heard Brian say, "On our broadcast tonight . . . "

The floor manager called to Alicia, "We're clear."

She got up, said, "Thanks, everybody," and raced to the makeup room to change into her clothes.

When she was dressed, Agnes the makeup woman touched up her eye shadow and gave her a quick comb out.

Alicia grabbed the box of chocolates that Suzy had brought her, threw her day clothes into her carryall, and hurried out of the building.

Carson and Cyndi were waiting in a car, as planned, at the Rainbow Room entrance.

"You had to do that, didn't you," she said to Cyndi as she climbed into the backseat, kissed her, and then Carson.

"Do what?"

The driver pulled the car into traffic.

"Outdress me."

Cyndi was wearing black suede shorts, a black Versace camisole, a red bolero jacket, and red Trussardi boots.

"Just a little outfit I picked up at Sports Authority," she said.

Carson warned, "If you two can't play nicely together . . . "

Now Alicia told Carson, "There's good news and there's bad news."

"What?" he asked.

"The bad news is that I have to do a ten-minute sit-down with Clinton."

"Some girls have all the luck," Cyndi complained.

"It's a party," Carson said.

"It's for *Nightly*."

"What's the good news?" he asked.

"The good news is that, apparently, Cameron Diaz is there. So be my guest. She's yours while Bill is mine."

Now Cyndi moaned, "Some boys have all the luck."

41

Antonia spent a few hours back in the office putting together the calculations Anthony Gallicano had asked for, amortizing various New Jersey properties, but the second she finished that, she hurried out the door.

It was just after five.

She took the subway uptown, picked up a pizza for dinner, and carried it into her apartment. She changed into sweatpants and a T-shirt, turned on her printer, put the pizza box on her bed to the left, and had plenty of napkins at the ready on her right. She bolstered up her pillows behind her, carefully placed a bottle of beer between her alarm clock and the lamp on her night table, positioned her laptop, logged onto her Gmail account, and then logged onto the 35Tango site.

Clicking on the 35Tango links she'd sent to *jerseyhot1983*, she printed all of them. Then she returned to the beginning of her search for information on Katarina Essenbach and started going through those files.

By the time she'd finished two slices of pizza and the bottle of beer, she was only halfway through the fourth page of references.

There were a dozen more go to.

She was fascinated with what she'd discovered about the suspected murder of Mrs. Essenbach's husband in Alaska, all of her lawsuits, and the stories she dug up on the woman's latest husband, the fraudster from Chile. But a lot of what she was finding now duplicated what she'd already seen, and what worried her was how much deeper she would have to dig to get new material.

Come on, Antonia, keep your eye on the prize.

Another slice and another beer later, she was asking herself, *how much more does Antonia need?*

She reminded herself, *Antonia only needs to make sure that Mrs. Essenbach is motivated.*

She thought about another slice of pizza but settled for her third bottle of beer.

She reassured herself, *Antonia only needs enough to be certain that her Lady Macbeth will kill the king.*

The King.

She thought about Belasco.

Now she opened a fourth bottle of beer, went to the search page at 35Tango, and typed in his name.

PIERRE BELASCO motioned to his couch and shut his office door. "Timmins doesn't come on for a few hours, so I said, no problem, that we could do this alone."

"How can I help?" Forbes asked, dressed as he always seemed to be in his dark-green bomber jacket. But this time, instead of a University of West Virginia baseball hat, he was wearing one that said, Marist Basketball.

Taking two DVDs off his desk, Belasco put the first one in the machine. "Watch this," he said and clicked it on.

The camera panned around Rebecca Battelli's trashed office.

"This is what the place looked like when she got there this morning. Riordan's people shot it."

"Forced entry?"

"No."

"The work of several people," Forbes said. "How'd they get into the Tower and then upstairs?"

"I'll show you." Belasco switched off that DVD and put the other one into the machine.

It was a CCTV composite that showed the two men coming into Trump Tower, going upstairs, and then leaving.

"So, he had a pass," Forbes said when one of the men flashed something to the security guard and was allowed into the elevator. "No sign of forced entry into the office? That means he also had a key. This has all the markings of an inside job."

Belasco suggested, "Let's start with her late husband's cousin Johnny."

"Have you automatically ruled out Mrs. Battelli?"

"What?"

He repeated the question. "Have you automatically ruled out Mrs. Battelli?

I presume she has a building pass and that she has a front door key. Probably several."

"You think she broke into her own showroom?"

"No. But how about she paid someone to trash the place?"

"That's ridiculous. Why would she do that?"

"Insurance?"

"No," he rejected the idea outright. "There's no way."

"In these types of cases," Forbes explained, "you have to look at everybody. You start with the full deck, then discard, one by one. It would help a lot if we knew what the two men took out."

"Took out?" he asked, "You mean, brought in."

"They didn't bring in anything. They took something out."

"How can you be so sure?"

"What would they bring in?"

"I don't know." Belasco suggested, "Burglar tools?"

"Like in the movies, a crowbar? You said there was no forced entry. Maybe if they'd have torched the place, you know, arson . . . but all they did was rip it apart. And take something out. What were they looking for?"

"I still don't know how you can be so sure they took something out?"

"The raincoats."

Belasco thought about that for a long time. "If the cousin . . . "

"You're ruling out Mrs. Battelli."

"Yes. Absolutely."

"Okay, then, for the sake of argument . . . "

"Yes, for the sake of argument," Belasco said. "The cousin wanted to take over the family business, said that it was his, and that Mrs. Battelli had to give it to him. So he had the place trashed because he's angry with her. That's what Bill Riordan said. That someone was angry with her. The police agreed. That points to the cousin."

Forbes shrugged, "Maybe."

"Who else?"

"I don't know. Maybe the cousin. Maybe somebody she's not telling you about. Maybe nobody."

"Have you met the woman? How can you possibly think Mrs. Battelli had something to do with this?"

"For the sake of argument?"

Belasco started shaking his head. "The woman just lost her husband. She's vulnerable. She's fighting to keep her sanity. There's no way . . . "

"Then maybe no one is angry at her."

"But they trashed her place."

"Maybe whoever did it wants you to think they're angry. Maybe there is something else going on."

"Like what?"

"Like," Forbes said, "whatever those two men took out hidden under their raincoats."

"What would they take out?"

"There are really only two things. Goods and information."

"You mean . . . shoe samples?"

"That often happens to major designers when they're about ready to announce their new collection. Someone steals samples, they counterfeit them in China and Eastern Europe, then sell the goods at street markets in the West. It's intellectual property theft."

"I don't think that's the case here. She's not a designer . . . she's an importer. A wholesaler."

"Who's her competition? Who does she owe money to? Who would benefit most if she went out of business?"

"Certainly not her husband's cousin," Belasco said. "She goes out of business and he loses."

Forbes suggested, "Then what about computers? Electronic files? Cash? Checkbooks? Accounting records? Is there a secret bank account somewhere? Is there information . . . was there information . . . that could be used to blackmail someone?"

Belasco admitted, "I don't know."

"Find out what's missing, and you're a big step closer to finding out who did this."

"The police aren't going to do much. I want to help this woman. My accountant is coming in to look through her books. Maybe he'll be able to tell us something."

"So," Forbes asked, "what do you want me to do?"

Belasco answered, "Whatever the police can't, or won't."

ANTONIA ONLY *needs enough to be certain that Lady Macbeth will kill the king,* she repeated.

She suddenly found herself confronted with references to more than thirty different Pierre Belascos.

She'd had no trouble finding the links to herself, or to Katarina Essenbach, or to her parents. Now she couldn't believe there were so many men with the same name. Next to "Pierre Belasco" she added "French," but that didn't do any good. She tried "France" and that didn't do much good either. When she put in the words, "Trump Tower," sure enough, several links came up, but they were professional links—office address, phone number, that sort of thing—and didn't contain anything personal.

It was obvious from the way the search terms were laid out that Belasco's social security number would make things easier. But she didn't have it, and even though she could get it, she worried that IT might catch her logging on from home and ask her what she was doing.

Belasco's New York address would help too—she knew he lived somewhere in the Village—but when she Googled him, it didn't come up.

Back at those business listings, she tried to find something that might work. She read each one carefully and came across the same information repeated and repeated and repeated. It was frustrating, and she was on the verge of giving up when she spotted an entry in one file that read, "(b) 1958, Crans Montana (Valais) Switz."

Immediately, she added "Switzerland" and "1958" to qualify her search for "Pierre Belasco," and up came three pages of links.

Gotcha!

There were references to the hotels where he'd worked, a few interviews with him that were in French and Italian, and all sorts of things she hadn't been able to find yet, like his New York address *and* his social security number.

There were cross-references to hundreds of people she'd never heard of—obviously people he'd worked with—and several cross-references to people she knew, like Donald Trump and Anthony Gallicano.

She sorted through names, looking for something that might help her find new links. And deep down on the third page of the links, she spotted the name Camille Chastain Belasco.

It wasn't a business link, she could tell that much, because there were some dates following that name.

Next to it was the name Christian Chastain Belasco.

She couldn't figure out what it was—brother, sister, mother, father—so she went back to her original search, "Pierre Belasco" and started by adding the qualifier, "Camille Chastain."

That brought up a few other links, which led her to what appeared to be a photo image of a newspaper article.

It was in French. Something about Paris. She saw the words, Hôtel de Crillon.

Antonia could speak the language passably, having worked in France for a year, but reading French was not the same thing as passably speaking it.

Her high-school and college Spanish was no help at all.

What's more, the image of the newspaper cutting was very dark.

She tried to brighten her screen, but that didn't work. So she pushed print, and tried to read it off the page.

It seemed to be dated 1986.

She knew he'd worked at the Crillon in Paris around that time, but the print was too small. She tried to print it larger, but she couldn't get the printer to understand what she wanted to do, and after nearly fifteen minutes of fooling with it, she had to settle for the first copy that came off the machine.

Taking the printed page over to a lamp, she squinted and saw the word *femme* and the word *fils* and then the word *voiture*.

That's when she realized what it was saying.

Oh my God . . . Antonia. She put her hand over her mouth. *Oh my God.*

In Paris in 1986, Pierre Belasco's wife, Camille, and infant son, Christian, had been killed in a car accident.

42

Three hundred handpicked guests had received the beautifully printed invitation that read, "Bill Clinton cordially requests the honor of your company for cocktails and finger food on the Iris and B. Gerald Cantor Roof Garden of the Metropolitan Museum of Art in aid of the Clinton Foundation initiative, 'New York Loves Haiti.'"

Dress was "smart casual," and the time was indicated as 6 to 9 p.m. In the corner of the invitation it said RSVP and warned "admission strictly by invitation." Underneath that was written, "Donations Beginning at $25,000."

For Alicia and Carson, this created a minor problem because she couldn't figure out if it meant twenty-five grand per couple or per person. Carson argued that because the invitation was addressed to Mr. and Mrs., it was twenty-five grand per couple. But Alicia decided that, because this was Bill, they really should err on the side of caution. She told Carson that he needed to write a check from their charity account to the Clinton Foundation for $50,000.

He did.

That same night, Cyndi phoned to say she'd been invited and presumed Alicia and Carson had been as well. Alicia said yes, then explained her dilemma about the donation.

Cyndi said, "Well, if you guys are in for fifty, I'll write a check . . . hold on . . ." She went to get her checkbook and, when she had it, she came back on the phone to say she was writing it now to the Clinton Foundation for $49,999.

Alicia asked, "What are you talking about?"

Cyndi reminded her, "You guys are paying fifty."

"So?"

"So," Cyndi said, "I shouldn't have to pay as much as you because I eat less."

THE NEW YORK Police Department had roped off traffic along Fifth Avenue from Eighty-Fourth Street to Eightieth Street in front of the museum and set up a perimeter behind it, too. No one could get close to the building, except on foot.

Then, before any of the guests could enter the building, they had to show their invitations, wait while their names were checked off the official list, and pass through security machines.

Alicia, Cyndi and Carson arrived at the museum's steps—shuttled there from the designated drop-off point at the corner of Fifth Avenue and Eightieth Street in golf carts decorated with NY (Heart) Haiti signs, and escorted by musicians up and down the block, playing traditional Haitian méringue—only to find a long line waiting to go through security.

Photographers were everywhere, snapping photos, and television news crews were all over the steps, too. They rushed to photograph Cyndi and Alicia, with Carson standing proudly in the middle, then just as quickly abandoned them when the next golf cart arrived, this time with Will Smith and Jada Pinkett Smith.

Behind the Smiths were Ellen DeGeneres and Portia de Rossi.

Behind them was James Gandolfini, sharing a golf cart with Hugh Jackman and his wife.

Steve Buscemi and his wife were near the front of the line, and so was Sienna Miller, who was deep in conversation with Barbara Walters.

For the press, it was a feeding frenzy.

Meagan O'Donnell spotted Alicia and wanted her to do a piece to camera, but Alicia sidestepped the interview by saying, "You don't want me, you want Liza Minnelli," who happened to be standing twenty yards away talking to Bette Midler.

Jimmy Fallon and Meredith Vieira were waiting to get in, and so was the rap singer 50 Cent. Not far away Matt Lauer was talking to Charlie Rose, who was on line in front of Jerry Stiller and his wife, Anne Meara.

Behind them was the legendary black soul singer Monserrat Madyson. And when she spotted Cyndi, Monserrat put her hands on her hips, shook her head, and called out loud enough for everybody to hear, "Honey, you are too damn beautiful. You ruin it for the rest of us. Girl . . . look at you . . . damn . . . don't you ever eat?"

That wound up being the teaser into the Clinton party segment the next morning on *Good Morning America*.

Once guests got inside the museum, police officers and museum officials guided them to elevators that took them up to the roof garden, where their names were checked a second time.

And, for the second time, everyone had to go through security.

But as soon as they stepped outside, five floors above the treetops, the city of New York at dusk surrounded them.

There was Harlem beyond the park to the north, and midtown below the park to the south, the elegance of Fifth Avenue apartments staring back at them on the eastside, and the towered silhouettes of stately buildings lining Central Park to the west.

A band was playing Haitian minijazz on the far side of the roof, while waiters and waitresses in white dinner jackets circulated everywhere, carrying drinks and platters with fifty different types of hors d'oeuvres.

Everything was prepared right there, in a special outdoor kitchen constructed under the trellis, where a dozen toque-headed cooks moved frantically back and forth to the commands of Micelo Sydney, the Haitian-born, French-trained chef whose restaurant, Cap-Haïtien, a few blocks away on Madison Avenue, had recently won a second Michelin star.

The air smelled of lime and grilled fish and French perfume.

Alicia went to check on her crew for the interview, while Carson and Cyndi wound their way through the crowd and found David and Tina. They chatted until Alicia came back, and a few minutes after that, Bill Clinton—who can work a room better than anybody else on the planet—sidled up to them to say hello.

"We watch you every night at six," Bill told Alicia. "And Hillary thinks you're the best."

"Don't *you*?" Carson challenged him.

He put his finger to his lips. "Shhhh," and whispered, "I do."

Now he turned to Cyndi. "When Chelsea was growing up . . . one Christmas . . . this must have been just after we left the White House, she wanted some of your perfume. She said it's called À Poil. Well, I knew what À Poil means, and there was no way . . . "

"Wanna know a secret?" Cyndi leaned close to him. "Chelsea knew, too."

He roared with laughter.

Turning to David and Tina, Bill told her, "You're much too beautiful and much too smart for a fellow like David."

"There's truth in humor," she said flatly, then forced a smile so that everyone would think she was joking.

"And from what I hear," Clinton said to David, "you're still not telling the truth about your handicap."

"What . . . y'all do?" David asked.

He smiled broadly. "Knowing what we know about each other's game, let's play sometime soon."

"I can't afford you," David protested. "A couple of strokes, maybe. But last time, you claimed to be a twenty-two, except y'all play to thirteen."

"I had to say that," Bill insisted, "'cause you claimed to be a nine when I know you-all play scratch."

"Trump plays to two, but he gives me four."

"Yeah, well," Bill took Cyndi's arm and wrapped it in his, "if The Donald ever becomes president, he'll claim to play to fifteen. It's what we do."

Now, with Cyndi on his arm, the former president headed for Robert De Niro and Julia Roberts, who were talking to Zeke Gimbel.

"Tell me something," Cyndi said before they joined that group. "Do you ever sign text messages George?"

He gave her an odd look. "No. Why?"

She shrugged, "I live in hope."

All over the roof garden, women in Gucci, Chanel, Dior and Valentino were drinking mango champagne cocktails.

And men in Armani, Zegna, Paul Smith and Prada—and several in designer jeans, a T-shirt, blue blazers, and sockless in Ferragamo loafers—were asking waiters in evening clothes, "What's that?" and when they were told, "*pikliz griot*" and "*tasot cabrit*" and "*poul fri*" and "*banan peze*," they took a chance, lifted whatever it was off the silver platter, and popped it into their mouths.

Steven Spielberg and his wife were talking to Stevie Wonder and Kathleen Turner, while Nicole Kidman and Cameron Diaz were listening to Antoine de Maisonneuve tell them about the museum's dress collection. "They have a 1935 Chanel evening ensemble that is to die for, and if you don't see anything else, there's a bright red Halston gown from the late 1970s . . . darlings, even I would wear that."

Matt Damon was trying to taste whatever it was that Halle Berry was eating, while Jennifer Hudson was describing her favorite restaurant in Miami to Mary J. Blige.

Jennifer Lopez was talking to Juliana Margulies, Caroline Kennedy Schlossberg was laughing with Yoko Ono, while Bono was pointing across the park to some towers on the top of an apartment building along Central Park West, telling Kelly Ripa and Coldplay's Chris Martin, "I'm right there."

The evening was still young when people started clinking their glasses for quiet and cleared a space in the middle of the roof for Bill Clinton, microphone in hand, to make a little speech.

Working in the round like the seasoned performer that he is, Clinton told his guests that he was very grateful for everything they were doing for Haiti, but reminded them that people were still dying there.

"It doesn't end when you write a big check and drink some champagne," he said. "It won't end till the dying stops and the schools are open and the hospitals are open and the water is clean and the tent cities are turned into homes and hundreds of thousands of lives are rebuilt. It won't end if you leave here tonight and think, now I've done my part."

He spoke for nearly ten minutes, off the cuff and with great passion, and when he was finished, everyone on the roof applauded him for nearly as long as he'd spoken.

That's when Alicia's segment producer found her to say it was time.

Together, they stole the former president away from the crowd and went to the corner of the roof where NBC had set up two cameras, lit two stools, and angled them with the lights of midtown Manhattan glistening behind them.

Alicia and Bill sat down. A makeup woman briefly stood in front of them and offered a light dusting of powder. The segment producer briefed Alicia one final time, and the cameras started rolling.

She said to Bill, "Start with the misery that you still see in Haiti after all this time."

And Bill was off and running.

Some people stood around and watched. Others went back to air-kissing hello, the finger food and the drinks. And all over the roof you could hear guests asking waiters, "What is it?" And after they were told and still didn't know, they tasted it. And all over the roof you could hear guests saying, "Wow, this is great . . . but what is it?"

Tom Hanks was talking to Derek Jeter when Michael J. Fox and his wife, Tracy Pollan, walked by. Jeter reached out for him and hugged him, and when Alex Rodríguez saw that, he came over to hug Fox, too.

Yankee center-fielder Roberto "El Espíritu" Santos—the ball player they called the Holy Ghost—was standing nearby, alone, taking it all in.

Zeke now wandered over to where Carson was standing, watching Alicia, and asked him, "How did things work out when you were signed with Sovereign Shields?"

Carson was surprised. "How did you know about that?"

"We're buying the agency and I saw your name on the client list from . . . ten years ago?"

"They sent me out one time for a shaving commercial. But I never even got to the soapy-face test. Sponsor took one look at me and decided I was wrong."

"Who represents Alicia?"

"William Morris Endeavor."

"Any chance we can steal her away?"

"How well do you know Ari Emmanuel?" Carson asked, referring to the man running the agency.

"Very well."

"Then you know there's not a prayer in the world."

Zeke smiled. "Can't blame a guy for trying," patted Carson's arm, and walked away to speak to Tina Fey and Alec Baldwin, who were describing an outtake from *30 Rock* to Anderson Cooper.

Carson drifted off to the side of the roof and looked around at the city. He did a three-sixty, then looked at Trump Tower and tried to count the floors to find their apartment. He thought he could see the gym—because from the gym he could certainly see the museum—then turned to find himself standing next to a tall, slim, young woman with deep green eyes and long, dark hair.

He smiled.

"*Bonsoir*," she said.

"Oh . . . okay . . . *bonsoir*."

She introduced herself in English, with a heavy French accent, "I am Amelie Laure Moreau. And who are you?"

He said, "I'm Carson Haynes. Nice to meet you."

She nodded, "Likewise," then asked, "And who are you here with?"

He pointed to where Alicia was sitting with President Clinton.

"Oh. I am impressed," she said. "Did you work with him when he was president?"

"No," Carson grinned, "not him . . . her."

"Ah . . . " She tilted her head slightly and pursed her lips, "Why am I not surprised? She is very beautiful. You brought her . . . "

"I did."

"But tell me . . . " She gave him a very intense stare . . . "do you have to go home with her?"

"Actually . . . I do. She pays my rent." He grinned. "I'm her toy boy."

"Alas . . . " She gave him a very knowing smile.

"And you? Who did you come here with?"

Looking around, she tried to find her escort, but couldn't. "Someone who is obviously too busy for me."

"He's a fool."

"My sentiments exactly."

"Your English is very good."

"I learned in England."

"At school?"

"I danced there for five years."

"Danced?"

She got up on her toes for a couple of seconds. "Not easy with heels. But then, at the Royal Ballet I did not wear heels."

"Oh," he said. "The Royal Ballet? That's Covent Garden, right? Are you still . . . "

"Yes it is, and no, I'm not. Now I am with the Opéra de Paris. Do you like the ballet?"

He nodded, "I do."

"And do you like ballet dancers?"

He grinned, "I'm sure that I do."

"And do you ever come to Paris?"

"I know Paris. I mean, I've been there a lot . . . "

"Do you want to come with me tomorrow?"

"Huh?"

"Tomorrow. Air France to Paris. The flight leaves at around seven. Buy a ticket. Come with me."

He chuckled. "That, ah . . . that happens to be the best offer I've ever had on a roof. Ever. But . . . alas, as you say . . . I can't. And even if I could, I'm going to Japan tomorrow."

"And . . . next time?"

"Next time on a roof?"

"No, next time you are in Paris. You can remember my name? Amelie Laure Moreau? Next time you are in Paris . . . find me. Call the Opéra, ask for the stage door, and leave a message. Say it's the man from the roof. Find me. I will remember, I promise. And then I will show you *les toits de Paris.*"

He smiled. "The roofs of Paris?"

"Yes . . . we will start with the roofs of Paris. *À bientôt, j'espère*"—soon, I hope—she lightly touched his arm and walked away.

"Tell me, Mr. Haynes," Cyndi whispered in Carson's ear, "how old were you when you took up ballet?"

He spun around. "I think I just got hit on."

"I guarantee you did. Mademoiselle Moreau is quite the babe."

He started to laugh. "Babe?"

"In French the word is *nana.* And she is a very well-known *nana.*"

"I'll have to remember that. *Nana.*"

"I'm sure that Alicia will be impressed with your French."

He put on his best stern face. "You wouldn't dare mention this to her."

"She's my best friend and my sister and my earth mother all rolled into one. Of course, I will."

"But I didn't do anything."

"But you're a guy . . . and you would have."

A waiter came by with a platter of small leaves wrapped around something. Carson took one. So did Cyndi.

"This is great, whatever it is," Carson said, and turned toward the waiter for another one, but as he did, a tall man with short hair, light tan skin, and a very pleasant round face stepped in front of him. "Oh . . . excuse me."

"Sorry," the man said.

Carson looked at him. "I think we're neighbors in Trump Tower." He extended his hand. "I'm Carson Haynes . . . this is our friend Cyndi Benson."

The man smiled shyly and shook both their hands. "I'm Roberto Santos."

"I've seen you play," Carson said.

He smiled, almost as if he was embarrassed. "I know who you are . . . although, I'm sorry, I never saw you play. And I know who Miss Benson is. Everybody does. But . . . aren't you married to the lady on television?"

"Alicia Melendez." He pointed to where she was interviewing Bill Clinton.

Roberto nodded. "My mother watches her every evening."

"Your mother?"

"Yes," he said, then added almost apologetically, "I'm not usually home at that hour."

"You could always TiVo Alicia," Cyndi suggested, "and watch her on your iPhone in the bullpen."

Roberto didn't realize she was joking. "I'm afraid I don't get to spend a lot of time in the bullpen. I take it you're not a baseball fan."

She teased him. "Grown men running around in their pajamas?"

"Don't take that personally, Roberto," Carson cut in. "I assure you, Cyndi has no problem with grown men in pajamas."

Roberto smiled politely.

Cyndi touched Roberto's arm. "Never mind him. I have it on good authority that he doesn't wear pajamas. But, then, neither do I. Do you?"

He smiled again, obviously trying to hide the fact that he had no idea how to respond to her.

Out of the corner of his eye, Carson noticed that Alicia and Clinton were now standing up. The interview had ended.

"Gotta rescue my bride," he said. "It was nice to finally meet you. Come by one night, we'll do dinner."

He nodded, "Thank you."

Carson shook Roberto's hand—"If Cyndi asks about the infield fly rule, don't bother"—winked at Cyndi and walked away.

"At Trump Tower," Cyndi said to Roberto, "we never have flies infield."

Again, Roberto just smiled.

Alicia thanked Clinton, who hugged her and left to continue working the room.

"How did that go?" Carson asked, taking her hand.

"Bill's Bill," she said. "If he hadn't gone into politics, he could have hosted the *Tonight Show*."

He kissed the side of her face, she thanked the crew, and the two of them moved away from the little set.

Now she asked Carson, "Becoming a patron of the ballet, are we?"

He started chuckling, "You never miss a thing."

"You do know who she is," Alicia said, certain that he did.

"Yeah. Used to dance with the Royal Ballet in London."

"No." Alicia shook her head. "She was prima ballerina at the Royal Ballet and is now prima ballerina with the Paris Opéra. She is a very big deal."

He shrugged, "Shows you what I know."

She glared at him, "I know what you know."

Carson realized Alicia wasn't finding this funny. "Frankly, I'm more impressed with Cyndi's new best friend." He pointed to where she was talking with Roberto Santos.

"Cyndi and the Holy Ghost?"

He nodded. "Sounds like a fable worthy of Corinthians."

"Or perhaps . . . " she suggested, "a choreographed ballet?"

He looked at her. "Come on."

"Come on, what?"

"I'm your number-one groupie. What are you worried about?"

"I know a predator when I spot one flirting with my husband." She took his arm. "Let's say hello to Brian."

The *NBC Nightly News* anchor was deep in conversation with the noted philanthropists and collectors Jay and Jean Kislak.

The subject of ballet was not mentioned again for the rest of the night.

THE PARTY broke up just before nine.

Alicia, Cyndi and Carson had a car and offered Roberto a ride back to Trump Tower.

He accepted.

But the night was mild, and Cyndi suggested they walk.

So the four of them started down Fifth Avenue but only got as far as Seventy-Sixth Street when Cyndi announced, "How about the Carlyle? I don't know what time the show starts, but I'm sure they'll let us in."

Alicia pointed to Cyndi's black suede shorts. "Us, maybe, but . . . you?"

"Trust me," she nodded confidently.

Alicia looked at Carson, who looked at Roberto, and the three of them shrugged, "Sure," at the same time. So they turned into Seventy-Sixth, went one block to Madison and walked into the Carlyle.

The show had already started, and they could hear the voice of the jazz legend Marva Josie.

"She's wonderful," Carson said. "Do you know that she used to be Earl Fatha Hines' band singer? We're talking real pedigree."

"You're older than you look," Cyndi said.

"I like this place," Roberto told them. "I have Marion McPartland's album *Live at the Carlyle* on my iPod."

"Who?" Cyndi asked.

Carson said, "And you're younger than you look."

Alicia pointed to the large, framed portrait in the lobby of the entertainer Bobby Short who, single-handedly, made the Café Carlyle famous.

"I interviewed him once in Miami," she said. "He did a concert there with the symphony. Bobby invented charm."

"May I help you?" A man in a tuxedo greeted them.

"Are we too late for the show?" Carson asked.

He looked at Cyndi's shorts.

She curtsied and smiled.

He hesitated, then nodded, "The four of you are always welcome," he said, and brought them inside. The place was crowded, but he found them a table.

They weren't hungry enough for a meal, but they ordered dessert and a bottle of champagne—although Roberto stayed with water—and after Marva's set ended, she came to the table to say hello.

She told Roberto that she recognized him from his rookie year with the Pittsburgh Pirates.

He told Marva that her version of "Something" was the best rendition of the song since the Beatles.

When the check finally came, Carson reached for it, but Roberto beat him to it.

"Come on," Carson insisted, "let me have that . . . please."

"No," Roberto said. "This is the nicest evening I've had in a long time."

Cyndi looked at him. "Really?"

"Yes." Then he shrugged, "Except a few nights ago in Chicago when I went four for four, which included a walk-off home run."

Alicia, Cyndi, and Carson laughed.

Then Carson announced, "I hate to be a party pooper, but I'm off to Japan tomorrow."

"And we get to play the Blue Jays. Would you like to come to the game?"

Alicia and Cyndi looked at each other, then at Carson.

"Can we take a rain check?" Cyndi said. "I can't tomorrow or Thursday . . . another time?"

Roberto smiled. "Sure. Another time."

"Really . . . we'd love to come to a game," Alicia said, still looking at Cyndi. "Maybe next week?"

"Sure," Roberto nodded, "maybe next week."

They left the Carlyle and walked down Madison Avenue all the way to Fifty-Sixth Street, talking about nothing in particular, most of the time with Alicia arm in arm with Cyndi, and Carson walking with Roberto.

"Why don't you want to go to a game with him?" Alicia whispered.

Cyndi reminded her, in a whisper, "I don't do first dates."

They turned onto Fifty-Sixth Street.

Now Cyndi stepped back and took Roberto's arm. "This has been really nice. Thank you."

He said, quietly, "You're welcome."

They walked into the lobby together and headed for the elevators.

Ricardo was standing in front of an open elevator and said, "Good evening."

The four of them got in and Ricardo closed the doors. "Fifty-two, fifty-nine, and sixty-one?" he asked, referring to Carson and Alicia's floor, Cyndi's floor and Roberto's floor.

"I'm fifty-two also," Cyndi said.

Alicia shot a look at her.

When they got to that floor, Cyndi stepped out with Alicia and Carson, then turned and said good night and thank you, again, to Roberto.

The elevator door closed.

Carson unlocked the door and asked Cyndi, "You coming in?"

"Nope, going home." She kissed Alicia and Carson, "Night night," and rang for the elevator.

Alicia stood there staring at Cyndi. "Since when did you become a fourteen-year-old virgin?"

She smiled, "Isn't it fun that he's so shy?"

WEDNESDAY

43

Antonia had hardly slept.

She'd dozed off sometime around two but was awake again at five because she wanted to keep playing on the 35Tango site before her one-day subscription expired.

Rummaging around everything there was to find about Pierre Belasco, she began printing out all the links she'd bookmarked.

Wife and son killed in a car accident.

As the pages came off her printer, she kept asking herself, *how does Antonia use that?*

After all the Belasco files printed, she turned to Katarina Essenbach and printed everything she could find about her various husbands, especially the one from Chile, and the mysterious death of her husband in Alaska.

How does Antonia use that?

By the time all those pages were printed, she had to start thinking about going to the office. But she still had the rest of the morning left on her subscription.

Antonia needs to keep going. Antonia shouldn't stop now.

So she e-mailed Anthony to say she'd be working from home this morning and promised to be in around lunchtime.

Back on the 35Tango site, she tried to think of who else to look at.

The woman who owned the shoe company. In Antonia's mind, Belasco had seemed protective of her. But the name Rebecca Battelli in the search box only resulted in links to clippings about her husband's death.

Carlos Vela. Belasco had defended him at the staff meeting. But when she put his name in the system, nothing came up.

Who else? Come on, Antonia, who else?

Cyndi Benson. Except for the fact that Trump Tower showed up as her address, there didn't seem to be anything in the forty pages of links about her career that connected her on a personal basis with Belasco or Essenbach.

But there was that little problem Pierre had solved for Cyndi.

Belasco didn't want Antonia to know, but Riordan's report spelled it out.

So now Antonia went looking for whatever she could find on Tommy Seasons.

DAVID OPENED his eyes, saw that the sun wasn't yet up, and moved close to Tina, who was still asleep. He reached for her and started moving his hands all over her body.

She groaned slightly, then moved closer to him and, with her eyes still closed, reached for him, too.

He woke her that way and afterward whispered, "Go back to sleep."

Then he got up and made her breakfast, which he delivered on a tray.

"Why are you being so nice to me?" she asked. "How guilty do you feel?"

"Not guilty at all. I'm being nice 'cause I love you."

"In case you haven't yet figured it out . . . sex, coffee and a *croissant* isn't going to change my mind about your getting involved with the Colombians."

His BlackBerry rang.

"It's going to be fine," he promised. "Who the hell is that at this hour?"

The caller ID flashed "RD."

He told his uncle, "You're up early."

"Nope, up late. On my way home. Your pals in Mexico . . . give 'em a call, will you? Let's do that deal."

"I'm on it." He hung up and looked at Tina, "RD's looking to do a deal with some Mexicans. I guess the Colombians will have to wait."

"David, we don't need them."

He blew her a kiss. "Not this morning, we don't."

ODETTE WALKED into the residents' lobby, already dressed for the day. She was wearing a long, sequined evening gown, with a fox-head fur collar wrapped around her neck.

"Good morning, Madame," Shannon said, staring incredulously at the fox-head fur collar.

She nodded and smiled. "Is Monsieur Belasco in his office?"

"Not yet. I don't expect him for another few hours."

"Pity. Perhaps I should leave a message."

"Of course, Madame." Shannon took some paper and a pen and handed it to her.

Odette leaned on the desk and started to write, then realized that Shannon could see, so she moved a little to her right to shield the note.

Anyway, she wrote it in French.

"Cher Monsieur Belasco, When you have a moment, can you please tell me how I can find YouTube on my television as I wish to view the tape made of Mrs. Essenbach's husband leaving the building the other night in his underwear. Please know that I send you my distinguished sentiments."

ALICIA GOT UP early to go to the gym with Carson. They worked the machines together, although she stopped running before he did, and then, sweaty and wrapped in their towels, they came back upstairs.

She said, "Take your shower first," and went to make coffee, but as soon as she heard the water running, she got out of her clothes and surprised him.

"Oh, hello . . . " he said, his head soapy with shampoo.

"Keep washing your hair," she instructed, took a handful of bath gel and touched him.

"Oh hello," he said again, this time in a different tone.

"Just a little trick that ballet dancers don't know."

He let the remark pass.

THE PHONE woke Cyndi.

She answered it with a groggy, "Hello?"

It was His Excellency calling from Kuwait, and he was crying. "Cyndi, help, please . . . help . . . "

"What's wrong? What's happened?"

He was weeping, nearly out of control. "Help me . . . please . . . I can't . . . help . . . this is terrible . . . "

"What's happened? Where are you?"

"It's Najeeba."

"Where's that?"

"No. Najeeba. My wife. She is going to leave me."

That woke her up. "What? Why? What have you done to her?"

The last thing in the world Cyndi wanted was for his wife to walk out and then him show up in New York thinking he could marry her. "You must not let her leave. Where is she now?"

"Umayma . . . it started with Umayma but now there is Karida . . . Umayma and Karida."

She didn't know where or what or who he was talking about. "Calm down. Take a deep breath. Take a drink of water. Calm down and tell me what's happened."

"Umayma . . . Umayma and Karida . . . Najeeba . . . my wives."

"Please . . . calm down." It took her nearly ten minutes to stop him babbling and get the story out of him.

Najeeba was his first wife and the mother of his three children. Umayma was his second wife, but they could not have children. That suited Najeeba because it meant her children would never have to share anything with Umayma's children. Their father's wealth was all for them.

Then, he said, he'd recently married his distant cousin's daughter, Karida—

it was the first Cyndi heard about that—and Karida got pregnant very quickly. Najeeba was furious because that meant Karida would move up a notch in the pecking order, which challenged her own position. At the same time, Umayma was displeased because, childless, she'd now be reduced to the role of occasional concubine.

So Umayma had issued him an ultimatum, which was get rid of wives one and three or she wanted out.

Najeeba, being wife number one, heard that, assumed he was considering it, and had, only this morning, issued an ultimatum of her own. She said, get rid of wives two and three or she'd leave.

As Karida, being wife number three was, technically, his own cousin, the family on her side had also issued a warning, insisting that if he divorced Karida, they would petition the ruling family—which happened to be on that side of the family—to divest him of his wealth and give it to her.

"Okay . . . okay . . . listen to me . . . " Cyndi tried to think of something. "You've got to make it right with all three of your wives."

"I can't . . . they won't . . . " He was crying again. "My life with them is over."

"No, no, no, no, no . . . " She knew she needed to think of something before he thought of rebounding from them to her. "You must make it right with all three."

"How? You tell me. I don't know how. You're a woman . . . "

"Yes . . . well . . . women who feel they have been rejected . . . they need attention. They need love. They need . . . " Out of the blue she decided, "Roses . . . "

"What?"

"Roses. And Diamonds. All women who feel rejected need roses and diamonds."

There was a long pause. "Roses and diamonds?"

She hoped he'd buy into this. "Is there a florist near you? And a jeweler?"

"I don't know . . . yes . . . maybe . . . there must be."

"All right. Now listen . . . " Cyndi had no idea if this would work in the Arab world and wasn't convinced it would in the Western world either, but if he didn't think too deeply about this, at least it sounded good. "Go buy three dozen roses. No, make it six dozen. Or twelve dozen. Buy as many roses as you can. Then go buy three very big diamond somethings . . . like a broach. Not a ring. A broach. Or a diamond necklace. Make sure they're not the same. Three different broaches or necklaces . . . or earrings or watches . . . whatever. And they have to be the same size. Then, take one bunch of roses . . . a third of whatever you can buy . . . and deliver them to your first wife. Get down on your hands and knees and tell her that she is the love of your life and that you cannot live without her. Beg forgiveness. Give her the roses and the diamond thing and then make love to her."

"But what if . . . "

"Don't worry about that," she said because she didn't know, what if. "Then get the second batch of roses and the second diamond thing and take one of your little blue pills. Remember those? Go to see your third wife. Start with the first one, then go to the third one. Give her the roses and the diamond thing, get down on your hands and knees, and tell her that you will love her forever. Beg forgiveness and then make love to her."

"To her, too?"

"I'm a woman, I know about these things."

"Najeeba . . . and then Karida . . . in that order."

"That's right. In that order. Then, take another little blue pill, or maybe even two little blue pills . . . it is very important that you can perform . . . and bring the rest of the roses and the third diamond thing to your second wife, the one without the children."

"Umayma."

"Right. Get down on your hands and knees, tell her you love her the way you have never loved another woman, beg forgiveness, and spend the rest of the night making love to her."

"I can't. I'll be dead."

"You must," she said, "all night. Those pills will help you. Go on, go buy as many roses as you can and three really gorgeous diamond things."

There was a long pause. "This will really work?"

"It will really work," she said, then mumbled to herself, *or not. Either way, it's better for him than sitting around crying and watching all three women walk out of his life. At least he'll be getting laid.*

"Cyndi . . . Cyndi . . . you are such a good friend . . . "

His Excellency hung up.

And where are you from, Cyndi Benson? She asked herself out loud, as if she were being interviewed as a contestant on a quiz show.

I'm originally from Taos, New Mexico.

That's nice, she said in her quiz show MC voice, *and where do you live now? Now . . . I live in Bizarro World.*

She lay back, closed her eyes, and tried to go to sleep.

In her head she envisioned His Excellency, his arms full of roses and his pockets bulging with diamonds, running away from three nagging women who were frantically shoving blue pills down his throat . . .

But she couldn't sleep.

Getting up, she threw on a robe and went into the kitchen to make breakfast.

That's when she saw it was 5:45.

"Yes? No?" She stared at her espresso machine, decided, "No," and went back to bed.

Now, when she closed her eyes she pictured the three women chasing him, except he was down on his hands and knees, and so were they . . .

She got up again and reached for her laptop to check her e-mail.

Seeing nothing special, she thought for a moment about last night, then Googled "Roberto Santos." There were a couple of thousand links that came up—she wasn't surprised that his Google search brought up more results than hers—and because the first one was his Wikipedia page, she started there.

She read through it, ignoring the baseball statistics and how well he'd played center field for the Yankees over the past twelve years, or how he was certainly going to retire in the next year or two. According to this, he was already thirty-six. Also according to this, he grew up in Texas, a first-generation American of Nicaraguan immigrants.

Further down, the page noted that he'd been married for ten years to his high school sweetheart. They were divorced and had two daughters whom he only saw occasionally because his wife had remarried, and she was jealously guarding custody of them.

Then, even further down, one line jumped off the page.

"Santo, famously, lives with his mother."

Cyndi read it and remembered what he'd said to Carson about her watching Alicia on television.

She lay back on her bed and stared up at her own smoked-glass reflection in the mirror that looked down on her.

He lives with his mother? I wonder what that means?

After a while, she couldn't decide, so she sat up again, took her laptop, got on the Net, did a search for "Marva Josie" and George Harrison's song "Something" and found an album of Marva's called *Forever*. She bought it on iTunes, set up a link so that Roberto could download it for his iPod, and handwrote a note to him on her own stationery.

"Thank you, again, for last night." She noted the iTunes link, and added, "Just 'Something' to make you smile."

She thought about signing it, "XXX, Cyndi," but at the last minute, left off the XXX.

Putting the note in an envelope, she addressed it to him and left it on the little table next to her front door. She'd have the concierge deliver it later.

Right now, she decided, *I'm going back to sleep.*

This time she managed it.

44

Zeke Gimbel's *pied-à-terre* on the thirty-ninth floor of Trump Tower had originally been a two-bedroom apartment. But after he and Miriam split up, his accountant convinced him that he needed to turn the whole thing into a business expense. So Zeke broke down the wall to the second bedroom and expanded the living room into a large office.

He bought a huge Georgian mahogany partner's desk, installed it in front of the floor-to-ceiling windows that faced Central Park, turned the couches toward the desk, and re-angled the dining room table that, for tax purposes, was inventoried as a conference table.

When he took over First National Artists and moved all of his New York people into their big offices on Fifty-First Street, his accountant warned him that if he started going there to work, or even if he maintained a desk there for an occasional visit, he'd lose his home office deduction.

Around the same time, Zoey and Max tried to convince him that, since he already had an office in Manhattan, anyway, if he could rebuild the second bedroom, then they could have their own place in New York. He had to remind them that teenaged school kids in California didn't actually need their own place in New York.

Then Birgitta suggested that if they put the second bedroom back, she could bring her sisters over from Stockholm for regular visits. Her parents, too. And maybe even her best friends.

Next, his mother, Hattie, began saying that it would be nice if there was room for her so that she could come to New York once in a while.

After that, his sister called to ask if it was true that he was building a second bedroom in Trump Tower for Hattie and, if so, could she and her husband use it occasionally.

That's it, he decided, *the office stays an office. No in-laws. No kids. No family. No friends of the family. Just me.*

And his art.

"Whatever you put in your office," his accountant told him when he bought the partner's desk, "is a legitimate expense."

Asking himself, *what would I like to own if the government is paying for it?,* he started going to art auctions in New York and very quickly got hooked.

He bought a Giacometti *Walking Man* for the entrance, and a Giacometti *Dog,* which lived on a marble pedestal next to his desk in the corner of the big room. For the wall, he bought a huge Arman accumulation of paintbrushes. For the floor-to-ceiling bookcases that he'd built facing that, he'd bought several small sculptures, including two by Elizabeth Frink, one by Henry Moore, two by Jean Arp, and a Jasper Johns "Ballantine XXX" beer can bronze.

He bought a Rauschenberg to hang over his bed and a Lichtenstein for the wall inside the door. He bought a Jim Dine *Heart* for the hallway and put a Jean Dubuffet face next to it. He had a small Wesselmann nude in his bathroom and a small Robert Indiana *Love* pencil drawing in the guest bathroom. There was also a Jim Dine *Bathrobe* in his kitchen, which would otherwise be an unsuitable place for a painting, except no one ever cooked there.

Soon out of wall space, he stashed more than two dozen other paintings in closets—including works by Frank Stella, Ed Ruscha, Larry Poons, and Cy Twombly—still wrapped the way they'd come from the auction house.

With two homes in California, he had plenty of places to hang them if he'd wanted to, the way he'd found room to hang two Warhols—a Campbell's can of vegetarian vegetable soup and an Elvis—and his Julian Schnabels. But keeping them in New York maintained their "business expense" status.

Anyway, hanging paintings had long ago ceased to be the object of the game. This was all about buying and selling and, especially, upgrading.

AFTER THE PARTY at the museum, Zeke had invited a bunch of friends to Rools, a private dining club on the East Side, near Sutton Place.

Audra Kaleigh Harris and her husband, Romain Neal, came along. She was a client of the agency and had just opened a biopic based on the life of the entertainer Pearl Bailey. And he was in his fourth season with the Knicks.

Solly Green and his wife, Belinda, were also there. He'd just sold his Green Room Music label to CBS for $1.7 billion.

So was Zeke's old law school friend, Natie Whitestone who, with his wife Ruth, was the largest-single taxi fleet owner in the country, having more than sixteen thousand cabs on the road in eighteen cities.

When they finished supper, he'd taken them all to Doubles—the private club in the basement of the Sherry Netherland—for a nightcap. It suited Zeke because he didn't have to be up early and could walk home from there.

He'd gotten to bed at three and had set his alarm for 8:45, but the phone rang at seven.

"This is James Malcolm Isbister. Good morning to you."

"Oh." Zeke was half asleep. "Good morning." He didn't realize that Isbister had his New York number.

"Would it be possible to meet this morning?"

"This morning?" He looked at the time. "Ah . . . I guess I could do breakfast but in . . . like an hour?"

"Unfortunately, I can't. I received the real estate—only plan from Mr. Lerner on Monday night. We reviewed it yesterday and need to make a decision today."

"The rest of the morning is a little tough for me." Zeke couldn't recall ever mentioning to him that he'd be in New York today. "Do you always work this fast? Can't it wait a few . . ."

"Everything with us happens in real time. It's always been our policy that whatever comes in needs to go right back out. We never put things off because other things are always coming in to get in the way. Could we meet at eleven? I apologize that I can't do any other time."

"Ah . . . yeah . . . all right. But you'll have to come to me." He gave Isbister the address. "Second floor. It's a big room, and there will be a lot of people, but you'll find me. I always stand off to the side."

WALKING INTO that big room on the second floor at 9:50, Zeke was greeted by Caroline Tomblay, a hefty, middle-aged woman with girlish bangs. She handed him a catalog and a cardboard paddle—like an oversized Ping-Pong paddle—with the number 512 across the front of it, and assured him, "I am quietly optimistic."

Zeke looked around at row after row of empty chairs and worried that the place wasn't yet even half full.

Quietly optimistic, he decided, *could cost me a lot of money.*

At exactly ten, a gray-haired gentleman of a certain age, wearing a well-tailored suit and carrying a small, round, wooden gavel head in his left hand took his place behind the large, polished wooden podium that sat on a raised platform at the front of the room.

"Ladies and gentlemen," he adjusted the microphone on the podium, "good morning."

There was a high desk to the right of the podium where four young men stood facing the room. To the left of the podium there were tables with a dozen telephones where several young men and women took bids.

"This morning's sale of contemporary art consists of one hundred and forty-three lots, and bidding in the room is by paddle. If you have not yet signed in and received your paddle, we have several people scattered around the room to help you."

The room finally began filling up.

"We will begin at the beginning," the man said. "Lot number one . . ."

Large screens on the walls suddenly lit up with a black-and-white drawing of a man sitting on a chair.

" . . . David Hockney, seated man, ink on tracing paper, signed with the artist's initials DH in the lower right. We will start the bidding at fifteen thousand dollars. I have fifteen. Thank you. Seventeen . . . twenty . . ."

A large screen over the auctioneer's head constantly updated the bid price in dollars, euros, Sterling, yen, Swiss francs, Hong Kong dollars and rubles.

" . . . twenty-two thousand dollars . . . and twenty-five . . . twenty-eight . . . and thirty . . . "

The sale was off and running.

For the next three-quarters of an hour, Zeke watched as most of the lots appeared to sell. Although a couple that Zeke was sure would sell went unsold, and a few that he doubted would ever sell somehow managed to find buyers.

Now the auctioneer announced, "Lot number forty-five . . . Alexander Calder, gouache on paper, untitled . . . "

A series of red-and-yellow circles appeared on the big screens.

This was the first of the four lots Zeke was selling.

The catalog estimate was $20,000 to $24,000, but he'd set a reserve price of $18,000, meaning that he wouldn't accept anything less than that. Obviously, no one in the room knew what his reserve price was.

"We will begin bidding," the auctioneer said, "at ten thousand dollars . . . "

Immediately, Zeke worried that starting so low was a sign of limited interest.

"I have ten thousand . . . " The auctioneer moved quickly through the numbers. " . . . eleven . . . twelve . . . thirteen . . . fourteen . . . fifteen . . . "

A few cardboard paddles rose and fell, but not that many, as the auctioneer pointed to various parts of the room.

"Seventeen . . . eighteen . . . In the room at eighteen thousand." He stopped.

And Zeke's heart dropped.

The auctioneer was obliged to offer the piece at the reserve price. But if there were no bids, if the lot went unsold, that didn't portend a healthy enough sale for Zeke to buy the piece he wanted using the money he made selling these four.

"Eighteen thousand dollars . . . " the auctioneer paused . . . "eighteen thousand . . . "

That's when one of the young men at the desk pointed to a gentleman in the second row.

The auctioneer spotted the bidder. "Now nineteen . . . thank you. Twenty thousand, to you?" He pointed to someone in the middle of the room. "Thank you, I have twenty thousand in the room on my left . . . "

Zeke sighed in relief.

A woman working one of the phones raised her hand.

"Twenty-two thousand here . . . twenty-four in the room . . . twenty-six on the phone . . . " The auctioneer stared at a man in the second row. "Twenty-eight, sir?"

The man nodded.

"I have twenty-eight in the room . . . " He looked at the woman on the phone. "Thirty thousand dollars to you."

The woman spoke with her hand hiding her mouth to whomever it was on the other end.

The auctioneer repeated, "I have twenty-eight . . . selling at twenty-eight thousand dollars in the room."

The woman nodded at the auctioneer.

"Thirty thousand dollars on the phone." He looked at the man in the second row who thought for a moment, then shook his head. "Thirty thousand dollars on the phone . . . any advance on thirty thousand dollars? No more?" He banged down his gavel.

Not bad, Zeke thought.

The auctioneer announced, "Lot number forty-six . . . Keith Haring."

An ink-on-paper series of black-and-white squiggles, circles and lines that combined to look something like a maze, Zeke's reserve price was $30,000. It was sold for $55,000.

Next was a Milton Avery nude, a very pink woman lying on her side on a divan, that Zeke offered with a $50,000 reserve. It went for $85,000.

Zeke now had $170,000 in his pocket, but to justify in his own head what he would have to spend for the lot he wanted, he really needed this last lot to go through the roof.

"Tom Wesselmann," the auctioneer announced. "From the series 'Great American Nude,' this is oil, printed fabric, foil and printed-paper collage on panel."

His reserve was $125,000.

The auctioneer started the bidding at $110,000 and with paddles going up and down all over the room, the price rapidly climbed to $250,000. Bidding stalled there for a moment, then picked up again.

"Two hundred fifty-five thousand dollars on the phone . . . thank you. Two sixty? Two sixty-five . . . "

Old bidders dropped out and new bidders came in and the auctioneer got the price up to $320,000.

"Any advance on three hundred twenty thousand dollars? Fair warning, selling now to the gentleman in the very rear of the room for three hundred twenty thousand . . . " He waited for something to happen and when nothing did, he banged down his gavel. "To you sir, for three hundred twenty thousand dollars."

Zeke's total came to $490,000. But the estimate on the item he wanted to buy, lot eighty-six, was $500,000 to $700,000.

And just as that was about to come up, James Malcolm Isbister walked into the room.

He found Zeke, shook his hand and asked, "Shall we step into the hallway to talk?"

"I'm going to bid on something," Zeke explained.

Dressed as he had been two days before in LA—in a somber suit, with a white shirt and dark tie—Isbister told him, "Unfortunately, I need to be elsewhere in less than quarter of an hour and was hoping to get this matter settled."

The auctioneer called out, "Lot eighty-six . . . showing on the screens . . . "

"This is mine."

Isbister didn't seem to care. "We continue to have antitrust concerns with your proposal."

"Robert Motherwell," the auctioneer announced, "polymer on canvas with charcoal . . . "

An almost solid square of crimson with a faint charcoal line in it came up on the screen.

"Signed with the artist's initials . . . I have several commissioned bids, so we will begin at six hundred and twenty thousand dollars. In the room, I have six twenty . . . now six fifty, thank you, now six seventy. . . ."

Zeke could see this was going to cost him more than he wanted to pay.

"The document that Bobby Lerner sent you," he whispered to Isbister, "sets up a real estate–only proposal."

"But it stipulates you won't be cross-collateralizing any assets."

The auctioneer continued at a brisk pace. " . . . I will accept six ninety, thank you . . . now seven hundred . . . on the phones at seven ten . . . seven twenty . . . seven thirty . . . seven forty at the side . . . "

Outwardly annoyed that there was too much interest in the Motherwell, he said to Isbister, "Of course not."

But Isbister must have thought Zeke's annoyance was with him. "Then that's that. It's a nonstarter for us."

The way Zeke and Bobby were designing the deal, each asset was being added into the mix as a separate company. This way, if something went wrong in one place—say, the New York production facilities didn't work—they were limiting the assets that creditors could claim. Any monies owed by the facilities in New York could only be collected by creditors against the New York assets. But it was standard practice to secure each loan with a specific asset, and Zeke couldn't understand why Isbister apparently didn't understand.

"What do you mean, that's that?"

The auctioneer went on. " . . . seven fifty . . . now seven seventy . . . thank you, seven eighty . . . and seven ninety . . . eight hundred thousand . . . yes sir, the bid is with you at eight hundred thousand dollars . . . in the room at eight hundred thousand dollars . . . now eight ten on the phones . . . "

260 JEFFREY ROBINSON

Isbister said, "You are exposing us to a limitless downside."

"If you come in as a lender, that's one thing." Zeke checked the room to see where the competition was. "But our plan was to bring you in as a partner, so it suits you, as well." He started to move down the aisle, "Excuse me for a second."

Isbister followed him. "We understand partnerships very well as our main businesses are built on them."

The auctioneer pointed to the phones, "Eight hundred ten thousand dollars on the telephone . . . any more at eight hundred ten thousand dollars . . . " He paused, then raised his left hand with the wooden gavel head. "Selling now at eight hundred ten thousand dollars."

Zeke raised his paddle.

"Eight twenty." The auctioneer spotted him. "New bidder in the room, thank you sir, at eight hundred twenty thousand dollars."

"Additionally," Isbister said, "there might also be some moral dilemmas we would not wish to confront."

One of the people on the phones called out, "Eight thirty."

"Moral dilemmas?"

"Eight thirty on the phones." The auctioneer looked at Zeke, "Eight forty to you."

Zeke nodded.

"Eight forty in the room." He turned to the phones. "Eight hundred and fifty thousand dollars to you."

"You're in the motion picture and television business," Isbister went on. "If you set up this studio, you will be making motion pictures and television shows that cater to the public taste."

The auctioneer said, "Thank you," and turned to Zeke. "Eight sixty?"

"Yes," Zeke nodded to the auctioneer, then agreed with Isbister. "Yes."

"Eight seventy?" The auctioneer pointed to the phone table.

"But the public taste is not necessarily our taste," Isbister claimed.

"Eight eighty to you," the auctioneer said to Zeke.

He nodded.

"Eight ninety?" The auctioneer looked toward the phones. "Eight hundred ninety thousand dollars."

Zeke said to Isbister, "Moral dilemmas? I don't get you."

"Eight hundred ninety thousand dollars," the auctioneer repeated to the person on the phone.

"The public taste and our taste do not necessarily go hand in glove," Isbister said. "In fact, in today's climate, it often doesn't."

"Yes? No?" The auctioneer asked again to the person on the phone, "Eight hundred ninety thousand dollars?"

There was a long pause.

Quit! Zeke stared at the person taking the phone bid.

The auctioneer said, "Yes or no, please."

Staring directly at the person on the phone, Zeke said to Isbister, "You make Mr. Farmer's business sound like a religion."

Isbister paused for a moment before saying, "Those of us involved with the day-to-day running of this business are religious men."

"Selling, then, in the room," the auctioneer said, "at eight hundred eighty thousand dollars . . . "

"I don't see religion and show business as mutually exclusive entities."

"Selling now, ladies and gentlemen . . . "

Come on. Zeke couldn't wait to hear the auctioneer's gavel bang.

Isbister shook his head, "I'm sure you don't."

"Selling now . . . "

"Eight ninety," someone shouted at the rear of the room.

"Oh fuck," Zeke said a little too loud.

"New bidder at the rear of the room." The auctioneer looked at Zeke. "Nine hundred thousand now to you, sir."

Isbister said, "I rest my case."

Zeke didn't know the man bidding against him but made eye contact and glared while he raised his paddle for the auctioneer to see.

"Thank you, sir." The auctioneer took his bid. "Nine ten to you sir in the rear of the room . . . yes sir, to you."

Still staring at the other bidder, Zeke said to Isbister, "If the idea is to wash your hands . . . " He stopped and immediately corrected himself, "to divest yourself of any moral conflicts . . . "

The auctioneer accepted the man's bid. "I have nine ten in the rear of the room, nine twenty to you sir?"

Zeke raised his paddle again.

"Thank you," the auctioneer said. "Nine thirty to you sir?"

"Yes," Isbister agreed, "divest is a better word."

"Frankly, I don't see a problem with the real estate, only the partnership proposal that Bobby sent you."

"Nine thirty? Thank you," the auctioneer said. "Nine forty?"

Zeke raised his paddle again.

"Except," Isbister said, "that it gives us the status of a bank or mortgage lender, without any of the real benefits of partnership."

"With risk comes reward," Zeke reminded him. "It's difficult to have it both ways."

"Nine fifty to you sir?" The auctioneer pointed to the rear of the room.

"Mr. Gimbel," Isbister said, "I don't need a lecture on risk and rewards."

Zeke's eyes narrowed angrily as he looked at the man in the rear of the room and decided not to answer Isbister.

The auctioneer tried again, "Nine hundred fifty thousand dollars?"

"Thank you for your time this morning," Isbister said.

"Thank you," the auctioneer took the bid. "Nine sixty to you, sir?"

Zeke raised his paddle way over his head and decided to keep it raised.

"I have nine hundred sixty thousand dollars at the side of the room," he pointed to the man in the rear of the room. "Nine seventy to you, sir."

There was a long pause.

The auctioneer repeated, "Nine hundred seventy thousand . . . any advance on nine hundred sixty thousand dollars?" The auctioneer glanced quickly around the room, and then at the phones, and then around the room again. "Selling now . . . at nine hundred sixty thousand dollars . . . "

"We will be in touch with you forthwith," Isbister said.

The gavel came down.

Isbister left.

"Sold at nine hundred sixty thousand dollars . . . " The auctioneer pointed to Zeke.

Zeke brought his paddle down and turned to Isbister.

But he was gone.

And with him, Zeke realized, a possible $1.6 billion in funding. He'd also spent nearly half a million dollars more than he'd hoped to.

"Lot sixty-nine," the auctioneer announced. "Showing on the screens . . . "

Now Zeke asked himself, *what the hell just happened?*

45

Shannon greeted Pierre Belasco as he walked into the residents' lobby, "Good morning," then handed him Madame Odette's handwritten message.

"What's this?"

"Our favorite resident."

He read it standing right there in the lobby. "How does she always find out about this sort of thing?"

Once Carson left for the airport, Alicia got on her computer and went back to the files she was compiling on L. Arthur Farmer. But no matter where she looked, she couldn't come up with any connection that he might have had to Trump Tower.

Pouring herself a second cup of coffee, she sorted through the photocopies she'd made yesterday. Flexural components? Shear-wall core? Concrete hat-truss? There were far too many technical terms that she didn't understand. But then she spotted something she did understand. On one of the forms, and on only one—it was some sort of construction permit—there was a reference not to Trump Tower but to Tiffany Tower.

And when she fed "Tiffany Tower" and "L. Arthur Farmer" into the NBC database, a dozen links appeared.

A PHONE NUMBER popped up in one of the 35Tango search links. Antonia stared at it and wondered what would happen if she dialed it.

It's too early and Antonia will wake him.

But she really wanted to call.

Antonia knows it's foolish to call him like this.

Unable to control herself, she dialed the number.

It rang several times before Tommy Seasons answered it. "What?"

She tried to say something but couldn't.

"Who's there?"

She couldn't.

"Come on," he said, "who the fuck is calling at this hour?"

She took a deep breath, "It's . . . my name is Antonia Lawrence . . . from Trump Tower."

He demanded, "Who?"

In the background she heard a woman's voice asking, "Who is it?"

"I don't know," he told the woman, then said to Antonia, "Who are you? And what do you want?"

"I'm from Trump Tower. My name is Antonia. I want to speak to you about . . . a man named Pierre Belasco."

"The fucker threw Tommy out," he said. "The fucker banned Tommy."

"I know, I know . . . and maybe I can help you get unbanned."

"How are you going to do that?" He asked her, then said to the woman he was with, "Hey darling, take care of this, will you?"

Antonia didn't understand. "What?"

"Nothing," he said. "So how are you going to get Tommy unbanned?"

"I need to talk to you . . . about Pierre Belasco . . . then I'll know how I can help."

"Yeah, okay. What do you look like?"

"What?"

"What do you look like? How old are you? Married? Single? Fat? Gorgeous?"

"Why?"

He said to the woman he was with, "Harder baby, harder," and she whimpered, "No, you do me," and he answered her, "Keep doing that while I'm on the phone," then asked Antonia again, "Tell me what you look like?"

"I . . . ah . . ." She was beginning to understand what was happening on the other end of the line. "I look . . . fine. I mean, I'm twenty-nine and single. People tell me I look like Minnie . . ."

"Big tits or small tits?"

"What?"

"Write this down." He gave her a phone number. "That's my dressing room. Call me tomorrow night after the show."

"Come on," the woman with him said. "Tommy . . . do me . . ."

She imagined what the woman was doing.

"Call me tomorrow night . . . Thursday night. Okay?"

She wrote down the number. "Okay."

"Okay," he said and put the phone down, but he didn't hang up.

"Me, Tommy," the woman said, "yeah . . . do me . . ."

Antonia couldn't move.

"That's good, Tommy," the woman started moaning. "Tommy . . . there . . . good . . ."

For Antonia, it was as if the phone was glued to her ear.

"Tommy . . ." the woman moaned.

Tommy grunted, "Good . . . now . . . more . . . come on . . ."

It was nearly half an hour before Tommy hung up.

ALICIA CALLED Carson on her way to the office.

"He was the first buyer here. Tina mentioned last week that she didn't think the original name was Trump Tower, and I didn't pick up on that, but when I found Tiffany Tower . . ."

"Good on you," he said. "That's great. But . . ." he asked, "what does this have to do with the book?"

"It has to do with L. Arthur Farmer."

"And?"

"And what?"

"Are you starting to confuse the two?"

"Farmer is my big story."

"But Farmer isn't your book on Trump Tower."

"I thought you'd be as excited as I am."

"I am. I think it's great. But that was, what, nineteen seventy-eight? Seventy-nine? Where is he now? And what about the Finfuckers, or whatever they're called. So he might have been the Tower's first resident. Or the first one to buy in. But . . . then what?"

"Why would you suddenly rain on my parade like this?"

"I'm not, Alicia, honestly. I'm trying to tell you, keep your eyes on the prize."

"And I'm trying to tell you that I'm starting at the beginning."

"I love you."

She took a deep breath. "Your flight on time?"

"No, delayed."

"I've got to go. Have a good flight."

"I still love you."

"Me too," she said and hung up.

She walked into the newsroom just as Greg Mandel was calling people in for the morning meeting.

After a fast e-mail check—there was a note from the segment producer at *Nightly* who'd been with her for the Clinton interview to say, "Come on down whenever you're ready"—she headed for the conference room.

Greg smiled and stared at her as she walked in.

She smiled back. "What?"

"Just . . . good morning," he said.

She said, "Okay, just good morning to you, too."

Then she saw it.

Right there in the middle of the table was a large platter of Thin Mint Girl Scout cookies.

CYNDI STAYED asleep until the phone rang again, and Shannon downstairs announced, "There's a delivery for you."

"Huh? Okay. Please send it up."

Pulling herself out of bed, feeling better now than the first time she got up, she went to the kitchen to make an espresso. But before she even poured the water into the machine, Miguel, the elevator operator, was at the door with a smallish bag.

He handed it to her, saluted, and started to walk away.

"Oh . . . one second." She gave him the envelope for Roberto. "Would you please shove this under his door?"

"I will deliver this now," he said. "Thank you."

"Thank you." She shut the door, looked inside the bag, and found a box. And inside the box was a Patek Philippe "Twenty-4" diamond watch.

"Oh my God . . . "

The watch was made up almost entirely of diamonds.

"Oh my God . . . "

She sat down right there on the floor.

A little booklet explained that this was an eighteen-jewel, manual-winding movement. The case was 18-karat rose gold and set with 192 diamonds. The bracelet was set with 1,128 round diamonds and the *pavé diamant* dial was set with 147 diamonds.

Her hands were shaking so much that she had trouble putting the watch on.

"Oh my God . . . "

The note that came with it read, "Two down, two little blue pills, and one night to go. You are truly a wonderful friend."

It was unsigned, but it didn't have to be signed.

And all she could say was, "Oh my God . . . "

AFTER THE MORNING meeting, Alicia thought of phoning Carson again to see if he was still delayed but decided not to. Instead, she made a few rough notes on the story rundown they'd decided in the meeting, then yanked herself away from her newsroom to go downstairs to *Nightly*.

Sandy gave her a desk so she could watch the raw footage of her interview with Clinton. After that, he introduced her to one of the editors, and two hours later the piece was a four-minute-forty-second segment.

She showed it to Sandy and Brian, and both of them said they loved it.

Sandy announced, "We'll 'and finally' it."

"Really?" She smiled proudly. It was going to be the piece . . . "And finally . . . " that closed the broadcast.

"Really," he said.

On her way out, Brian said to her, "Welcome aboard."

Back in her own newsroom, she was feeling pretty good about herself.

Welcome aboard.

Her cell phone rang.

Seeing who it was, she picked it up and said, "Welcome aboard."

And Cyndi screamed, "Oh my God. . . ."

CARSON HAD ARRIVED at Kennedy Airport by ten, had checked in his one bag, and had gotten through security in no time.

Upstairs, the woman who ran the airline's third-floor First Class lounge told him, "Flight's running a little late. Probably about an hour. So you've got plenty of time. You know where everything is . . . "

He said thank you and carried his shoulder bag to one of the large, uphol-stered chairs next to the windows.

Dropping it there, he went to get a cup of coffee and took a muffin, as well. There was also fruit, so he helped himself to some sliced peaches and a piece of melon and returned to his seat.

That's when he'd spoken to Alicia.

"Keep your eyes on the prize."

"I'm starting at the beginning."

"I love you."

"Your flight on time?"

He told himself, *when she gets in that mood . . .*

Now he rang Tony Arcarro. They talked for quite a while because Arcarro was having trouble with HSBC in London on a deal he was trying to finance in Italy.

Next, he called Ken Warring but got voice mail and left a message that he'd try again before takeoff, otherwise he'd speak to him from Tokyo.

Sitting back, he stared out the window, quickly got bored with the view of a taxiway, and went to get some newspapers. On the way back to his chair, he decided to have a little more fruit and helped himself to some sliced guava. When he finished that, he started thinking about Mr. Shigetada and how hard he might have to press the man.

He took his phone and called Milt McKeever at EXIT. "What's going on with Shigetada?"

McKeever answered, "Nothing since you came in. There was that one bite, and that was all."

"Please let me know if and when."

"I will," McKeever promised.

Carson hung up, stood up, walked over to the magazine rack against the far wall, and flicked through a couple of magazines. Nothing interested him, so he went to the buffet bar to think about a second muffin. He decided, no.

The lounge was filling up.

Some of these people will be on my flight, he told himself, *and the rest will be going to . . .*

He sat down and tried to guess where everyone else was going.

There was a young couple with a three- or four-year-old kid. *Miami.* There were two men in suits, much older than him, sitting nearby. *They're on my flight.* There was a young guy with a young blonde woman.

He looked at her for a long time.

She caught him staring.

He smiled, looked away, then peeked back at her.

Blonde hair.

Now he took his laptop out of his bag, and when it was ready, he went to Google.

In the search box he typed, "Amelie Laure Moreau."

46

Unlike LA and Malibu, Zeke didn't have live-in help in New York. He used a bonded valet service that furnished a housekeeper named Christina to come in when he was in town. She would clean, shop, make the bed, and, if need be, serve a meal. Otherwise, she'd come by once a week to make certain the apartment was always ready for him whenever he showed up.

Christina was there straightening up when he walked in. "Hello sir, welcome back."

"Nice to see you," he said. "Family good?"

"Yes, sir. Everyone is fine. I am changing the sheets and towels, sir, do you want me to go shopping?"

"No," he said. "I'm leaving this afternoon . . . "

"And how is your wife?" she asked.

"Everyone is fine," he said, not wanting to discuss Birgitta.

He kicked off his shoes, threw himself onto a couch and rang Bobby Lerner. "I might have blown the deal with that Isbister guy. The one representing L. Arthur Farmer."

"What happened?"

Zeke told him.

"How weird," Bobby said. "Who the hell does a one-point-six-billion-dollar deal in thirty-six hours? Nah, you didn't blow it, he was looking for an excuse to stay out."

"You think so?"

"Come on, cross-collateralization? He knows better."

Zeke thought about that. "I guess you're right. What else is happening?"

"You want the good news or the bad news?"

"You mean better news and worser news? Start with worser."

"We got the list of demands from Birgitta's lawyers."

"Already? Talk about doing deals in thirty-six hours."

"My bet is that she had them drawn up a long time ago. She's hired Spelman Meyers Fisher."

"That good or bad?"

"Expensive. There's no way a firm with their reputation ever does anything without first billing hundreds of hours."

"Am I paying for it?"

"You could be."

"What's her list look like?"

"Like everything you own."

"What's she going to settle for?"

"A whole lot less. The pre-nup is solid."

"Bobby . . . " He took a deep breath. "I can't deal with this now. Tell me what else."

"The better news? The Truman brothers are signing this morning. You now own a sports agency."

"Ah shit," Zeke said.

"You sound thrilled."

"No . . . last night . . . how dumb. At the party. Roberto Santos was there. He's a Sovereign Shields client. I had it in my head to tell him . . . and I completely forgot."

"Doesn't he live in Trump Tower?"

"Yeah. I'll call him. Or tell him next time. Let me phone Perry and Monica. We'll deal with Birgitta tomorrow."

Now he dialed his office in LA and spent the next hour and a half on the phone with the two young lawyers who would be running the sports side of the agency.

"Take nice premises," he said, "but don't go wild. I want to see a request for anything and everything that costs more than a hundred bucks. Furniture. Stationery. Scotch tape. Paper clips. Water bill. Trips. Lunches. I don't care what it is. If it's more than a hundred bucks, you need my approval. Take your secretaries with you, and each of you chooses an assistant. How many agents from Sovereign do you intend to keep?"

"We're making up a short list now of about a dozen," Perry Griswald said.

Monica Rosenblatt warned, "Obviously the ones we let go will set up on their own."

"Obviously. So what you do is offer them first rights on the deadwood. We'll keep a core base of their clients, then see what we can get for the ones we don't want. Sell whoever you don't want or can't use. But don't bilk the old staff. Give them a chance to survive."

Monica wanted to know, "What happens when they wind up killing us because we didn't kill them first?"

"You get fired for not doing your job well enough."

Perry suggested, "A little harsh, no?"

"What's the line from Jerry McGuire? This isn't show friends, this is show business." He paused for effect. "I want to set up an advisory board. Make up a short list of old clients, men and women . . . retired . . . and put them on a sensible retainer. Some of them may still be viable clients, some of them may bring in new clients. But if we get the right people on the advisory board, it gives us the cred that the former management lost."

"Sounds good," Perry said and Monica agreed.

"First name on that list," Zeke added, "is Carson Haynes."

"Who's he?" Monica asked.

"Find out for yourself. If you're going to survive in this business, you need to know the players."

"I never heard of him, either," Perry said. "And I know all the players."

"He's a player because I made him a player. Also, set up a pitch to sign Romain Neal. I had dinner with him last night."

"The guy's married to Audra Kaleigh Harris?" Monica said. "See, I know the players when they're players."

"I'm back tomorrow. By then I'll try to come up with more players you never heard of."

While he was on the phone with LA, half a dozen calls came in, mostly to his cell, and at least twenty e-mails did as well. The only call that seemed important was from his New York office, so hanging up with Perry and Monica, he called over there and spent another hour on the line taking care of his New York business.

There were contracts they wanted him to see and a financial statement to go over. He asked them to send it over to Trump Tower right away and promised he'd read everything on the plane home.

He was still on the line with the New York office when Christina said she was leaving. He waved to her, "See you next time, and thank you."

More calls came in, and more e-mails came in, too, and after he hung up with New York, he checked his voice mail and skimmed through his e-mail and finally decided, the hell with it.

Assuring himself, *everything can wait until tomorrow*, he phoned his pilot. "Let's go home." The pilot said he'd arrange to have a car pick him up at Trump Tower right away.

Then he phoned his mother. She was complaining about something, and he heard himself repeating over and over again, "Everything will be all right."

After that, he phoned his kids.

He got Zoey's voice mail and left a message.

But he managed to find Max. "How you doing?"

"Fine."

"What's new?"

"Nothing."

"Where's your sister?"

"Dunno."

He almost phoned Miriam but decided he'd had enough for one day.

Walking into his bedroom, he thought about taking clothes back to LA, decided no, then checked the kitchen. He was running low on mineral water and beer and made a note to have some delivered.

While he was putting his shoes back on, a fax came in from the auction house summing up his four sales and one purchase, and invoicing him for the difference. He didn't even look at it. He simply folded it and put it into his attaché case.

Then Felicity rang from downstairs to say there was a large envelope waiting for him at the front desk. "Shall I send it up?"

"No," he said. "I'll pick it up on my way out."

He checked the apartment one last time to make sure the lights were off and that he could leave.

That's when someone knocked on the door.

I told her I'd pick it up, he grumbled, and opened the door to find a young man in a drab suit, with a white shirt and dark tie.

He'd never seen this man before. "Can I help you?"

"Excuse me for disturbing you like this. My name is Eric Arnold Ronaldsay. Mr. Isbister asked me to stop by and give this to you."

It was a manila envelope. Zeke took it. "Thank you very much."

The man turned and walked away.

Closing the door, Zeke opened the envelope and found several dozen pages inside. On the first page, the typed title read, "Our counter-proposal for the full financing of your project." The first line of the second page read, "Why we have decided to forgo our preference for cross-collateralization."

He said out loud, "These guys are too fucking strange for me," and put the envelope in his attaché case.

Downstairs, Felicity handed him a large envelope from his office. He thanked her and said, "See you next time through."

David, the doorman, saluted, "Your car is there, sir."

"Thanks," Zeke said and left Trump Tower.

It was only when he got to Teterboro Airport and climbed into his plane that he wondered, how come the fellow that Isbister sent didn't get announced by the front desk?

47

Rebecca Battelli called to tell Pierre Belasco, "I'm going to shut down the business. I didn't sleep last night. I'm looking at this mess again today. I can't cope."

"Don't make that decision yet," he urged her. "I know this is very difficult for you, but we're trying to help."

"My husband's cousin Johnny called me from Florida late last night. He said he'd heard about the break-in and was glad that I wasn't hurt."

"He actually said that?"

"Yes."

To Belasco, that sounded like a veiled threat. "Have you heard anything from the police yet?"

"Nothing."

His second line rang.

"Rebecca . . . Mrs. Battelli . . . "

The caller ID read, "Private Number."

"Rebecca," she corrected him.

"You're upstairs?"

"Yes."

The phone rang again.

"Private Number" could be any of a hundred people he knew, including Donald Trump. But not everybody who hid their number from caller ID knew the number of his second line. "I've got to take this call. I'll be right up."

"It's such a mess."

"I'm on my way," he promised, hung up with her, and picked up the incoming call.

It was Forbes.

Belasco told him, "I was waiting for Timmins to wake up so that he could phone you and we could have a chat."

"Normally that's best," he said. "But I'll tell you what . . . write down this number . . . " Forbes gave him one with an area code he didn't recognize—855—which turned out to be a toll-free number. "No one will answer and you won't hear a message. All you get is a beep. Leave a voice mail and I'll phone you back, usually within two hours. Any longer than that, someone else will be in touch with you."

"Yes, okay, thank you. I've got it."

"The reason I phoned . . . I was down at One Hogan . . . you know, police headquarters . . . and they've decided there's nothing they can do about the Battelli matter."

Belasco was astonished. "How about, they can investigate a crime."

"You know the word, triage? It's French. They look at everything that comes in and decide where to allocate resources. They see this one . . . no violence, no obvious motives, the suspects are not known and probably never will be, no clues, no one even knows if anything's been stolen . . . and how much time do you think they can spend on it? They put resources into crimes where there's been violence, where someone has been hurt, where there is a real possibility of a result. Sorry to say it, but like everything else in this world, it boils down to return on investment. They spend their time working crimes they think they can solve."

"Unbelievable. Just gets tossed into the wastepaper basket."

"Nope. Footnoted as a statistic."

"That's pathetic."

"That's reality."

He wanted Forbes to know, "The husband's cousin, Johnny, threatened her last night. He phoned her, said he'd heard about the break in, and said he was glad that she didn't get hurt."

Forbes paused. "Then what?"

"Then . . . nothing."

"Sounds to me like condolences."

"Sounds to me exactly like a threat."

"A threat is, give me your wallet or I'll kill you."

"A threat is having hoodlums tear your place to bits, then telling you, I'm glad you weren't hurt. That's saying, next time it will be you."

Forbes wasn't having it. "That call doesn't prove a thing."

"You need to talk to her."

"I have talked to her. Trust me on this, unless she's involved, there's nothing she can say that can move this forward."

"That's it? That's the end? One day later and everyone has already washed their hands of it?"

"The cops have. But whoever is behind this hasn't. For that person, or those persons, it's not over."

"You think they're coming back?"

"We need to find out what they took. Then we can figure out what they're going to do next."

WHEN BELASCO walked into Scarpe Pietrasanta, he was surprised to see that nothing had been done. The place was still a mess.

Rebecca was sitting in a nearly broken chair, her head in her hands. Carlos Vela was standing in the corner.

Bill Riordan was also there.

"This man," he pointed to Vela, "what's he doing in the building? He says she hired him. She says you recommended him."

"That's right," Belasco went to Rebecca. "You okay?"

She shook her head, no.

"You're out of here," Riordan ordered Vela. "Right now. Or I call the cops and have you arrested."

"No," Belasco said. "You'll do nothing of the kind. Mr. Vela works for Mrs. Battelli."

"He's on the Chapman list?"

"No he's not."

"Then I'll put him on the Chapman list."

"No, you won't. I run Trump Tower. I decide who goes on the list."

Riordan glared at Belasco. "You're not the only one with the boss' ear." He pointed to Vela, "Get out of Trump Tower now, or I will have you arrested." With that, Riordan turned on his heels and left.

Rebecca looked up at Belasco. "It's all gotten out of hand." She turned to Vela. "You're a very nice young man, and I'm truly sorry that you've found yourself in the middle . . . "

"I'll worry about Mr. Riordan," Belasco said. "But first things first. We need to find out who's trying to hurt you and to stop them. If you walk away now, they win."

"I don't think I care anymore."

He dared, "I heard your daughter say that she does."

Rebecca stood up. "My daughter has her own life. This is mine. I'm sorry." She looked at Vela, "I will see that you get paid for this week . . . I'm sorry . . . "

And then she walked out.

"Señor?" Vela shrugged. "I must leave, too."

He looked around at the mess.

All sorts of questions ran through his mind.

If Rebecca wants out, why shouldn't she walk away? If the police aren't going to bother, why should I? If Vela is afraid to stay in the building because Riordan is threatening to have him arrested, why shouldn't he leave? If Riordan is looking for a fight, why should I accommodate him?

"Señor?"

He turned to Vela. "Have you got a cell phone? Let me have the number."

Vela gave it to him, and Belasco typed it into his BlackBerry.

"Stay here and start cleaning up. You will not be arrested. I give you my word. But lock the door. If Mrs. Battelli needs to come back, she has a key. If I need you, I'll call your cell. Take my number." Belasco gave it to him. "If someone tries to get in, phone me immediately. If Mr. Riordan shows up, or if he contacts you, phone me."

"Señor," Vela was obviously afraid. "I have a wife and a baby. I need to find a job."

"For the time being, you have one. Start putting this mess into order. When you get hungry, you know, lunchtime, call me, and I'll see that you get food. I'll check in on you later. But stay here and do what you can. I promise, you will be all right."

Vela still wasn't sure. "If Mr. Riordan calls the police . . . "

"I will take care of the police, and I will take care of Mr. Riordan."

Vela stared at Belasco. "I didn't steal that coat from that woman."

"I know you didn't."

"And this woman . . . Mrs. Battelli . . . she is a very nice woman."

"I know she is," Belasco nodded. "Go on, get to work. Lock the door behind me and don't worry."

BELASCO GOT A NUMBER for the main switchboard at Sarah Lawrence in Bronxville, New York, rang it, and asked how he could get in touch with a student named Gabriella Battelli.

The call was passed to a secretary in some office.

"My name is Pierre Belasco," he said, "and I am the general manager of Trump Tower in New York. Miss Battelli's parents have a business in the building, and I need to speak to her, please, about a business matter, rather urgently."

"I'm sure that you understand we don't give out any personal information about students or staff," the woman said, "But if you leave me your number, I will pass along the message."

He left the necessary information and hoped she'd phone back soon.

That's when Carlos Vela phoned. "The police are here."

Racing back upstairs, he found two uniformed officers standing in the showroom with Bill Riordan. "What's going on?"

"This man will be escorted from the building," Riordan said, pointing to Vela. "And if you get in the way . . . " he motioned toward the officers . . . "I will ask them to arrest you for obstruction."

Belasco demanded to know, "What authority do you think you have?" He reached into his pocket and handed one of the officers his business card. "I am the general manager here, and Mr. Riordan reports to me. He has no authority whatsoever to overrule any decision I make. Mr. Vela is an employee of this company. He has his employer's permission to be here, and he has my permission to be here. If you like, I will have our company lawyer come here and spell it out for you."

The two officers looked at each other, and one of them shrugged, "Sounds like a domestic dispute, gentlemen. You probably should work this out between yourselves." He said to Riordan, "If you need us, call us. But . . . right now . . . this isn't any of our business."

"Thank you," Belasco said, and watched them leave. Then he warned Riordan, "Don't you ever try anything like that again."

"It's not over Pierre."

"Yes it is."

And Riordan assured him, "No it is not."

48

David had phoned the Rojas brothers in Mexico, just the way Uncle RD had asked him to, and had done the deal with Gonzolo. He was the youngest of the three.

But in David's mind, Gonzolo was also the least trustworthy.

Hector, the middle brother, had phoned back to say they'd been in touch with RD and everything was great.

RD had also phoned to confirm the deal, adding that the Rojas brothers had agreed to a one percent facilitator's fee for David.

Late in the day, the third Rojas brother, Liberio, had phoned to ask for wiring instructions to David's account and, a few minutes later, Liberio had announced, $47,500 was on its way.

David said, "Thanks," and Liberio promised, "If something else comes up, amigo, we will be in touch."

Now, first thing in the morning, Liberio was back on the phone. "This is between my brothers and you. No Uncle RD this time."

"What y'all got?"

"Heavy crude. Whole tanker full."

"Where's it coming from?"

"Wherever."

David knew that meant Iran. "What's the manifest say?"

"Manifest says Mina Al Bakr, Iraq."

"How much?"

"Four hundred sixty thousand barrels."

"Where's it going?"

"Trinidad."

"How much you need?"

"The *hombres* we're talking to are looking for twenty. We're looking at spot minus fifteen percent. Call it, thirty plus. That's ten for us . . . we'll take two . . . you walk away with eight."

David thought about it. "Send me what you've got, and I'll call y'all back."

Almost immediately, an e-mail arrived from Liberio with the shipping and cargo information. Based on that, he started shopping it around. He hoped he could get it for less than $20 million, sell it on somewhere right away, and make a few extra points.

But everybody he spoke with was onto the manifest switch, and David knew better than to push his luck when it came to embargoed oil.

He looked at the paperwork again.

This wasn't the megadeal he was hoping to do, like a supertanker with two million barrels. It wasn't even, technically, a distressed cargo. It was a bunch of cowboys trying to offload contraband. He didn't even know who the sellers were.

What's more, paying $20 million for $30 million worth of contraband was looking too steep. He reckoned if he could get it for pennies on the dollar, then that would make it really interesting. Otherwise . . .

He thought about the Colombians.

If he took it on as a straight oil deal and put it through the "Curaçao Trading One" account, then, at least in his mind, this wasn't actually costing him anything. Even at $20 million, taking the Colombians' profit out of this, David reassured himself, *this could be my first $10 million day*.

He phoned Liberio. "For twenty mil they can keep it. Too risky. Tell them I'm in for five."

"No way."

"It's contraband."

"It's heavy crude."

"It was born in the wrong place."

"They're going to say no."

"Then that's what they say. Let me know." He hung up, sat back in his chair, and stared at his phone.

It wasn't long before Liberio came back to him. "They may go for eighteen."

"Five," David insisted.

Liberio hung up, and a few minutes later called back. "Seventeen, last offer."

David said no, "But maybe seven."

Liberio said no but added that his amigos might be willing to do sixteen.

David went to nine. Liberio's friends came down to fourteen. David went up to eleven. They settled at thirteen.

Putting the trade through a shell company he'd incorporated years ago in Antigua, Sivle-Sevil Trading Partners—backward it spells Elvis Lives—David did the deal.

He e-mailed Wayne Grannum at the New York office of Caymans Comtrad, a private offshore bank, and asked him to wire $13 million out of his newly opened Curaçao Trading One account.

That was the overdraft account backed by the Colombians.

"What's going on?" Tina came into the office and sat down at her trading desk.

"Nothing much," he said. "How would you like to have a yacht?"

She gave him a strange look. "Yesterday it was coffee, a *croissant* and sex. Today it's a yacht?"

"There may be some crude looking for a home. I'm thinking, if I can get in low enough and move it fast enough . . . and you once said you wanted a boat . . . "

"I also once said I wanted to screw Robert De Niro, but I don't see you offering him up on a platter."

"Why do you have to . . . " He shrugged her off, "Fuck it, Tina, I was looking at this cargo and saw that there was a lot of room and thought I'd buy you something nice."

She logged on to her computer. "No problem. How about if I get on it?"

"It's only another crude cargo . . . y'all find something really good for you to work and I'll shop this around myself."

"No, put it up on the screen. I want to see it."

He showed her.

"So fucking suspicious of everything. Okay, it's there. Now, like I said, I'll take care of this one, and you find something else."

She backed off and started checking the markets.

And he began putting out feelers to dump the cargo.

He contacted all the usual suspects, offering it up as Iraqi crude, figuring that whoever took it off his hands could work out the manifest switch in Trinidad.

There were no takers.

"You see any other crude moving anywhere?" he asked her.

She switched screens and looked. "Yeah. Cargoes all over the place. One. Two. Three." She switched screens again and showed him. "There's four. I thought you said the market was flat."

"It was."

"It isn't now."

"No, it isn't," he conceded.

In fact, the more he looked, the more the market appeared to be pretty average. Nothing spectacular. But there were cargoes to be had, and there were players in the game.

He wasn't even getting a nibble on this. And that didn't make sense to him. His price was where it should be. Of course, he could always drop his price down to undercut the other sellers—owning this cargo outright meant he had plenty of room—but he worried that if no one was biting, potential buyers might be seeing something he wasn't.

Going back to the shipping information Liberio had forwarded, he put the tanker's name into the shipping database at Lloyd's of London. The *Moghul King Humayun* had been built in 1981 by some guys in Pakistan who still owned it, along with six other tankers. He checked them out, and they struck him as legit. At least, they'd been in business a long time.

The ship flew a Panamanian flag. So he got on the Panama ship register and that confirmed what the Lloyd's database had.

From what he could see, this cargo appeared to have been owned by a company operating out of Dubai. But the company turned out to be nothing more than a plaque on the wall of some registration office on the Caribbean islands of Saint Kitts and Nevis.

Hiding deals like this behind shell companies was par for the course.

Logging on to a global tracking website to obtain a live position—a map came up on one of his screens—he found the *Moghul King Humayun* half a day out of Trinidad.

Tina looked up at the screen. "What's that?"

"The crude cargo."

"You got it?"

"Trying to figure it out," he said, hoping to avoid a straight answer.

"You got it or not?"

He hesitated . . . "Yeah."

She clicked on to the global tracking screen and hit the ship's link. When she saw the name come up, she put it into a bunch of chat rooms. "Let's see . . . "

One of their big trading screens now split into four with chat-room gossip scrolling through them until . . .

They both saw it at the same time.

"Fuck," he shouted.

Tina enlarged that quarter screen to full screen.

A chat room billing itself "strictly need to know" was highlighting this particular cargo with a red "high danger" flag.

"Shit," Tina yelled. "David . . . "

He immediately brought up the flagged comment. "Embargoed oil. Shadowed by US warships. Imminent arrest."

"Fuck me," David said, his throat going dry and his stomach knotting into a tight wad. "Fuck me. . . . "

"Do you really have this?"

"Yeah." He started checking the other chat rooms. "This is only a rumor . . . they don't know for sure . . . look, no one else has it . . . don't panic."

"Don't panic? Are you fucking out of your mind? How much did you put down?"

"Let me see if I can stop it," he said to her, grabbed the phone and called Wayne Grannum at the bank. "That money I sent out from Curaçao Trading One, get it back."

"I can't get it back. It's gone."

"Then put a stop on it."

"What are you talking about? There's no way . . . "

"Try," he shouted at Grannum. "Try to stop it. Try to get it back."

He hung up and dialed Liberio Rojas.

Gonzolo took the call.

"Where's your brother?" David demanded.

"Gone. Won't be back today."

"What's his cell number?"

"What's wrong?"

"He fucked me, that's what's wrong."

"What are you talking about?"

David told Gonzolo that the crude he'd bought through Liberio was about to be seized. "Your fucking brother knew. Give me his fucking cell."

"Hold on, *hombre* . . . I said, he's not here. So you tell me . . . "

"Listen to me, you little shit, find Liberio and tell him to call me *pronto*, because if I find him first . . . "

"Don't threaten me, *hombre*."

"Find him, motherfucker." He banged down the phone.

Tina was staring at him. "How much?" She asked softly.

"I'll take care of it." He tried to catch his breath.

"How much?"

"I said I'll . . . "

"David . . . " She suddenly screamed, "How much?"

He rubbed his hands over his eyes, then said quietly, "Thirteen."

"Oh fuck, David." She stood up and walked to the window to stare outside.

"I'm taking care of it."

She turned to look at him. "Which account?"

He confessed, "Curaçao Trading One."

"The Colombians' money? You pissed away . . . "

"I didn't piss away anything."

"How much is left?"

"I don't know."

"How much?"

"I'm telling you, I don't know."

"Then find out."

Seeing how angry she was and knowing her well enough not to challenge her any more than he had to, he picked up the phone, got Grannum back on the line and asked him, "How much is left in the guarantee account that backs Curaçao Trading One?"

"Lawyer's client account?" Grannum typed on his keyboard to open the account. "Got it."

"How much?"

"Nothing."

"What?"

"Nothing. It's empty."

"It can't be. We opened it with . . . "

"It is, I'm afraid," Grannum said. "There was an initial deposit of . . . let's see . . . forty-five million."

"Yeah, that's right."

"But that was withdrawn."

"Impossible."

"First thing this morning."

49

After reassuring Vela again that he would not be arrested, Belasco went straight to Carole Ann Mendelsohn's office.

A no-nonsense woman in her midforties, she'd spent five years at the Justice Department dealing with blue-collar crime before going to work for Trump's old college friend Stenny Bayliss at his Wall Street law firm Crowther, Bayliss, Evers. "She's the best there is," Stenny had bragged.

So when Trump needed someone, he hired her.

"Why would you steal her away from me?" Stenny wanted to know.

Trump shrugged. "You said it yourself. She's the best there is."

Carole Ann sat down on the couch next to Belasco. "We need to talk about Mrs. Essenbach."

"I know. But before we do . . . " He told her what had occurred with Bill Riordan.

"I'll call him, and we'll set up a meeting to redefine his parameters. We don't want dissension, and we certainly don't want him exposing us to lawsuits by calling the police when it's not warranted."

"Thank you."

She nodded like a schoolteacher to show him that part of this discussion was finished. "Now you need to get me up to speed on Mrs. Essenbach."

Belasco outlined what had taken place on Monday night, after the residents' board meeting.

She took notes, then asked, "Did you at any time, or in any way, make any sort of promise to her, or say anything that she might construe or even misconstrue as a promise to act on her behalf?"

"No."

"Did you at any time suggest that the residents' board decision could be influenced in any way?"

"No."

"Do you have any idea why she might believe that you had promised to influence the vote or help obtain a different result?"

"No."

"Do you have any sort of personal relationship, whatsoever, with Mrs. Essenbach?"

He gave her an odd look. "Absolutely not."

"How would you describe your relationship with Mrs. Essenbach?"

"Relationship? We don't have a relationship, other than a business relationship."

"Have you ever visited her alone in her apartment at other than business hours?"

"Yes. As I said, I went to see her after the residents' board meeting."

"And that was to advise her of the board's decision?"

"Yes."

"Where did you meet with her?"

"In her library."

"Was anyone else present?"

"No."

"Where was her husband?"

"I have no idea. Although, he must have been in the apartment because . . . you've seen the CCTV footage, haven't you?"

"Yes," she said. "During your meeting, was any food or drink served?"

"She offered me champagne, but I said no."

"And . . . " she looked closely at him . . . "during this meeting, what was Mrs. Essenbach wearing?"

He was shocked. "What are you trying to say?"

"What was she wearing?"

"It was ten o'clock at night. She was in a housecoat . . . a dressing gown."

"Surely you can see what I'm trying to say."

He became defensive. "You're trying to insinuate that I had some sort of relationship with her. I did not. I have never acted unprofessionally with her or, in fact, with anyone at Trump Tower."

"And yet, you visited her in her apartment after business hours, or what might be called unprofessional hours, to speak to her about the residents' decision to deny her the right to construct . . . a rain forest? This, despite the fact that you do not sit on the board, have no influence over the board's decisions, and claim that you have no relationship with Mrs. Essenbach, other than a business relationship?"

"Yes."

"How many other clients with whom you have a business relationship have you visited at home, alone, after normal business hours?"

"I resent this."

"As well you might. But believe it or not, I'm on your side."

"You have an odd way of showing it."

"Wait till you see how the other side shows it."

"What other side?"

"One of my former colleagues, someone with whom I have remained very close, works at a firm called Dregger Simmons. They're a boutique firm that specializes in David-Goliath lawsuits."

"What's that?"

"Poor people who want to take on rich people. Occasionally, they also represent rich people who want to take on extremely rich people. You see, if Goliath sues David, Goliath wins because he can outspend David. But when David sues Goliath, even if David is very rich, as long as Goliath is much richer, the costs of getting into the game can still be prohibitive. Goliath spends what he has to in order to lock David out. So David needs a pretty big stone. And Dregger Simmons have very big stones."

Belasco was surprised that she would make reference like that. "What does this have to do with me?"

"Your contract with the Trump Organization contains a clause that protects you from certain liability during your employment. As long as you have acted properly, it falls on us . . . on me and my office . . . to protect your rights and defend you against any actions. Obviously, if you have at any time acted outside the boundaries, if there have been improprieties, that's a game changer. But as of right now, we will defend you."

"From what?"

"From Mrs. Essenbach and Dregger Simmons. My friend there has given me a heads up that Mrs. Essenbach is going to file a lawsuit against you. Apparently she will claim in her suit that, as her lover, you promised to use your influence with the residents' board to grant her application for this rain forest project. She will also claim that, when she recently rejected your advances, you acted out of spite, using your influence to assure that her request was rejected."

He was dumbfounded. "That's absurd. It's preposterous. It's a total lie."

"It wouldn't be the first time someone involved in a lawsuit lied."

"Totally, absolutely, and one hundred percent lying."

"If she is," the lawyer assured him, "there is recourse. On the other hand . . . "

"On the other hand, what?"

"On the other hand," she said with no emotion, "there is also recourse."

At the same time that Belasco was meeting with Carole Ann Mendelsohn, Bill Riordan was sending a scathing e-mail to Anthony Gallicano.

"Mr. Belasco refused to place a fired employee, Carlos Vela, on the Tower's persona non grata list, and subsequently proceeded to help him find a job at an office in the Tower. A man who was fired for theft therefore continues to work here. Furthermore, I believe that Mr. Belasco has overstepped his authority by intervening in the investigation by my office into a crime committed on the premises and has, furthermore, hampered the police in their duties when asked by a competent authority to have someone removed from the premises. I respectfully suggest that Mr. Belasco's behavior must not be tolerated."

ACROSS TOWN at Columbus Circle, Antonia was sneaking into Anthony Gallicano's office to peek at his e-mail in-box.

She discovered Riordan's e-mail about Belasco.

Immediately, she forwarded it to her secret Gmail account, then erased both Riordan's original and the sent copy she'd forwarded to herself.

In her office, she went into her Gmail account and re-sent Riordan's e-mail back to Gallicano—being very careful to make sure that Riordan's return address showed in the sender box—but this time, she added to the recipient's box, "cc: DJT."

50

David was absolutely beside himself. "What do y'all mean there's no suite sixty-five oh one?"

The security guard in the lobby at 500 Fifth Avenue repeated, "What I mean is, there's no suite sixty-five oh one. There is no sixty-fifth floor."

"Bastard," he screamed, went outside, and grabbed the first taxi he found. "Plaza Hotel."

Arriving at the main entrance on Central Park South, David took the steps two by two, charged through the lobby and stormed into the Champagne Bar.

"May I help you sir?" a waiter wanted to know.

He looked around until he spotted the waiter who'd served them. "You . . . I was in here the other day with a guy named Zhadanov . . . "

The waiter came over to him, "Yes, sir, I remember."

"How do I find him?"

"I don't know."

"He comes in here all the time, right? Y'all must know . . . "

"Never saw him before, sir."

"What do you mean? Y'all said something like, nice to see you again. You knew his name. He asked for his usual."

"Sir . . . " The waiter seemed genuinely embarrassed. "That sort of thing happens a lot. The guy gave me fifty bucks to pretend I knew him."

David exclaimed loudly, "Ah . . . fuck," and stormed out.

"Bastard set us up," he said coming into his apartment.

Tina was livid. "I warned you this would happen. I warned you not to get involved with these people." She berated him, "You're a fucking idiot."

"He said he knew Asil . . . "

"Why didn't you call Asil to check? No, you're too smart for that. Too worried that Asil was going to make money off your back. Okay, now, call Asil and see if he'll shell up for your fucking stupidity."

He looked at his watch—"What time is it in Istanbul?"—then grabbed the phone. "Fuck it."

In fact, it was just after three in the morning.

"Asil, it's David . . . David Cove . . . I'm looking for Vasyl Zhadanov."

"David . . . do you know what time it is?"

"Asil, I need to get in touch immediately with Vasyl Zhadanov."

"Who?"

"Vasyl Zhadanov. The lawyer."

"I never heard of such a person."

"Don't tell me that . . . he said y'all gave him my name and number . . . "

"What is his name?"

"Vasyl . . . Zhadanov."

"I may be asleep, but I promise I don't know anyone with that name."

"You must know him."

"I don't."

"Then how did he get my name and number?"

"David, I have never heard of such a person."

"Fuck you, Asil." He slammed down the phone.

"That's right," Tina yelled at him. "Blame everybody else."

"Fuck you, too!"

"Yeah, right." She reached for the phone and dialed a number.

"Who are you calling?"

She ignored him and waited for someone to answer.

"Hello?"

She said, "Uncle RD, it's Tina. Sorry to bother you, but your nephew is an asshole. He's fucked up big-time and you need to know about it. Hold on." She looked at David, forced a smile, and shoved the phone to him. "Go on, big shot."

David gave her a nasty look. "It's nothing," he said to RD, "everything is under control."

He responded, "Clearly, boy, it isn't."

"It's okay. It's all right. Tina's having her period."

"Fuck you," she shouted at him.

"Fuck you, too," he screamed back.

"Sounds to me," RD said, "you're having yours. This about the Colombians?"

"No. Well, sort of. The Rojas brothers put me onto a deal. I financed it with the Colombians' money, and then the lawyer who put me onto them disappeared with their money."

"I warned you, boy. I said, you get your ass whipped on this, and we're gonna leave you swinging in the wind."

"It's not the same thing. The Colombians are cool. This is that lawyer guy and the Rojas brothers. He's disappeared, and they fucked me. I keep calling Liberio, but he's not returning my calls."

"How do they know each other?"

"They don't."

"Then why are you telling me about both of them?"

"I'm telling you because . . . listen, the first thing that happened is the lawyer disappeared with the Colombians' money. Then the Rojas brothers . . . "

"And y'all owe that money to the Colombians?"

"Not me. The lawyer."

"Better hope they see it that way, too, son. Now what was the deal with the Rojas brothers?"

"It was some heavy crude coming out of Iran, remanifested as Iraqi . . . "

"The one that was due to land in Trinidad and got arrested?"

"Yeah, that's it."

"You are one fucking idiot, boy. Those three sleazebag brothers have been shopping that cargo around for two days."

"So where do I find Liberio?"

"Why? Y'all think you're gonna get your money back?"

"I'm sure gonna try."

"Good luck."

"You know, y'all could help me, a bit."

"I warned you the first time."

He hung up.

"Fuck you, too," David slammed down the phone. "Goddamned miserable old prick." He turned to Tina . . .

She wasn't there.

"Tina?"

There was no answer.

He walked into their bedroom. "Where are you?" Then he went downstairs, "Tina?"

She was gone.

WHEN DAVID finally got Liberio on the phone, he didn't hold back. "Listen to me, shithead, that cargo you stuck me with . . . "

"My brother told me you were calling . . . "

"And did your brother say I've been trying to find you all day?"

"No, he said you would call me back."

"He's a fucking liar, and so are you. That Iranian crude bound for Trinidad . . . "

"I heard about that this afternoon," Liberio said, "I was shocked."

"Y'all sure will be shocked if I don't get my money back."

"I don't have your money."

"I don't care who has it. I sent it to you. You send it back to me. The account is with you, pal. You've got twenty-four hours."

There was a long pause. "Or what?"

"Or . . . " David hesitated, and as soon as he said it he knew he'd made a mistake . . . "or I'm putting a down payment on your ass."

51

Alicia watched the piece running on her monitor as Phyllis the makeup lady lightly powdered her forehead.

"Coming to you in ten," she heard the director, Paul, say in her earpiece.

She nodded to the camera so that he could see on his monitor in the control room that she'd heard him, then sat up straight and licked her lips.

That was a little trick she'd learned from listening to a Bette Davis interview a long time ago—"Lick your lips before the camera rolls"—and Alicia always did.

"In three . . . to camera one . . . " Paul said, "In two . . . in one . . . Alicia."

She looked up from her monitor and smiled. "That's it from us. Thank you for watching. From all of us here at *News Four New York*, we look forward to seeing you tomorrow night at six. Brian Williams and *NBC Nightly News* . . . starts now."

Smiling to camera, she paused, then looked down at her script and waited like that until she heard the intro to *NBC Nightly*.

"We're clear," Paul said.

Alicia looked up at the big monitor in the studio and saw Brian start the program, "On our broadcast tonight . . . "

Tracy the floor manager called out, "Night, Alicia."

"Good night," she said, "thanks."

A few other people said good night, and within twenty seconds the studio was empty.

Then the lights went off.

Alicia stayed where she was, behind the news desk, in the dark, alone in the studio.

"And later," Brian said, "our exclusive one-to-one with former president Bill Clinton. You won't want to miss this. But first . . . "

She clenched her fist and grinned. "Yes."

Behind her, she knew, the newsroom was now probably already empty. No one ever lingered.

That's when she heard Greg's voice. "You're allowed to go home."

She pointed to the monitor where she was watching the program. "My debut."

He walked into the studio. "Want company?"

"Sure."

He fell into the chair next to the news desk where the sports guy usually sat, kicked his feet up onto the desk, and leaned back.

Neither of them spoke while they watched the program.

And then there were only six and a half minutes left.

"When we come back," Brian said going to a commercial, "our exclusive sit-down with former president Bill Clinton."

The monitor went to black. It was a studio monitor, not an air monitor, so it didn't show any commercials.

Alicia took a deep breath.

Greg looked at her and grinned, reassuringly.

And neither of them spoke.

Then Brian was back.

"Last night, Bill Clinton hosted a party on the roof garden of the Metropolitan Museum here in New York City. It was a charity event . . . the kind of big, glamorous, star-studded evening you might expect . . . which the Clinton Initiative called "New York Loves Haiti." In the middle of last night's shindig . . . which raised more than seventeen million dollars to help our Caribbean neighbor so devastated by an earthquake in twenty ten . . . the former president took time away from his guests to sit down and speak with our own Alicia Melendez."

The shot cut to Alicia and Clinton sitting with Manhattan at dusk behind them.

Alicia said to him, "Start with the misery that you still see in Haiti after all this time."

For the next four minutes and forty seconds, the two of them talked about Haiti, and about what Clinton was trying to do there, about where he was succeeding, about where he was failing, and about what the future held.

It ended with Alicia asking, "One wish . . . what would it be?"

"Only one?" He laughed and tilted his head, the way he does when he's amused. "Make it right for ten million people down there whose own wishes have not yet come true."

The shot cut to Brian Williams who looked up from his monitor and smiled warmly. "That's our broadcast for this Wednesday evening . . . "

Alicia turned to Greg and he looked at her and, at the very same moment, alone in the dark studio, the two of them started applauding.

52

Tina banged on the door, and kept banging on the door until somebody finally opened it.

There was loud music playing, and she could see a lot of people in the living room getting stoned and playing music.

"What?" said the guy who'd opened the door. "What?"

"Where's Ricky?"

"And to whom does he owe the honor?"

"Fuck you," she said, shoved him out of the way and stormed into the apartment.

"Close the door shithead," someone shouted, "before the cat gets out."

He closed it.

She looked around. "Where's Ricky?"

A guy pointed to his bedroom. "Ricky?"

He came out carrying a bass guitar, wearing Bermudas that were too big for him and a Brentwood FC soccer shirt. "What?" Then he saw Tina and smiled. "If it isn't me visiting nurse service."

She walked up to him and grabbed his arm. "Come do me."

"What a good idea," he said. "Don't mind if I do."

One of the women in the living room asked, "Can we watch?"

The guy next to her suggested, "Maybe we should film it."

"Fuck you," Tina said to them and dragged Ricky back into his bedroom.

"Nice to see you," Ricky said to her, "to see you, nice."

"Shut up, Ricky. Put the guitar down and lock the door."

He did.

By that time, she was naked and on his bed.

"Little randy this evening, are we?"

"A lot pissed off. Come here."

"Always glad to oblige the inflicted," he said. "No prescription necessary."

SHE SPENT the night with Ricky and in the morning didn't seem in her usual hurry to leave.

"What's for breakfast?"

"Breakfast, luv? I don't really know. I'm hardly ever up for breakfast."

She got out of bed and started for the door. "Have you got coffee?"

"Don't know luv . . . but . . . " He warned, "I wouldn't do that. Not with all them people out there."

She started looking for a robe. "Who are they?"

"Don't know."

"Where did they come from?"

"Don't know."

"Why do you let them stay?"

"Don't know, do I?" He shrugged, "I reckon if they had someplace else to be, they wouldn't be here. So, I suppose, that means they have no place else to be."

She found an old silk robe in one of his closets, put it on and opened the door.

The ocelot raced in.

"What's that?" she screamed.

Ricky threw a pillow at it.

She turned around and tried to find it.

The ocelot dove under the bed.

"Fucking cat . . . " Ricky grabbed another pillow. "I'm going to drown it as soon as I can catch it."

Tina bent down and looked under the bed. "It's not a cat . . . and it's trembling with fear." She made some soft kissing sounds. "Come here . . . come on . . . "

"His name is Billy."

"Come on . . . come on . . . it's okay . . . "

And very slowly, the ocelot came into her arms.

"It's okay . . . it's all right . . . " Tina lifted it up gently. "She's scared and much too thin . . . don't you ever feed her?"

"Billy's a bloke."

"Okay," she kept rubbing its neck, "don't you ever feed him?"

"Nah . . . I hate him. I'm going to drown him. Or cut him up and have him stuffed and made into a cushion."

"Stop it." She looked closely at Billy. "What is he?"

"Someone said he's an ocelot. I think of him as a cat."

"You can't keep him in an apartment," she said. "You've got to call a zoo or something. Ricky, this animal is going to die here."

"I didn't want him, someone brought him, and now I'm stuck with him."

"Have you got any milk?"

"He eats barbecued chicken. Or at least that's what he found in the fridge. And I think he found some pizza the other night."

"This is awful," she said. "I'll go out now and buy him some milk and . . . I don't know, maybe some cat food. Then when those assholes in your living room wake up, they have to take him to a zoo or an animal rescue shelter."

"There's a zoo in Central Park."

"Ricky, I'm serious." She stroked the animal again. "If you don't do it today, I'm going to turn you in to the animal welfare people."

"No reason to do that, luv."

"I'll get the food. You take him to the zoo. And you better do it."

"All right, luv . . . I promise."

She carefully put the ocelot down on the bed and, immediately, he raced under it to hide.

THURSDAY

53

Gabriella Battelli phoned Pierre Belasco, and when he said to her, "I need you to convince your mother to keep the business open," she agreed. "My father would be heartbroken if she closed it."

"Tell me about your father's cousin."

"There's not much to tell. My grandfather didn't want him in the business and paid him to stay away. Every now and then Johnny would get in touch with my father and demand money. My father would remind him that he'd signed an agreement to stay away from the business, but Johnny would say it's not worth the paper it's printed on, and they'd fight until my father would send him more money."

"How did Johnny get along with your mother?"

She hesitated, then said quietly, "He was the one who told her . . . when my father died . . . he called her and told her . . . " She stopped.

"Told her what?"

"I probably shouldn't be talking to you about this . . . if my mother ever found out . . . "

"Gabriella . . . you're right that we shouldn't be talking. But I have to go behind her back because she doesn't want to deal with this. She wants to run away from it."

She blurted out, "That my father had a girlfriend."

Belasco waited a few seconds before he asked, "Why would he do that? Why would he deliberately want to hurt your mother? Especially right after your dad passed away."

"My dad wrote a letter," she went on, "to my mother and me. He said if anything ever happened to him, we were to make sure that Johnny was kept away from the business."

"Please don't mention this call to your mother. She's not in the mood to understand just yet. The time will come when we can tell her. And we should tell her. But not yet."

"I understand."

"Convince her to keep the business."

"I'll try," she said, then added, "She's not acting like herself."

"Don't give up on her."

"I won't . . . if you won't," Gabriella said, "but honestly, I don't hold out much hope."

NOW HE DIALED the 855 number Forbes had given him and left a message. "It's Pierre Belasco. If you would be kind enough to call me, please, I'm in the office. Thank you."

When Forbes didn't return the call within half an hour, he went upstairs to Scarpe Pietrasanta.

The door was locked.

He knocked on it but nothing happened.

Then he took his phone and rang Carlos Vela's number.

"*Hola,*" the man answered in Spanish.

"Carlos, it's Pierre Belasco. Where are you?"

"I am home, Señor."

That surprised him. "I need you to come into Trump Tower."

"I was there this morning, Señor, but the security man downstairs at the elevators confiscated my pass. He wouldn't let me upstairs."

"You should have called me."

"I called Mrs. Battelli. She said not to worry, that I did not any longer have to come in. She said the office was closed."

"Can you come to my office this morning?"

"Señor . . . if I come in . . . you know how Mr. Riordan said . . . "

"Please come in," he said. "I will take care of Mr. Riordan."

An hour later when Vela showed up, Belasco said, "Give me your key, please."

Vela confessed, "I don't have a key. The security man downstairs took it with my pass."

"All right," Belasco shook his head in frustration. "Come with me."

The two of them went to the twenty-fourth floor and walked straight into Bill Riordan's office.

"His pass and the key to the door at Scarpe Pietrasanta," Belasco demanded.

Riordan answered, "Mr. Vela's pass has been destroyed. Normally, Mrs. Battelli would have to request another one. But that won't happen now, either. As for the key, that is no longer operative."

Belasco managed to keep his anger in tow. "Get me a pass for him and a door key."

"I can't," he said. "I spoke with Mrs. Battelli early this morning, and she informed me that the business is closed. Anyway, she is delinquent with the rent and charges. So, acting entirely within my job description, all of the passes that had been issued to her have been rendered void, and the locks on her front door have been changed. If you want to go in there, seeing as how the business is defunct and in default, you will have to speak with Mrs. Mendelsohn. It's out of my hands."

Belasco turned to Vela, said, "Come with me," and went to Carole Ann Mendelsohn's office.

"I need access to the Scarpe Pietrasanta premises," he said. "And I need a pass authorized for Mr. Vela here. According to Bill Riordan, neither is possible without you signing off on it."

She gave him an odd look. "You're in charge of Trump Tower, you run the place, you can authorize anyone you want to have a pass. As for access to the premises, ditto."

"Apparently the company is in default."

"That has nothing to do with me. Go see accounting."

"But Bill Riordan said . . . "

"But Bill Riordan doesn't seem to know what he's talking about."

"Thank you."

Belasco took Vela back to the staff offices, this time to Harriet's desk, where he told her, "I need a building pass for Mr. Vela."

She made a face. "I have been ordered, expressly, not to do that."

"By?"

She pointed to Riordan's office.

"He doesn't get to decide. I do. So please cut a pass for him. Also, do you have keys for the Scarpe Pietrasanta office?"

She pointed again to Riordan's office.

"No problem," he said. "Send Mr. Vela's pass down to my office. And if he interferes, tell him I said . . . " He stopped, then decided, "Never mind. I'll tell him myself."

Leaving Vela at Harriet's desk, Belasco went into Riordan's office. "If you interfere, ever again, with something I am trying to do, or something I want, or something I have asked someone else to do, I will personally take it up with the boss and recommend that you be summarily fired."

Riordan didn't seem in the least bothered by that. "Take your best shot, pal."

"I will," Belasco said, "and it will be good enough."

Walking away, he motioned to Vela to follow him. Once they were outside the office, Belasco phoned Big Sam, the building engineer in charge of all maintenance, and said he was on his way down to his office.

When he stepped into the long, windowless room, deep in the bowels of Trump Tower, not far from the boiler plant—it was filled with tools and generator parts and the walls were covered with blueprints and engineering designs—Big Sam was shocked to see Carlos Vela.

"What's he doing here? He's on the Chapman."

"No, he's not," Belasco said. "He works upstairs at Scarpe Pietrasanta on the nineteenth floor."

Big Sam looked at Vela and nodded. "How you doing, Carlos?"

Vela nodded back shyly. "Okay, Señor."

"I need someone to open the door and change the locks and give me three sets of keys. No one else is to have them."

"But Bill Riordan said . . . "

"But you don't work for Bill Riordan."

"No problem, boss." Big Sam held up his hands to show him he was cool with that. "I'll send someone up right now."

Belasco turned to Vela. "Go upstairs with whoever changes the locks, take all three sets of keys, and hold onto them. I will collect them from you later. Then go inside, lock the door, and go back to work. Got that?"

"Okay, Señor," he said to Belasco but looked at Big Sam.

"It's all right, Carlos," Big Sam reassured him. "Come on, you and I will find somebody and get that locked changed. Like old times, yes?"

WHEN HE got back to his own office, Belasco found a voice mail from Rebecca Battelli. He dialed her number, apologized for missing her call, then asked, "How are you?"

"It gets better and better," she said. "Your office called to say that they're putting the company into default."

"Who phoned you?"

"Mr. Riordan. He said the locks have been changed . . . "

"Well, here's the good news. Your company is not being put into default. Mr. Riordan has no authority to do anything of the kind. I'm having new locks put on the door and no one else will have the keys except you and Carlos and me."

"Why Carlos?"

"Because he's upstairs now cleaning up the office."

"I told him not to come in."

"That's when you thought we were putting you in default. I called him and asked him to come back."

There was a long pause. "This morning I arranged for a cleanup crew to get everything out of there. I will find some money, and you will be paid for back rent and however much the rent will be . . . you know, for those months during which we have to give you notice."

"Don't worry about that. We can work it out . . . "

"Pierre . . . I'm not sure I want to work it out."

He thought fast. "I'm afraid that someone from the company will have to . . . you know, authorize access for the cleanup crew."

"You have my permission to be that person."

He lied, "There are also some . . . there are some papers that need to be signed. Authorizations. Perhaps if your daughter were here?"

"Yes. Fine. I'll send Gabriella." She paused, and then said, "Thank you for what you've been trying to do. Goodbye." And she hung up.

He quickly went to his phone and checked the day's incoming caller IDs until he found Gabriella's number.

"I just got off the phone with your mother."

"I'm sorry that I haven't had a chance to talk to her yet."

"Plan B. She wants to clear out the office. I said we needed authorization. She said she'll send you. When you speak to her, tell her that you'll handle everything. When can you come in?"

"I have no classes tomorrow."

"Good. Pick a time."

"Noon?"

"Come to the residents' lobby on Fifty-Sixth Street. That's where my office is . . . "

"Hold on . . . my mother's on the other line . . . hold on . . . " She clicked off.

Belasco waited.

It was several minutes before Gabriella came back. "Sorry about that. She's not being rational. I've never seen her like this. She keeps saying she can't cope anymore. I tried to talk to her, but she didn't want to know. She said, go see Mr. Belasco and sign whatever needs to be signed."

He smiled. "See you tomorrow at noon."

Hanging up with her, he tried the 855 number for Forbes again and left another message.

This time Forbes phoned back.

"What's up?"

"The guys who broke into Scarpe Pietrasanta. I know what they were looking for."

54

Tina walked into the apartment as if nothing had happened.

"Luisa," she called for her housekeeper.

David demanded, "Where the hell were you last night?"

"Out," she responded. "Luisa?"

He wanted to know, "Out where?"

"What difference does it make?"

Luisa arrived. "Yes, ma'am, good morning."

Tina smiled at her. "Would you bring me coffee and one buttered toast, please? I'll be upstairs."

David waited for Luisa to say, "Yes, ma'am," and hurry off.

"What difference does it make? I'm your husband, and I have every right in the world to know where my wife is sleeping, that's what difference it makes."

She pulled her arm out of his grip. "If you must know, I was screwing a wild animal trainer."

He moved in front of her to stop her walking away. "Dammit, where were you?"

She lied, "At Cyndi's."

"And if I pick up the phone right now and call Cyndi, she's going to verify that?"

"Be my guest."

He stared at her, then stepped out of her way.

Tina went upstairs and David went into the office.

He had to do something, but he didn't know what to do. There was no way he could call the police because they'd start asking a lot of questions about the Colombians. Nor could he tell them about how the Rojas brothers had sold him a cargo of illegal crude. The only thing he could think of was phoning his old buddy in Houston, Oscar Mack Moore.

"Law offices," the operator answered.

"Mack around yet this morning? It's David Cove in New York."

"Putting you through," she said.

Right away, Moore came on the line. "Tell me you're in town and I'm leaving on the next freight train out."

"Y'all can stay put," David said. "But I got me a little problem and I need some free advice."

"Free? Hardly. What's happening?"

David told him everything.

When he was done, Moore said, "I always knew you were one dumb son of a bitch, but I never knew how dumb."

"Yeah, rub it in."

"You want me to tell you it's gonna be all right? It ain't. You've got jeopardy written all over your sorry ass."

"I want my money back from the Rojas brothers, fast, so I can pay the fuckers in Colombia before they find out their money is gone."

"Now you know why, when you do business with criminals and they screw you, there's nobody you can complain to." He barked, "Fucking idiot," then asked, "How'd you leave it with the Rojas boys?"

"I phoned Liberio and made him understand . . . no doubts . . . that if I didn't get my money back I'd have him killed."

"Key-rist . . . David . . . didn't your mama ever tell you to think before open-ing your mouth? You got yourself a real win-win situation going on. Either you have him killed, which means you never get your money. Or he has you killed first, which means you never get your money. Any other bright ideas?"

"Can we sue him in Mexico?"

"Sure. But you're asking the wrong question. You should be asking, if we sue him in Mexico can we win? The answer to that is, no way, José. If the Rojas boys don't already own all the judges down there, they'll buy a dozen first thing in the morning. And then, to hedge their bet, they'll kill you."

David leaned way back in his chair and shut his eyes. "You got any better ideas?"

"Uncle RD might have some influence. But I never supposed the Rojas boys were very charitable. I don't see them giving you your money back just be-cause ol' RD says pretty please."

"How about a private detective to hunt down Zhadanov?"

"Hold on." David could hear Mack moving some papers on his desk, then typing on his keyboard. Then he came back on the line to say, "Try this guy. Name is Renny Regis. Ex-FBI. Knows his way around the playground."

Mack gave David a number in Austin, Texas.

"Lot of good this is going to do me in New York City."

"You asked if I knew someone. Frankly, from what you're telling me, even Dick Tracy in New York City isn't going to do much good."

"You saying I'm fucked?"

"Got that right."

David took a deep breath. "Let me tell you, Mack, there are three types of friends in the world. One who tells you the glass is half-full. One who tells you the glass is half-empty. And then there's you, who says the fucking glass ain't even there no more."

"Got that wrong, pal. There are people who will tell you what you want to hear. And there are people who tell you the truth, no matter what. Only one of them is your friend. You decide for yourself which is which."

With that, Moore hung up.

David heard the phone go dead. "Fuck you, too."

Looking up at the trading screens, he spotted a bunch of small deals sitting there waiting to be had. Aluminum in Indonesia. Cement in Papua New Guinea. Newsprint in Gulfport. Potatoes, of all things, in Angola. He knew he could make some money getting in and out fast, but with a big hole blown in his finances, he had enough sense not to start trading. If he got in the game without being able to cover his downside, and then somehow got caught short, he'd be dead as a trader. Best-case scenario was that no one would ever trade with him again. Worst-case scenario was that the cops would show up and arrest him for fraud.

"Win-win my ass," he said, and tried to think of some way to come up with fast money.

He phoned Uncle RD, but couldn't get through. He left a voice mail, but Uncle RD didn't phone back.

Then he called Carson.

Someone in his office said, "He's out of the country."

"When will he be back?"

That person answered, "Not this week."

David wondered for a moment if he should e-mail Carson and try to set up a phone call. But he knew that was a nonstarter. When you're trying to borrow money, you can't do it in an e-mail or over the phone. He needed to sit down with Carson and discuss his predicament face to face.

Next he took a deep breath and called Wayne Grannum at Caymans Comtrad.

"I'm looking to extend my line of credit . . . short term . . . a couple of months. What kind of rate can I get?"

Grannum shook his head. "David . . . looking at the hole you're in with us right now . . . "

"Short term," he reiterated. "How long have I been with the bank?"

"I hear what you're saying, David . . . "

"People who say that never do. Just . . . yes or no."

"Sorry, David . . . no."

Now he started calling around to other banks where he had relationships. He phoned JP Morgan Chase, Citi, ING, Deutsche Bank and Credit Suisse. His contacts there were more receptive than Grannum, but when he said he was looking for upward of fifty million, each of them said he'd have to show that much in assets stashed away somewhere else.

Each of them said, "If the assets are there, no problem, we'd be happy to do business with you."

Except it was a problem because they'd inevitably check with Caymans Comtrad and see that his ship was taking on water. Instead of manning the buckets, they'd do what banks typically do—head for the lifeboats and call in his outstanding debts.

Then he wondered, if instead of getting fifty from one bank, what would happen if he tried to get ten on his signature from five of them? Or, he might even be able to double-talk ten of them into five each.

One of the office lines rang.

Caller ID said, "Private Number."

David hoped it was RD.

Instead, when he answered it, a man said, "David, long time no hear."

"Who's that?" he asked.

"Pepe Forero."

Oh, fuck me! David took a deep breath. "Pepe, how are you?"

"How am I? To tell the truth, I'm a worried man."

"What are you worried about?"

"When I send someone a lot of money and that person doesn't let me know how things are going, I worry."

"It's only been a few days. Y'all still in Curaçao?"

"No," he answered. "Tell me what's happening."

Not sure what Don Pepe already knew, David tried, "Have y'all spoken to our mutual friend, Mr. Zhadanov?"

"Have you?"

"No."

"Any idea where he is?"

Shit, David thought. "No. You?"

"And our money?"

Fuck me, here it comes. "What about your money?"

"Playing coy does not suit you, my friend. Where is our money?"

He didn't want to be caught in a lie but, at the same time, he didn't want to tell Don Pepe the truth. "I put a call into our mutual friend first thing this morning . . . "

"That's not what I asked."

"When I speak to Zhadanov, I'll let you know immediately . . . "

"That's not the way deals work, as I understand it."

"As you understand it?"

"As I understand it, my money was transferred into an account you call Curaçao Trading One at Caymans Comtrad Bank. Where is it now?"

"Hold on," David said. "That's not quite right. He held the money in his client account, and I used my account . . . listen, y'all got to speak to Zhadanov."

"No," Don Pepe said calmly. "You don't seem to understand that the moment you used my money, then my money becomes your problem."

David lashed out, "But I didn't use your money . . . "

"We don't need to hear from Mr. Zhadanov. Perhaps you do. But we already know who owes us this money."

"Y'all can't look to me. As soon as I find that little fucker . . . "

"As I said," Don Pepe went on in a quiet voice, "our money was entrusted to you. We want it back . . . from you."

"I never saw a penny of your fucking money. Zhadanov . . . "

"Mr. Cove, what is it you don't understand?" Don Pepe's voice was now almost in a whisper. "This is not about Mr. Zhadanov. This is about you returning my money within twenty-four hours. Please don't miss the deadline, Mr. Cove, because if you do, this will turn, decidedly, ugly."

"Y'all don't know who you're threatening," David yelled.

"Yes, I do," Don Pepe said. "Twenty-four hours . . . you all."

And then he hung up.

"Fuck you." David slammed down the phone. "Fuck you." And for a long time he sat there cursing, "Fuck you. Fuck you. Fuck you."

55

"You're the designated driver," Ricky told his son. "Take off your shoe."

"You can't do this," Joey objected.

Ricky insisted, "But that's what we're going to do."

"And what if they don't want him?"

"They're a zoo . . . of course they want him."

Joey appealed to Ricky's friend Neville. "You tell him."

"Not my place, mate."

"Come on," Ricky said, "take off your shoe."

"What happens if I say no?"

A woman sleeping on a couch turned around and looked at them. "Can't a girl get some sleep without everyone arguing all the bleeding time?"

"Somebody has to do it," Ricky said to Joey, ignoring the woman. "How else can I get out of here?"

Another woman came out of the third bedroom carrying Billy. "He's the cutest cat. He's been purring all afternoon."

"Did he finish that cat food?" Ricky asked.

"And drank all his milk, he did."

"All right then, someone get me a rucksack."

"You're fucking daft," Joey said to his father, pulling off his right shoe.

Ricky asked, "Where do we keep our rucksacks?"

Joey answered, "We don't have one."

"Then get a suitcase," Ricky said.

Neville worried, "How's Billy going to breathe in a suitcase?"

Ricky shook his head. "Obviously, we're going to poke holes in it."

"Oh yeah," Neville nodded. "Good thinking."

"Wot, you want a rucksack?" The woman on the couch stirred. "You can take mine."

"Where is it, luv?" Ricky asked.

She pointed toward the hallway, turned over, and went back to sleep.

"Where?" Ricky looked but couldn't find it.

"I got it," the other woman said, pulling it from behind a couch.

Ricky saw it and said, "That's perfect."

It was a Simpsons backpack, except it was obviously a bootlegged one, because the drawing on the side was Marge, naked on her knees in front of a naked smiling Homer.

Ricky studied it—"I love it"—then opened it to pull all of her stuff out. He found a small collection of sex toys, some underwear, toothpaste and deodorant.

"Your bird comes prepared," he said to Joey.

"Not my bird. Never saw her before."

Ricky looked at the other woman, "She your mate?"

That woman shrugged and said the same thing, "Never saw her before."

"So then," Ricky wanted to know, "how did she fucking get here?"

Joey said, "Don't have a clue, mate. Assumed she was your bird."

"Yeah, well . . . " Ricky went to look at her closely and nodded to show the others that she wasn't too bad. "Here, take all this," he dumped the backpack's contents onto the floor, "and put it on my bed. When she wakes up, if I'm not here, tell her to get into my bed and I'll be back."

The woman nodded, "Sure, Rick."

He sat down on the floor opposite Joey and took off his right shoe. Joey put his feet together with his father's, then twisted it so Ricky's right heel was touching Joey's right toes.

"Go on Neville," Ricky said, and Neville bent down to slide the ankle bracelet over Ricky's heel and onto Joey's toes.

It was very tight, and scraped both their feet, but as it came off Ricky's foot, it slid snugly onto Joey's foot, then up his ankle.

"Got it," Ricky said triumphantly, rubbing his ankle where the bracelet had been. "Don't know why they insist on making it so hard to get off." He stood up and stepped back into his shoe, "My foot feels a stone lighter."

He did a little jig to show the others that he was free of the bracelet, then said, "Get some of them cat biscuits, or whatever they are, and drop them in the bottom of the rucksack . . . "

When Neville did that, Ricky picked up the ocelot and slipped him into the backpack.

"It works," Neville said.

"Of course it works," Ricky said. "Let's go."

With the ocelot's head sticking out over the top, Ricky handed the backpack to Neville.

"Why me?"

"Because of me ankle," Ricky said. "I can't put any weight on it . . . you know, after the bracelet being there and all . . . can I."

Neville accepted the excuse.

The woman reminded Ricky that if he went outside, breaking the rules of his house arrest, and someone spotted him, he'd be in trouble. "You need a disguise."

She gave him her baseball cap and big red sunglasses.

"And don't forget," she said, "to put the cat's head inside the rucksack and keep it zipped up while you're out."

"Right." Ricky nodded to Neville.

"Right," Neville said, hoisting the backpack over his shoulders.

"Right," Joey said, "right fucking daft."

THEY GOT out of Trump Tower and headed up Fifth Avenue, and all the time Neville kept saying, "Do you think anyone's on to us yet, mate?"

Ricky kept answering, "Nah, mate, we're sweet as a nut."

But when they got to the Central Park Zoo, two policemen were standing near the entrance.

Ricky quickly turned Neville around. "The Old Bill, mate," and together they walked into the park.

"Phew," Neville said, "that was close."

"Yeah." Ricky kept looking back to see if the cops were following them, which they weren't. "We'll never get past them."

"So what do you suggest?"

He looked around. "This path . . . let's go."

"Where does it lead?"

"Wherever it leads." He started taking deep breaths. "It's really cool to be outside, taking a stroll like this after all that time being shut in."

When they got to Eightieth Street, Ricky saw a little path turning off the drive to their left. Following it, they found themselves walking across a great expanse of lawn, near the Turtle Pond.

Ricky looked around and off in the near distance spotted some tall brush. "Over there," he said. So they went there and Ricky decided, "This is as good a place as any."

"But I thought . . . what about the zoo?"

"Can't do it, can we, not surrounded by coppers, like that. If they spot me out here they'll nick me and they'll nick you for stealing an animal from the zoo."

"We didn't steal nothing," Neville said.

"Tell it to the judge." Ricky took the backpack from him, opened it and bent down to pour the ocelot out. "Go on, Billy . . . go on . . . "

First, it poked its head out, then it jumped out . . .

"Go on, Billy, scat."

. . . then it raced for the bushes.

"Free at last," Ricky said.

Neville looked at the bushes. "I kind of miss him already."

"We better get out of here." Ricky motioned. Neville didn't move. "Come on." He tugged at Neville's arm, and the two of them hurried back to Fifth Avenue.

"Being able to walk outside is pretty good," Ricky said.

"You don't have much time left now."

"Not a lot. Eight or nine days? I should show you my countdown clock."

As they stepped into the residents' lobby, Ricky took off the sunglasses and the baseball hat.

"Hey Mr. Lips, long time no see," Jaime the doorman said.

"Look who's there." Schaune, the concierge on duty, waved to him. "Nice to see you."

Ricky waved back, "To see you, nice."

Upstairs, Ricky and Joey put their feet together and slipped the bracelet back on Ricky's ankle.

"What did they say at the zoo?" Joey wanted to know.

Ricky looked at him, then at Neville, then back at Joey. "They said . . . free at last."

"Free at last?"

"Yeah." Ricky knew the rest of the famous speech because it was part of the lyrics to one of the Still Fools' songs. "Free at last. Thank God Almighty, we are free at last!"

56

Antonia paced the floor of her living room, looking at the clock in her tiny kitchen every few minutes.

She'd already checked the papers, but they only announced the time when the curtain went up, so she'd phoned the box office and learned that, on most nights, the show usually ended around 10:20.

It was now 9:30.

She went into her bedroom, turned on the television, but couldn't sit still long enough to watch anything. She came back into the living room, then went back to her bedroom. Eventually, she got it into her head that she should try again to rearrange the furniture.

If Antonia moves her desk from under the window and puts the couch there instead, what should Antonia do with the bookcase on the wall where the couch is now?

She'd been through this before, several Saturday nights in a row, but was still not happy with the outcome. So she pulled the desk into the middle of the living room, shoved it off to the side, grabbed the couch with both hands, and dragged it from the far wall to the window.

It was facing the wrong way, but because it was so heavy, she needed to catch her breath before she turned it around.

She fell into it, sat there for a few seconds thinking about the apartment, then glanced up and began staring out the window.

From her fifth-floor apartment, she could see lights on in the apartments across West Eighty-Eighth Street.

A fat woman was carrying a baby. An old man standing in his kitchen was talking to someone. Two young boys in their room were arguing about something.

Fascinated, she leaned forward and began counting how many windows she could peek into.

There were those three, and there were another two a few doors to the left—in one she could see a wide-screen television hanging on a wall, and in the other it looked like there were bunk beds—and then a light came on to her right and she saw a man taking off his shirt.

She watched him. But once he had his shirt off, he moved away. She waited for him to come back. He didn't.

Then a light one floor below went on, and now a young guy—she figured he was probably eighteen or nineteen—took off his jeans and walked around in a pair of white jockey shorts.

She waited for more. "Come on, take it off," she whispered.

But the light in his room snapped off and didn't come back on again.

This is fun, she said to herself, looking at the clock in her kitchen and seeing that she had plenty of time before making her call.

Antonia needs to buy binoculars.

Hurrying off the couch, she pushed it right up to the window, turned off all her lights, then crawled back onto the couch, sitting there on her knees, watching lights come on and go off all over the block.

A woman walked in front of a window, took off her bra, and moved away.

A couple kissed in the middle of a room, then disappeared. She figured they fell onto a couch or a bed, and she waited for them to reappear, but they didn't.

Binoculars. Where can Antonia buy binoculars? There must be a place on Broadway . . . the hardware store . . . Antonia can buy binoculars and be back real quick . . .

A light came on almost directly right across from her window, and a man with a towel tied around his waist went to a set of drawers and took out some underpants.

She held her breath, anxious to see what he was going to do.

He tossed the underpants onto something . . . she figured it was his bed . . . then turned around, with his back to her, and the towel came off.

"Oh . . ." She couldn't believe how exciting this was. "Turn around."

She couldn't see what he was doing, but he stood there like that for a long time as she stared at his bare backside.

"Turn around . . . please . . ."

Then he did.

"Oh . . ."

He was standing there, naked.

Binoculars. Antonia must buy binoculars tonight.

Her phone rang.

The man was still there, naked in the window.

The phone rang a second time.

Then, suddenly, the man shut the blinds.

He was gone and her show was over.

The phone rang a third time, and this time she lunged off the couch to grab it.

"Hello?"

"I told you to call me."

"What?" She carried the phone back to the couch to watch the windows across the street.

"I told you to call me after my show."

"Your show? Oh . . ."

She looked at the clock in the kitchen. It was now nearly eleven. "Tommy. I'm sorry. I was busy. I was going to call . . ."

He asked, "What are you doing?"

"How did you get my number?"

"I can get anybody's number. What are you doing?"

"Ah . . . reading," she lied. "I was reading. I was going to call you . . . really. Did the show go well tonight? What are you doing?"

"I'm in my dressing room," he said. "What are you wearing?"

"What do you mean?"

"What are you wearing?"

"Ah . . ." He flustered her. "A pair of jeans and a sweatshirt."

"And where are you?"

"At home."

"But where? In your bedroom?"

"In my living room."

"What does your living room look like?"

She didn't know what to tell him. "It's . . . I don't know . . . it's square and there's a door . . . "

"Is there a couch or a chair?"

"Yeah, sure . . . there's a couch and a couple of chairs . . . "

"Where's the couch?"

"In my living room."

"Where in the living room?"

"Under the window."

"Are all the lights on or off?"

"They're . . . one of them is on," she lied, again.

"Turn them all on."

"What?"

"Turn on all the lights. Every one of them. Go on."

She asked, "Why?"

"Do it."

She hesitated, then said, "Okay," and turned on all the lights.

"Now . . . stand up on the couch, facing the window."

"What?"

"Stand up on the couch facing the window. And open the blinds all the way."

"What for?"

"Do as I tell you. Stand on the couch and open the blinds."

She didn't move. "Why?"

"Go on."

Slowly, she did what he told her to do.

"Are you standing up on the couch?"

"Yes."

"Facing the window?"

Her mouth was getting very dry. "Why?"

"Are the blinds open?"

"Yes."

"Now put your phone on speaker, put it down on the window ledge and face the window."

"Why?"

"Do as I tell you."

She fumbled with the phone, found the speaker button, and put it on the ledge. "Can you see out the window?"

"Yes."

"Can people out there see you?"

Her breathing was getting heavier because she realized what was going to happen. "Yes."

"Now take off your sweatshirt."

She didn't budge.

"Take off your sweatshirt," he said again.

Her hands were trembling. "No."

"Yes," he said. "Take off your sweatshirt."

She reached for the bottom of her sweatshirt, but all she could do was hold onto it. "No."

"Yes."

"I can't."

"Yes you can. Do as I tell you. Take off your sweatshirt."

She tried to swallow, but her mouth was totally dry. "I can't . . . "

"Do it. Take off your sweatshirt. Do as I tell you."

She closed her eyes, hesitated, then pulled off her sweatshirt.

"Did you do it?"

"Yes."

"Now . . . take off your jeans . . . "

"No . . . "

"Yes. Take off your jeans. Go on."

Almost in a trance, she unbuttoned her jeans, opened them, and let them fall to her ankles.

"What are you wearing now?" he asked.

She kept her eyes shut tight and whispered, "My bra and panties."

"Now take off your bra."

Her hands were shaking as she reached behind her and did what he wanted her to do.

"Yes?" he asked.

"Yes," she said and let her bra fall to the couch.

"Now take off your panties."

She didn't budge.

"Go on," he said. "Roll your panties down slowly . . . very very slowly . . . roll them down."

With her eyes still shut, she put her hands on the sides of her panties and then, slowly, rolled them down her hips.

"Pull them all the way down."

She did.

"Are you naked?"

She was barely able to say, "Yes."

"Can people across the street see you in the window?"

Again, she only barely managed to say, "Yes."

"Now," he said, "put your hands there . . . "

She couldn't move.

"Go on . . . put your hands there . . . "

In a whisper she said, "Where?"

"You know where . . . go on . . . "

She moved her hands and touched herself and now her knees were so weak that she couldn't stand up anymore, and she fell onto the couch, still touching herself.

He kept whispering to her, and she couldn't stop.

"Tommy . . . " she groaned. "Tommy . . . Antonia wants Tommy . . . "

"Antonia is going to have Tommy," he said. "Tonight. Tommy is coming to Antonia's apartment and Tommy will ring the bell, and Antonia is going to open the door for Tommy, completely naked . . . "

"Yes," she groaned.

"Yes, Antonia?"

"Yes . . . yes . . . completely naked."

"And do whatever Tommy wants."

"Yes." She couldn't stop. "Whatever Tommy wants."

"Whatever Tommy wants."

"Yes . . . yes," she said it very loudly. "Whatever Tommy wants. Antonia wants. Whatever Tommy wants. Antonia wants. Yes."

She waited for him like for the rest of the night, and finally fell asleep around three.

He showed up at five.

FRIDAY

57

When she saw Arthur's caller ID come up on her phone, Cyndi grabbed it and asked, "How's my favorite agent?"

He asked, "And how's my favorite client?"

"That's what you say to all the girls."

"No, I don't. I say to all the girls, how's my second-favorite client? And they say, is Cyndi still your favorite? And I say, she will always be my favorite."

"But will you still love me when I'm old and wrinkly?"

"You? Old? I promise, at a hundred and ten, you will still be the most beautiful girl on the catwalks and the most wonderful woman in the world."

"Can we be a hundred and ten together? I'd like that."

"If that's what you want, but you've got a lot of catching up to do. I'll be a hundred and nine next August."

"Are there catwalk shows for Zimmer frame designers?"

He laughed, then said, carefully, "And speaking of catwalks . . . we've had a very cool offer."

"If it's Fashion Week in New York, my answer is the same. No."

"Don't say that until you hear what's on the table."

"I don't want to work in New York, ever again."

"I know. But we're talking unheard-of money. One show, six changes. You open with an evening gown. You close with the bridal gown. No prêt. All one-offs. No bikinis, no underwear. Big opening. Big finish." He paused, then reminded her, "Cyndi . . . we're talking one million dollars."

She didn't hesitate. "Arthur . . . not New York."

"Next spring. Last show of the week. Major designer. Major finale. Everybody who is anybody. And, of course, there's the closing party. I think we can probably work a tie-in with your perfume. You will light up the entire city."

"Been there, done that, hated it. I'm never going through again what I went through three years ago. Whatever happened to Rome? You said Giancarlo asked for me. Rome is fun. I'll go to Rome anytime."

"Giancarlo thought you'd work cheap because you love him. We said no."

"I do love him. And I'd be happy to work for him anytime. I also love his mother. She cooks linguini primavera for me. Remember that shoot in Sardinia when I caught the flu? She came down from Rome, all by herself, and sat in the villa with me for a week, holding my hand and cooking. She also taught me how to play *Machiavelli*. It's an Italian card game. I have no one to play cards with in New York, so tell Giancarlo yes."

"No."

"Arthur, it's not the money."

"Cyndi, it's always got to be the money. Food or no food, *Machiavelli* or pinochle. You'll kill your brand by underpricing it. That's what you pay me to protect. You can't work for Giancarlo for no money. But this offer is real money. A million bucks. No one else can get even close to what he's willing to pay you. Every girl in New York, London, Paris, Rome, anywhere . . . Moscow, Tokyo, name it . . . they'd kill for this. One day. You open. Six changes. You close. And the party . . . "

"I hate those parties."

"All right. You won't have to go. We'll stipulate that in the contract. Listen to me, nothing could be easier . . . "

Now she asked, suspiciously, "Who is it?"

"Morning walkthrough," he went on. "Afternoon dress, makeup, hair . . . curtain at eight, biggest show of the week, home by nine thirty with a million bucks."

She asked again, "Arthur . . . who?"

He hesitated. "Loic."

Closing her eyes—no one had mentioned that name in a very long time—she said quietly, "Never."

"Cyndi . . . "

"No. Not New York. And never, ever, him."

Arthur was silent for a long time. "I guess deep down I knew you wouldn't. I probably shouldn't have asked."

Suddenly, she blurted out, "The fucking bastard hasn't shown a stitch of design in nine years, and now one day, just like that, out of the blue, he decides to come back into the business? So his fucking whore wife must have finally dumped him. So Monsieur de la Grange decides to make his comeback in New York . . . not in Paris or London . . . but in New York. And Monsieur de la Grange thinks that a million bucks is going to buy my ass back. Well, Monsieur de la Grange can fuck himself. I spent enough time doing it for him. He can take his million bucks and . . . " she stopped.

Her eyes got very red.

There was another long silence before Arthur said, "Please forgive me. I'm sorry. I should have known better."

"Oh . . . Arthur . . . dear sweet Arthur . . . I've already given enough blood. Never again. Not him. Not in this life. Not even in the next life."

"Cyndi . . . if I was thirty-five years younger and could stay awake past nine o'clock, I would whisk you away in my pumpkin coach."

She smiled. "And if I didn't love your wife so much, and she hadn't told me how you snore . . . "

"She said that?"

"Thank you, Arthur. I love you."

She hung up and closed her eyes again.

She didn't want to remember Loic. She didn't want him anywhere near her life. She'd spent so many years learning how to forget him and everything about him, and everything about them.

Except one thing.

That was all she allowed herself. A single charm on her bracelet of memories from a very long time ago.

Only one thing.

Their first kiss.

Barefoot on the beach at Cannes on a chilly September night. There was still traffic roaring up and down the *Croisette*, and lights were on in the rooms and suites of the Majestic and the Carlton and the Martinez. Water lapped quietly on the shore and a full moon hung over the sea, casting a beam of light along the sea that came right to them.

He took the sweater that was wrapped around his neck and put it over her, and held his arm around her.

Then, very slowly, he turned her face toward his and put his lips barely against hers. They stayed like that, staring into each other's eyes, until she finally took his face in her hands and closed her eyes and she kissed him.

And now, for one brief instant, other kisses and other beaches began to fill her head. Rio and Tahiti. Cap d'Antibes and Maui. Costa Rica and St. Martin.

"Stop it," she said out loud, fighting with herself not to cry. "Stop." She stood up and took several deep breaths. "I am not going to do this to myself. Stop."

Grabbing her phone, she called Alicia's cell. "Where are you?"

"At work."

"Oh . . . " She wanted Alicia to be home. "Sorry . . . never mind."

"What's wrong?"

"Nothing."

"I can hear it in your voice. Tell me."

She sighed loudly. "What do you do when your memory starts screwing around with your memory? When you start remembering things you really don't want to remember?"

"Good memories or bad memories?"

"They were wonderful at the time. Sort of. You know . . . but now . . . "

"Him?"

She admitted, "Yes, him."

Alicia suggested, "Do my television trick. Run the videotape backward at quadruple speed with no sound. You'll be surprised what you see that you didn't see the first time."

"Like what?"

"Like . . . how he used to wear really thick, really embarrassing geeky glasses. Or how he picked his teeth after breakfast in bed? Or his socks? Everybody's naked except he's still got his sweat socks on."

Cyndi tried, "Or how he wouldn't make love to you until the first half ended, and then you had to be done before the second half kick-off?"

Alicia laughed. "Or how about when he says, you know what, darlin', I still have fantasies about that night I poured champagne into your belly button and drank it. And you have to tell him, sorry, chum, but that wasn't me."

Cyndi laughed. "Or how about when you lie awake thinking of some guy who tattooed your name on his arm and years later you bump into him and suddenly the tattoo reads, 'Harley Hog Heaven.'"

"Really?"

"I swear I remembered my name there."

"Then how about . . . New Year's Eve in the Laurentian Mountains, that's in Canada, and we were skiing. Here I am, barely old enough to cross a state line, a Miami girl who's never been in really cold weather, and years later I bump into him and tell him, I never forgot that New Year's Eve. And he says, I never forgot it either, and every now and then, every few years, I try to relive it by going back to Bermuda."

Cyndi began to sing, "We dined at eight, we dined at nine, you were late, I was on time . . . "

"Ah yes," Alicia joined in, "I remember it well."

"I loved *Gigi*," Cyndi said.

"It was *West Side Story*."

"It was *Bye Bye Birdie*."

"It was the Laurentian Mountains."

"It was Bermuda."

"Ah yes," they sang together, "I remember it well."

Alicia asked, "Feeling better?"

"I love you."

"I love you too."

Cyndi hung up.

Did we dine at eight or was it nine? A chilly September night? A full moon?

She went to her laptop and found a perpetual calendar. She knew the date and she knew the year, and the calendar noted that the full moon had happened . . .

. . . two weeks before?

She couldn't believe it. The beach? The night? The moon?

But there was no full moon.

She started to laugh.

Thank you Alicia.

Fuck you Loic.

"Ah yes," she sang out loud, "I remember it well."

58

Antonia opened the door naked, the way he'd told her she had to, and as soon as Tommy stepped inside, he took her right there on the living room floor.

It was the first time they ever actually saw each other. Neither one of them even said hello.

She couldn't get enough of him. But then, after only two times, they went into her bedroom and he fell asleep. She lay there watching him, hoping he would wake up so they could do it again. Eventually, she fell asleep, too.

Now, opening her eyes, she saw it was after nine. She was exhausted and already late for work.

She didn't want to leave him. *Antonia has a Broadway star in her bed.* Then she remembered Belasco's weekly staff meeting. "Tommy . . . Tommy . . ." She gently touched his shoulder. "Antonia needs to go to a meeting . . . "

He stirred and reached for her.

"No Tommy, not now . . . I have to go to work."

But he didn't listen to her, and it didn't take long before she was moaning, "Antonia wants Tommy."

"YOU CALLED ME," the man said. "Name's Renny Regis."

"Oh, yeah," David said. "Yeah. I'm an old buddy of Oscar Mack Moore in Houston. That's how I got your name."

"What can I do for you?"

"Help me find someone who owes me a lot of money."

"Tell me who, what, when, where and why," Regis said, "and I'll tell you how much."

David related the entire story but deliberately left out the fact that the Colombians were Colombians. He referred to them as, "foreign business contacts."

Regis asked, "Have the police been called in yet?"

"No."

"Good," he said. "Five grand a day for the first two weeks, not counting expenses. Saturdays and Sundays are prorated extra. Then we move onto an hourly rate of five hundred, not counting expenses. One week up front. Signed contract by fax. If that's not okay, it's been nice talking to you. If it is, when do you want me to start?"

David said, "Right now."

After they hung up, David's cell phone rang. The caller ID said, "Private Number," and David worried that it would be Don Pepe again. He thought about not answering it, but if it was Uncle RD . . .

"Hello?"

A man asked, "Is this Mr. Cove?"

"Who's this?"

"Your new best friend."

"Who?"

"Your new best friend."

"Who are you and what do you want?"

"I told you who I am. What I want is to look after your health, and the health of your loved ones."

David didn't like the tone of this. "Listen asshole . . . "

"Mr. Cove, this is a courtesy call so I will be courteous. A mutual friend wants his money back. If he doesn't get it in the time allotted, when we speak next, it will be face to face . . . and not very courteous."

"Don't you fucking threaten me," he yelled.

"Mr. Cove," the man said calmly, "this is strictly business. Nothing personal . . . yet. Still . . . wherever you go in the next twenty-four hours, look around. You and your loved ones won't be alone. Have a nice day."

"Fuck you," David screamed into the phone. "Fuck you."

In a rage, he went looking for Don Pepe's number, and when he found it he dialed it. But the call went no further than an operator's voice saying, "The number you have dialed is no longer in service."

"Fuck you, too." He threw his phone against the wall, smashing it.

"What's going on?" Tina was standing in the doorway with her arms crossed. "David . . . I need to know what the fuck is going on?"

"Leave me alone," he yelled at her. "Just leave me alone."

She stared at him for several moments, then nodded, "Fine," and walked away.

WHILE ANTONIA and Tommy took a shower together, she said she wanted to help him get even with Pierre Belasco for banning him from Trump Tower.

"Antonia has a plan. There is somebody we should meet with. If we leave now, I can sneak you in. There's a staff meeting I'm supposed to be at. But Antonia can't go now. Antonia will make some excuse later. It runs from ten to eleven. It means Belasco won't be in his office. I can sneak you in."

He reached for her. "Watch me sneak myself in right now."

"No, we don't." She moved quickly away before he got her going again. "I've got to make a call."

She got Katarina Essenbach on the line.

"This is Antonia . . . you know, Antonia Lawrence . . . good morning. I have someone you need to meet. May I bring him up in, say, half an hour?"

The woman said yes.

"We need to hurry," Antonia told Tommy.

He reached for her again.

"No, no, not now. Later. Antonia promises."

"Tommy doesn't like it when people don't keep their promises."

They got dressed. But before they left her apartment, she worried that if someone spotted him, she'd get into trouble. So she found an old hooded sweatshirt and made him put it on. It was a tight fit but it served the purpose. Then she insisted he also wear sunglasses. He said he didn't have any with him, so she gave him an old pair of hers.

Dressed like that, she walked him through the residents' lobby at Trump Tower and right past Belasco's empty office, without anybody recognizing him or asking any questions.

On the forty-second floor, one of the maids opened the door and brought them into the main living room where Mrs. Essenbach was sitting with a heavyset, jowly man wearing an ill-fitting brown suit.

"Hey, ain't you Tommy Seasons?" the man asked.

"Oh my goodness," Mrs. Essenbach gushed all over him. "I was there opening night and thought you were far better than Burton. I knew Richard. And you gave the role new meaning."

"Yeah, thanks," he said, not caring what she thought.

"You made that movie," the man said. "The one where you . . . whatever, I forget, but I saw it on television . . . you were a taxi driver or something in Miami or someplace . . . "

"Yeah," he nodded, "thanks."

Antonia extended her hand to the man. "I'm Antonia Lawrence . . . I'm with the Trump Organization . . . "

"Oh?" The man shot a look at Mrs. Essenbach. "Then I think it's time for me to leave." He stood up. "Nice meeting you," he said to Tommy, merely nodded to Antonia, then said to Mrs. Essenbach, "I'll be in touch on that matter we discussed."

"I'll see you out," Mrs. Essenbach said and escorted him to the door.

"Who the fuck was that asshole?" Tommy whispered to Antonia, then wanted to know, "And who's this ugly bitch?"

"Be nice. She wants to help us."

"How can she walk around with a face like that?"

Coming back into the living room, Mrs. Essenbach motioned to them to sit down, then confided in Antonia, "That was Clarence O'Bannion. You must know who he is . . . very important in the building trade . . . some sort of inspector or controller or something. I'm not really sure. After you and I spoke about Mr. Belasco, I got in touch with Mr. O'Bannion to see if he could help us."

"That's good," Antonia said. "Tommy also wants to help. He's very angry with Mr. Belasco."

"The more the merrier," she said. "Just one word of caution, please, Mr. O'Bannion would rather that you not mention his visit here to anyone."

"Of course not," Antonia promised. "But what does he have to do with . . . "

"Steel mesh," she said.

"What is steel mesh?"

"Your Mr. Trump is building all over the city of New York. And in New Jersey. And in Connecticut. He has so many projects all over the place, and he buys a lot of steel mesh. If Mr. Trump doesn't fire Mr. Belasco, then Mr. O'Bannion is going to turn off all the steel mesh that goes into cement that goes into Mr. Trump's various projects."

DAVID RACKED his brains for people he could call.

He knew that the guy who ran the US side of the Trade and Industry Banking Corporation of China lived in Trump Tower. But when he did a fast Google and saw that it was the government's official commercial investment bank, he knew banging on that door was a nonstarter.

Then he remembered someone else in the building.

They'd met in the elevator a year or so ago, and Tina even went to have tea with her once. He knew she was loaded and, he thought, *it's worth a shot even if I only get her to introduce me to her bankers.*

He found a number for Katarina Essenbach and rung her.

"I know this is short notice," David said, "but Tina and I heard how y'all got screwed by the residents' board the other night. And we think that really stinks. We wanted to commiserate. So when I had a last-minute cancellation for lunch, I said to Tina, how about we see if Katarina can join us downstairs. Y'all up for something light at say, one?"

"How very sweet of you," she said. "I'd love to see you both."

He didn't bother finding Tina to tell her.

322   JEFFREY ROBINSON

KNOWING THAT the staff meeting was in full swing, Antonia brought Tommy back to the residents' lobby and out onto Fifty-Sixth Street.

"I have to go to the office," she said. "Antonia is so late. When will I see you again?"

"Come with me."

"I can't. I've got to . . . "

"Come with Tommy." He took her arm and started leading her down the block toward Fifth Avenue. "Tommy doesn't like it when people make promises . . . "

"Where are we going?" Then she realized what he was saying. "When I said later I meant . . . like later tonight? After the show. We can spend the whole weekend . . . "

He took her by the arm down Fifth Avenue.

"Tommy . . . I have a meeting . . . where are we going?"

"Tommy's taking you someplace special," he said.

At Forty-Fifth Street, they turned right, went a few blocks to Schubert Alley, turned left into the alley and came out at Forty-Fourth, where they turned right.

"Seriously, Tommy . . . I'll keep my promise . . . "

A few hundred yards down the block, at the side entrance to the David Merrick Theater, he escorted her in through the stage door.

"Tommy . . . please . . . I've got to go . . . "

He nodded to the guard at the door, took her up a long flight of stairs, which came out behind the stage, then up a shorter set of stairs that led to his dressing room.

"You made Tommy a promise," he said.

"Tommy, Antonia will keep her promise later . . . "

Before she could finish the sentence, he locked the door and started taking off her clothes.

DAVID WAS sitting at a table on the patio in front of the restaurant on the lower-level arcade at Trump Tower, nursing a bourbon and branch, when Mrs. Essenbach arrived. He apologized that Tina had a call and couldn't make it. "So it's just us kids," he smiled and asked what she wanted to drink.

She ordered a white wine spritzer.

When it arrived he proposed the toast, "To your health, and eventually, your Brazilian tropical forest," then said he wanted to know more about how the residents' committee had turned her down.

They both ordered salads, and while they ate Mrs. Essenbach went on and on about the committee and about how Pierre Belasco had promised her everything would be all right.

David sat there taking it all in, agreeing with every opinion she expressed.

At one point, a man seemed to pass very close to their table, and David was distracted briefly by him. But he didn't think twice about it.

When he and Mrs. Essenbach finished their salad, he asked her if she wanted dessert and coffee.

She said, "Neither."

"I'll have coffee," he said, and was about to change the subject to money, when she suddenly stood up and announced, "So nice to see you again. Please send my love to Tina. And do come for a meal one evening. Thank you for lunch. I shall be in touch."

She patted his head and left.

Goddamn. He was annoyed with himself for wasting all that time listening to her ramble on about her jungle.

Now his cell phone beeped that a message had come in.

It was a photo taken very close by of him sitting at that table with Mrs. Essenbach.

The text message with it said, "The health of you and your loved ones."

Oh fuck! He looked around.

That man who'd walked so close by the table.

He was nowhere to be seen.

In a panic, David dialed his pilot Barry at home.

Putting his hand over his mouth so no one could hear him, he said, "Sorry to call you on short notice like this. But I need you to gas up the plane."

"Where we going?"

"File a flight plan to Houston."

"Okay, boss. We overnighting in Houston?"

"We're not going to Houston."

"But you said . . . "

"I know what I said. But I don't know where we're going. I'll think of something once we get off the ground."

ALONE IN the office, Tina moved her trading account offshore to the Caymans, then moved half of what was left in her joint account with David—a little under $600,000—into one of her own offshore accounts in the Bahamas.

All told, between those accounts, another account in the Caymans, and the trust account in Liechtenstein, she figured she was cash rich to the tune of roughly $16.5 million.

She owned the apartment jointly with David, had six investment rental properties in her own name in Calgary, Canada, four chalets she rented out in Breckenridge, Colorado, plus a five-bedroom house that she also rented in San Francisco's Sea Cliff neighborhood.

That will do, she said to herself, not even bothering to add in her stock portfolio because whatever she had tied up in the markets was at the whim and mercy of the markets and, by her way of thinking, it wasn't worth anything until she cashed out.

Then, she took her jewelry, put everything in a carryall, walked two blocks to the bank where she rented a large safety deposit box and put the carryall inside. Back at Trump Tower, she told Luisa, "I need you to help me pack, please."

"Is madam going on a trip?"

"Yes. For a little while."

While Luisa was packing, Tina phoned her old school friend Li Ming. When she answered, Tina said, "I hope I didn't wake you, but if I did, I know that you will forgive me."

"Where are you?"

"On my way to see you."

"You're coming to Hong Kong?"

"I'll e-mail you when I've got a flight number and arrival time."

"This is so exciting. To what do we owe the honor?"

"No big deal," she said. "I'm leaving David."

59

He hurried through the staff meeting.

Little Sam, the human resources section head, noted that Antonia wasn't present. "Is everything all right?"

"Everything's fine," Belasco maintained. "She's not required to be here." He looked around the table. "If no one else has anything . . . "

"Scarpe Pietrasanta," Harriet said, "they're still delinquent."

"I'm aware. But there have been several problems, not the least of which is a break-in on their premises. I'm dealing with it and we're going to give them some breathing space." He pointed to Riordan, "You want to add anything about the break-in?"

"Police are dealing with it," Riordan said, reaching into a folder and handing everyone around the table a CCTV photo of two men. "We believe this is the pair that caused the break-in. Show it around and see if anybody recognizes them." He ended by looking at Belasco, "My office is on the case and will continue to do whatever is necessary to maintain security here . . . whatever is necessary . . . no matter what."

Without responding, Belasco adjourned the meeting.

As he was leaving the conference room, Riordan handed him several copies of the two photos. "You forgot these. Please show them to your staff."

Belasco took them, "Thank you," and left.

Before he got to the elevators to go back downstairs, Carole Ann Mendelsohn caught up with him. "Pierre, you need to know that we received notice from Dregger Simmons that they intend to sue on behalf of Katarina Essenbach."

"No surprise," he shrugged. "You said yesterday you knew they would."

"Yes. And in their brief outline of particulars, it seems to be pretty much along the lines of what we expected. But what is unexpected is that you're the only party named."

He didn't understand. "And the significance of that is . . . what?"

"She's suing you, not us."

He still didn't understand. "Okay . . . so?"

"So she is suing you, not in your professional capacity, but personally."

"Does it matter? After all, I haven't done anything."

"It does matter that she's suing you personally, and it doesn't matter that you say you haven't done anything."

"It's a nuisance suit."

"It's more serious than that."

"What does she want?"

"One hundred million dollars."

He was astonished. "That's absurd."

"Of course, it is."

"Completely absurd. With that kind of money, even if she wins, she loses. After all . . . if she was suing me for a million dollars I'd worry. But a hundred million? You can't get milk from a stone."

"Obviously not."

"What is she playing at? Does she think I'll settle for half?"

"I agree," Mendelsohn conceded, "and if she was suing us . . . except she isn't. We're not party to this in any way. She's suing you personally, which says to me that, in her mind, this is strictly personal."

"She's hallucinating."

"Whether she is or isn't hardly matters to Dregger Simmons. They know that money is no object for their client. In other words, they have no incentive to settle this at all. Quite the opposite."

"They have a cash cow, she's delusional, and I'm caught in the middle. This is a nightmare."

"You've summed it up perfectly."

"What can I do to make this go away?"

"Not much."

"I need to find a way. There must be something."

"Not that's legal."

"How about if someone throws her off the Fifty-Ninth Street Bridge?"

"This is not something you should talk about, even if it is a joke. I will disregard that question, as if it was never asked."

"You're saying that she's coming after me personally and there's nothing I can do about it? I cannot . . . will not . . . accept that."

"It's only natural that you're upset . . . "

"I'm more than upset. I'm bewildered and I'm angry. I'm pretty far out of my comfort zone and I don't understand how I got here."

"As I see it, you have two options. You can resign your position here and hope that satisfies her."

"I will not."

"Don't shoot the messenger."

"That's not an option."

"It has to be. This woman knows she is never going to get a huge amount of money out of you and, plainly, she doesn't need what little she might get. Because this is personal, she wants to inflict pain. Forcing you out might satisfy her. On the other hand, it might not. I'm not advising you one way or the other. I'm merely setting out your options."

"It's not going to happen. What's option two?"

"You can fight it."

"Then that's what I'll do."

"Then we need to get you a lawyer. Our insurance will cover this to some extent. But you will be out of pocket."

"How much?"

"I told you yesterday that Dregger Simmons specializes in going after people who can afford to fight. Imagine how much pain they can inflict when you're David and they're Goliath."

"As I remember the story, David won."

"I believe one definition of the word fable is myth."

He stared at her for a long time. "I'd be grateful if you could find me a lawyer, please . . . with a big slingshot and a lot of stones."

Downstairs, Belasco handed the photos Riordan had given him to Pierro. He explained who the men were and wanted to make sure that the entire lobby staff, on all three shifts, saw them.

Just before noon, Belasco headed upstairs to Scarpe Pietrasanta.

Gabriella was there with Carlos clearing the floor space in the showroom. She told Belasco that her mother was still talking about closing the business. "When she gets something in her head like that, she can be very stubborn."

That's when Forbes arrived. Belasco introduced Gabriella to him as someone who was going to help them but didn't go into any detail about who he was or exactly what he would be doing.

Belasco asked Gabriella, "Did your father keep any business files at home?"

She said, "Not that I know of. But I don't think so."

"What about your mother? Did she bring files home?"

"Again, I don't think so. She might have, but I doubt it. I never saw any office files at home."

"That means what we're looking for has to be here. Tell Mr. Forbes about your father's letter to his cousin, and the one he wrote to you and your mother."

She did.

Belasco turned to Forbes. "We find those letters here, and it's not the cousin. We don't find them, and that's what the guys who broke into this place came to destroy."

60

Although Carson's flight to Tokyo had left an hour late on Wednesday, the pilot was able to make up a little time and they'd landed at Narita Airport at around four on Thursday afternoon.

At the Peninsula Hotel, the front desk manager had personally welcomed him back and had escorted him to the huge Peninsula Suite on the twenty-third floor, overlooking Hibiya Park and the Imperial Palace Gardens.

The bedroom featured a double king–sized bed with an enormous en suite dark, marble bathroom, a large whirlpool bath and a gorgeous view of the city while you were soaking in it.

There was a big living room and very handsome dining room—both with spectacular views—plus an outdoor balcony, an office, a tea ceremony area, a minigym, and a fully equipped kitchen and pantry. And in every room throughout the suite there were forty-two-inch plasma television screens.

As soon as he'd unpacked, he'd gotten onto the NBC Nightly News site and watched Alicia's interview with Clinton. Then he'd phoned her.

"It was terrific. I loved it."

"Apparently everybody else did, too. Even Bill. His office called and left a message. After I edited it, Brian said he liked it, and as I was leaving the newsroom he said to me, 'welcome aboard.'"

"I'm really proud of you." Then he'd broached the subject of her book. "What's happening with your friend Mr. Farmer?"

All she'd say was, "It's under control."

At 7:30, the feng shui expert—a very small, very round man who reminded

Carson of Buddha—had arrived at his door and, without a word, had gone about rearranging the dining room.

He'd removed the table and all the chairs from the room, as well as the decorative pottery and vases on the shelves.

He'd then placed two chairs in very specific spots—the slightly larger one facing the window, the smaller with its back to the window—and had moved a low coffee table between the two.

Carson had shown him where he wanted to put his laptop, open to him so that Mr. Shigetada could not see it from the smaller chair, and after that was done, the little man had placed two glasses and one bottle of still water on the table. Next, he'd turned on the overhead light and all the room lamps, then he'd shut them off one by one, until there was only one lamp left on. It was in the far corner and slightly behind where Carson would sit.

Stepping back, the little man had surveyed the room, bowed and left the suite.

Carson sat in both chairs, slowly understanding what he'd accomplished. The bigger chair, his chair, was more comfortable. He'd be more likely to want to stay longer. It also had a view out the window. The smaller chair, Shigetada's, was less comfortable and with nothing else to focus on but Carson. He'd be more likely to want to leave sooner.

Did that mean Shigetada would be more likely to settle this in Warring's favor? Carson didn't know. But he could see that from the way the lamp would cast shadows, Shigetada was supposed to feel that he was no longer in charge.

ON FRIDAY, he'd had a pleasant lunch with the Japanese lawyers at a private dining club in the Ginza. After that, he'd climbed into bed and slept through dinner.

An hour before Mr. Shigetada arrived, he'd showered and shaved, dressed in a suit, then Skyped Kenneth Warring in Omaha to rehearse their banter.

Now, at three in the morning Tokyo time—Saturday morning in Japan but still Friday afternoon in the United States—Carson Haynes stared at the short, flat-faced man with a large, bald head and bulging eyes, sitting opposite him in the suite's near-empty dining room.

"Our answer to that," Carson said yet again, "is no."

Mr. Shigetada stared back at Carson, not giving anything away.

"This is bullshit," Warring growled from the screen on Carson's laptop. "We're getting nowhere."

Mr. Shigetada showed no emotion.

For three hours, he had not budged from his original position. "I will not sell. There is no reason for me to buy. And I will not permit you to walk away.

I am insisting that you honor your commitment."

Finally, Warring announced he'd had enough. "I'm going home."

Carson looked at the screen—which Mr. Shigetada could not see—and watched Warring cleaning his nails with a letter opener.

"On Monday morning," Warring went on, "short and simple, we're going to liquidate the company."

Slowly at first, then with ever-increasing anger, Mr. Shigetada began shaking his head.

"You cannot. You cannot. I built this business . . . " For the first time all night, he came dangerously close to losing his temper. "My father and I built this together. I will not permit you to dishonor his memory . . . "

Warring snapped, "I turned your father's business into something neither you nor he ever dreamed of. You brought us in because you needed us and we came in because we saw potential. I found your father to be an honorable man. But you, pal, are not your father."

Mr. Shigetada's eyes narrowed as he stared at Carson. "I will not permit you . . . "

"Sell your shares to me," Warring demanded, "or buy ours. But you'd better let me know right now. I'm standing up and walking out of my office, and as soon as I shut off my lights, I turn off your lights."

Carson saw Warring put the letter opener down, lean back in his chair and toss his legs on top of his desk.

"This is not the way I do business," Mr. Shigetada insisted. "It is not the way we do business in Japan."

"Forty-two or forty-six," Warring said. "Or *sayonara*."

Mr. Shigetada blurted out, "I give you forty, the same price you offer me."

"No, you give me forty-six."

Mr. Shigetada repeated, "Forty. And if you don't accept my offer right now, it will come down to thirty-eight."

"I love it when people think they can threaten me." Warring reached forward, grabbed an open bottle of beer that was sitting on his desk and took a swig. "Carson . . . tell him that I'm standing at the door and that I'm two seconds away from turning off the lights. This is the moment of truth. Deal or no deal?"

Carson looked at Mr. Shigetada and gestured. "What do you want to do?"

Mr. Shigetada simply stared back at Carson.

Carson waited a long time before he said to Warring, "Mr. Shigetada's answer is no answer."

"Okay," Warring said. "No answer, no deal. Carson, shut down your computer, I'm going home. Have a good weekend."

"Forty-two," Mr. Shigetada announced. "Final offer."

Warring said, "Too late. Monday morning, it's over. Fire-sale prices. We don't care."

"Then I buy back at fire-sale prices."

"Not quite, because we're not going to sell to you. It will be a private sale. There are several interested parties, including Kami whatever they're called."

That was Mr. Shigetada's biggest rival.

He suddenly stood up and yelled a word in Japanese.

Carson didn't know what the word meant or what Mr. Shigetada was going to do.

"Forty-four," he shouted angrily at Carson's computer, "Forty-four. Not one penny more. Take it or leave it."

Warring said calmly, "All cash."

Mr. Shigetada nodded at Carson.

"That's a yes," Carson told Warring. "Forty-four . . . all cash."

"Done," Warring said.

Carson looked at Mr. Shigetada. "Done?"

Mr. Shigetada pointed at Carson, then at Carson's computer, yelled that same word in Japanese, and stormed out of the suite.

"He's gone," Carson told Warring.

"Do you know what he said before he left?"

"It sounded like it might be the Japanese equivalent of 'fuck you.'"

"It wasn't that polite." Warring raised the beer bottle in a toast. "Mission accomplished. Good job, my friend. Have a great weekend. Get home safely. We'll talk Monday."

Carson said goodbye, e-mailed the lawyers to draw up the contract, shut off his laptop, and stared at the nighttime shadows as they moved across the Tokyo skyline.

"Mission accomplished," he said to himself, then checked his watch, which was still on New York time.

Alicia wasn't on the air yet, but he knew at this hour she wouldn't have a lot of time to talk. Still, he dialed her cell.

She saw his caller ID and answered right away. "How did it go?"

"Not good," he said.

"Why? What happened?"

He said, "Shigetada is impossible. He's dug in his heels and won't budge. I've been up all night, and we don't have a deal. Warring is furious. We're meeting again tonight and will probably be locked into this all day Sunday."

"You'll be in Tokyo all weekend?"

"Blame it on Mr. Shigetada. I'm sorry. But he won't sell and he won't buy and . . . it ain't good. I'll talk to you over the weekend."

"Oh well, if you're stuck in Tokyo, maybe I'll fly down to my mother's." She said, "I miss you," and he said, "I miss you too," and they both hung up.

Carson calculated that if he left a wake-up call for seven, that would give him time for a short nap now, then a light workout, a fast whirlpool and some breakfast. But he'd also need some time to pack.

He dialed the front desk. "I'd like to leave a wake-up call for six thirty."

The woman there promised to wake him on time.

Then he asked for the night concierge. "Is that ticket confirmed?"

"Yes, sir," the concierge said. "We'll have a car ready for you at . . . how's eight thirty? Flight leaves at eleven fifty. You arrive tonight at ten to six, Paris time."

61

The newsroom was going into countdown mode with less than an hour to air.

Alicia was finishing her copy for the lead story when Greg Mandel shouted from across the room, "We can't go live from the park."

"That's idiotic," she called back. "It's a public park."

"We're not fighting City Hall. It's the Feds."

"What have the Feds got to do with this?"

"Park rangers had to call in the Fish and Wildlife guys. And they're the ones who said no to us."

"Why is Fish and Wildlife involved?"

"Because turning one of these things loose in the park may be a federal crime. Something about importing dangerous animals. Trust me, we tried."

"So where's Peter going to be?"

"Walk and talk from Belvedere Castle to the Turtle Pond. That's where we think the action is."

"How late can we hold the live feed?"

"For the lead?" He shrugged, "If Peter's not in place by quarter to, we'll have to can it."

She stopped working on her copy, brought Google Maps up on her screen, and typed "Central Park" in the search box.

The area north of the Turtle Pond was heavily wooded. There would be no way to see it from outside the park on Fifth Avenue. But then, she noticed, several tourist attractions were listed on the bottom right-hand corner of the map, including St. Patrick's Cathedral, the Radio City Music Hall . . . and Trump Tower.

"Screw 'em," she shouted back to Greg. "I have a better idea. Let me make one call."

She dialed Pierre Belasco. "I need a really big favor."

"Of course," he said, "for you, anything."

"Can I send my camera crew and a reporter to the gym? We're doing a story about the park and they won't let us shoot live there."

"Is Trump Tower or the Trump Organization involved in the story in any way? Will either be mentioned at any time?"

"No."

"Because if Trump Tower or the Trump Organization is mentioned, you will need permission, which means bringing in our media people."

"Honestly Pierre, all we want is the view of the park."

"If that's all, then it will be my pleasure. When can I expect them?"

"Right away." She hung up and called to Greg, "Trump Tower . . . residents' entrance on Fifty-Sixth Street. Ask for Mr. Belasco. The Trump name cannot be used. The vantage point cannot be identified."

"Done," Greg shouted back, and reached for his phone to redirect the reporter and the crew.

Alicia went back to writing her copy, changing the lead-in to, "Live from a vantage point overlooking Central Park . . . "

That's when Carson phoned from Japan to say he was stuck there.

No sooner had she hung up with him, when Greg shouted to her, "Peter's on the line."

She grabbed the phone. "Peter . . . you mention Trump Tower and I will personally feed you to the monster."

"I promise, I won't."

"This is a big favor they're doing for me and I am warning you . . . "

"Okay, okay. Tell me what to say and I will say it."

"My intro says, live from a vantage point overlooking Central Park."

"Then I will throw it back to you by saying the same thing."

"Peter, screw me on this and I guarantee one of us won't be working here on Monday."

"Alicia . . . I promise."

She hung up with him, then dialed Cyndi.

"You feeling better?"

"I'm okay."

"Sure?"

"Just about."

"Listen, Carson called to say he's stuck in Tokyo. Pack a bag. I'll phone Maria and have her pack a bag for me. Pick it up from her, get a car and meet me at the Rainbow Room entrance at six thirty-five. You and I . . . how about a dirty weekend?"

"I don't have anything to wear."

"You probably won't need much," Alicia said. "I'll buy us some airplane tickets right now."

SHE READ HER INTRO to the piece, then said, "We go live to Peter Bennett at a vantage point high above Central Park. Peter?"

On the monitor, a tight shot came up of a young man in a blue blazer with a blue shirt and dark blue tie standing close to a window with the park in the background.

"Alicia, city officials are concerned this evening that a wild animal is on the loose in Central Park. It is believed to be an ocelot . . . which belongs to the leopard family. They are native to South and Central America and sometimes roam as far north as Texas. But, as you said in your introduction, we don't find them in New York. While the animal has not yet been spotted, there are reports of birds, rabbits and even a raccoon being killed. We learned a few minutes ago that the carcass of a small red fox has been found. And we can also report tonight that the Central Park Zoo is in lockdown. Animals that normally live outside have been brought into shelters to protect them. Alicia?"

The screen split in two, with Alicia on the left and Peter on the right.

"Peter, is there any danger to the public?"

"Alicia, this is a wild animal. Although it is nocturnal, which means it hunts for food at night . . . "

A slide of an ocelot came up on the screen.

" . . . and the park is closed at night . . . the public is being advised that anyone who sees the animal should not approach it. They should notify the police or the park rangers immediately. This is not a friendly little pussycat."

The screen went back to the two shot.

He continued, "This animal is a long way from home and . . . presumably . . . very frightened. There is no way to predict how it will react to humans. Alicia?"

"Peter, we've learned this evening that the federal government is now involved in this. Why?"

"Normally, the park rangers handle stray animals. Snakes, for example, are a common problem, and not long ago someone set a pet python free in Central Park. But an ocelot is another thing, altogether. There are concerns that it may have been imported into the country illegally . . . and that raises questions that the United States Fish and Wildlife Service, part of the Department of

Interior, must deal with. So they have become the lead agency in the hunt for the animal."

"Finally, Peter, does anyone know yet how it got in the park?"

"Authorities are telling us there are only two reasonable explanations. Either it was a pet that escaped from an apartment. Or, someone brought it to the park and turned it loose. They want to find out because . . . if someone did turn it loose in the park . . . that could constitute a crime. Alicia?"

"Peter Bennett," she said, "reporting tonight from high above Central Park. Thank you Peter."

The shot went full screen to her.

"The MTA is back in the news . . . "

BY THE TIME Alicia signed off the air, Cyndi was waiting with a car and driver at the Rainbow Room entrance.

The driver said, "Kennedy Airport?"

Cyndi said, "This is exciting but . . . where are we going?"

Alicia asked, "How's Paris?"

62

Most of Birgitta's clothes were already gone by the time Zeke got home from New York, although a lot of her other things—furniture she put in the room she called her office, several laptops, some art, a closet filled with hats and shoes, family photo albums, books, a huge collection of CDs and DVDs, her tennis gear, her golf clubs, six sets of fine china, silver tableware, and one of her two cars—were still at the house.

A note from her read, "I'll get the rest when I send movers to collect everything."

He didn't know if something had been lost in translation from the original Swedish, or if she was making some sort of veiled threat. In any case, he saved the note to give to Bobby Lerner.

At the office, he faxed copies of the proposal he'd been handed from James Malcolm Isbister to Carl Kravitz, Lenny Silverberg, Harry Kahn, Bing O'Leary, Ken Warring and Bobby. He then spent the morning locked in a meeting with Perry Griswald and Monica Rosenblatt, going over their plans for the new business. When he came out of that meeting, there was a message from O'Leary saying, "Harry and I look forward to seeing you tonight." There was also a message from Silverberg saying the same thing.

Not having heard from Kravitz or Warring, he phoned Warring first.

"With a few minor changes," Warring said, "the guy's proposal is worth pursuing. After all, if he's willing to throw that much money into the pot, we should be willing to talk to him."

He then related Warring's advice to Kravitz who offered to call Isbister to set up a meeting with Zeke. "How's Tuesday in New York?"

Zeke had an early lunch at Nate and Al's deli on Beverly Drive with Larry King—now that King was semiretired, Zeke made a point of having lunch with him a couple of times a month, and they always talked baseball—and after that, he drove home. He went for a quick swim, sat by the pool with a beer and made his usual round of calls—to Zoey and Max, to Hattie and to Miriam—then talked for the third time that day to Bobby.

That's when Kravitz called to say, "He can't do Tuesday morning but could do Wednesday afternoon at four. He said he can come to you."

"Trump Tower . . . Wednesday at four."

Thinking he'd fly east on Tuesday, he found a number for Roberto Santos and, when a woman answered in Spanish, Zeke announced in English who he was. She said, "Not home." He left his name and number.

Five minutes later, Santos was on the line. "My mother tells everyone I'm not home, even when I am."

"I was afraid you'd be on your way to the ballpark."

"I'm already here in the clubhouse."

"The reason I'm calling . . . I'm in LA . . . and I wanted you to know that we've taken over Sovereign Shields. You're now my client, which means you're a tax deduction. I can afford to take you out for a meal. As long as you don't eat too much. I'm back in New York next week. Where are you Wednesday or Thursday? I'd love it if we could get together. You guys home or on the road?"

"We're at home Tuesday night, play Wednesday afternoon, then go out for the next ten days."

"If I come in Monday night, how's Tuesday lunch?"

"I don't do lunch when there's a game at night . . . but why don't you come to the game Tuesday night? I'll arrange tickets."

"I'd love to."

"No problem," Roberto said, then added, "The other night I met Carson and Alicia and their friend Cyndi . . . I invited them to come to a game. So maybe . . . maybe you could bring them along?"

"Sounds good to me."

"Do you mind? I mean, maybe you could call them?"

"You want me to arrange it? Sure. I'll do it now." Zeke phoned Carson in the office, but was told he was out of the country. So he phoned Alicia at home, and the maid suggested he try NBC. But then someone at NBC said she'd just left for the night, so he found her cell phone and dialed that.

She was in the car on the way to Kennedy.

He told her about the invitation for Tuesday night and she said, "Hold on, I'll check with Cyndi."

Cyndi nodded, "Sure. Grown men in pajamas."

"You're on," Alicia said, but wanted to know, "How come Roberto didn't call himself?"

"Maybe he was afraid you'd say no."

"Ah, I get it. Not me . . . Cyndi. He's so shy." Then she added, "By the way, I have to pay for my own ticket. NBC rules."

"Okay. But I got the impression that Roberto is comping us."

"That's up to you guys. No problem for Carson and Cyndi, but make sure he knows I'm paying for my ticket."

After speaking with her, Zeke took a short nap, then showered and dressed— white suit, white shoes, white shirt—for the Kahns' wear-only-white party.

He remembered to take the gift—a 24 x 16–inch antique English silver picture frame, hallmarked London 1877, into which he had fitted a rare photo he'd managed to dig up of Harry and Ilsa first arriving in Los Angeles—got into his 1957 Inca-silver Corvette convertible and drove to Marina del Rey, where *Goose Chase IV* was waiting.

The Kahns' 157-foot yacht had originally been called the *Nickelodeon* when Carl Laemmle, legendary founder of Hollywood's Universal Studios, commissioned it in Great Britain in 1937. Unfortunately, Laemmle never saw her because he died in 1939.

When World War II broke out, she was requisitioned by the Royal Navy and converted into a submarine chaser. After the war she sat in dry dock until she was bought, in the early 1950s, by the Greek shipping magnate Aristotle Onassis. He owned her for less than a year, trading up instead to the 325-foot *Christina*.

Onassis sold the decommissioned subchaser to Gaylord Dunwoody Bulloch, at the time the largest cotton merchant in Georgia, who dubbed her *Cotton Picker II*. On his passing, she changed hands several times, eventually falling into disrepair and winding up in a ship chandler's yard in Punta del Este, Uruguay.

The Kahns had owned three boats since the mid-1980s, each one bigger, faster and more modern than the previous one. In 2005, Harry had decided to build a new boat, which he'd planned to be the biggest, fastest and most modern seagoing yacht on the West Coast. That is, until a broker mentioned this one. He and Ilsa flew to Uruguay to see her, fell in love with her immediately and freightered her back to the United States where he spent $3.6 million refitting her.

She slept ten, carried a crew of eight and featured a fifty-foot main dining room and salon. Normally they moored her at Santa Barbara, where the Kahns had a home. But this was Ilsa's seventy-fifth birthday, and *Goose Chase IV* was sailing tonight promptly at seven around Catalina while seventy-five guests had dinner and danced.

As Zeke pulled up to the gangplank, a young guy valet parking attendant opened his door and said, "Cool car. I just parked a red one exactly like it."

Zeke rolled his eyes because he'd owned his longer than Jay Leno had owned the red one.

A receptionist in a white tuxedo greeted him at the bottom of the gangplank, checked his name off the guest list and wished him a pleasant evening. Waiters and waitresses—all in white tuxedos—were lined up at the top of the gangplank to welcome him aboard with mimosa cocktails.

A jazz band was playing on the aft deck, where Harry and Ilsa were greeting their guests.

Zeke kissed Ilsa and hugged Harry and handed her the gift.

"Thank you, so much, darling," Ilsa said, wearing a flowing white Ralph Lauren taffeta gown. "I take it that Birgitta isn't with you this evening. Harry told me. I'm so sorry."

"It happens in the best of families," he said.

She handed the gift to a young man who was standing at her side for just that purpose. "You know, of course, you could have brought a date. Miriam, perhaps?"

Thanking her and wishing her happy birthday again, he stepped aside so that Tom Hanks and his wife could wish Ilsa a happy birthday, too.

Zeke went to remind Leno and his wife, Mavis, that he'd bought his Corvette first.

The major studio execs were there—he chatted briefly with Hertz Monroe and Frank Lacosta and Ti Wrigley—then greeted Ron Howard and his wife who was talking to Steven Spielberg and his wife.

Next to them, the legendary comedy writer Chris Bearde and his wife, Caroline, were talking to Arnold Schwarzenegger.

Bearde reminded Zeke, "Arnie's unemployed and could use a job."

Arnie nodded. "I'm very good around the house . . . plumbing . . . painting . . . gardening?"

Waiters moved through the crowd carrying trays with drinks, followed by waitresses moving through the crowd carrying trays of hors d'oeuvres.

Nearby, Demi Moore was talking to Forest Whitaker and his wife, Keisha.

Then Zeke spotted two great old pals. He went across to the other side of the aft deck where Carl Reiner . . . wearing a flat sailor's cap . . . was standing with Mel Brooks, director and screenwriter Phil Alden Robinson and Phil's wife, Paulette Bartlett.

He hugged them all, then said to Reiner, "I didn't know you were a sailor."

"Harry has made so many C-pictures," Reiner smiled, punning the rating "C" for the word "sea," "that I enlisted."

All of a sudden, the ship's bells sounded and the captain's voice came over a loudspeaker. "Ladies and gentleman, all ashore who's going ashore. Gangplank away."

The ship's horn blasted twice and as music blared over the speakers—a recording of the US Navy Band playing "Anchors Aweigh"—*Goose Chase IV* slipped its moorings and headed into the harbor.

Over dinner, Zeke sat at the table with Lenny Silverberg, who'd flown to the coast especially for the event, this time bringing his wife, Sylvia, with him.

They couldn't really chat during the meal—which was cooked by Rene Theriault, whose tiny restaurant in Santa Barbara, appropriately named *Douze* because there were only twelve tables, had won its third Michelin star—but Sylvia changed places with Zeke during dessert.

Of course, they talked about the meal.

Theriault had designed it entirely around oranges. Beginning with a tossed salad of prawns, mandarins, and walnuts, there was a choice of three main courses—an orange spring salad for the vegetarians, grilled deep-sea perch in an orange vinaigrette sauce for anyone who wanted fish, or duck in orange sauce for anyone who wanted meat. Dessert was a triple-orange Grand Marnier soufflé, made with California mandarins, Florida bloods, and Spanish Murcias.

"I could probably cook like this," Silverberg bragged to Zeke, "except Sylvia would have to show me first where the kitchen is."

"I don't cook at all," Zeke admitted. "Do you?"

"Does toasting a bagel count?"

Now Zeke asked, "You see the proposition from that guy, Isbister?"

"I say, go for it. What the hell. Although Bobby should back him away from his insistence that we use his auditors. If he wants to audit the books, that's his business. But our auditors need to be our guys."

"You're right," Zeke said, and was about to ask Silverberg whether or not they should reconsider including the Bronx property in the deal, when the lights in the room dimmed and the waiters appeared carrying an enormous dark chocolate and orange birthday cake, alit with candles.

Everyone sang happy birthday, then Harry got up and made a little speech—telling Ilsa that she would always be the love of his life—and as champagne was poured into every glass in the room, everyone on board toasted Ilsa.

The six jazz musicians now moved into place on the bandstand, presumably so that the evening of dancing could begin while the cake was being served, but then Bing O'Leary and his wife, Ilene, got up to speak.

"Ilsa," Bing said, "when I stole your only daughter, you welcomed me with open arms and an open heart into your family."

Everyone in the room knew that wasn't quite true, but no one was going to say as much.

"And as you are the love of Harry's life," he went on, "Ilene is the love of my life. And she has now revealed the family secret."

Ilene took the microphone. "Yes, there is a family secret. Mom, you and I both know that. Now Bing knows it too. Remember that night, I was about sixteen, and I said that I had a crush on Danny Rabinowitz . . . "

"Wait," Bing cut in. "I never heard this part before."

"Don't worry," she said to her husband, obviously having rehearsed this bit, "nothing ever happened. But . . . don't get too comfortable because Danny is a very successful orthodontist and I know how to find him."

He mugged a face and everyone laughed.

"That night at the dinner table," Ilene continued, "I said if Danny wanted to go steady, I would never leave him . . . except if Paul Bloomberg asked me first because he was the guy I really liked. So Dad asked Mom, would you ever leave me? And she said, no, never . . . except for one person."

"Harry . . . hold on to Ilsa . . . " Bing announced, "that one person is here tonight. Ladies and gentlemen, please welcome . . . mister . . . Tony Bennett."

The band struck up the music, and Tony Bennett sang for an hour.

Champagne was still being poured as *Goose Chase IV* slipped back into the marina at one in the morning.

Zeke was standing near the rails, watching the mooring with Matt Damon and his wife, Luciana, when someone came up behind him, put his arms around him, and kissed the back of his neck.

He turned around to find Mikey Glass.

"That was pretty friendly of you," he said.

"Why not?" Mikey announced. "You're my favorite person in the whole wide world of Learjet Sixties." He smiled at the Damons, "I guess you can tell it's not our first date."

Luciana kissed Mikey hello and Matt hugged him.

"Quite a party," Mikey said.

"It certainly is," Zeke agreed.

He looked at Zeke, "Going back to New York any time soon?"

Zeke knew enough to be vague. "Hard to say. Not tonight, in any case."

"Too bad," Mikey said. "I'm going tomorrow. Otherwise I would love to have invited myself for another ride." He said to the Damons, "No in-flight movies, but the taps in the bathroom run hot and cold Perrier."

Zeke told him, "You're a brave man going back to the lion's den."

Mikey shrugged it off. "Trying to apologize to the wife."

"That's good. I'm proud of you."

"Has nothing to do with me," he confessed. "My accountants came up with a number, you know, what it would cost if I didn't. Apologies are part of my five-year economic plan."

Zeke looked at Matt and Luciana, "If he's nothing else, Mikey is utilitarian."

"Is that like being a Unitarian?" He looked around. "I'm not, but if I were, I'd be outnumbered two hundred to one. Aren't there any Protestants left in Hollywood?"

Zeke decided to change the subject. "I didn't realize you were close to the Kahns."

"Harry and Ilsa?" Mikey bragged, "They've been like second parents to me."

"I didn't know that," Zeke said.

And later, when Zeke mentioned it to Harry, he said the same thing. "I didn't know that, either."

SATURDAY

63

In the taxi from Charles de Gaulle Airport to the Ritz Hotel, Cyndi got on her cell phone and made a call. She spoke softly in her fluent French with a slight American accent, always keeping her hand over her mouth so the driver couldn't hear what she was saying.

All the time she was on the phone, happy and laughing like an excited schoolgirl, Alicia noticed that the driver kept looking at Cyndi in his rearview mirror, as if he knew her but couldn't figure out who she was.

Par for the course, Alicia thought. After all, it hadn't been all that long ago when Cyndi was one of the most famous faces in Europe.

Just as they were coming into Paris, Cyndi pointed to a huge billboard showing the face of an extremely handsome, slightly weathered man with dark green eyes and pursed lips. In bold letters across the bottom was the word *Convoitise.*

"What? That?" Alicia looked at the huge sign as they passed it.

"Him."

"Him?"

"On the phone."

"Oh." Alicia turned to take a closer look.

Cyndi nodded. "Picking me up at the hotel this evening for dinner. Hope you don't mind. Means you've got the room all to yourself . . . or something like that."

"Or something like that," she grinned. "What does that word on the billboard mean?"

"*Convoitise*? It's his new film. It means . . . " She opened her eyes wide, "Lust. Appropriate, no?"

The taxi pulled into the *Place Vendôme* and up to the front of the hotel. The smartly uniformed doorman came up, opened the door and tipped his hat. "*Bonjour mesdames et bienvenu.*"—Good morning ladies and welcome.

Then he recognized Cyndi and screamed, "*Mademoiselle Benson, c'est vous? C'est pas vrai.*" Is that you? It's not true.

She hugged him and said in French, "Gaston, you are the love of my life."

"Where have you been? We haven't seen you in such a long time." He nodded to Alicia, "*Bonjour madame*," then went back to gushing over Cyndi. "Seeing you is like a vision . . . " He signaled for a groom—a young boy in a blue jacket and dark blue *kepi*—who couldn't take his eyes off Cyndi.

Gaston had to remind the boy to fetch the luggage in the trunk.

Escorting them inside the hotel, Gaston called to the head concierge who looked up from what he was doing and saw Cyndi. "*C'est pas vrai.*" He raced around his desk and into the lobby to hug her. "*Mademoiselle . . . c'est pas vrai. C'est pas vrai.*"

"Jean-Pierre . . . " she said in French, "you are more handsome than ever."

While they were hugging, Gaston called to the reception desk clerk, "Tell Monsieur Fournier to come quickly. Right away. Immediately."

Jean-Pierre nodded to Alicia, "*Bonjour madame, bienvenu*"—welcome— then turned back to Cyndi. "Why have you been such a stranger? When was the last time you were here? Paris is not Paris without Cyndi Benson."

"That's true," Gaston agreed, "very true. Paris needs you."

"And I need Paris." Cyndi started telling both of them in French why she hadn't been back in nearly four years, when a booming voice came from down the hallway, "*C'est pas vrai.*"

A large man with a trimmed goatee in a perfectly cut charcoal-gray suit came galloping up and hugged her. He kissed Cyndi on both cheeks, hugged her again and kissed the side of her face again.

Cyndi introduced Alicia. "Monsieur Fournier is the *directeur général* of the Ritz. He is the man who makes everything happen . . . not just here but in all of Paris."

He took Alicia's hand, bowed, and almost kissed it. "*Bonjour madame*, welcome to the Ritz Hotel." Then he turned back to Cyndi and started asking all the same questions that Gaston and Jean-Pierre had. "Where have you been . . . why haven't we seen you in such a long time . . . "

The reunion in the lobby attracted quite a bit of attention from other guests and soon included the *maître d'* from the restaurant, the chef, the bartender from the Hemingway Bar and the head housekeeper.

When they saw her, each of them exclaimed, loudly, "*C'est pas vrai*," and although they were polite and welcoming to Alicia, after they said, "*bonjour madame,*" to her, they immediately turned back to Cyndi to ask where she had been for so long.

An older American woman, obviously a tourist, leaned over to Alicia. "Who is she? A French movie star?"

Alicia whispered, "She owns the joint."

The woman nodded, "Looks like it," and walked away.

Eventually Monsieur Fournier excused himself, went to the desk, spoke quietly with the receptionist, and came back with two key cards. He said to

Cyndi in French, "Unfortunately, the suite of Madame Chanel is occupied. Had we known in advance that you were arriving . . . I hope you won't mind the alternative."

He escorted them into the elevator, up one flight and into a private entrance.

Stepping through the door, they walked into an absolutely gorgeous living room that ran along the front of the hotel, with huge French windows draped in silk facing the *Place Vendôme*.

It was filled with Louis XIV furniture and fine antiques.

Fournier then brought them into the master bedroom with its wonderful four-poster canopy bed and said to Alicia in English, "Madame, this is an exact replica of Marie Antoinette's *chambre*."

Cyndi assured Alicia, "Not to worry, they didn't chop her head off in this bedroom. An exact replica of the guillotine is in the next room."

"There is, of course, a second bedroom," Monsieur Fournier nodded to Alicia, as if to say, *Cyndi gets the great one, you get the merely very good one.* He even showed it to them. It was beautiful, Alicia thought, but not as imposing as the main bedroom.

He also showed them the main bathroom with the largest marble bathtub Alicia had ever seen.

"This is called the Imperial Suite," Cyndi said to Alicia, "because the Czar used to stay here. The tub is that big so that when the Czar was out for an evening of clubbing, raping and pillaging, the Czarina could take baths with the Cossacks."

"Speaking of Cossacks . . . " Monsieur Fournier raised his finger to make a point, then motioned for them to follow him. He led them to a secret passageway near the front door with a tiny balcony inside the suite that overlooked the entrance. "This is actually where the Cossacks stood guard to protect the Czar when he was here."

The luggage quickly arrived, and with it a huge basket of fruit, two bottles of champagne, several vases of fresh-cut flowers and an enormous box of chocolates.

Monsieur Fournier assured Alicia if she needed anything at all, it would be his honor to serve her. He then bent down and almost kissed Alicia's hand, but took Cyndi in his arms and kissed both sides of her face. "You are a breath of fresh air. May you never ever change."

When he was gone, Alicia extended her arms to Cyndi, inviting her to dance, and began singing softly, "Never never change, keep that breathless charm . . . "

Cyndi sang with her, " . . . won't you please arrange it 'cause I love you . . . "

The two of them nearly fell over with laughter.

"Chocolates!" Alicia ripped open the box. "Not bad digs for two girls from the sticks."

"Champagne?" Cyndi took two glasses while Alicia opened the bottle and poured.

"The suite where Coco lived," Cyndi explained, "is much smaller. And anyway, it's not the same one she had at the end of her life. It's nice, but I have always preferred this one."

"Always?"

"Always."

"Always?" Alicia poured them both a second glass. "How many alwayses have you spent in this museum to French . . . *convoitise*?"

A grin came across Cyndi's face. "More than a few."

"With who?"

"More than a few."

"At the same time?"

"More than a few," she giggled. "Let's take a bath."

"Where are the Cossacks when you need them?"

"Bring the champagne."

"And the chocolates."

Cyndi ran the water in the huge tub—it took some time to fill because it was so big—while Alicia found bottles of bubble bath and emptied four of them in the tub. Then she filled their glasses, popped a chocolate into Cyndi's mouth, took one for herself, and the two of them raced out of their clothes.

Alicia lay back at one end, and Cyndi lay back at the other, facing her, champagne glass in hand. But even as big as the tub was, the spout was in the way and Cyndi couldn't get comfortable. So she sat up and, careful not to spill any champagne, crawled next to Alicia.

"Better," she said, taking Alicia's left arm and wrapping it around herself.

Alicia filled up their glasses again, then sang in a whisper, "Yes you're lovely, with your smile so warm . . . "

Cyndi looked up at Alicia and kissed her lightly on the mouth. "You are the sister I never had . . . and the mother I never had . . . and the best friend in the entire universe I always dreamed of having. I love you so much."

"I love you, too."

Cuddled up close like that in the hot bubbly water, the two of them drank more champagne, sang slowly and softly, and within a few minutes, both of them were asleep.

"FIRST THINGS FIRST," Cyndi announced once they woke up, soaped off, dried off, and got dressed, "*Les Deux Magots*."

Alicia wore her Missoni jeans, one of Carson's button-down Oxford white shirts, tied at the waist and a New York Yankees baseball jacket.

Cyndi wore white Chanel jockey pants tucked into white Chanel knee-length boots, a white sweatshirt that read "*Bon Marche*" in big black letters—it means "bargain"—a little white jockey's cap, and big dark sunglasses.

Downstairs they hired a car for the afternoon.

It was a little after two when their driver, Roland, delivered them in his brand-new Mercedes to the entrance of the famous Left Bank Café on the Boulevard Saint-Germain. Some of the Saturday lunch crowd had already left. But for Alicia, arriving there with Cyndi was like arriving at the Ritz all over again.

"*C'est pas vrai.*" A tall older gentleman in a suit and tie with a bushy gray mustache came running up to her. "*Mon amour . . . mon amour . . .* "—my love—"*Mon amour . . .* " He hugged her and kissed her and brought her to his table at the back, along the far wall.

Cyndi introduced Monsieur Pelletier. Alicia had no idea who this man was, except that everybody seemed to show him great deference. He ordered champagne and French onion soup and snails for them. The waiters fawned over Cyndi and obeyed every one of Monsieur Pelletier's commands.

Before long, they were joined by two other men in their seventies and two women around the same age. Cyndi whispered to Alicia that one of the women was a famous old actress and the man with her had been Minister of the Interior. She said that the other man was France's greatest opera star. But everyone was speaking French so fast and there were so many people hovering around the table that all Alicia could do was eat her soup, drink her champagne and feel really happy that Cyndi was having so much fun.

Then another man arrived, and he was carrying a huge photo album. He kissed Cyndi hello, slid onto the banquette next to her, thumbed through the album and started showing everyone at the table photos.

Cyndi pointed to Alicia and he showed the photos to her, too.

There was Cyndi in the *Deux Magots* laughing with Charles Aznavour, Jean-Paul Belmondo and Jane Birkin, pretending to pose with the photographer Henri Cartier-Bresson, clowning with Catherine Deneuve and Gérard Depardieu, making faces with an absolutely stunning Princess Caroline of Monaco, singing with Vanessa Paradis and Johnny Depp, and on point with the famous ballerina Rosella Hightower. There was Cyndi in the *Deux Magots* in the arms of the fashion legend Pierre Cardin, and with Jean-Paul Gaultier and Inès de la Fressange, in the arms of the director Roger Vadim, arm in arm with President Mitterand, leaning on the shoulder of the French soccer star Zinedine Zidane, sharing a secret with Carla Bruni, and lip to lip with the dancer Mikhail Baryshnikov.

Alicia watched Cyndi laughing and babbling away in French with people she'd known in some previous life.

When Cyndi looked up and saw Alicia staring at her, she whispered, "And the laugh that wrinkles your nose . . . "

Alicia thought she was going to cry.

Before long, Cyndi whispered again, "We've got to go," so Alicia motioned to the waiter for the bill.

Immediately Monsieur Pelletier waved her off. "Not when you are here with my lovely Cyndi."

It took them nearly ten minutes of goodbyes to leave.

From *Deux Magots*, Roland took them to Hermès on the *Rue du Faubourg Saint-Honoré*.

The two of them walked through the front door, and suddenly there was a shriek. It sounded like someone was being stabbed. A woman of a certain age, elegantly dressed, came running through the room with her arms open. "*Mon enfant*"—my child—"Cyndi . . . *mon enfant* . . . "

The woman threw her arms around Cyndi and began to cry.

Now Cyndi was crying too.

As the two women wept in each other's arms, she introduced Madame Bergenoir to Alicia—"the legendary queen of Hermès"—and the woman insisted that they have tea with her.

Cyndi said, "Of course, we would love to," then pointed upstairs.

"Yes, yes, good idea," Madame Bergenoir nodded, took Cyndi's hand and motioned for Alicia to follow.

"You'll like this," Cyndi promised Alicia.

Upstairs, Madame Bergenoir brought them into a good-sized room that overlooked the Faubourg Saint-Honoré and was filled with antiques, most of them in leather.

The woman said that this was the private collection of Thierry Hermès, who founded the company—he was the official saddle maker to the Russian Czars—and his grandson Emile.

Not surprisingly, there were several dozen saddles, including a rare Persian saddle in ten different colors and dripping in gems, and lots of bridles, even a pair of stirrups used by Napoleon. But there were writing desks, including Emile Hermès' own large leather desk, and there was a rocking horse, and there were small carriages, and baby strollers, trunks, travel cases, purses, shoes and boots.

There was also a large floor-to-ceiling bookcase filled with leather-bound books. Except, when Alicia looked more closely, it turned out to be a false front to a secret passageway.

"The Cossacks were everywhere." Cyndi said.

After tea in the private Hermès museum, Madame Bergenoir brought them into a private showroom off the main floor where the day's shopping began.

Alicia bought a pink crocodile Kelly bag and two pairs of shoes. Cyndi passed on a Kelly bag—"I have seven"—but bought half a dozen scarves because, "You never know when that's all you want to wear."

As they left, Madame Bergenoir handed them both a small Hermès bag. "Some things for you and for the men in your lives." There was perfume and eau de cologne and two Hermès leather notepads.

They put their shopping bags in the trunk of Roland's Mercedes and jumped in the backseat. Cyndi announced the next address. Roland took them down the *Rue Royale*, along the *Champs-Élysées*, around the *Arc de Triomphe* and into the *Avenue Montaigne*, stopping right in front of Dior.

"This was their very first store," Cyndi said. "Bring your new bag," and after Alicia took it from the trunk, Cyndi led her inside.

"Why do I need the bag?" Alicia asked, but didn't get the question answered because walking into Dior with Cyndi was the same as walking in everywhere else with her. There were screams and hugs and kisses and all sorts of people shaking their heads, "*C'est pas vrai.*"

A tall man in his sixties, wonderfully overdressed for a Saturday afternoon, came rushing over to Cyndi and wouldn't stop hugging and kissing her.

When she introduced him to Alicia as, "The one and only Thibaut de Saint Marc."

He told Alicia, with his perfectly practiced British accent, "And this is the only woman in the world who has ever broken my heart."

"Oh, really?" Alicia said, getting the joke.

"Oh, really. Cyndi came to Dior from . . . them," he said with disdain, referring to Chanel . . . "and I was over the moon. Ecstatic. A young boy falling in love for the first time. But . . . " He made an elaborate gesture, "But . . . alas, she left me for . . . them . . . and I have never been straight since."

Cyndi got up on her toes and kissed the side of his face, then pointed to Alicia's bag. "Lipstick to match."

He looked at the bag, "I know the color you want, but not here. It's impossible to find." He nodded to Alicia. "I shall have it made for you and send it to you. Nail polish, too."

"Custom-made lipstick?" Alicia had never heard of that before.

"And custom-made nail polish." He assured her, "When you're with Cyndi, everything is possible."

"Black cocktail dress for Alicia and belts for me," Cyndi said, "that is, if you don't mind dealing with the public yourself."

"It has been a very long time," he assured her, and showed Alicia a gorgeous black cocktail dress. She bought it and Cyndi bought two wonderfully ornate belts.

"You can't stop there," Cyndi said to Alicia, and motioned to Thibaut, "Shoes for the dress, please." But when he said to them, "Follow me," Cyndi said something to him in French. He nodded and she told Alicia, "Be right back."

She assumed Cyndi was going to the ladies' room.

Alicia tried on several pairs and was torn between two, then realized it had been some time since Cyndi left.

"Where is she?"

"She's fine," Thibaut said.

That's when Cyndi reappeared carrying a Jimmy Choo bag.

"Where did you go?"

"Next door." She pulled out a pair of black-and-yellow catwalk sandals with plexi heels that had flashing lights inside them.

"Fantastic," Thibaut said, "model them."

Cyndi put them on and walked up and down the floor with them—"Once a catwalk girl always a catwalk girl," Alicia said—and after Thibaut applauded, Cyndi studied the two pairs of shoes that Alicia was considering.

"What's the problem," she asked Alicia. "They're gorgeous."

"I don't know which one . . . "

"Alicia, this is Paris . . . these are shoes. When in doubt . . . " She looked at Thibaut, "She'll take them both."

Thibaut escorted them back to the car and waved to someone inside the shop who came out with two Dior bags for them. "Something to remember me by," he kissed them both.

Inside each were two bottles of perfume, a beautiful enameled bracelet and a pair of pearl earrings.

He helped them load their packages into the trunk.

Out of the corner of her eye, Alicia saw Thibaut hand a small package to Cyndi, which she quickly put into the Jimmy Choo bag.

Roland asked, "Next stop?"

Cyndi thought for a moment, looked down the block, and told Roland, "Don't move." She took Thibaut's hand and Alicia's hand and walked them into Vuitton.

Thibaut called out to a woman in English, "Claude, my dear, look who the cat dragged in."

The woman, who was much older than Thibaut, turned around and said with a heavy French accent, "I do not believe my eyes."

She came to Cyndi and hugged her and sure enough—because, by now, Alicia was waiting for it—the woman shook her head with a huge smile, *"C'est pas vrai."*

Looking around, Alicia spotted a beautiful black leather attaché case and knew Carson would love that, so she bought it.

What she didn't see was that, while she was buying the attaché case, Cyndi was buying a suitcase.

"What are you doing?"

Cyndi shrugged, "How did you think we were going to get all this stuff home?"

Thibaut helped them load everything into the trunk and then, with tears in his eyes—and Cyndi's too—they said *au revoir*.

"Last stop." Back in the car, Cyndi gave Roland an address, then warned Alicia, "Be prepared."

"For what?"

"You'll see."

As soon as Roland pulled up to the last stop, Alicia understood.

It was Chanel.

Now, the commotion Cyndi caused surpassed anything that Alicia had yet seen. It went on for almost fifteen minutes as one person after another came up to hug and kiss her. And before long, calls went out to other Chanel boutiques and people came by from there to hug and kiss her.

It was starting to get late, but Cyndi insisted on buying a pair of aqua patent-leather-strapped shoes and talked Alicia into the same pair but in red. Cyndi bought two pairs of sunglasses for herself and one as a present to Carson.

Alicia found a pair of light-blue jeans with a matching denim jacket decorated with jeweled buttons. She tried it on and wasn't sure, so Cyndi asked a young woman working there to get something, and when she came back, it was a beaded shell and pearl belt.

That clinched the sale.

After that Alicia found a pink cruise dress with a matching top and loose knit shawl, which she loved.

Then she found white slacks and a matching cotton top that looked kind of like a judo costume, with a big black velvet belt—that tied like a scarf—and was held tight with a large enameled pearl and glass broach.

"Enough," Alicia now declared. "*Basta*. That's all. Done. Finished. Any more and we'll need therapy."

Cyndi reminded her, "This is therapy," and discovered a silk crepon see-thru ensemble—slacks and a dress-length top—decorated in multicolored candy patterns. To go with it, she took a pair of sandals with gold chains that strapped around her ankles and were decorated in pearls, but looked as if she wasn't wearing any shoes at all.

The entire staff accompanied them to the curb where the trunk filled up, and Roland had to put the overflow on the front passenger seat.

A woman handed them both a large Chanel bag.

"A little something . . . " she said.

Inside each there was perfume, and two men's ties, a Chanel silk scarf and a miniskirt-length silk bathrobe.

After a long series of teary goodbyes, they made their way back to the Ritz.

"This has to qualify for *convoitise*." Alicia admitted to Cyndi, "We ought to be ashamed of ourselves."

Cyndi shook her head. "This is Paris so it isn't *convoitise*. It's *débauche du samedi*." She translated, "Saturday debauchery."

64

Even though it was Saturday, Belasco came uptown to check on Gabriella, Forbes and Carlos.

He walked into Trump Tower from the Fifth Avenue entrance, went upstairs to nineteen, knocked on the door and was surprised when Rebecca opened it.

"Good morning," he smiled.

"Gabriella told me . . . " she stepped aside to let him in . . . "how you and she have been plotting behind my back. I'm not sure I like that."

He forced a smile. "I think plotting is a bit harsh. But our intentions were honorable. Nothing was ever intended to be kept secret."

"Except that it was a secret. No one said anything to me . . . "

"Until now," he pointed out. "You haven't exactly been in the mood . . . "

She looked at him, then admitted, "I know," and walked away.

He followed her into the showroom.

Forbes and Gabriella were sitting on the floor going through a mountain of files. Carlos was reconstructing some shelves.

"Any luck?"

"Depends on how you define luck," Forbes said. "Sometimes finding something is lucky. Sometimes finding nothing is lucky. So far we've found nothing."

"Don't find anything and we know," Belasco said.

Rebecca shook her head, "I'm not so sure."

Forbes looked at her. "I am."

BELASCO STAYED there with them for a little while, then announced that he was going to his office, but offered, "I'll have lunch sent up in a few hours. Twelve thirty, okay?"

He went back down to the main hall, then down the escalator to the lower-ground food court where he ordered four Caesar salads to be sent up to Scarpe Pietrasanta. He added some water, iced teas, and four slices of carrot cake to the order, and paid for the food himself.

Turning back toward the escalator, he saw Odette at the pastry counter helping herself to three donuts then leaving without paying for them.

He went over to her, "*Bonjour madame,*" and asked in French, "Is that breakfast or lunch?"

"Silly of me," she said handing him the napkin with the donuts on top. "I shouldn't be eating between meals, you are quite correct."

"Quite right," he said. "After all, you must keep your figure."

She was dressed in a pale blue flapper skirt, with her hair in a chignon. "Keep my figure?" She did a twirl. "I've tried my best."

"You've done very well."

"My public expects nothing less," she said, then came close to Belasco and whispered, "I didn't know that Mr. Cove even knew Mrs. Essenbach."

He was very curious. "Mr. Cove and Mrs. Essenbach?"

She nodded with great assurance.

"They must have met at some point," he presumed. "Everybody in Trump Tower knows everybody else."

"Cher Monsieur Belasco," she whispered, "does everybody who knows everybody else in Trump Tower have romantic little lunches together?"

Bizarre, he thought. "You're referring to Mr. Cove on forty-five and forty-six? Married to a young Chinese American woman?"

"I am."

"And . . . romantic? With Mrs. Essenbach?" He couldn't possibly imagine that.

"There is more going on here," Odette asserted, "than meets the eye." She wished him, "A very pleasant Saturday to you," and walked to the escalator to go up to the atrium.

Looking down at the three donuts he was holding in the napkin, he went to the counter to pay for them—"No, sorry we can't take them back once a client touches them"—then spotted a woman sitting at a table with two children. He took two extra napkins, wrapped each donut individually, and walked up to their table. "Mr. Trump himself would personally like you to have these donuts for being the best-looking children in Trump Tower today."

The woman was too startled to say thank you. The kids grabbed the donuts and started eating.

Belasco smiled and walked away.

Upstairs, he took the fire station shortcut into the residents' lobby. Just as he got there, Mrs. Essenbach stepped out of the elevator.

"Good morning," he said.

"Oh," she smiled, "dear, sweet Pierre. How is everything? Are you well?" She put her hand on his left arm. "How nice to see you," turned and left the Tower.

Still standing there, he berated himself for not having said something to her—something like, *why are you suing me when you know your story is one big lie*—and wondered why she'd touched his arm like that, almost affectionately.

"Is everything all right?" Schaune asked from the concierge desk.

"Yes," he said, "fine," and headed for his office. Then he stopped, walked back to the spot where he'd been standing when she touched his arm and looked up at the CCTV camera.

That angle would be the side view.

Trying to imagine it, he saw himself saying something to Mrs. Essenbach and her coming over to . . .

He suddenly understood.

From that angle, it would look like she was calming him down.

He told himself, *there is no way she could have thought of that. No way she could have known.*

Yet, she touched his arm deliberately like that.

And for the first time since this all began, he started to realize what, until now, he'd been denying—that Mrs. Essenbach could cost him his job.

65

Back at the hotel, it took two grooms to help them bring all the packages and bags, plus the brand-new Vuitton suitcase, up to the suite.

"Where do we begin?" Alicia asked, looking at the day's shopping, which filled the living room. "Do we pack or unpack?"

"C . . . none of the above." Cyndi announced, "We go for a swim."

Alicia reminded her, "No swimsuits."

"In the Ritz pool?" Cyndi shrugged, "Wouldn't be the first time."

"Really?"

"Really. But seeing as how you're such a prude, I suggest matching underwear, and no one will know the difference."

"Oh . . . I'm sure they will."

"Oh . . . this is Paris, I'm sure they won't."

"*Vive la France,*" Alicia said, and found a panty and bra that almost worked. Cyndi found something that almost worked even less.

Wearing the terry cloth robes that were hanging in the bathroom, they went downstairs to the swimming pool. A dozen people were there, and Cyndi was right, when she and Alicia slipped off their robes, no one paid them any attention.

They swam for half an hour, then went back to the suite and took a shower.

"I'm going to be late," Cyndi said. "Will you be all right? And you really don't mind? It's that I never get a chance to see him anymore, not since he got married again."

As Cyndi jumped into the silk crepon see-thru ensemble she'd just bought, Alicia asked, "Did he cheat on wife number one with you, too?"

"It's not cheating because I was there long before either of his wives. It's only cheating if it's new. You know, like when you take a book out of the library? When you renew the book, it's not the same thing."

"I suppose that's logical," Alicia nodded, "but only if you're Cyndi Benson."

She checked herself in the full-length mirror, nodded, then sat down on the bed to put on the shoes she'd also just bought, the ones that didn't look like she was wearing shoes. "I am."

"Where are you going for dinner?"

"The *Moulin de Mougins*. We're spending the night there."

"Where is it? In Paris? Outside of Paris?"

"Mougins. It's in the hills behind Cannes." She stood up, gave herself a spray of Chanel No. 5, did a pirouette, waited for Alicia to approve of her outfit and hair, then kissed her. "I love you. See you tomorrow," and headed for the door.

"Cannes? That's in the south of France."

"Yes," she said as if everyone went 650 miles for dinner.

And she was gone.

THE PINK cruise dress looked fantastic, but Alicia decided it wasn't dressy enough. The Chanel ensemble that resembled a judo costume was sensational, but definitely not dressy enough. Then she tried on the black Dior dress. And that was perfect.

Slipping it off, she went looking for the right underwear.

She asked herself, *where is all that Firenzi stuff when you need it*?

There was a silk thong and matching bra in her suitcase, but when she put it on and inspected herself in the mirror, it wasn't the right look.

When in doubt, don't, and decided, no underwear.

She put the dress back on, stepped into her new red shoes, sorted through all the various perfumes she'd been given, settled on the Hermès 24 Faubourg, put on her Cartier watch, her wedding band, and her big diamond ring, then added her new Dior earrings and the enameled bracelet.

Fumbling through Cyndi's suitcase, she borrowed a little red evening bag, dropped her key card in it, and left the suite.

THE HEMINGWAY BAR at the back of the Ritz is wood paneled, with green leather stools in front of the bar and green leather chairs at the dark wood tables scattered around the smallish room.

There were couples sitting at tables and several men hanging at the bar, all of whom noticed her when she walked in.

Looking around, feeling very sexy with nothing on under her dress, she went to a table in the corner to her left.

A waiter came by and asked what she wanted. She ordered a Campari soda. He quickly came back with the drink, some olives, and a plate filled with small Spanish tapas.

Sipping her drink, she sat back to wait.

A middle-aged man, who'd been with two other men at the bar, walked over. "Excuse me." He was American. "My friends and I were wondering if . . . I mean, if you're alone . . . could we buy you a drink?"

She smiled at him, then pointed to the ring on the fourth finger of his left hand. "What would she say?"

He seemed embarrassed. "She'd say . . . when in Rome."

Alicia smiled, "But this is Paris."

He forced a grin and returned to the bar where his friends began teasing him.

Next, a younger man came from across the room and apologized to her. "I am sorry that the gentleman embarrassed you," he spoke with an accent she didn't recognize.

"I don't embarrass easily."

"Perhaps I could buy you a drink."

"I already have a drink."

"Would you like another?"

"I haven't finished this one."

He wondered, "Do you always play so hard to get?"

She asked, "Do I strike you as easy to get?"

He raised his hands in surrender, "*Bonsoir*," and walked away.

Now two good-looking men in their forties walked into the bar, and one of them stared at her. "Don't I know you?"

She shrugged, "I don't think I've ever been there."

"I'm Lamar Jackson from Dallas, Texas. This is my partner Rainer Martin."

"His poor partner," Martin said.

She smiled. "Good evening."

"And you are?" Jackson wanted to know.

She told them, "Dolores del Rio."

Martin hesitated. "Like the old movie actress?"

"Do I look like an old movie actress?"

"Matter of fact, you look like a gorgeous young movie actress. Are you an actress?"

"Actually," she said, "I run my family's scaffolding business in Miami, Florida."

The two guys stared at her then looked at each other.

"Scaffolding?" Jackson said, "You're joking."

"I never joke about scaffolding."

The waiter came by to ask what the gentlemen wanted to drink.

Still standing in front of her table, Jackson asked Alicia, "How about a bottle of champagne?"

"Thank you," she said, "but I never drink champagne with two men at the same time . . . until I've known them for at least an hour."

"Okay," Jackson smiled, then said to the waiter. "Scotch on the rocks for us, and the lady here will have . . . "

Alicia answered, "Campari soda, please."

The waiter nodded.

"And then," Jackson said to him while checking his watch, "It's quarter to eight. So at quarter to nine you can bring us that champagne."

The two men sat down at her table.

Jackson smiled at Alicia.

She smiled back at him.

"So tell us, Dolores," Martin wanted to know, "what brings a gorgeous woman like you to Paris all by herself?"

With a straight face she answered, "Scaffolding. And you? What do you do as partners? Everything? Or is it strictly business."

Jackson looked at Martin and grinned. "We, ah . . . we're in green fuels. You know, like ethanol."

Martin cut in, "Was that you this afternoon down at the pool with the blonde chick?"

"Chick?" Alicia gave him a strange look.

"Girl," he corrected.

"Girl?"

He got flustered. "Woman. Young woman. Younger woman."

"Younger than who?"

"I meant . . . "

"Keep that up," Alicia said, "and you're never going to get to the champagne."

Martin shook his head, "For a gorgeous woman, you sure are tough."

"I take that as a compliment." She raised her first glass and finished it. "So what brings two married guys to Paris, all the way from Texas, without their wives?"

"Divorced," Jackson showed her, "See? No more ring." He said to Martin, "You'll have to do your own lying," then he pointed to Alicia's left hand. "Speaking of rings, that's a pretty good-sized rock."

She shrugged it off with, "A friendship ring."

"You must have a pretty good friend."

"As a matter of fact, I do," she said. "But let's not talk about me. Let's talk about ethanol."

66

Carson's JAL flight from Tokyo landed half an hour ahead of schedule. While they were taxiing to the gate, the pilot welcomed his passengers to Paris—in Japanese, French and English—wished everyone a pleasant stay and announced that the local time was 5:40 pm.

Carson reset his watch.

He'd managed to get some sleep on the flight and had written an e-mail that he would send to Ken Warring from the hotel, outlining the next steps they'd need to take to finish the Shigetada deal.

After thanking the cabin attendants, he stepped off the plane and walked for what seemed like a very long time until he got to Immigration. From there, he picked up his luggage, went through the nothing-to-declare line at customs and found the taxi stand.

He told the driver, "The Ritz Hotel."

The driver said, "*Place Vendôme, oui monsieur,*" and drove him into town.

Arriving at the hotel, the doorman welcomed him, signaled for a groom to fetch his luggage, and escorted him to the front desk. A woman there handed him a registration form to fill out, then escorted him to a lovely suite toward the rear of the hotel, overlooking a small garden.

The furniture was Louis XV and the walls were covered in a warm beige silk fabric. It was considerably smaller than the suite he'd left in Tokyo. But then, that one could have been anywhere in the Orient. This one could only be in Paris.

After his luggage arrived, Carson opened the French doors in the living room that led to a tiny balcony, stepped outside and stood there for a moment gazing at the surrounding buildings.

He thought to himself, *les toits de Paris*, then checked his watch, wondered if he had time for a fast swim downstairs, decided he probably didn't, and took a very long, very hot shower instead.

After he sent his e-mail to Warring, he unpacked, picked out a fresh white shirt, put on a dark blue suit and chose a pale blue tie.

Taking one of his two key cards, he sat down at the desk in the living room, addressed an envelope, wrote his room number on the stationery, then slipped the key card and stationery into the envelope and sealed it.

He stopped in the bathroom to check himself in the full-length mirror there, and finally added a light spray of his current favorite eau de cologne, Ambre Topkapi. It was a complex mix of bergamot, grapefruit, cinnamon, cardamom, ginger, sandalwood, leather, musk, vanilla and a dozen other spices. At $600 a bottle, every time he used it, he thought to himself, *this is as far away as a man can possibly get from his teenaged years of Canoe.*

Feeling very grown up, and on time at exactly eight o'clock, he left the room.

The elevator brought him down to the ground floor, where he handed the envelope to the woman at the front desk—"In case she asks"—then went to the main restaurant.

The *maître d'* greeted him, "*Bonsoir, monsieur.*"

"*Bonsoir.*" Carson looked around the candlelit room. "You see that table over there . . . in the corner." He pointed to it. "That table right there strikes me as being a very romantic table."

"I would say, monsieur, it is the most romantic table in the room."

"Eight thirty? Mr. Haynes and guest."

"Of course."

"And . . . please put a bottle of champagne on ice at the table."

"Any choice of champagne?"

"Cristal. You choose the vintage."

"With pleasure, monsieur."

He smiled, "*Merci,*" started to walk away, then stopped and came back. "Ah . . . when I say, you choose the vintage, that means within the past, say, seven to ten years."

"May I ask about your dinner companion?"

"I have it on good authority that she is an exceptional woman." He remembered the word Cyndi taught him. "A very beautiful . . . *nana.*"

The *maître d'* gave him an odd look. "*Nana*? Perhaps what Monsieur really means is, *une très belle femme.*" A very beautiful woman.

"Yes. *Une très belle femme.* But she's also a babe."

The *maître d'* suggested, "If monsieur is looking for an exceptional vintage to go along with an exceptional woman, may I suggest the ninety-six."

"Exceptional?"

"Yes, monsieur, I assure you, exceptional."

He nodded, "That sounds, I assure you, very appropriate. Thank you." He started to walk away, then stopped and came back again. "So that there are no surprises . . . that is nineteen ninety-six, not eighteen ninety-six."

The *maître d'* grinned broadly and reassured him. "*Oui, monsieur.*"

Carson said, "Thank you," left the restaurant, walked through the long corridor to the back of the hotel and stepped into the Hemingway Bar.

67

The 911 call was panicky, as most of them usually are.

"It's a body . . . we found a body . . . I think the person is dead."

"All right sir . . . " the woman working the call said with practiced calm . . . "please tell me your name and where you are."

"We're in Central Park. My girlfriend and I are in Central Park. We were taking a walk . . . "

"And what is your name?"

"Ah . . . why do you need my name?"

"My name is Janet, sir, and I want to help you. What's yours?"

"Ah . . . okay . . . I'm . . . " He stopped and asked his girlfriend, "What?" Then he told Janet, "My girlfriend says we shouldn't give our names. We don't want to get involved."

Janet saw the man's cell phone number come up on her screen, along with his name and address. "That's all right, sir, I understand. Now . . . where in Central Park are you?"

"You know the Boat House? There are some woods to the north of that . . . "

Janet brought up a map of Central Park on her screen. "Sir, tell me, are you closer to the Fifth Avenue side or the Central Park West side?"

"We came in at Seventy-Seventh Street . . . and Central Park West."

"Are you on . . . " she checked the map, "West Drive?"

"What's West Drive?"

"That's the road inside the park that runs north and south. If you came in at West Seventy-Seventh, there's a road . . . "

"Yes, that's right. We turned left on that road . . . wait . . . what?" He spoke to his girlfriend, then came back, "She says that the Swedish Cottage is up there."

"All right, sir. Thank you for that. Now, where did you find the body? And where are you now?"

"Just off the drive, below the theater, in the woods . . . but please, we don't want to get involved, we were walking and we found . . . it's horrible . . . the person is dead . . . "

"Sir, from where you're standing, can you see West Road?"

"No."

"All right, sir . . . I'm sending the police to you now . . . but I would appreciate it very much if you or your friend would please go to West Road and wait there so that the police can find you. And . . . sir . . . please stay on the line with me."

"Ah . . . really . . . we don't want to get involved . . . "

"I understand sir. Don't worry about that. Everything will be fine. But please . . . stay on the line with me . . . "

The man said to his girlfriend, "Don't do that. Come here. Move away. What?" Then he said to Janet, "Oh my God . . . my friend took a close look . . . she says this person has been shot through the head."

68

There was an empty stool at the end of the bar, so Carson went there, ordered a vodka and sat with his back against the bar to watch the room.

"It's nothing new," Jackson was explaining, "the original Model T . . . you know, Henry Ford's car . . . it ran on ethanol."

"I never knew that," Alicia said, pretending to be interested.

"Then along came Prohibition." Martin picked up the story, "and the government ruled that ethanol was like some kind of moonshine and had to be outlawed."

"So that," she said, "was the end of that until you two came along."

"Not us two, exactly," Jackson said.

Carson sipped half his drink and checked his watch. He didn't want to be late at the restaurant. So now he got off the stool, walked halfway through the bar, then turned and looked at Alicia.

Still listening to the two men, she looked up at him.

"Ah . . . excuse me . . . " Carson started toward the table. "Excuse me . . . I'm sorry to interrupt but . . . aren't you part of the del Rio family from Miami? Scaffolding, right?"

She smiled politely.

Jackson looked uneasily at Martin.

Carson extended his hand to her. "Do you have a sister named Cyndi?" He grinned at the two men sitting there. "I'm sorry to interrupt like this . . . " He looked again at Alicia. "Cyndi is your sister, right?"

She nodded, "That's right."

"I'll be. Who'd a thunk it. I come all this way . . . " He smiled again at Martin and Jackson. "My name is Lewis A. Riley . . . "

Which happened to be the name of the last husband of the actress Dolores del Rio.

" . . . I can't believe I'm in Paris and you're in Paris."

"Hi Lewis," Alicia said. "This is Mr. Jackson and Mr. Martin. They're in ethanol."

He shook Alicia's hand, then shook both theirs. And while Alicia was still smiling, the two men were not hiding their impatience.

"How is Cyndi? I haven't seen her in years. Is she still working in the business?" He looked at Jackson and Martin, "Her family is in scaffolding, and I'm in fasteners, that's how I met Cyndi, and that's how I sort of know Dolores here."

"Well," Martin nodded. "That's real interesting to know. I hope you have a pleasant stay in Paris."

Carson pointed to Alicia, "The last time I saw you . . . what's the place in Miami with the stone crabs . . . down at the beach . . . "

"Joe's."

"That's right. You remember? You were having dinner at Joe's . . . " He smiled at Martin and Jackson—"You like stone crabs?"—then sat down. "I'll only be a minute," he nodded and continued talking. "You were having dinner . . . "

"Look, Mr. Lewis . . . " Jackson tried to cut in.

"It's Riley," Carson said. "Lewis Riley."

"Sorry that my friend got your name wrong," Martin said, "but you see, we're here with the lady . . . "

"You in scaffolding too?" Carson asked. "No, that's right, you're in ethanol. Damn but it's a small world." Carson signaled to the waiter, "I'll have another vodka. You having something?" He asked Alicia.

"I'm good," she said.

"Look pal," Jackson was getting annoyed, "we're here with the lady, so why don't you take your drink . . . "

"No need to be rude about it, friend." Carson said. "It's just because we're sort of in the same business and I know Cyndi . . . "

"It's all right," Alicia reassured Jackson and Martin. "He'll have one drink." She asked Carson, "That's right, isn't it?"

"One drink," he said. "Unless, of course, you'd like to have dinner with me."

"The lady's taken," Jackson said.

"Yeah, pal," Martin added, "we were here first . . . "

"The lady's taken?" Alicia looked at them. "You were here first?"

Jackson tried to reel that back. "I meant that we were having this nice conversation, you know, just the three of us . . . "

"That's right," Martin said. "We weren't claiming you . . . not like Mount Everest and planting a flag . . . "

"Planting your flag?" Alicia asked. "Have you always had a way with women?"

"No . . . not that . . . nothing like that at all," Jackson assured her. He turned to Carson, "Sure, if you want to have that drink with us . . . "

"No problem." He waved at the waiter. "Cancel that vodka please. I'll take a bill. In fact, give me the whole bill for the table."

"That's okay," Martin said.

"I insist."

When the waiter brought the bill, Carson paid it.

"I'm sorry about interrupting. Anyway, I'm hungry. I've been flying all day." He smiled at Alicia, "Would you like to join me for dinner?"

Martin waved his finger. "We keep telling you the lady is taken . . . "

Alicia wanted to know, "Shouldn't the lady decide?"

"Of course," Martin said. "We were about to invite you out . . . there's a great place we know . . . "

"Thank you," she said to them, then smiled at Carson. "I'd love to."

She stood up. "It's been very nice talking to you."

Neither Jackson nor Martin knew whether to argue or just sit there.

Alicia and Carson left the bar.

"I am so turned on," Alicia whispered.

"Should we find a cloakroom?"

"Like at Elliott and Linda's wedding?"

"I'm up for it if you are."

She pinched his arm. "Is up the right word? I hope so because I'm not wearing a single thing under this dress."

"*Bonsoir madame, bonsoir monsieur.*" The *maître d'* greeted them. "This way monsieur . . . for you and for this exceptional woman."

Alicia nodded thank you as he brought them to their table.

Carson slipped him fifty euros. "I told you she was a *nana.*"

They sat down and as the champagne was poured, Alicia slipped one shoe off and ran it up the leg of Carson's pants.

"I don't know how we're going to get through this meal," he said.

She assured him, "As horny as I am for you right now, we're not."

"Plan B." He signaled for the *maître d'*. When he came to their table, Carson told him, "Here's what we're going to do. We'll both start with the snails."

Alicia nodded.

"And then . . . fish for you?" He asked Alicia.

She nodded again.

"The *dorade* for the lady and the *maigret de canard* for me."

"And how would you like your duck, sir?"

"Rare," he said. "For dessert, we'll do the soufflé. Raspberry for the lady, strawberry for me."

"Yes, of course sir."

"But . . . " Carson looked at him. "It's take-away."

He didn't understand. "Sir?"

"Send it up with room service."

The *maître d'* almost smiled because he understood. "Certainly sir. The room number?"

Alicia answered, "The Imperial suite."

"Yes, of course, *madame* . . . but it may take up to forty-five minutes."

"Give it a full hour," Carson said, "don't rush," took the champagne bottle, stood up, pulled Alicia's chair away from the table and slipped the *maître d'* another fifty euros.

In the elevator, Carson said, "Really? The Imperial suite?"

"We may not get there in time." She put her mouth full on his.

While the elevator doors were still closing, she was already tugging at his belt buckle.

"Wait till you see this place." Getting off the elevator on the first floor, she fumbled with her key card, opened the door to the suite, dragged him by the belt along the private corridor, then opened the living room door.

By that point she'd pulled down his trousers.

"Jesus," he looked around as he kicked off his shoes and stepped out of his pants. "We could live here."

"This is what happens when you travel to Paris with Cyndi Benson." Now she was taking off his jacket and undoing his tie and pulling off his shirt.

He let her undress him completely, and when he was standing there with nothing but the champagne bottle, she said, "Come with me."

Leading him out the living room door, she brought him back into the private corridor. "Wait here."

She shut the door, disappeared, then quickly reappeared on the little balcony that looked down on the corridor. "This is where the Cossacks used to stand guard for the Czar."

He looked up at her there. "That's cool."

"But the Cossacks never did this." Very slowly, she slipped out of the little black dress.

She was wearing nothing but her red shoes.

"How do I climb up there?"

She pointed at him, "With that thing at full mast, I wouldn't suggest climbing anywhere except on top of me. Meet you halfway."

She raced down the steps. He was waiting for her as she came out of the secret door. And they fell onto the floor together.

By the time room service arrived, they were wearing terry cloth robes, finishing the champagne and filling the bathtub.

"That was better than the time in Hong Kong," he said.

"Poor bastards from Texas . . . "

They ate dinner in the tub.

"Did both of them really think . . . "

"If I'd have uncrossed my legs . . . I mean, one guy was already starting to breathe so heavy . . . "

After they emptied a second bottle of champagne . . . "Here's to ethanol," Alicia toasted . . . they made love again, splashing water all over the floor.

"Poor bastards from Texas," she repeated.

"Remember that time in Buenos Aires?"

Getting out, they sort of dried off, and Carson carried their soufflés into bed.

That's when Alicia saw a small red box on the pillow.

"Classy place," Carson said, admiring the room.

"Marie Antoinette almost slept here," Alicia said. "Most hotels turn down your bed and then leave chocolates on your pillow."

"They did," he pointed.

The moment she picked up the box, she realized what it was.

It was the box she'd seen Cyndi slip into her shopping bag at Dior.

"Why don't you open it?" Carson asked.

She did.

A little card read, "Thank you so much for bringing me to Paris. I love you. C."

Inside was a red, diamond-studded Dior cell phone.

SUNDAY

69

The priest's voice rang out. And the congregation answered in unison. That's when his phone began to vibrate in his pocket.

No one ever called him this early on a Sunday morning.

He took his phone out of his pocket and saw that a text message had come in. *Oh my God . . . dear Jesus . . .*

He crossed himself, hurried out of the church, found a cab right away, and told the driver, "Trump Tower."

Two patrol cars and several unmarked police cars were parked on Fifty-Sixth Street in front of the residents' lobby.

Jumping out of the taxi, Belasco went to the front door, where a uniformed officer stopped him. "Sir?"

"It's all right," David the relief doorman said, "he's the boss."

Inside, four men in suits, each with a gold detective's shield hanging on a lanyard, were standing in the lobby.

"I'm Pierre Belasco," he said to them. "General manager of Trump Tower."

Two of the men looked at each other—one was short and heavyset, the other was not much taller but shaved his head—and it was the short heavyset man who asked, "Is there some place we can talk?"

"My office." Belasco brought them in.

"Detective Lazaro," he introduced himself. "My partner . . . " the one who shaved his head, " . . . Detective Stoyanov."

Neither offered to shake hands.

"Yesterday afternoon," Lazaro reported, "a body was found in Central Park. Victim was shot once through the head. Nine-millimeter automatic pistol. Close range. Shot through the right temple. Coroner only got around to identifying the body this morning. Name is . . . " he looked at his notepad, "Katarina Laszlo Bartok Essenbach?"

"This is terrible," Belasco said. "I can't believe it."

"How long has she lived here?"

"Many years. I don't know exactly. At least twenty, maybe twenty-two, something like that. I can get you the exact dates. She has the entire forty-second floor and half of the forty-first."

"Was she well liked?"

He shook his head. "Quite the opposite. I think it's fair to say that she was universally disliked."

"So she had enemies."

He thought about that. "I don't know that you could call them enemies. But she didn't have . . . as far as I know . . . many friends."

"What about her husband?"

"There was a strange incident last week. They must have had a fight about something, because she threw him out in his underwear."

Lazaro glanced at Stoyanov.

"We have CCTV footage," Belasco volunteered. "I can get it for you. Our head of security, Mr. Riordan . . . "

"He's on his way in," Lazaro said. "I presume that there are plenty of CCTV cameras around here. A place like this . . . "

"Yes," Belasco assured him. "Security is very tight. It's Fort Knox. I'm sure you can understand why."

"So there will be footage of her leaving the building?"

"Yes."

"And people coming in?" He pointed to the lobby. "Camera out there? What about front doors? Elevators? On each floor? We'll need to see whatever you've got."

"We'll make everything available to you."

Now, Stoyanov spoke for the first time. "How did you and the victim get along? What was your relationship with her like?"

"Relationship?" He told them the truth, "Strictly business but contentious."

"And when was the last time you saw her?"

"Yesterday afternoon."

"Where?"

"Here. In the lobby. Early afternoon."

"Are you always in the office on Saturdays?"

"Not always . . . but often. I came in yesterday because one of our commercial clients has a problem and I wanted to check on her. I bumped into Mrs. Essenbach when I came back downstairs. She was on her way out."

"Thank you. We appreciate your help," Lazaro said. "We'd like you to come upstairs with us." He motioned for Belasco to follow him. "Please."

The three men got into the elevator and went to the forty-second floor where a uniformed officer was guarding Mrs. Essenbach's front door. He opened it and they stepped inside.

Another detective came to greet them.

"This is Mr. Belasco," Lazaro said to him.

"I'm Detective Wytola . . . I recognize you."

Belasco wanted to know, "From where?"

"Follow me and I'll show you." Wytola led Belasco and the other two men around to the rear of the apartment and into a windowless laundry room where there was an industrial-sized washing machine and equally large dryer, a huge sink, a folding table, and two ironing boards.

And taped on the walls were dozens of photographs of Belasco.

He was speechless.

Taken clandestinely, they showed him walking down the street, in the lobby, in neighborhood shops, in the atrium and in the main entrance to Trump Tower. There were also photos of him taken secretly in front of his apartment in the Village, and in various places around his neighborhood. There was even one taken of him sitting in church.

"This is . . . beyond bizarre. It's . . . " He couldn't find the words.

"Let's talk about this photo right here," Wytola pointed.

Black and white, blown up and grainy, obviously taken from a hidden camera high up in Mrs. Essenbach's study, it showed her sprawled out across the couch, wearing a fur dressing gown and Belasco pouring her a glass of champagne.

BY THE TIME Bill Riordan arrived at Trump Tower, Belasco was back in his office with Lazaro and Stoyanov.

They briefed Riordan on what had happened to Mrs. Essenbach. He and two other detectives then went to the CCTV monitoring room to begin reviewing footage.

Now Lazaro wanted to know, "On Saturday, after you met Mrs. Essenbach in the lobby and she left the building, what did you do?"

"I came here to my office."

"How long did you stay?"

"Not long."

"Where did you go from here? Specifically, where were you between, say, noon and five o'clock yesterday?"

Suddenly, his offhanded remark to Carole Ann Mendelsohn flew into his head.

How about if someone throws her off the Fifty-Ninth Street Bridge?

He shook his head, "Surely, you can't think that I had anything to do with this?"

Stoyanov asked point blank. "Did you?"

"No. Of course not."

"But you had a personal relationship with her."

"No. Not a personal relationship. I did not. It was a strictly business relationship."

Lazaro suggested, "Champagne says otherwise."

"What you would see if there was videotape in her hidden camera is that I didn't take a glass of champagne for myself. I didn't stay there. She asked me to pour a glass for her, I did, then I left. I wasn't in her apartment more than five minutes total. You'll be able to see from the CCTV footage when I arrived and when I left. Not even five minutes. It was right after I left when her husband got thrown out in his underwear."

"What sort of a relationship did you have with him?"

"Until recently, I didn't even know she had a husband."

"Never met him?"

"Never."

"Do you know anything about him, like where he's from?"

"No."

"He's from Chile. Are you aware that there's a warrant out for his arrest?"

"No. What for?"

Stoyanov disregarded Belasco's question. "Are there many people living here for twenty or twenty-two years that you have never met?"

"There is at least one," he glared at the officer. "But what is he wanted for?"

"It's political," Lazaro said. "Did you ever see Mr. and Mrs. Essenbach together?"

"No."

"Did she ever mention her husband?"

"No. Except that night. She said . . . I don't remember, something that included the words, my husband."

The two detectives continued asking Belasco questions for nearly an hour, until Detective Wytola phoned and asked them to come back upstairs.

Wytola met them carrying a large carton of photos. "This woman had more closets than most people have rooms. There are even closets inside other closets."

"Like secret closets?" Lazaro asked.

"Yeah," Wytola answered. "Like right out of some horror movie. We dig through a closet and find a door behind it leading into another closet."

"What's she hiding?"

"Mainly clothes. She had a lot of clothes. But then we found this." He motioned for them to follow him, put the carton down on the big dining room table and asked Belasco, "Recognize any of these people?"

They were photos of Mrs. Essenbach, mostly standing next to or with her arms around younger men.

The first photo Belasco recognized was the same photo he'd spotted in her apartment—the snapshot that showed Mrs. Essenbach in a black leotard with her arms cozily around a bare-chested Alejandro.

"This one," he handed it to Wytola. "He's a personal trainer in our gym."

While Wytola looked at it, then passed it to Lazaro and Stoyanov, Belasco tried to remember her comment to him when he'd first seen it.

A mere child . . . hardly the man that you are.

But he didn't volunteer that information to the police.

"We'll need to know his hours," Wytola said to Belasco.

"We can get you his time sheets . . . no problem."

"Anyone else?" Wytola asked.

Belasco continued sifting through the box until he found another one. "This man's name is Tomas Tejeda. He was an elevator operator. But he no longer works here."

Wytola said, "We'll need an address for him."

"Sure," Belasco said.

Lazaro nodded toward Wytola, "Thanks . . . we'll be in Mr. Belasco's office," and started to walk to the front door.

"Just a second," Belasco said to him, then turned to Wytola. "These closets inside closets. Can I see them?"

Wytola looked to Lazaro for an answer.

"Why?" Lazaro asked.

Belasco asked Wytola, "You say the closets inside the other closets are filled with clothes?"

"Yeah."

"You wouldn't happen to have found a vicuna coat, would you?"

"What's the significance of that?"

Belasco told them the story of Carlos Vela and promised that looking in the closets would only take a moment or two. Lazaro shrugged, Wytola nodded okay, and Lazaro warned Belasco, "You don't touch anything."

"No problem," Belasco said.

It was in the second hidden closet that he found Mrs. Essenbach's vicuna coat.

BACK DOWNSTAIRS, Lazaro wanted Belasco to answer more questions.

"Where were you . . . and what did you do between . . . say, noon and five . . . yesterday?"

He responded, "I ordered lunch for some people in the food court at twelve thirty or so, then came back here, which is when I bumped into her . . . Mrs. Essenbach. She was on her way out. That might have been . . . quarter to one? I stayed here until one thirty . . . no, probably not that late . . . then walked over to Madison Avenue. I poked my head into a few galleries."

"Which ones?"

"I don't know . . . " Belasco shrugged, "I was just walking. Up in the sixties or seventies. Then, sometime around three thirty or so I took the subway downtown to Union Square. I went to the market to buy some cheese. I usually do that on Saturdays. From there I walked home."

"Which train and which station did you take it from?" Lazaro asked.

"The number six. I got it at Seventy-Seventh . . . I think."

"You use a Metro Card?"

"Yes."

"May I have it please?"

"What for?"

"Because we can use it to find out where it was used and what time it was used."

"Seriously . . . " he looked at both the officers . . . "You can't possibly think . . . "

"If we could borrow your Metro Card please," Stoyanov said.

Belasco reached for his wallet and looked inside. "I ah . . . " It wasn't there. "I don't seem to have it."

Lazaro stared at him. "Do you own a gun?"

"No."

"Have you fired a gun in the past twenty-four hours?"

"Detective, I really resent this . . . "

"Why's that?"

"Because I didn't have anything to do with this . . . and I take exception to you questioning me as if I did."

"We're only doing our job," Stoyanov reminded him. "Seeing as how you don't have your Metro Card, how about, in a little while, we drive you home? At that point, would you mind if we looked around your place?"

"As a matter of fact, I would mind." He didn't like this at all. "Why do you want to look around my place?"

"It's what we do," Lazaro reminded him. "Most homicide victims are killed by someone they know. So we start with everybody who knew the victim and eliminate people one by one. You're not a suspect, you're someone we want to eliminate from our investigation, which, therefore, might bring us one step closer to whoever did this."

"It wasn't me."

"But we don't know that," Lazaro said, "until we know that."

"This is absolutely ridiculous. No more. You're barking up the wrong tree. I think this interview is over."

"No problem," Lazaro shrugged. "But the interview isn't over, it's merely postponed. It isn't actually over until we decide it's over."

That's when Stoyanov's cell phone rang. He took the call, hung up, and said to Belasco, "The CCTV monitoring room. We need to take a look at some things. Can you show us where it is?"

Belasco took them through the fire station shortcut into the main hall and then upstairs to the monitoring room. Two plainclothes officers, one of them considerably older than the other, were sitting with Riordan and the CCTV security guy on duty. Lazaro, Stoyanov and Belasco crowded into the narrow space behind them.

"This is Friday," the older guy said. "It's the hallway in front of Mrs. Essenbach's front door."

The main screen showed Antonia and Tommy coming to her door and being let in.

"You know these people?" Lazaro asked.

"Her name is Antonia Lawrence. She works for the company. He's Tommy Seasons."

"The actor?"

"Yes."

Riordan volunteered, "But he shouldn't be in the building. He's on a banned list."

"And who's this?" the older officer asked as the shot changed to a man stepping out of Mrs. Essenbach's apartment and giving her a long, deep kiss before leaving.

"Don't know," Belasco said.

"Take another look." The shot changed to the residents' lobby as the man walked out.

"Never saw him before."

"And this? Watch. The woman and the man leave. Then someone else shows up."

It was Carlos Vela. He and Mrs. Essenbach seemed to be having a brief but heated discussion at her door.

Riordan said, "That man was banned and Pierre unbanned him."

"The vicuna coat?" Belasco said. "It's upstairs. Vela didn't steal anything."

"What do you mean?"

"We found it in her closet, where it always was."

Riordan turned to Lazaro. "That true?"

"That's true," he said, "but you two ladies can argue about it on your own time." He tapped the older officer on the shoulder. "What else you got?"

"There's this on Friday," the older officer continued. The shot in the food court showed Mrs. Essenbach at the table with David Cove. "But watch what happens when we enlarge it and run it slow."

Someone moved in front of the table where they were eating, stopped for a second with something in his hand, then quickly moved away.

"A cell phone," the sergeant said. "He used it to take a photo."

Belasco didn't understand. "Why?"

"Good question," the older officer said. "Someone takes her picture secretly . . . and the next day she turns up dead? We'd like to know why, too." He motioned to the security guy to change the shot. "This is Friday after midnight. Recognize anyone?"

A man came into the garage from the street, got into the service elevator, and went up to twenty-four. He then transferred into one of the residence elevators and rode up to forty-two. There, he knocked on Mrs. Essenbach's door and went inside. Two hours later, he left, taking the same route down and out of the building.

Belasco nodded. "He's the guy from the box of photos. The ex-elevator operator, Tomas Tejeda."

The older officer said, "There's something else we want you to see."

A shot from the camera in the lobby, time-coded Saturday, 12:51 p.m., showed Belasco and Mrs. Essenbach speaking, and before she walked away, she put her hand on his arm affectionately.

IT WAS well after seven that evening when the two detectives drove Belasco home.

In the car, Lazaro said, "You need to come clean about your personal relationship with the victim."

"I did not have a relationship with the victim," Belasco insisted. "Everything was strictly business. There was no personal relationship."

"That video of you and her in the lobby . . . "

"I did not have a personal relationship with her."

When they got to his place, he reluctantly brought them inside. "You wanted to look around . . . be my guest."

"Actually, that probably won't be necessary," Stoyanov said. "But the dark suit you were wearing yesterday. We'd like to borrow it."

"What for?"

"Gun residue."

He snapped, "I said to you that I had nothing to do with . . . "

"Then why would you mind?" Lazaro asked.

Belasco glared at the two men, turned, walked into his bedroom, took his suit from yesterday out of his closet and handed it to Stoyanov on the hanger. "Anything else? Underwear? Socks? Toothbrush?"

"Thank you for your cooperation," Lazaro said. "We'll be in touch."

"I'm sure you will." Belasco saw them out.

Annoyed with them and tired from having wasted his entire day going through this, he walked back into his bedroom and emptied his pockets, putting his wallet, some change, his keys and his BlackBerry on the dresser. And right there, under the piece of paper that listed the prices of paintings on show at a gallery on Madison Avenue, he found his Metro Card.

70

The party was in full swing.

There must have been two dozen people in Ricky's apartment, some of them drinking, some of them sitting on the floor getting stoned.

Music was blaring, and at least one young woman—a redhead whom Ricky had never seen before—was already half-naked.

"You can't let her be the only one." A very stoned Mikey Glass was going up to every other woman in the room. "You know how embarrassing it is to be the only naked person in a room? Trust me, I know. But . . . two naked people . . . that makes it so much easier for everyone else . . . so would you please step out of your clothes . . . "

Ricky was parading through the living room, showing everyone his NASA countdown clock. "Look at that . . . " It was moving down from 17:17:49 . . . "Seventeen hours plus value-added tax."

"Only that many hours left, Rick?" Some woman asked. "How are you going to celebrate?"

"We're doing it now." He kissed her full on the mouth, and she put her arms around him and kissed him back.

"We only have . . . " He looked at his countdown clock . . . " . . . seventeen hours, sixteen minutes, and twelve seconds. Then, like on New Year's Eve when it reaches midnight . . . we can start celebrating from the beginning." He kissed her again. "Four seconds, three seconds, two seconds, one second . . . look . . . only seventeen hours, fifteen minutes, and fifty-nine seconds to go . . . "

Joey stepped out of his bedroom with a young blonde woman who was laughing nonstop.

Mikey walked up to her. "Don't let Wendy be the only one . . . "

"Who's Wendy?"

He pointed to the half-naked woman. "Sharon, over there."

"I thought you said her name was Wendy."

"The left one is Wendy, the right one is Sharon. What do you call yours?"

Laughing, she yanked up her sweater and, braless, showed him a small tattoo on the side of each of her breasts. "Left . . . and right."

"How cool is that," Mikey said, helping her out of her sweater.

"Hey," Joey objected, "this is my new girlfriend."

"No, pal," Mikey insisted, "this woman's left and right belongs to the ages." He took her hand and began parading her around the room, showing everyone her tattoos.

The phone rang. After someone answered it, Ricky asked, "Who was it?"

The person who answered it shouted back, "Whoever it was."

Ricky nodded. "Makes sense to me."

A couple of minutes later, the doorbell rang and in walked King Windsor and his girlfriend Tyne. Ricky shouted out his name and went to kiss her hello, full on the mouth.

"Hey man," King hugged Ricky. "We got us a problem. Where's Billy?"

"Who?"

"Billy. The cat."

"Oh yeah . . . he went to live on a farm."

King was shocked. "He's not here? I've got to take him back."

"You can't take Billy back," Ricky reminded King, "you gave him to me."

"Well, I've got to take him back, don't I? That's why I came here." King looked at Tyne. "Go find him, luv."

"Billy don't live here," Ricky insisted. "He lives on a farm . . . sort of . . . I took him there me-self."

"Well, then," King towered over him, "you've got to take us there bleeding fast 'cause the bloke who lost him wants him back."

"What bloke who lost him?"

"Yeah, that bloke. So where's this farm?"

Ricky pointed toward the park. "There."

"Where? Central bloody fucking Park?"

"Yeah."

Tyne looked at Ricky, "You can't turn a bleeding cat like that loose . . . "

"We've got to find him," King said. "Let's go, right now."

"I can't, can I," he objected, "not with all me-guests here. After the party. It's only going to last another . . . " He showed them the countdown clock . . . "sixteen hours . . . "

"I'm warning you mate," King shoved a finger in Ricky's chest.

"Can't leave, can I, not with this thing."

"Find yourself a designated driver, like you call 'em, and let's go."

Realizing he didn't have much of a choice, Ricky looked around, saw Joey making out with some woman, didn't want to interrupt, then spotted Mikey.

"Do me a favor mate, I've got to run out . . . take off your right shoe and socks . . . wear this thing for me for half an hour, one hour tops."

"Sure Ricky," Mikey fell onto the floor.

Ricky sat down opposite him, got Mikey to twist his foot the proper way, and slipped the ankle bracelet off his leg and onto Mikey's.

"Half-hour, one hour tops," Ricky assured him, then turned to the nearest woman. "Do me a favor luv, take care of my mate Mikey here until I get back. One hour tops."

Mikey said to the woman, "See those two women there who don't have most of their clothes on? You know how embarrassing it is to be the only two? Trust me, I know. But if there were three . . . "

Ricky put his shoe and sock back on—"Need to grab my disguise . . . "— found sunglasses and a baseball cap, then stopped in the kitchen for a paper bag. "Something to put Billy in."

"Great," King said, "let's go," and the three of them left.

The woman standing with Mikey decided, why not, and started to take off her clothes when Mikey grabbed her hand and asked, "Have you ever been naked with a television star in a rock star's bedroom?" He led her inside to Ricky's bedroom and locked the door behind them.

AFTER THE WOMAN fell asleep, Mikey came out, looked around and saw there were at least six women not wearing tops.

He proclaimed, "I'm dead. I've gone to boob heaven."

The doorbell rang.

"Somebody get that," he said, but no one was paying any attention to him— "Too many boobs in one room are very distracting," he decided—so he opened the door himself.

A young girl was standing there. "Is Joey here?"

"He is," Mikey said. "But no one can come in if they're still wearing a top."

"What?"

"No tops. No bras. Sorry, that's the price of admission."

"I want to see Joey . . . "

"If you're down to your bra, you can see him. But only see him. I'll point him out. But if you want to come in and actually speak with him . . . "

She stared at Mikey. "Please tell Joey . . . "

"Bra," he said, then started clapping, "bra . . . bra . . . bra . . . "

She took a deep breath suddenly ripped off her shirt and stood there very nervously in a small, pink bra. "Joey . . . " she said breathlessly . . . "where's Joey?"

"I'll page him." Mikey turned and screamed, "Joey . . . Joey . . . where are you?"

Joey was still making out with that woman when he glanced up, then jumped up, and screamed, "Pocahontas . . . " He raced to the door. "What are you doing . . . get dressed . . . " He pulled her shirt back over her head, then screamed at Mikey, "Are you fucking out of your skull?"

"Nice to meet you," Mikey said.

Joey was frantic. "Pocahontas . . . you can't stay here . . . "

Amvi threw her arms around Joey and started kissing him. "I love you . . . "

"No," Joey said. "You've got to go home . . . go on . . . " With his arms around her back, Joey picked her up and carried her to the elevators. "You've got to go home . . . " He pushed the elevator button. "Come on, I'm taking you home . . . you've got to go home."

When the elevator arrived, Joey carried Amvi inside.

Mikey watched as the elevator doors closed and waited there.

But they didn't come back.

Walking inside, he tried to find the woman he'd just been with, had trouble remembering exactly which one she was, then recalled that they'd been together in Ricky's bedroom. That's where he found her, still naked, but snoring and fast asleep.

"I remember you," he said.

Back in the living room, he noticed that some people were leaving.

"Isn't anybody going to get naked?" He asked two women on their way out, "Come on girls . . . "

They left.

"Aw come on . . . anyone? Someone? You? You?" He pointed to one woman, then another, turned around and then another. And soon he found himself turning round and round. "You? . . . you? . . . going . . . going . . . gone."

Dizzy, he fell to the floor.

"What kind of a party is this when the world won't stop spinning."

Getting onto his hands and knees, he crawled over to a woman who was standing at the door. When she saw him there, she opened the door and asked, "Where are you off to, then?"

"I was thinking of . . . I don't know . . . " He looked up at her. "Where can we crawl to together?"

"My place?"

"Sure. Where's that?"

"New Jersey."

"Can't get there from here."

"How about your place?"

"No, no, no. Not if we both want to live to tell the tale."

"Then where?"

"Where are we now?"

"Trump Tower."

"Been there, done that," he said. "Speaking of which, we're right around the corner from the Plaza. Ever been there?"

"Not with you."

He crawled into the hallway, over to the elevators, and pushed the call button. When Ricardo arrived, Mikey—still wearing Ricky's ankle bracelet—crawled in with the woman walking beside him and announced, "The Plaza Hotel please, and step on it."

MONDAY

71

Carson walked into the office two hours later than usual.

"Where the hell have you been?" Tony Arcarro wanted to know.

"When? Last Week? Yesterday? Last night?"

"This morning."

"Why? You taking attendance?"

"No. Raising the alarm."

"What alarm?"

"Better get onto voice mail. You got yourself a real problem."

TWENTY-FOUR HOURS before, Carson and Alicia had ordered a leisurely breakfast—two big café lattes with fresh *croissants*—gotten back into the tub and had spent nearly an hour making love there until Alicia announced, "I have to pack . . . for Cyndi, too."

They'd put all their luggage together, then gotten Roland to drive them to *Fouquet's* to meet up with Cyndi.

There, they had lunch on the private club terrace off the *Champs Élysées*, along the *Avenue George V*—Carson couldn't get over the fact that just about everybody on the terrace came up to kiss Cyndi hello—before going to the airport and flying back to New York together.

No sooner had the three of them arrived home at Trump Tower when Alicia remembered that she and Carson had, weeks ago, accepted a dinner invitation at the Park Avenue penthouse home of Fleming and Elizabeth Scranton.

A couple they'd only recently met, the Scrantons privately owned Decorators' Depot, a chain of 180 big-box stores around the country.

So Alicia and Carson rushed out of their traveling clothes—"Lucky for us that we spent so much time taking baths in Paris," she said—got into dinner-party clothes and managed to get to the Scranton's place almost on time.

Not surprisingly, between his jetlag from having come full circle around the world in only five days plus the late night, Carson had overslept.

It was the wrong morning to have done that.

"YOU GOT yourself a real problem."

Carson wanted to know, "Who or what or why?"

Arcarro told him, "Omaha."

That woke him up.

Instead of ordering his usual juice and bialy, Carson punched up his voice mail and listened to the message from Warring, which simply said, "He fucked us."

He returned the call immediately. "It's Carson."

Warring demanded to know, "Where the fuck have you been?"

"I just got back . . . last night."

"Yeah, well, I needed you on the phone with Japan this morning while Japan was still open. Now they're closed."

Carson asked, "What's the problem?"

"The problem is," Warring said angrily, "he fucked us . . . And you're asleep at the switch."

"Hold on . . . Ken . . . calm down . . . "

"Don't ever tell me to calm down."

"Sorry," he said, taking a deep breath. "I'm sorry. Please tell me what happened."

"He reneged. Fucking flat-out refused to sign. Said he changed his mind. Said if we didn't like it, we could take him to court or fuck ourselves, or both."

Carson pulled his keyboard closer and checked the Shigetada share price on the Tokyo Exchange. "Closed down two-thirds. Who else knows?"

"Who knows what?"

"That he wants us out?"

"How do I know? Lawyers had everything set to sign the initial intent, and the fucker sends a message that the deal's off. I try to get in touch with you because we need to do something fast . . . and I can't find you . . . "

"What did the lawyers say?"

"What do you want them to say?"

"Okay." Carson understood that Warring was in no mood to have a conversation. "Let me find out what's going on and where we stand and figure out what we can do."

"You don't need to figure out what we can do. We need to ruin the fucker. That's what you have to do when somebody tries to screw you. Screw them back fifteen times so they never do it again. Screw them back fifteen times worse and your reputation gets out there and the next guy thinking about it says to himself, *I better leave this prick alone.*"

"I understand," Carson said.

"You can never let some son of a bitch get away with anything because if you do, you only invite others to try."

"I'm on the case," Carson said. "I'll call you in an hour."

"Yeah, and when you call . . . you better have something to say."

Carson hung up and screamed loud enough for everyone in the office to hear, "Shit!"

"What?" Arcarro was standing in his doorway.

"Shigetada went away. Refused to sign."

"I thought the fat lady already sang."

"Wrong song. And Warring is seriously pissed off."

"At us?"

"At me. At Shigetada. At everybody."

Arcarro fell onto Carson's couch and took up all of it. "What now?"

"I don't have a clue." He checked the time. "It's too late to get the lawyers on the phone in Tokyo. And, I don't have any home numbers for them. I could phone Shigetada . . . I don't know. Ken is furious. What do you think?"

"Don't ask me. Ask J. R. Ewing what he would do."

Carson smiled at the *Dallas* reference. "Yeah . . . J. R. Ewing's art of the deal. Besides blackmailing somebody's ass, J. R. would probably say that we've got three choices. We buy . . . we sell . . . we do nothing."

"Right. J. R. would look for a girlfriend, a boyfriend, a donkey, whatever. So get something on Shigetada and blackmail the shit out of him."

"Knowing Warring," Carson suggested, "he wouldn't automatically say no. But short of blackmail . . . what else you got?"

Arcarro thought for a while. "Shift your defense. This is an away game. Go zone."

"You don't score playing defense."

"Tie goes to the base runner. If he doesn't score, he loses."

"Too many mixed sports metaphors . . . makes no sense at all. If we don't score, either . . . "

"You're not following me. He can buy, he can sell, he can do nothing. So, prepare the ground for all three eventualities. If he's buying, you've got to be selling high. If he's selling, you've got to be buying low. If he's doing nothing, you've got to kick him in the ass and make him do something."

"He's suddenly not selling," Carson said, "but that doesn't mean he's necessarily buying. Easy enough to find out, I guess. But what happens to us if Shigetada's doing nothing?"

"If he's doing nothing, maybe he's waiting for the market to tell him what to do."

He looked at Arcarro. "You're saying I should force the market?"

"That's step number two."

"And, step number one is?"

"After all the time you've spent putting this deal together, you've got to know him and his company inside out."

"I do."

"So step number one is . . . find out what you don't know."

AT EIGHT O'CLOCK New York time, Carson phoned Warring to say the only thing that seemed to make any sense. "I'm working on it."

Warring's mood hadn't changed. "Don't bullshit me."

Carson promised, "I'm not going to let you down."

Warring warned him, "I'm not going to sit around listening to bullshit for very long," and slammed down the phone.

CARSON CORRALLED Mesumi and one of Arcarro's traders, a fellow named Matthew who'd been with them for four months, sat them down in the conference room with their laptops and said, "Shigetada Industries. Find me a way in."

"Like what?" Matthew wanted to know.

"Like anything and everything. Go to analysts' reports, pink sheets, Internet rumors, intel, out-tel, under-tel." He sat down with them. "Whatever there is." He pointed to Mesumi, "You get the Japanese pages."

At ten Arcarro stopped in to ask, "How goes it?"

Carson answered, "Nothing yet."

At 10:30, Matthew stepped out to do a conference call that he'd set up days ago and didn't come back for over an hour.

By noon, they still hadn't found anything on Shigetada Industries that Carson could use.

"I wish we knew what we were supposed to be looking for," Matthew said, motioning toward the printouts that were now cluttering up the conference table.

Carson thought about calling Warring but didn't. He was afraid of what Warring might say.

At two, Matthew stood up and announced, "I'm getting cross-eyed. I need to take a walk."

Now there was only Mesumi and Carson in the conference room.

At three, Mesumi finally decided, "Matthew's right. Maybe if we knew what we were looking for."

"Anything and everything."

"Which is why we've got nothing and nothing."

"I can't tell you because . . . " he admitted, "I don't know."

"Not very helpful."

He leaned all the way back in his chair, then swung his legs onto the table, spilling some papers onto the floor. "Fuck it."

Mesumi pushed her chair back from the table, stood up and stretched. "Maybe we're looking for the wrong things."

"I'll know it when I see it . . . but I can't tell you what it is until I see it."

"We're looking for a way in."

"And found nothing."

"So let's pretend we're already in . . . "

He finished the sentence for her. "And look for a way out?"

She nodded. "Thank you, Princeton."

"What would get us out?" He thought for a moment. "What would get us to sell?"

"Labor unrest."

"None."

"Negative analysts reports, falling share prices . . . various ratios going the wrong way, tax problems, diminishing asset base, pending government regulations, other sellers . . . "

"Stop." He sat up and started fumbling through the piles of printouts on the table.

"Other sellers?" Mesumi asked.

"Tax problems. Ten years ago. Old man Shigetada had a tax problem." He hunted through a pile of printouts. "Here. Just a blurb. Went to court, then quickly settled it. The old man paid out. But then look at this . . . " He fumbled through more printouts until he found what he was looking for. "This intel report shows considerably less trading in Shigetada shares right after the tax case when Junior suddenly took a prolonged vacation."

"Which means?"

"Which means the old man was pissed at his son because Junior was playing the market. He was doing all the trading. What's the Japanese version of Lexis?"

"Lexus? The car? It is Japanese."

"Not the car. LexisNexis. The legal database."

"I think . . . there must be a Japanese version of Lexis."

"Get on it," he said. "Or whatever you can, and find out what happened when old man Shigetada went to court."

It took a while, but she found it. "Trading profits on the company's books . . . offset by various things so that no tax was paid."

Carson looked at her. "And?"

"And apparently the courts said this was private trading. Nothing to do with the business."

"The son?"

"Doesn't say. But it sure looks like that."

"I wonder if he's still a player?"

Now the two of them dove headfirst into every historical database they could find that noted short selling of Shigetada shares. There was nothing of any note after Shigetada senior's tax problems, until three years ago, when it picked up with regularity.

"Why three years ago?" Mesumi looked at Carson.

"That's when old man Shigetada died and Junior could play again."

"So this is what we've been looking for."

"I think so." But he wasn't sure so he kept looking, until he spotted some buying through Chiba, the investment bank owned by Shigetada's cousins. "Bingo. This is him."

At four, Carson phoned Warring on his cell, but got voice mail. He left a message.

At five, he phoned back, got voice mail again, and now rang Warring's office. His secretary Stella answered. "He's flying. I'll get a message to him and he'll call you when he lands."

At six Warring phoned. "What have you got?"

"The way out . . . and back in."

"Huh?"

"Shigetada's a player. He got caught doing it ten years ago when his old man was running the show. He was forced to stop. But when the old man died, he got back into the game."

"How do you know this?"

"Historical analysis."

"And you're sure it's him?"

"Yeah. We don't know what name he's using but some of the recent fooling around has been through an operation owned by his cousins. Chiba Investment Bank. It's him."

"You're betting on that with my money," Warring said flatly.

"With our money and my ass."

"As long as you put it that way . . . "

"Normally, we both have three choices. Buy, sell, wait out the other one. What we know, pretty much for sure, is that he doesn't want to sell. If he did, he would have."

"Maybe it's a question of the price."

"I doubt it. Shigetada grew up in a society where honor matters. He gave his word to us. Backing out is dishonorable. He wouldn't go there if it was only about money."

"So what's he thinking?"

"He's thinking we were more dishonorable than him by trying to railroad him out of his daddy's company."

"Not sure about the dishonorable part," Warring said, "but he's right about the railroading."

"What he doesn't know is what you want. My guess is he's waiting on you to take one last shot, then you bail out."

"So he's gonna run up the price."

"No," Carson said. "He's going to do nothing until you hit the sell button, then he's going to sink the price like a stone. He's going to sell short every-thing he owns so that you're selling at a loss."

"If it starts getting that low, why wouldn't we become buyers again?"

"'Cause if you start buying the shares he's selling short, he'll change gears and run up the price again. He's betting he can control the market. It's not that liquid to begin with, and because he's in Tokyo and you're in no place he ever heard of called Omaha, he takes you for a schmuck."

"In the meantime," Warring asked skeptically, "what are we doing?"

"Playing the dark pools to set the trap," Carson said. "We've got more than enough shares to manipulate the price. Hiding behind shells and dummy companies, we lay in wait for him to go crazy selling short. He will. He'll be counting on you to sell into a sinking market, not realizing that we're control-ling it. A couple of big banks come in, hedge funds, too, and when it's enough that everybody's starting to scramble for shares to cover their short selling, we rush back in and dry up all the liquidity."

"So we're going to suffocate the bastard."

"It's not going to be pretty."

"You can pull this off?"

"A short squeeze? Yeah, I can."

"Without sinking us at the same time?"

"If we start drawing water, don't panic."

"You got a good term-life policy?"

Carson wanted to know, "What for?"

Warring told him, "So that if we go under, Alicia can become a very rich widow."

72

"It doesn't matter where the coat was," Riordan got into Belasco's face. "What you have never gotten through your head is that when it comes to the security of Trump Tower and the people who live here, and the people who work here, and the people who walk through the front door because they want to see what it looks like inside . . . I'm in charge."

"I never said you weren't."

"You have consistently undermined me and consistently gotten in the way of letting me do what I know is right."

"Bill . . . I have never done anything of the kind."

"Then why did you have that woman hire Carlos Vela?"

"Because he was innocent. I knew it then, and you know it now. And Essen-bach knew it, as well."

"It doesn't matter who knew what or when. It doesn't matter that you found the coat. Security isn't some television courtroom drama. In the real world, everybody is presumed guilty until proven otherwise."

"He has been proven otherwise."

"When this first happened, you made a big to-do about how innocent he was. You then undermined my authority by allowing him back into the building. Your actions are all the more galling now that it turns out you secretly thought he was guilty. Believe me, you still have a lot of questions to answer to me . . . "

"What are you talking about? I never thought he was guilty."

"The hell you didn't."

"Not at all."

"Then how do you account for this?" He handed Belasco an e-mail from Anthony Gallicano to Donald Trump. "Concerning the employee in question, Carlos Vela, Belasco reports there is sufficient evidence for dismissal. The resident is adamant. Your call."

"I never said that."

"It's right there."

"Anthony's got it wrong." Belasco reached for his phone and called Gallicano. "The Carlos Vela matter? Maintenance guy we dismissed on Mrs. Essenbach's insistence over a vicuna coat? Do you happen to recall what I said about the evidence against him?"

"No."

He reminded him, "Remember, Mrs. Essenbach was adamant. But I wasn't so sure about the evidence."

"Yes. I guess I do remember that. She was adamant. That rings a bell. You said something about there being insufficient evidence against him."

"But Bill Riordan showed me an e-mail you sent to DJT quoting me as saying there is sufficient evidence."

"Not me."

"I have it right in front of me."

"I never said that. I told the boss what you told me."

Now he wondered, "Who else has access to your e-mail account?"

"No one," Gallicano said. "No one at all."

"Hold on." He passed the phone to Riordan. "Something's not right here."

Those two men talked until Riordan assured Gallicano, "I'll check." He hung up and said to Belasco, "We have back-ups of everything," and left the office.

REBECCA BATTELLI stepped into Belasco's office.

"Have you got two seconds for me?"

He smiled. "Of course I do."

"We've been looking for those letters. The ones my husband wrote. We've been through almost everything. They're gone."

"What's the next step?"

"Good morning," Forbes said, standing in the doorway with Belasco's suit.

"You're timing is perfect," Belasco pointed to his suit. "Where did you get that?"

"Our mutual friends." He handed the suit to Belasco then said hello to Rebecca. "How are you getting on?"

"Fine . . . better . . . well, okay," she said.

"Am I interrupting?" When they both shook their heads, no, he said to Belasco, "You and I have a lot to talk about," then turned to Rebecca. "But first, you should expect a call today from your husband's cousin Johnny."

"Oh?"

"He's going to tell you that he had nothing to do with the break-in. He will then tell you that his lawyer will draw up a letter to you renouncing any claim to the business."

She was astonished. "How do you know this?"

"Some people visited him early yesterday evening in Florida," he said. "You are clear to continue the business without worrying about anyone else interfering ever again."

Belasco offered, "Perhaps now's a good time to call my accountant. Let him see what the state of the business looks like. At that point, you'll be in a better position to make a decision."

After a few seconds she said, "I don't know. Carlos is still fixing up the office . . . I'm thinking I may go away for a little while. Can it wait?"

"Yes."

"I'll call you." She forced a smile, nodded and walked out.

Belasco took a deep breath, then asked Forbes, "Where did you get my suit?" He hung it in the small closet behind the office door. "I presume it tested negative . . . for whatever it was they tested it for."

"It did."

That's when Bill Riordan stepped through Belasco's doorway and handed him an envelope. "Some printouts you will want to see."

Belasco opened the envelope and saw what they were. "If you don't mind, Bill, I'd like to handle this myself."

"If you don't want to, I'd be happy to."

"I can do it, thank you."

"If you need me," Riordan said to him, "we are, in fact, on the same side."

"I know. Thank you."

Riordan left.

"Okay," Forbes said. "Here's the deal. The police have now issued an arrest warrant for Mrs. Essenbach's husband. Apparently his name is . . . " He took out a notepad and read it from there . . . "Julio de Garcia-Gutierrez. He's a former Chilean diplomat. There's an Interpol Red Notice on him, issued by the Spanish government for theft. Nasty piece of work tied in to the late General Pinochet. That brings the Feebs into the game."

"The Feebs?"

"FBI," Forbes nodded, then continued. "The husband is officially considered a person of interest in his wife's murder. At the same time, they want to talk to David and Tina Cove. She left the country on Friday night, kind of suddenly, and boarded a flight to Hong Kong. David also left suddenly sometime on Friday. He's got a plane at Teterboro. The pilot filed a flight plan for Houston but never arrived. The police located his car at the airport in long-term parking but haven't located him yet. Whether the Coves have anything to do with Mrs. Essenbach . . . who knows. A coincidence? The cops don't know . . . yet."

Belasco asked, "What about the vicuna-coat kid, Carlos Vela?"

"He's clear. He told the cops he went to see Mrs. Essenbach because he wanted her to know he never took anything from her."

"And he didn't," Belasco reiterated.

"As for the elevator operator, Tejeda, he was banging her. Apparently, he wasn't the only one on the staff. Seems she liked young guys."

Belasco reached into his pocket and took out his Metro Card. "The cops wanted to see this. I found it at home."

Forbes waved him off. "They've seen the CCTV tape at Seventy-Seventh Street. You were there. They also dropped your phone LUDs. In case you might have called some Mafia creep to knock her off."

"I don't know any Mafia creeps."

"After checking your phone calls for the past thirty days, they couldn't find any, either."

"Thirty days? They checked every call I made?"

"And received," he added. "They've eliminated that woman who works here, Antonia something, and the actor Seasons. But there are three things that continue to interest them."

"Which are?"

"First, the man coming out of Essenbach's apartment after Antonia arrives with Seasons. She kissed him in the CCTV footage. Name's Clarence O'Bannion. He comes up on radar screens as a minor hood. Pretends to be well connected but probably isn't. He's now a person of interest."

"Second?"

"The guy who appears to be taking a photo of Cove and Essenbach downstairs in the food court."

"You really think he's taking a photo? Maybe he's just walking by."

"Turns out your friend Mr. Cove has friends in Colombia and Mexico."

Belasco shrugged, "Just because he knows people who . . . "

"Does business with them. Makes money? Loses money? Steals money? What if he cheated someone and Mrs. Essenbach turns up with him in the wrong place at the wrong time?"

He hadn't thought of that. "You mean somebody thinks she's involved with him, and she winds up getting murdered by mistake?"

"Odds are long . . . but, then, every guy who wins a hundred million bucks playing the lottery says, I never thought it would happen to me."

Belasco tried to take it all in, then fell onto his couch. He looked at Forbes and sighed. "I sometimes wonder . . . you know . . . if God really does have a plan for the universe. Doesn't look like it most days. Maybe all he does is sit there and roll the dice and move the little pieces around the board."

"Sorry, pal, metaphysics is above my pay grade."

He grinned. "What's the third thing?"

"You."

"Me?"

"The cop who shaves his head, Stoyanov, he's bothered by the fact that you didn't tell them that Mrs. Essenbach was going to sue you."

"No, I didn't."

"Why not?"

"I didn't think it was relevant."

Forbes warned him, "Motives for murder are always relevant."

BELASCO WAITED until the end of the day before he phoned Antonia to say he wanted to speak with her immediately. She started making excuses about being too busy, about being too upset about Mrs. Essenbach, about having a conflicting appointment with her dentist. But he told her, "Five thirty," in no uncertain terms, and she showed up on time.

"This is awful about Mrs. Essenbach. And before you say it, I was wrong bringing Tommy into the building. But Mrs. Essenbach said to me that she was a huge fan, so I thought if I introduced them . . . "

He handed her two printouts from the envelope Riordan had given him. "I need you to explain these."

The first was Tony Gallicano's original e-mail to Donald Trump saying that Belasco reported "insufficient" grounds for Carlos Vela's dismissal. The second was the e-mail actually sent from Gallicano's computer where the word "insufficient" was changed to "sufficient."

She read them, "I don't know anything about this," and tossed them onto Belasco's desk.

He handed her another printout. "You see the time you logged into your computer? That's when you got to the office that morning."

"So what?" She was becoming nervously defiant. "What does any of this have to do with me?"

"Look at the log-in times. Your computer stayed on for the entire day. His was only on for two minutes. Then eight minutes later, someone logs onto his computer again and stays on for the entire day."

"This has nothing to do with me. You need to speak with Tony . . . "

"This has everything to do with you." He handed her another printout. "Those are the computers on your floor. Yours was the first logged-on that morning. Except for the two minutes that Mr. Gallicano's computer was on, none of the others logged on for eight minutes. That's Mr. Gallicano. It's fifteen minutes later before anyone else on the floor is logged on."

"So what? This doesn't prove . . . "

"You were alone in the office. You logged on to Mr. Gallicano's computer, hacked his e-mails, changed insufficient to sufficient and logged off."

She crossed her arms and stared past him. "Antonia did nothing of the kind. You can't prove that Antonia . . . "

"Then why . . . " he handed her yet another printout . . . "did Antonia receive an e-mail in her private Gmail account from Mr. Gallicano's computer during those two minutes when he was logged on?"

She didn't say a word.

He reminded her, "Everything is backed up. I've got incontrovertible evidence that violates any number of company rules. What's more, you have, probably, also broken the law."

She scowled, then warned him, "And I know everything about you."

"What does that mean?"

"It means I know everything. Absolutely everything. I know about . . . " She blurted out, "I know about your wife and son."

"What?" He felt the blood rushing out of his face.

"That's right . . . everything there is to know about you. If you make trouble for me . . . "

He had to fight hard to control his temper. "You have two choices. Tender your resignation, or I take this to Anthony Gallicano who will summarily fire you. Along with your firing will come a formal investigation into all of your activities during your employment here. At that time, I will recommend that the police be brought in."

"You do that," she snapped, "and Antonia goes public with what Antonia knows about you. When people find out . . . when Antonia tells them . . . "

"When Antonia tells them what?"

"Everything."

He exploded, "That my wife was killed?"

"Everything."

"That I lost my child?"

"Everything."

He paused for a second, then said in a softer tone, "Antonia, you need serious help."

She railed, "Antonia will get even."

"But Antonia won't be working here anymore."

"Why are you doing this to me?"

He pointed toward the door. "You resign . . . or you're fired. Either way, clear out of your office within twenty-four hours."

She leaned forward and then screamed at him at the top of her lungs, "Antonia says, fuck you," and stormed out of his office.

It took him a while to calm down.

Eventually, he opened his laptop and began writing a report, outlining everything she'd done. If she didn't resign, he intended to send it to Donald Trump, Anthony Gallicano and Carole Ann Mendelsohn.

But long before he finished writing this, he sat back and thought about what had happened all those years ago on a rainy night in Paris.

He'd never discussed it with anyone here. He never wanted anyone here to know. But now, someone knew.

And for one slight moment, he thought, *maybe it's time.*

In an odd way, it was as if this thing that he'd carried inside him for all these years had suddenly been set free.

Someone here knows.

It is no longer a secret.

He finished writing that report, saved it, but didn't send it, and went home.

Rummaging through a carton at the back of the closet in the hallway, he found the silver picture frame he'd put away a very long time ago.

He hadn't looked at it in years.

His eyes filled with tears.

No longer a secret.

For the longest time, he clung to that photo.

And after a while, he stopped crying.

Then, before he went to bed, he cleared a space on his night table, put the frame there, and angled it so that he could see it.

No longer a secret.

He fell asleep looking at the beautiful, young, smiling wife who stood next to her husband, so proudly holding their newborn son.

TUESDAY

73

Zeke had his usual car and driver take Cyndi, Carson and him up to Yankee Stadium at five o'clock, then rush back downtown to be at NBC at 6:30 for Alicia.

Getting out at Gate 4, they made their way past several security checkpoints—the guards all loved Cyndi's Yankee uniform, which looked real except for the pinstriped hot pants—and to the entrance of the ultraprivate Legends' Suite.

Given wristbands to show they had access, they were escorted by a Yankee hostess through a series of blue-lit dining rooms—with flat-screen TVs everywhere—to a table where, the hostess reminded them, everything was free.

"It always tastes better that way," Cyndi remarked.

On one side of the room there was a huge buffet with meat, fish, salads, vegetables, fruit, and desserts. Nearby was the largest mountain of every kind of candy that any of them had ever seen.

Zeke shook his head. "Dentists must love this place."

"Dentists are probably the only people who can afford it," Carson said. "This is Yankee fan heaven."

"Is this what the private side of Wimbledon is like?" Zeke asked him.

"Wimbledon is good, but the food is much better here. Look at this place. And no waiter at Wimbledon in the players' dining room would know what to do if you wanted . . . " he pointed to two young teenage boys walking away from the candy mountain, each juggling four boxes of Cracker Jacks . . . "that."

Someone from the staff reminded them, "If you don't want to eat now, we will bring you anything you want while in your seats during the game."

"That's another difference with Wimbledon," Carson said. "No way can you get a cheeseburger and a Bud at center court."

They debated the buffet, but after they ordered drinks at their table and a waiter came by to ask if he could bring them anything, Cyndi ordered a salad, Zeke went for the roast beef and Carson had the lamb.

The three of them sat eating their early dinner, looking out at the field, stopping every now and then to say hello to people who came by the table.

When a couple of middle-aged guys asked if Cyndi would take a photo with them, she said sure. Then two teenage boys nervously approached the table to ask if they could take a photo with her, too.

"Have you noticed," Carson said quietly to Zeke as Cyndi in her hot pants stood in between the two overgrinning boys, and one of the hostesses snapped the picture, "every time someone comes near the table, a hostess appears to ask if she can get something for us."

"Just the Yankees' way of making sure no one tries to cop a feel of Cyndi," Zeke said. "It's called personal attention."

Carson smiled. "Can you imagine what would happen if the airlines paid this much personal attention to their passengers who aren't Cyndi?"

"Yeah," Zeke assured him, "they'd be broke before the plane even took off."

At quarter to seven they decided to go to their seats.

"Powder room first," Cyndi stood up and looked around.

A female staff member rushed up to ask, "May I help you?"

"Ladies'?"

"This way please . . . " and the staff member led the way.

A few minutes later, Cyndi rushed back to the table to assure Carson and Zeke, "You will not believe what they have in there."

Carson tried, "Guys?"

"Better. High-def television screens set into the back of every sink so you can watch the game while you wash your hands."

Before they left the Legends' Suite, Alicia rang from the car to say, "I'm on my way." Carson told her where to pick up her ticket and how to find them.

An usher accompanied them out of the Legends' Suite, down past one level of box seats and to the very first row, immediately behind home plate.

"Waiting for my wife," Carson said, tipping him twenty dollars.

"I'll see that she finds you when she gets here."

The three of them sat down. The seats were like recliners.

As the Yankees warmed up, Derek Jeter walked by to say hello, and so did A-Rod.

Then a waiter appeared to ask if there was anything they wanted. Zeke and Carson ordered a beer. Cyndi said that mineral water would be fine. That's when Roberto stopped by. "I'm really glad you guys could come to a game," he said, looking at Cyndi. "I don't think they sell that uniform in our souvenir shop."

She turned around to show him that the shirt had his number on the back.

He nearly blushed. "The guys will never let me live this down."

The waiter returned with the drinks and at exactly seven o'clock, five minutes before the game was scheduled to begin, the Yankee announcer came over the loudspeaker.

"Ladies and gentlemen . . . and Yankee fans of all ages . . . may we direct your attention please to the jumbo-vision screen in the outfield . . . and all the other screens around Yankee Stadium."

Suddenly, there on the big screen was Roberto Santos standing next to a dozen kids in wheelchairs. "Hi, I'm Roberto Santos."

Subtitles rolled across the bottom of the screen in Spanish.

"As many of you know . . . when I first came here to the Yankees, I founded a charity called Gloves for Kids. I started it to help provide gloves, bats and balls for special-needs children all over the greater New York area."

A young boy in a wheelchair waved his glove at the camera. "I play first base." Another young boy raised a bat. "I'm like Roberto, I bat cleanup." A young girl threw a ball toward the cameras. "I'm a starting pitcher."

"Today," Roberto said, "we help bring baseball to more than twenty thousand special-needs kids all over the country, so they can play baseball too. Tonight, when you see one of our volunteers with the Gloves for Kids badge and the special collection cup, please . . . please give generously. Thank you."

All the kids around him waved their gloves and bats, threw balls at the camera and laughed, "Thank you."

Some people applauded.

The announcer then said, "Ladies and gentlemen, the New York Yankees are proud to participate in Roberto's Gloves for Kids drive. So on behalf of the Yankees, for every strike pitched by a New York Yankee, the club will donate fifty dollars to Gloves for Kids. And every time a Cleveland Indians pitcher throws a ball, the New York Yankees will donate another fifty dollars to Gloves for Kids. Please give generously. And now, will everyone please stand for the singing of the National Anthem."

More people applauded, the National Anthem was sung, and the announcer came back to say, "Please welcome, our New York Yankees as they take the field."

And the game began.

Alicia arrived at the top of the second inning, was brought to the front row by an usher, and slipped into the seat next to Cyndi. "I used to think that watching baseball was better at home, in bed, with a good book. I take it back."

"I don't know," Cyndi said, "watching baseball in bed with a shortstop probably isn't so bad . . . "

Carson reminded her, "The Holy Ghost plays center field."

"So," Cyndi shrugged, "a shortstop and a center fielder."

Zeke whispered to Carson, "She's joking, right?"

"Yeah," Carson said. "What she really means is a third baseman and a center fielder."

The Indians went ahead 2–0 in the third, and the Yankees caught up to make it 2–2 in the fifth.

Sitting right behind home plate like that, they could see where every pitch crossed the plate. In the bottom of the sixth, with Roberto at bat, when the umpire called a very high pitch a strike, Cyndi shouted out, "Come on ump, we can get fifty bucks for his balls."

The umpire actually turned around to look at her.

Roberto stepped off the plate, turned away, and Alicia thought she saw him blush.

"I was with your guy Warring recently," Zeke said to Carson. "He mentioned briefly that you were doing a big deal in Japan together."

"Which may or may not work. Ken's worse than these guys," he nodded toward the Yankees. "They hate losing. He really hates losing."

Cleveland came to bat in the top of the seventh and the lead-off guy got a single to right field.

"I don't blame him," Zeke said. "We brought him in on this studio project we're trying to put together. It's a great project if we can pull it off. And I think we can. I found one guy who might even be willing to foot the whole bill for us. Ever hear of L. Arthur Farmer?"

"Whoa," Carson said. "You've been dealing with Farmer?"

"Not with him directly. His people."

"Hold on." He reached across behind Zeke and tapped Alicia on the shoulder. "Ask Zeke about his new best friend."

The guy on first stole second and then Cleveland got another single to shallow center. The guy on second headed for third as Roberto raced in to take the ball on one hop. The base runner rounded third and headed for home. Roberto wound up and threw to the plate.

The crowd stood up.

The ball came right into the catcher's glove, and the base runner hurried back to third.

Standing and applauding Roberto's perfect throw, Alicia looked at Carson and then at Zeke. "New best friend?"

Zeke didn't understand what her interest was. "Ever hear of L. Arthur Farmer?"

Her eyes opened wide. "You know him?"

"Not him, his people."

They all sat down.

"I think he was the first buyer into Trump Tower." She said, "I'm writing a book for the thirtieth anniversary."

"I know. Remember? You wrote to ask if you could photograph my apartment . . ."

"Right. So I started looking at other people who have lived in the Tower, and his name came up. But I can't find anything about him. No one even knows if he's alive or dead."

The next batter knocked the ball out of Yankee Stadium and the Indians went ahead 5–2.

"I'm dealing with a strange guy named Isbister. I don't have his number but I'll try to get it for you. You can phone him and ask."

"Thank you," she said. "By strange . . . do you know if he's particularly religious?"

"In fact, he told me he is."

She smiled and nodded. "He's a Finfolkmen. Farmer is surrounded by them . . . "

"A what?"

"Finfolkmen. It's a small religion. Farmer is surrounded by these guys, like Howard Hughes was surrounded by Mormons."

"Finfolkmen? Never heard of them."

"I know a lot about them. Someday when you've got a week, I'll fill you in. But I'd really love to talk to this guy . . . "

"James Malcolm Isbister."

"I'm trying to figure out if Farmer was the first person to buy into Trump Tower and if he, or his people, maybe still live there. Nobody knows anything . . . "

"I hadn't thought of that," Zeke said. "Isbister had something delivered to my apartment. The guy who delivered it wasn't announced from the desk downstairs. No one called up. He just knocked on the door."

"Which . . . " she concluded, "he could only do if he was already in the building."

Three more batters came up, and the Yankees put them down, then did nothing in the bottom of the seventh. They did nothing in the eighth and now, in the bottom of the ninth, Roberto came to bat with no one on. He knocked the ball into the second tier in left field.

The stadium went wild, hoping for a late rally, and when Roberto stepped on home plate, he fist-pumped toward Cyndi.

But it wasn't enough and the Yankees lost 5–3.

On the way out, Zeke handed $500 to one of the Gloves for Kids donation volunteers. Carson gave them $500 as well. Alicia only had a few hundred on her and handed it all over. But Cyndi didn't put anything in the donation cup.

"That's for both of us," Alicia said, trying to cover up for Cyndi.

"It's okay," Cyndi said, "I have another idea," and left it like that.

BACK AT the concierge desk at Trump Tower, Cyndi, Zeke and Carson each wrote notes for Roberto to say thank you for a great night out. Then Cyndi, Zeke and Carson headed for the elevators, while Alicia stayed where she was. "I'll be right up."

When they were gone, Alicia asked Carlo, the night concierge, "Is Mr. Timmins on security tonight?"

"He is," Carlo answered.

"Would you give him a call please. I'd like to have a word with him."

Carlo dialed his extension and a few minutes later Timmins came downstairs to find Alicia.

"I never got a chance to thank you in person for what you did for Suzy," he said.

She took his elbow and led him outside to Fifty-Sixth Street, where they started walking toward Madison Avenue. "She's a great girl. She'll do fine at NBC. And you did thank me because she brought those chocolates."

"She thinks you're the best," Timmins said. "She's a terrific girl . . . and you gave her a chance . . . my wife and I are really very grateful."

Now Alicia changed the subject. "Tell me something . . . strictly off the record . . . between us . . . never to go any further . . . " She asked, "Does L. Arthur Farmer live in the building?"

"Who?"

"L. Arthur Farmer. He's a zillionaire recluse who owns or controls like a lot of the world's rice."

"Never heard of him," Timmins said.

"Honestly? Off the record . . . "

"Honestly, never heard of him."

"How about a man named Isbister?"

He shook his head. "Nope. Not that I know."

She thought for a moment, "When someone delivers something, they have to stop at the concierge and the concierge calls up to say there's a delivery."

"Right."

"So how could someone deliver something without calling up from downstairs?"

"They can't."

"Unless they're already in the building."

"Ah . . . yeah, sure, if someone was already in the building . . . but even then, if the elevator guy didn't know that person, he's supposed to ask, who the hell are you? Well, maybe not in those exact words . . . "

She smiled. "If I knew the time and date that someone delivered a package, what are the chances of having a quick look at the CCTV footage?"

"None," he said right away. "Please don't even ask. I mean, Miss Melendez, I'd do anything in the world for you . . . anything . . . except that. It's my ass if anybody ever found out."

"That's all right," she said. "Forget that I even thought of it."

"No problem." He turned around and headed for the entrance to Trump Tower. "I've got to get back to work."

She patted his arm. "Suzy is a great girl. You can be proud."

He said goodnight to her in the lobby.

Upstairs, Carson asked, "What was that all about?"

Alicia told him, "If L. Arthur Farmer ever lived here, no one is going to help me find out."

"How about," he asked, "if L. Arthur Farmer never lived here? Or doesn't live here? How about if you're barking up the wrong tree altogether?"

She reminded him, "When Zeke gets that Finfolkmen guy's phone number, I'll ask him."

"In the meantime?"

She stared at Carson for a second, smiled, then started slipping out of her clothes. "What did Cyndi say, fifty bucks for his balls? I'll give you a hundred."

74

On Wednesday morning, when Pierre Belasco walked into his office on the ground floor of Trump Tower, off the residents' lobby, he found a large, white envelope with his name on it.

Inside was a letter from Antonia Lawrence addressed to Donald J. Trump, Anthony Gallicano and him.

She wrote, "Circumstances beyond my control have intervened in my ability to carry out my duties with the Trump Organization. I regret any mistakes I might have made. Accordingly, I feel it is best for everyone involved that I herewith resign my duties. I thank you for the opportunities I have been given and wish everyone well."

IN THE master bedroom on the fifty-ninth floor, Cyndi Benson lay in bed alone, staring up at her own reflection in the mirrored ceiling. "Buy me some peanuts and Cracker Jacks . . . "

She smiled, then reached for her phone and called her lawyer, Sydney Feinberg.

"You're up early," he said. "I took care of that little matter . . . Arizona. I understand that your friend's friend is having treatment."

"And they don't know?"

"I made sure that it was covered six ways to breakfast. There's no way they'll ever know it came from you."

"Good. Thank you. Now I need to do it again. I'm sending you an envelope this morning. I'll write a note outlining everything. Please take care of it for me. And make sure no one ever finds out."

"Your secrets are always good with me," he said.

"I know. I love you." She pushed herself out of bed, went to the smaller of the two safes she had in the apartment—this one was in the floor in the second bathroom—opened it and pulled out the diamond watch that His Excellency had sent her. She put it in a padded envelope, which she addressed to Sydney.

Then she wrote him a note. "Please sell this for me, getting as close to the retail price as you can. Take the proceeds and donate it anonymously, absolutely and totally anonymously, to the Roberto Santos Gloves for Kids program/ xxx Cyndi."

IN THE dining room on their fifty-second-floor apartment, Alicia sat with her laptop trying to find anything she could about James Malcolm Isbister.

Nothing came up when she searched the terms, Isbister and Trump Tower. Nor did anything come up when she searched Isbister and L. Arthur Farmer. But hundreds of links came up when she searched Isbister and Finfolkmen, most of them noting that the name Isbister was an old Scots name, and examples of it could be found in the United States in some small communities bordering on Lake Superior in Michigan's Upper Peninsula.

So now she wrote a note to Donald Trump and Pierre Belasco, asking them if they've ever heard of L. Arthur Farmer, and whether or not Farmer ever had anything to do with Trump Tower.

DOWNSTAIRS, in the twenty-third-floor offices of First Ace Capital, things were moving even faster than Carson had imagined they could.

He was on the phone with Milt McKeever at EXIT-Strategies. "Time to set the trap?"

"Yeah. We confuse him with buying and selling. The increased traffic will peak his interest and then we wait to see how he reacts."

"If he buys, we sell and if he sells . . . "

"Not necessarily," McKeever said. "We just need to create confusion in the market. It's shallow enough so it shouldn't be a problem. But if he's seeing action from several different places, he won't know who or what, and that's going to scare the crap out of him."

"Which accounts do we use to go after him?"

"We should spread them as wide as we can."

Carson thought about that for a moment. "Caymans? Luxembourg? Hong Kong?"

"All of the above. And New York is okay, too, as long as it doesn't look like it's you. How about London? Can you work something with Tokyo?"

"I'm on it right now," he said. "You tell me what to do and when."

"Get everything set up as soon as possible. Like, right now. We'll aim for just after midnight, our time, tonight. That way, there won't be anyone he can find at work here. Europe will be closed, too. This will drive him crazy."

"How do I know when to push the button? Will you e-mail me?"

"No, I'll text your cell," McKeever said. "Harder to trace, just in case the SEC ever comes looking."

"Okay. Yeah . . . sure." Except Carson wasn't sure. "The SEC?"

"As long as none of the accounts can be traced back to you . . . "

"I'm not worried about that."

"Then don't worry about the SEC. Just follow my texts. I'll tell you what to do, to buy or sell, and I'll give you the pricing. You put the orders in. But be sure to use a different money source every time. You'll be selling into yourself, buying at the same time, so he can't ever get hold of any of your shares. The minute he understands he's on the outside looking in, he'll panic. That will unnerve other players."

"And then?"

"And then he'll make a mistake."

"Which will be?"

"No idea. But we'll know it when we see it."

IN HIS big living room office on the thirty-ninth floor, Zeke Gimbel was getting ready to meet with James Malcolm Isbister to firm up Farmer's participation in the studio project, when Isbister phoned.

"I'm terribly sorry about this. I'm running late."

"No problem," Zeke said. "By the way, as long as I've got you on the phone, I was out last night with Alicia Melendez . . . the anchorwoman at *News Four New York* . . . you know the local channel four. She told me she's writing a history of Trump Tower and thought that Mr. Farmer either once lived here or does live here, and I said I'd put you two together . . . if I gave you her number, would you be kind enough to phone her?"

"No," he said flatly. "Absolutely not."

"Oh." He was surprised at the man's tone. "I'll vouch for her . . . "

"I'm terribly sorry, Mr. Gimbel, but this is not something I appreciate."

"I didn't mean to insult you . . . "

"Mr. Gimbel, I'm afraid we can no longer discuss any business arrangements with you. Indiscretion is not something we tolerate, and when Mr. Farmer's name is brought up . . . "

"Hold on, all I did was say to a friend . . . "

"Please accept my sincerest apologies for canceling our meeting today and terminating our negotiations. I wish you luck in your endeavors and must now end this call. Goodbye, sir."

Isbister hung up.

For the longest time, Zeke stared at the phone in his hand. "What the fuck was that all about?"

THE FIRST text message from McKeever showed up on Carson's phone at 12:02, Thursday morning. *Sell at 40, buy it back.* Two minutes later another showed up. *Sell at 41, buy it back.* Then there were several in the space of the next minute. *Sell at 39. Sell at 38. Sell at 38. Sell at 39. Sell at 38. Keep buying.*

Carson did what he was told to.

At 12:11, his phone rang. It was McKeever to say, "There's action . . . a lot of it."

Carson clicked on his screen and saw the Shigetada share price dropping. "Looks like he's a worried man."

"He's certainly a confused man. He started shorting at forty. He came in with some real ambition at thirty-eight. He spooked the banks and they came in at thirty-seven. He dumped a big bundle at thirty-six. Hedge funds have forced it down to thirty-two. One bank is in heavy . . . Chiba. They're playing alongside Shigetada, and the two of them are going nuts. They're both sniffing around . . . hold on . . . wow, they've dropped as low as thirty. See that? You watching the screen? Everybody must be thinking the hedge funds are driving it even lower."

"I see it. At what point does Shigetada run out of cover?"

"This market?" McKeever suggested, "I say the minute he dips under thirty. Chiba might have deep pockets, but your guy's in quicksand. I mean, he's out of control. He's spinning the wheel nonstop."

"What does the liquidity look like?"

"Right now, besides you, there's next to nil."

"What do you want me to do?"

"Nothing yet. Just stay on the line with me. Then, suddenly, McKeever screamed, "Holy shit."

"What?"

"He's dumped the biggest bundle of all at twenty-nine. This guy is nuts. Hold on," McKeever said . . . "let me get this up . . . "

Carson could hear him typing on his keyboard.

"Here we go," McKeever said. "Ready? Now. Buy it all. Everything."

"Doing it," Carson said, and furiously put in orders using those accounts scattered around the world.

"Keep going," McKeever kept yelling. "Keep going . . . watch . . . look at your screen . . . keep going . . . "

Carson couldn't type instructions fast enough.

Two minutes later McKeever yelled, "Shot through the roof. I'm telling you, this is beyond awesome. I've never seen a market move like this. Japanese authorities are going to investigate this for the next fifty years."

"We're protected, right?"

"You're completely invisible. And this asshole is still sitting on shorts at twenty-nine. He got greedy."

"Does he have any idea it's us?"

"Who knows? Who cares? If this price keeps climbing . . . fuck me, Carson, there's zero liquidity left in the market . . . nothing . . . this is a bloodbath."

"You're the best," he said to McKeever, hung up with him and dialed Warring on his cell, "I don't know where you are or what time it is where you are, but Shigetada's finished."

"Great. Now get the company."

"Call you right back." Carson phoned his lawyers in Tokyo, "Tell Shigetada he surrenders or dies."

As soon as the lawyers called back, Carson got Warring on the line again. "Done."

"How bad?"

"Finished. It's over. He's wiped out."

"Good work," Warring said. "What else is going on?"

Carson couldn't believe it. "I pull off the deal of the century, take a company you were willing to buy in the mid-forties, steal it for you in the mid-thirties, destroy the guy fifteen times, and all you can ask is what else is going on?"

"Yeah," Warring said. "What do you want me to do, bake you a cake?"

"Strawberry shortcake is good," Carson said.

"We won," Warring said. "That's what is supposed to happen. Now, that's done, what's next?"

LATER THAT morning, and three and a half miles south of Trump Tower, on the second floor of the New York Criminal Court Building at 100 Center

Street, Richard Lipschitz . . . also known as Ricky Lips . . . accompanied by two attorneys, walked into the chambers of Judge Giovanni Vitali.

The prosecutor was already there with an assistant, as were the judge's two clerks.

"Your honor, thank you for handling this in camera," one of Ricky's lawyers said.

The judge looked up and scowled at Ricky, who was dressed in a suit and tie. He shook his head. "Mr. Lipschitz . . . are you fucking crazy?"

Ricky shrugged, "Got to admit judge, I came bleeding close."

"Close only counts in horseshoes and nuclear war. I could throw you in jail. But I always liked the band, so no jail time."

The assistant district attorney who'd been handling the case blurted out, "Rock-star justice, your honor?"

"You could call it that," the judge said. "House arrest, the ankle bracelet stays, another full six months. We're starting from the beginning, Mr. Lipschitz . . . count yourself lucky . . . and this time try to get it right. Goodbye."

"Your honor," Ricky's other lawyer said, "Please reconsider . . . "

"Goodbye," he said, and waved them out of his chambers.

BACK AT Trump Tower, before Alicia left for work, three handwritten notes were delivered to her.

The first was from Zeke Gimbel. "The fellow I mentioned, Farmer's guy, bailed out on me. Sorry, I tried. Won't talk to you or me anymore. I'll phone you later."

The second was from Pierre Belasco. "Although I have heard of Mr. Farmer, vaguely, if he ever was here it's way before my time."

The third was from Trump himself. "Alicia, I hate it when someone asks me to remember something from thirty or more years ago. You are much too gorgeous to force me to admit that I haven't thought about him in years. Ask me about Liberace. Him I remember. Donald."

She shrugged then started to laugh.

"Three strikes. I'm out. Mr. Farmer . . . and all you little Finfolkmen out there, somewhere, farming and Finfolking," she pushed the handwritten notes aside and shut down her computer. "I have to go to my day job now. I'll get back to you one of these days. Maybe. Just don't tell Carson he's sort of right."

TWENTY-NINE FLOORS below her, in the twenty-third-floor offices of First Ace Capital, a delivery boy arrived with a large box. "For Carson Haynes?" He opened it and the note that came with the huge strawberry shortcake read,

"Okay, okay, gloat. But when you're finished with the fucking cake, get back to me with the next deal."

NINE FLOORS above those offices, Ricky Lips stepped into his thirty-second-floor apartment where he found forty people singing, "For He's a Jolly Good Fellow . . ."

Ricky went around the room, planting a big wet kiss on the mouth of every woman there, who'd come to celebrate what they'd thought would be his release, and the return tour of Still Fools.

Little by little, the singing ended as more and more people in the room realized the bracelet was still on his ankle.

Ricky looked at them and simply shrugged, "No one knew how to get the bleeding thing off."

SEVEN FLOORS higher up, in his thirty-ninth-floor living room, Zeke was on a conference call with Lenny Silverberg, Bing O'Leary and Carl Kravitz.

"Don't go back to him," O'Leary said.

"I wouldn't either," Kravitz said.

"We can do the deal without this asshole," Silverberg agreed.

"Okay," Zeke said. "I thought if we needed Farmer's money . . . "

"We don't," Silverberg reiterated. "And anyway, what the fuck are Finfuckers?"

ON FRIDAY MORNING, Forbes walked into Pierre Belasco's ground-floor office at Trump Tower and told him, "You're out of jeopardy."

"What happened?"

"Mainly . . . time ran out on the investigation. Murders get forty-eight to seventy-two hours. If they're not done and dusted by then, they get put on the back shelf until something new comes up."

"They just stop?"

"They don't just stop, they move on to the next one."

"So that's all?"

"Where you're concerned, yes. They've written you off. You won't end up becoming a reality show on some cable channel . . . life on death row."

"Don't joke about that."

"I'd thought you'd be pleased."

"That I'm not being investigated for a murder I had nothing to do with? I would have been pleased if I'd never gotten involved in the first place."

Forbes patted Belasco on the back. "Call me if you need me."

"Thanks," he said as Forbes walked out. "I will."

Suddenly he heard some odd beeps. He went to his desk and found that it was his BlackBerry telling him the battery had run down. He found the charger he kept in the office, put it on a shelf and hooked up his phone.

That's when Gabriella Battelli called. "My mom's going away for about ten days. An old family friend has a house in Tuscany . . . she's leaving tonight and . . . "

"Please tell her I said I hope she has a good trip."

"I will. In the meantime, Carlos is still cleaning up. I'll stop by next week to see how he's getting on and maybe when she comes back . . . "

"The accountant?" Belasco told her, "I hope so."

"No . . . well, yes that too . . . but what I was really going to say was that . . . you know, maybe when she comes back, if you phoned her and suggested something like . . . maybe lunch some Sunday . . . "

NEARLY THREE THOUSAND miles away, David Cove sat in his suite at La Quinta, the Palm Springs hideaway in the shadow of the Santa Rosa Mountains.

Although his flight plan had originally been filed for Houston, David changed it in midair, hoping that way no one could follow him, and flew instead to Kansas City, where he boarded a commercial flight for San Diego. From there he rented a car and drove the rest of the way. He'd played La Quinta for years and knew the manager well enough that he was allowed to check in under a false name.

The first thing he did was get Regis on the phone.

And Regis announced, "I think I found your guy."

"That's great. Grab him and I'll get in the plane and meet you wherever."

"Don't bother. Miami police found a body yesterday meeting his description."

"Oh shit."

"What was the MO of the old lady?"

"What old lady? You mean, Essenbach?"

"How'd she get killed?"

"Papers said it was a single bullet to the temple."

"What caliber?"

"Ah . . . " David tried to remember. "Nine mil?"

"Which side?"

"How the hell do I know?"

"Presumably the right."

"Why? What difference does it make?"

"Same thing with your guy. Single nine mil to the right temple."

"Oh fuck. What do I do now?"

"My advice?" Regis said. "Don't look to your left."

BACK AT Trump Tower, Zeke was on the phone with Alicia. "I meant to call you yesterday. This Isbister guy won't talk to you."

"I got your note. Is he afraid I'll find something?"

"He's a schmuck."

"Do you think he lives in the building?"

"Frankly . . . no."

"Hey, where are you going to be at six thirty tonight? Anywhere near a television set?"

"No. I'm flying home today. Why?"

"Thought I'd ask. Oh well, listen, thanks, anyway."

"See you guys next time through." He hung up, checked to make sure that everything was turned off, locked the door, took his shoulder bag and rang for the elevator.

The elevator doors opened, Jaquim said, "Good morning, Mr. Gimbel," and from behind him came a familiar voice. "As I live and breathe."

Mikey Glass was standing there.

Zeke reminded him, "You're like a bad check that keeps bouncing back."

Mikey pointed to Zeke's shoulder bag, then down to his own. "You wouldn't by chance be flying back to LA today in that gorgeous airplane of yours, would you?"

Jaquim closed the doors and they headed down to the ground floor.

"You on the run again?"

"Not this time," Mikey bragged. "In good graces with the old lady . . . and I even paid my bill at the Commodore. I'm trying to get those circus performers booked into the hotel's cabaret."

"What circus performers?"

"At the Commodore. They love me there."

He nodded, "Someone has to."

"What time we taking off?"

Zeke shook his head and took a deep breath. "They're fueling up now."

The doors opened and the two of them walked through the lobby.

"Your car is waiting," Roberto the doorman said to Zeke.

Mikey put his arm around Zeke and did his best Bogart imitation. "Louie, I think this is the beginning of a beautiful friendship."

MUCH LATER that afternoon, seven and a half blocks south of Trump Tower, in Studio 3C at 30 Rockefeller Center, Michael Douglas' voice introduced *NBC Nightly News* with Brian Williams.

But it was Alicia sitting in Williams' place behind the big desk.

"Good evening," she said straight to camera, "I'm Alicia Melendez in for Brian Williams. On our broadcast tonight . . . "

Carson sat in the control room thinking to himself, *it's as if she's been doing this all her life.*

AT THE SAME time, on the sixty-first floor of Trump Tower, in a large living room with very little furniture, a woman in her early sixties who spoke almost no English sat on the couch with Cyndi, who was trying to tell her in Spanish that Alicia, the woman on the television, "*la mujer en television,*" was her best friend. "*Mi mejor amigo,*" and like her mother, "*como mi madre.*"

Roberto Santos' mother nodded several times, smiled and pointed to Alicia, then asked, "*Su madre?*"

"No," Cyndi said, pouring another cup of tea for the woman. "Not my mother. *Como mi madre,* like my mother."

She nodded several times. "*Su madre.*"

BACK AT NBC, when the final story ran, Alicia smiled warmly to camera. "That's our broadcast for this evening. Brian looks forward to seeing you back here on Monday night. For all of us at *NBC Nightly News,* thank you for watching . . . have a wonderful weekend. Good night."

The theme music came up.

Alicia looked down at her notes.

The on-air monitor in the control room went to commercial.

And someone said, "We're clear . . . thanks, Alicia . . . great job."

Carson applauded.

A woman in the control room turned, looked at him, and shook her head. "Bad form."

He shrugged, "I'm new at this."

The woman pointed to Alicia on the studio monitor. "But she's not."

And in that monitor Carson could see Alicia was still sitting at the big desk, grinning from ear to ear.

PIERRE BELASCO turned off the evening news and handwrote a note to Alicia. "You were wonderful."

He slipped it into an envelope, sealed it, addressed it and handed it to Shannon at the concierge's desk.

"Ms. Melendez?" She put it into the pigeonhole mailbox with the name Melendez/Haynes written on it. "You off, sir?"

"I am. Good night."

"Good night, sir."

He said good night to David, the on-duty doorman, and stepped out onto Fifty-Sixth Street.

It was one of those balmy New York spring evenings, so instead of looking for a taxi downtown, he started walking.

Sunday lunch, he thought. *Maybe. Or, maybe I'll just happen to pass by the showroom one afternoon . . .*

He smiled because he knew where to find her.

It was an hour later when he realized he'd actually walked all the way home. *First time in a long time for that,* he reminded himself.

Reaching for his key to the front door, he also realized something was missing.

He had his keys. He had his wallet. Then he remembered. *My BlackBerry.* He'd left it charging in the office.

He asked himself, *is it worth going all the way uptown for it?*

Without thinking twice, he said out loud, "No."

After all, what's that BlackBerry about? He answered his own question. *It's about managing Trump Tower. It's a tool. But it is not the end-all.*

He told himself, *I don't need my BlackBerry to hook me into my job twenty-four hours a day. Whatever comes in to me through that BlackBerry can wait another day. How do I know that?*

He said, out loud, "Because Donald Trump only *thinks* he rules Trump Tower . . . I do. So whatever it is, I will decide. And I have decided it can wait until Monday.

75

The BlackBerry still sitting in the charger in Pierre Belasco's now-darkened office at Trump Tower beeped and suddenly lit up.

An e-mail arrived addressed to Pierre Belasco and Anthony Gallicano.

The sender was "DJT."

And the message read, "Given all that her grandfather did for my father, I have decided not to accept Antonia Lawrence's letter of resignation."